JACK IN
THE BOX

JACK IN THE BOX

HANIA ALLEN

**FREIGHT
BOOKS**

First published April 2014

Freight Books
49-53 Virginia Street
Glasgow, G1 1TS
www.freightbooks.co.uk

A CIP catalogue reference for this book is available from the British Library

ISBN 978-1-908754-47-9
eISBN978-1-908754-48-6

Typeset by Freight in Garamond
Printed and bound by Bell and Bain, Glasgow

CREATIVE SCOTLAND

the publisher acknowledges investment from
Creative Scotland toward the publication of this book

I would like to thank the following people for reading the manuscript, and suggesting ways in which the novel could be improved: Andrea Bremner, Jenny Brown, Jonathan Cameron, Liz Cole-Hamilton, Dorothy Graham, Jane Greaves, Gaitee Hussain, Moira Jardine, Caroline McAdam, Anne McCreanor, Michael Pollak, Key Proudlock, Val Smith, Krystyna Szawelski, Annette Zimmermann, and Sarah Ames.

I owe a huge debt of gratitude to Allan Guthrie for his editorial help and advice. Heartfelt thanks also go to my agent, Jenny Brown, for all the support she has given me, and to Adrian Searle and everyone at Freight Books for taking on the publishing of this novel.

Chapter 1
LONDON, 1985

Dave was taking his time. Not like some of the others, the ones who couldn't get it over with quickly enough. Manny'd had to get things started, moving his hips till the guy got the hang of it. An amateur. The Iron Duke seemed to attract them. Manny'd seen him there before, laughing and drinking with the Irish lads. The regulars said he worked in the theatre. But that was probably a lie.

Manny had spotted him, a young guy sitting alone at the bar, nursing his vodka tonic. He had one of those plastic Jack in the Box bags that the whole of London seemed to be carrying. Manny smiled shyly, and he smiled back. His eyes were what Manny noticed first. Large, with long lashes, and soft, like a spaniel's. He shifted, turning his athletic body round. An invitation? Manny ambled over with his shandy, wary in case he'd misread the signal. He still had the scar from when he'd got it very wrong. But at this time of night, the only people left in the bar were the punters who wanted a boy.

His instincts were correct: the guy pushed a stool in his direction. They chatted. Exchanged names (fake, of course – this was the third 'Dave' he'd met that month). Had a couple of drinks, no rush. Then they left.

Preliminaries over, Dave's behaviour changed. He clutched Manny's arm, walking him briskly up Dean Street and across Oxford Street. Good. He'd be out cruising for another punter before the end of the night.

They went to Manny's place, an abandoned warehouse backing onto the shops on Tottenham Court Road. Convenient for his punters, even though it meant a climb over the gate. He'd made a living space in one corner behind a stack of cardboard boxes. Hauled a mattress from the skip, clean enough apart from one or two suspicious-looking stains. He'd had difficulty getting the full-length mirror in. The wooden frame had slipped from his hands and the glass cracked near the bottom. He'd propped it up by the window where the beam from the street lamp cast an amber light over the glass. The razor he'd filched from the barber's was lying open next to it. He'd shaved before coming out. Always did. The punters liked his skin smooth. Some asked him to wear make-up, lipstick mainly. But he didn't need to steal that. They brought it themselves.

Dave looked round, frowning. Fuck. If he didn't want to do it here, they'd have to go to the gents down the road, the one with the iffy lock. Some punters preferred the gents as the stench wasn't as bad as in here. But he seemed satisfied. He dragged the mattress over, then lifted the mirror and placed it against the wall. Manny had seen this before: sometimes they liked to watch themselves, or him. He'd kept his gloves on. They were nice gloves, black leather, like his jacket. Perhaps he'd take them off, and forget and leave them behind...

He removed Manny's anorak, and started to unzip his jeans.

'I don't do it without a johnny,' Manny said quickly.

Dave slid a condom from his pocket. He was nervous, fumbling with it before getting it on. His cock stood against his belly, an enormous dark thing. He'd shaved down there, but then some of them did that to make their cock look longer. He pulled Manny's trousers and pants down, then positioned him so he faced the mirror, and shoved him onto his hands and knees.

Manny waited. Dave removed the Jack in the Box from the bag

and turned it over in his hands. This was something new, using the toy. Manny knew what the clown inside would look like, he'd seen so many. Bright green clothes, and a grinning face with glass eyes. They gave him the jitters. But Dave didn't pop the box, just set it carefully on the mattress. Then he knelt and, with a steadying hand on Manny's back, forced his cock in. Manny gritted his teeth, trying not to flinch.

He rocked backwards and forwards rhythmically, watching in the mirror. Dave's eyelids were flickering, his lips slightly apart. His grunts grew louder. He leant forward and buried his fingers in Manny's hair, pulling his head back. Jesus, the guy was strong. Manny stared at Dave's reflection, neck muscles straining against the pull, eyes locked on his. The thrusts became faster and deeper until, with a cry that was more of a howl, Dave came like a train.

The surges lessened. He released his hold and Manny's head fell forward. It hadn't been too bad this time, he'd been able to relax. But, God Almighty, his neck hurt. He'd have to be more careful. One of these days, what had happened to Gilly and the others would happen to him. He couldn't complain, though. Full-on sex paid the best. And he'd be out on the street again in a few minutes.

Dave withdrew his cock. Manny watched as he peeled off the condom and wrapped it carefully in a handkerchief before putting it in his pocket. That was a first, a punter who tidied up after himself. He began to get to his feet, but felt a firm push on his shoulder. What the fuck was this? He stared into the mirror. Dave was leaning over him, a length of string in his hands. He looped it over Manny's neck and yanked it tight. Manny struggled, clawing frantically at his throat, unable to tear his gaze from the reflection. In desperation, he tried to reach behind him to grab Dave's wrists. His vision clouded, his struggles became weaker, and his arms dropped to his sides.

A second later, pain seared his eyes, and he felt the ooze of hot liquid down his cheeks. He had time to think, 'I'm dying', before *he slumped onto the mattress. As blackness closed over him, the last sound he heard was the doll's hideous cry: 'Jack-jack! Jack-jack!'*

Chapter 2

'The Chief Super wants to see you, ma'am.'

Von Valenti glanced up from the desk. 'What sort of mood is he in?'

A muscle in the constable's cheek twitched. 'He only has one mood, ma'am.'

She left the office, bracing herself for the meeting. She could guess what this was about. Chief Superintendent Richard Quincey was going to give her a new case. He wouldn't bother asking how many she had already. She could refuse, but he'd hold it against her, even make a note of it in her file. Either that, or she was going to get another bollocking because of the glacial pace of her existing cases.

She'd been at Clerkenwell CID for nearly five years, the last three under Richard Quincey, but she and Quincey had never developed the same easy relationship she'd had with her old governor. Quincey was a mystery to her and to the other officers, who resented and feared his hanging-judge demeanor. He'd made his name years before in the drugs squad, but left it to run Clerkenwell. Although she'd asked around – she liked to know what sort of a man she was working for – she'd discovered nothing solid about his private life. Rumour had it he'd married money, was a member of an expensive London club, and owned a racehorse. But she put little stock in rumours. She'd heard what the men said about her, after all. And continued to say. Although her skin had thickened, she still had scars in tender places.

The Chief Super's door was open. She knocked with her customary loudness, a habit formed after she'd once walked in on a couple of officers with their buttons undone.

'You asked to see me, sir.'

'Come in, Yvonne.'

Richard Quincey was standing staring out of the window. A well-built man, he held himself as if constantly on inspection. Although in his fifties, he'd kept his head of dark hair with just a touch of silver at the temples. A female junior had once described him as handsome in a conventional sort of way. Von studied his back. The junior could think what she wanted, she'd never seen him wither his subordinates with a look. He turned then, and she was shocked to see his face drained of colour, his pale eyes, dull. He seemed to be growing old in front of her.

He motioned to her to sit, and lowered himself heavily into his chair.

'You've a new case,' he said. 'This one's different.' He pushed a file in her direction, then swivelled round to gaze out of the window again. 'We haven't much, I'm afraid, but we know the identity of the victim.'

There was one page. She didn't have to read far to see it. 'Max Quincey?'

'My brother.'

'I'm sorry, sir,' she said, conscious of the slight tremor in her voice.

'Please spare me your sympathy.' He turned his strongly-boned face to hers. 'How many cases are you running?'

'Five, sir.'

'I'll reassign them, I want all your efforts on this.'

She tried to suppress her excitement. 'Yes, sir.' So she was back on the murder squad...

She couldn't remember a time when she hadn't wanted

to be a detective. As a girl growing up in the streets of Whitechapel, her favourite game was cops and robbers. Her two older brothers, who adored her, indulged her role-playing, particularly her little murder mysteries, and always made sure they were well and truly nicked at the end. The three of them left school early, the boys to start up their garage and she to join the Metropolitan Police. Her parents, recognising she was more talented than her brothers, were unhappy she hadn't stayed on to sixth form, but they soon came to accept her choice of career, and nearly burst with pride when she passed her exams. Her mother was constantly telling the neighbours that her daughter was 'an important police inspector in the Met'.

The Chief Super was looking at her coolly. 'Assemble your team, Yvonne, and draft in whoever you need. And take DI English.'

Her curiosity got the better of her. 'Why me, sir? There are any number of officers you could have picked.'

'Last month's enquiry seemed to suggest that the' – his mouth twisted – 'fiasco you were embroiled in may not have been entirely your fault. I've decided to give you another chance. But it's your last. I can't afford any more mistakes.'

Bastard. He takes every opportunity to remind me. 'I understand,' she said.

He spoke in clipped tones, the accent he worked so hard to disguise betraying his working-class roots. 'Something useful came out of that incident. It seems you're not overly interested in what your colleagues think of you. Some may view that as a weakness, but in my opinion it's a strength. A strength which I wish you to harness in this investigation.'

'Yes, sir.'

He stopped her at the door. 'I want a quick, clean result, Yvonne. I don't need to tell you why.'

The Toyota was pulling out of the station.

'A quick, clean result,' Von said, staring at Steve. 'What the hell does he mean?'

'No idea, boss. But I can tell you one thing. If you get this wrong, he'll ask you to fall on your sword.'

'Makes a change from being stabbed in the back.'

'You think there's a difference? It never feels that way.'

She was surprised at the bitterness in his voice.

Steve English had been her number two for a little over a year. He was a couple of years younger than her. Tall and lean, with brown hair as thick as fudge, he was popular with both the men and the women in the force. They'd worked together on her first big case when they were still detective sergeants. He was not long down from Scotland where, rumour had it, he'd had a bust-up with his superior officer. Their paths had crossed several times until they both found themselves posted to Clerkenwell. He'd finished his Inspector's course and she'd been made a DCI. At five foot two, she had to work hard to be taken seriously. She'd met them all: men who tolerated her presence, those who were openly hostile, and ones who actively tried to undermine her. Steve had congratulated her on her promotion, pumping her hand, sincerity shining from his eyes. She was relieved he would be working this case with her, her first murder case in nearly a year.

'It's good to see you, Steve.'

He said nothing but she caught his smile.

They turned into Farringdon Road and headed north. Steve switched on the radio, and they caught the tail end of the news. The main item for September 14th was the ongoing fuel protest, which had reached such a level that many petrol stations were reported to be empty. The NHS had been placed on red alert and supermarkets were rationing food.

'Brilliant,' Von said, tapping the arm rest. 'If Tony Blair

doesn't pull his finger out, we'll soon be walking to the scene of the crime.'

'I hear it'll all be different tomorrow,' Steve said smoothly.

'And the same in a hundred years.'

As they waited at the traffic lights, he said, 'You thought about the team?'

'We'll use the ones you had on your last murder case.'

'They're young.'

'They've had the benefit of working with you. You got anything against youth?'

'No, boss, I'm fighting to get mine back.'

They swung off King's Cross Road into a long terrace of identical four-storeyed houses.

'So what do we know about Max Quincey?' he said.

'Worked in the theatre, started out as an actor but gave it up to run a rep company, the Quincey Players. They've finished touring and now they're playing in London. The strange thing is that I met him only last Saturday, at some arty farty do at the National Gallery.'

'Didn't know art was your scene.'

'I went with Kenny. He pointed out I'm always dragging him to police functions.' At the mention of Kenny's name, she felt rather than saw Steve bristle. Steve and Kenny had never got on. Fortunately, their paths seldom crossed. 'The Chief Super was introducing his brother to everyone,' she said.

'What was he like?'

'He had a nice way with words.' *And a patronising manner.* As they'd talked, his eyes had wandered round the room, as though he were searching for someone more interesting. 'Clothes-wise, he was exactly my image of an actor. Velvet jacket and silk cravat.'

'And he lived here?' Steve was staring at the houses. The upper walls had been left in their original red brick but the ground-floor façades were plastered in white, most of them dirty and chipped with age. 'Rather down market for a velvet jacket. Looks like Coronation Street but with iron railings and window boxes.'

'This area's full of guest houses. Lots of touring actors bunk in this street.'

They stopped outside number fifteen. The sun had risen into a pink sky, shot through with threads of cloud. A nearby road was being resurfaced and acrid smoke, brought in on a light wind, stung Von's eyes.

She studied the building. The curtains on the top floor were drawn.

A short flight of steps led to the front door. They showed their warrant cards to the policeman, who stepped aside to let them pass.

In the narrow hallway, she consulted her file. 'There are six rooms. Max Quincey's is—'

A door opened suddenly to her right and a rake-thin woman emerged. She was joined by an elderly man, who slipped a protective arm round her shoulders.

'Who are you?' the woman said, in a tone so harsh it was almost a shriek. She clutched at the man, her huge eyes darting from Von to Steve.

'Police officers,' Von said quickly. 'We're with the Metropolitan Police.'

The man frowned. 'My sister's had a terrible shock. Must you do this today?'

'Are you Mrs Deacon?' Von said, addressing the woman.

She nodded, her wrinkled lips trembling so violently that Von could see the slight gap between her front teeth.

'We'll need to speak to you, Mrs Deacon.' Seeing the look on her face, she added gently, 'But we don't need to do it now.'

The man seemed relieved. 'Come on, Mavis,' he said, guiding

her back into the room. 'It's on the top floor,' he whispered to Von. 'You can't miss it. It's the only room on the landing.'

'It was the landlady who found the body,' Von said, after he'd closed the door. 'She became suspicious when she saw Quincey's curtains closed all day yesterday.'

Steve frowned. 'So he's been dead for a day?'

'At least.'

'Gee, I just love it when that happens.'

The narrow staircase was covered in a patterned carpet, threadbare where it curved over the steps. Several stair rods were loose.

'Three flights, Steve.' She peered up. 'Gee, I just love it when that happens.'

At the top of the house, a second policeman stood outside a door that was closed and taped off. He nodded at Von. 'The room's as we found it, ma'am. The door was closed.'

'Unlocked?'

'I'm afraid so, ma'am.'

'Just our bloody luck,' she muttered.

It meant that, for at least a day, anyone could have come into the room. It was what detectives dreaded most: a contaminated crime scene. In the hands of an experienced defence pathologist, any evidence painstakingly gathered could be rendered useless in court. Von had had a case like this blown wide open, and she was determined to avoid a repeat.

She ripped the cellophane packaging from the box in the corridor and removed white suits, latex gloves, and overshoes.

'Shouldn't we wait for Forensics, boss?' Steve said, pulling on gloves.

'We'll be careful.' She knew what would happen once Forensics arrived: the place would be like Piccadilly Circus. What she needed was that first impression of the crime scene which could give her a leg up in the investigation. Her old governor used to call it quality time with the corpse.

She opened the door and ducked under the tape.

The curtains were so thin, she had no difficulty distinguishing the objects in the room. Someone had made a bad job of erecting a partition to create an en-suite bathroom. A lacquered wardrobe towered in the corner, the doors hanging wide. Beside it was a matching chest. Its surface was littered with books and papers, the top drawer open, ties trailing from it like multi-coloured tongues. A cluttered table flanked by two armchairs stood against the opposite wall. The bedside cabinet and brass-framed double bed took up what space was left, and behind them hung the only picture in the room: a reproduction of one of the scenes from Hogarth's 'A Harlot's Progress'.

Something pricked her nostrils: the unmistakable stench of death. But overlaid with another odour. 'Can you smell tobacco, Steve?'

'Too sweet for cigarettes. Weed, perhaps?'

'Not a smell you'd forget, is it?'

She skirted the foot of the bed. With a rapid movement, she drew back the curtains.

Morning light streamed in, illuminating the body of Max Quincey.

He was lying on the bed, legs apart, naked except for the school tie. It was pulled tight, the knot half-hidden in the folds of flesh under his chin. His wrists were secured to the bed frame, hands bent forwards, fingers slightly curled. His lips and the tongue protruding from his mouth were pale blue. A trickle of blood from his left nostril had solidified into a black line that stopped at his upper lip. His chest hair was dark and tangled, and so profuse that the tie seemed to float above his body. The sheet between his legs was stained brown.

Von had worked on enough murder cases not to flinch when she saw a corpse. Nor did she behave like some of her male colleagues, whose insensitivity degenerated sometimes into gallows humour, masking their true feelings. Her initial reaction was, inexplicably, one of shame and she approached a corpse with respect bordering on reverence.

'He's been hit, Steve. See here? The swelling above the temple?' She flattened the hair with a fingertip and examined the cracked discoloured skin. 'But not hard enough to kill him.'

Steve motioned to the clothes scattered across the room. 'He undressed in a hurry. Or someone did it for him. Could it have been a sex romp that went wrong?'

'Erotic asphyxia? If it was, then I can understand what the Chief Super was trying to tell me. The press will have a field day with this.'

'I thought you said he wore cravats, boss. I've counted four ties round his wrists.'

'Maybe people who wear cravats also wear ties.' She jerked her head at the door. 'Any sign of forced entry?'

He examined the lock. 'Nope. Looks like he invited his killer in.'

'He doesn't seem to own much apart from clothes.'

'He's been touring, boss. Maybe he has a house somewhere.'

She scanned the room, trying to get an impression of what Max Quincey's life was like. If she was going to crack this case, she'd need to know everything about him. 'What's that on the table?' she said suddenly. 'On top of the newspaper.'

Steve turned. 'My God,' he whispered.

'Don't touch it. Just tell me what it is.'

It was several seconds before he spoke. 'Our Jack in the Box has popped up again.'

'Our what?'

'You've not heard of the Jack in the Box murders, boss?'

'Hold on. The year I was with the NYPD. The rent boys?'

'That's it. Each time, the killer left behind a Jack in the Box.

And its eyes were slashed.' He bent over the doll. 'Like this one.'

'Jesus,' she murmured. 'Ring Forensics and find out where the hell they are. Do it now.' She knelt beside the bed and brought her face close to Quincey's. His eyes were open, the cheeks streaked as though he'd been crying. There was something odd about the eyes, a squint that wasn't right. She moved nearer. With a jolt she realised that the eyeballs had collapsed. The streaks weren't tears – the contents of his eyes had leaked onto his face. 'And get Danni,' she shouted, jumping to her feet.

She bent over the table, studying the toy. It was grotesque, a parody of a doll with its coarsely painted face, scratched eyes, and red gash of a mouth. She pushed it back into its box. It sprang out with a ghastly squawk, 'Jack-jack! Jack-jack!'

Steve wheeled round. 'Christ, boss, you made me jump.'

She crammed the doll into the box and closed the lid. 'Tell me everything about the Jack in the Box murders,' she said softly.

'There were four of them, poor buggers, all rent boys. Strangled. Eyes slashed. One boy survived.'

'They didn't catch the killer, did they?'

'The senior investigating was DCI Harrower.' The corner of Steve's mouth twitched. 'Not the sharpest pencil in the box.'

'He had a good track record,' she said coldly, suddenly defensive of a man she'd never met.

'I didn't work with him, but his reputation reached Glasgow.'

She lifted an eyebrow. 'And that was?'

'His men would follow him anywhere, but only out of morbid curiosity.' Steve rubbed his neck. 'Mind you, in this case, the cards were stacked against him. The dolls were the only real clue. Unfortunately, most of London had them. People took them to work, walked down the street carrying them like children.'

'I remember. They called it Jack in the Box Fever.'

'Aye, you could buy the dolls everywhere, not just at the

theatre.'

'The theatre?'

'The one showing the play. That was the whole point, boss. During the period of the murders, a play called Jack in the Box was running in London. It was a Brian Rix type of farce. You know the kind, some man always in and out of women's bedrooms.'

She was only half listening. Her mind was back at the reception at the National Gallery. Max Quincey had told her about his new production of an old play. The play's name had meant nothing to her then.

But it meant something now – Jack in the Box.

Chapter 3

Von and Steve waited outside the room with the photographer and the Scene Of Crime Officer, watching through the open door as the pathologist examined the body.

Professor Sir Bernard Truscott-Hervey was kneeling beside the bed. Without turning, he beckoned to the photographer. Although it was normal practice for the photographer to finish before the pathologist began, Sir Bernard was notorious for doing things his way. 'A close-up of the face from this angle, please,' he said, through his mask. 'One more, and then I think we're done.'

As the senior pathologist at the Forensic Science Service, he had had more than his share of murder cases, and his years of experience would always make him Von's first choice. Unlike her colleagues, she wasn't put off by his appearance: his bald head, long neck and habit of bending low over a corpse, as though he were about to devour it, had earned him the nickname of The Vulture. When he wasn't working murder cases, he was a professor at London University, grooming the next generation of forensic scientists. But he had signalled his intention not to retire. Von suspected it wasn't love for the profession that made him want to continue working into his sixties. She'd met his overbearing tank of a wife.

Sir Bernard hauled himself to his feet and edged round the bed towards the door. He lowered his mask and snapped off his gloves.

'Is there anything you can tell me, Sir Bernard?' said Von.

He peered over his half-moon spectacles. 'Such as?'

'Time of death.'

'What are we today? Thursday the 14th.' He studied her face. 'Given the temperature in the room, the body temperature, and the fact that rigor's beginning to wear off, I'd say some time during the evening of Tuesday, the 12th. A more precise timing will have to wait till I get back to the lab. Do you happen to know whether the windows have been opened in the last couple of days?'

'I'll check with the landlady and have someone phone you.' She was determined to extract as much as she could before Sir Bernard disappeared. 'Am I right in saying that the blow to the head wasn't fatal?' she said.

'You are.' He motioned to the lamp lying beneath the armchair. 'I suspect that may be the culprit. Photograph it and bag it, please,' he said to the SOCO. 'It was a nasty crack, Chief Inspector, but he was conscious while he was being strangled.'

'Was he struck before or after he was tied up?' said Steve.

Sir Bernard rested his watery gaze on Steve, well aware of the detective's dislike of pathologists. 'Impossible to tell, as I'm sure you realise. All I can say is that he was tied up before rigor set in. I suggest you wait for an assessment from that dolly-bird psychologist.' He made a show of turning round as though looking for her. 'Where is she, by the way? Polishing her nails, I should imagine.'

'Is there anything else you can tell us?' Von said quietly, not rising to the bait.

'The tie round his neck is Sydney Sussex, if I'm not mistaken.' He added with a mocking bow, 'University of Cambridge.'

'You do surprise me,' said Steve. 'I could have sworn they were Aston Villa's colours.'

Sir Bernard ignored the remark. 'I've been asked to fast-track the post-mortem, Chief Inspector. I'll phone through the date.' A smile played about his lips. 'I know how much Inspector English likes attending.'

'Can prints be lifted from the tie?' Von said.

'We'll do what we can.'

'What about the eyes?'

'What about them?'

Why is it such hard work with him? I'm a police officer running a murder case, not one of his medical students. 'Can you confirm they've been cut?'

'Judging by the quantity of liquid on his face, I'd say that both the vitreous and aqueous humours have been compromised.'

'Post mortem?'

'Strangulation causes the capillary blood vessels round the eyes to haemorrhage. If the eyes were cut *after* strangulation, I'd expect an abnormal quantity of blood in the humours. I'll know after we've done the tests.' He turned to go.

'Can you tell what sort of implement was used?' she said, catching him by the arm.

'Not without more detailed examination. Now, Chief Inspector, you really must excuse me.'

'Thank you, Sir Bernard.'

They watched his retreating back. 'Well, he's mellowed,' murmured Steve.

'How can you tell?'

'He called Danni a psychologist. Last time, he used the word, quack.' He peered over the bannister. 'No sign of her, boss.'

'We can't wait, Steve. We've still to check the bathroom.'

The partition shook as she pulled at the flimsy door. She poked her head inside. 'No cupboards. A ledge above the wash-hand basin. Toothpaste, toothbrush, soap, shaving brush, safety razor.'

Steve was peering over the top of her head. 'The mirror's broken. Looks like he had his seven-years' bad luck all in one go.'

'Don't you know it's unlucky to be superstitious, Steve?' She signalled to the SOCO. 'We need Forensics back in to do the bathroom. I'm interested in the toothbrush. People sometimes share them. And bag the towels. We may get DNA other than Quincey's.'

'Anyone at home?' came a voice from the corridor.

Steve broke into a grin. 'Dr Mittelberg. So, did you pass him on the way out?'

'The Vulture? Certainly did.' Danni Mittelberg had removed her stilettos and was clambering into a pair of white overalls. 'Why are the Forensics boys waiting downstairs?'

'There's no room here to swing a cat,' said Von. 'They want us to finish before they take the place apart.' She watched Danni dress. 'Glad you could make it, Danni,' she said warmly.

Von had met Danni Mittelberg four years ago. As their careers progressed, they regularly worked together, recognising in each other the desire to succeed against the odds. But these days the gloss was starting to come off the relationship: Von found Danni's clear-eyed gaze uncomfortable. As part of Danni's research into the criminal mind, she had spent six months undercover in a psychiatric hospital. She shrugged off criticism that it was a gimmick, stunning the professional world by publishing a book which stayed in the bestseller list for over a year. Von had read the book, and suspected it was just a matter of time before she became the anonymous subject of Danni's next one.

Danni lifted the hood over her auburn hair and tucked in the stray curls. She pulled on a pair of overshoes and drew gloves over her long-fingered hands. 'I'm assuming everything's been catalogued and recorded?'

'It's okay to move things,' said Von.

Danni spoke in the clipped precise way she did when appraising a crime scene. 'Duvet and pillows on the floor. Clothes scattered everywhere.' She picked up a cream-coloured shirt. 'Strange style. Looks Elizabethan. Who was he? An actor?'

Von exchanged a glance with Steve. She was saying nothing. Danni would have to earn her money.

'Whatever he was, he was a clothes horse.' Danni fingered a peacock-blue jacket. 'Gieves and Hawkes. Expensive, yet flung onto the floor. He was in a hurry.'

'To have sex?' said Steve.

'To have sex. They could hardly wait to get their clothes off. And it wasn't a quick wham, bam, thank you, ma'am. They took their time. And they were practised at it.'

'You think they knew each other? This wasn't a tom he brought back home?'

'It was someone he knew.' She crossed to the chest of drawers and riffled through the papers before inspecting the books. 'Interesting mix. Complete Works of Shakespeare, Churchill's "The Gathering Storm", and Graham Greene's "Our Man in Havana".'

'He was educated,' said Von.

'Someone took a great deal of trouble to tie him up.' Danni was studying the corpse. 'It's tempting to think it was a sex prank that backfired, but it wasn't. A single restraint round each wrist is the norm in bondage cases.'

'And the knots?'

Danni looked appreciatively at her. 'You noticed them too. I guess you were in the Girl Guides, then.'

'Okay,' said Steve, 'I'll come clean and tell you I was in the Boy Scouts, but I can't tie knots like those.'

'They may look elaborate, but they aren't.' Danni grinned.

'If Girl Guides know them, then so should a Boy Scout.'

'You're saying whoever did this wouldn't need specialist knowledge?'

'They wouldn't, but the point I'm making is that these knots weren't tied by someone about to have sex. Whoever did this immobilised him for some other purpose.' She indicated the tie round Quincey's neck. 'May I look?'

'Go ahead,' said Von. 'He's been swabbed all over. And he's softening up, rigor has already left the neck.'

Danni placed her hands on either side of Quincey's head and turned it gently. 'This is an ordinary single knot. The kind you'd tie if you wanted to strangle someone.'

'Any significance in the tie itself?' said Steve. 'Apart from the colours, which are Aston Villa's.'

'He went to Sidney Sussex College.' She leant forward. 'He's been crying.'

'Those aren't tear streaks. Someone's pierced his eyes,' said Von.

Danni peered into the blue-grey face. 'Good God,' she breathed. 'What did The Vulture say about this?'

'Only that the cut was deep enough to empty the eyeballs. Nothing about how it was done.'

'Sir Bernard never commits before being sure.'

'We've conducted a systematic search of the room but there's nothing sharp enough to blind him.'

'Let me know if you find the weapon. It'll tell me more about the killer.' Danni straightened. 'This wasn't the result of a burglary that went wrong. I'm betting nothing was taken.'

'As far as we can tell, it's all here, wallet, credit cards. We found his mobile on the floor.'

'Whoever did this hadn't planned it. He or she was caught unawares, which is usually why people are strangled. Premeditated murder tends to be done differently.' Danni stared into the ruined eyes. 'But the blinding is something else. I need to see the post-mortem results as soon as they come in.'

'What can you tell us about the attacker? Single? Married? Family man?'

'Any of the above. Who found the body, by the way?'

'The landlady saw the drawn curtains. She came up and found the door closed. Suggests he didn't just run off. He was in control.' And that would make their job so much harder. A killer who didn't panic was more likely to clean up after himself.

'Could a woman have done it?' said Steve.

'Some women could,' Danni said. 'But I'm guessing this was a man's doing.'

'Will he kill again?'

'Impossible to tell without the motive.' She looked slowly round the room, stopping when she saw the table. 'What's that? The rainbow-striped box next to the ashtray.'

'A Jack in the Box.' Von opened the lid, and the doll sprang out, shrieking.

'The doll's eyes have been scratched too,' said Steve.

Danni stared at the painted face with its scarlet rictus. 'It's absolutely ghastly. Who would keep such a thing? What is it, anyway?'

'A toy,' he said. 'You push the doll in and it pops out on the end of this concertina thing. You wouldn't believe children once played with these. Now it's Grand Theft Auto.'

'So, the killer slashed the victim's eyes,' Danni said, half to herself. 'And also did the doll.' She fell silent.

'Well, what's his profile?' Von said impatiently. 'Who are we looking for?'

'Sorry, I need to see The Vulture's report first.'

Von studied her. *Oh, yes? Now who's not committing?*

Later that morning, everyone was crowded into Clerkenwell's

incident room, a depressing open-plan area decorated in regulation grey. A rushed paint job had caused the walls to blister, reinforcing the general impression of gloom. Someone had tried to lighten the atmosphere by replacing the office furniture with pine desks and brightly coloured plastic chairs, but the laminate had curled at the tables' edges and the backs had a tendency to come off the chairs. But Von wasn't complaining; she'd worked in incident rooms where the tables, as well as the chairs, regularly came to pieces.

Most investigating officers running a murder case dealt on a daily basis with a large team, but during the past year Von had been off the murder squad, managing her case loads largely from her office, and dealing only with the DIs. Steve apart, she hadn't worked with any of the twenty-odd people sitting in front of her and would have to hope that her reputation would be enough to earn her their respect. It was bad enough that, by the time she remembered all their names, the case would probably be over. But her opening briefing, the most important of the case, had gone well.

She turned to the young detective sergeant with the long hair and movie-star looks. He was sitting on the edge of his desk, legs swinging. 'Larry, could you unscrew that incident board? I want to use the whole wall.'

Larry nodded and jumped to his feet. She caught Steve's look of approval: a brisk tone was what the staff expected of the senior investigating.

'Right, gather round,' she said. 'First piece of information, we've established the victim's date of birth as July 13th 1955.'

She scrawled the date on the wall, then added in large letters:
MOTIVE
METHOD
OPPORTUNITY
Ignoring the titters of recognition that rippled through the

room, she said, 'And which is the most important?'

'Motive,' came the chorus.

Von was famous throughout the force for the maxim, learnt from her governor: Find the motive, and you find the murderer.

'The method seems clear,' she said, facing them, 'but we need to track down the weapon. You know what to do. Find out when rubbish is collected, the weapon may still be at Mrs Deacon's in a black bin bag. Check the rubbish bins and nearby skips. Widen the search if necessary.' She counted off on her fingers. 'Ascertain Quincey's movements up to and including the Tuesday evening. Someone may have seen him enter the house with another person. There's no CCTV in the street, unfortunately. Check out the taxis. And talk to the other tenants of number fifteen. I want to know who Quincey's friends were. But leave Mrs Deacon, the landlady. DI English and I will speak to her. Check phone records. Not just his mobile, there's a payphone on the ground floor. I want voicemail, texts, the lot.' She paused. 'Okay, what's wrong? You're giving each other looks.'

Larry broke the silence. 'What about his family? In a murder investigation, they're the first people you interview. The Chief Super—'

'I'll speak to the Chief Super,' she said, noting his reluctance. 'Now, does anyone know what the Jack in the Box murders are?'

There were blank looks.

'Sorry, ma'am,' someone said. 'Can we phone a friend?'

'It appears we've seen this MO before. That's why we need the entire wall. So get the file, Larry. It's from 1985.'

'Now, ma'am?'

'Now.'

Chapter 4

Von and Steve were in her office, having lunch. The word 'office' was a euphemism. Clerkenwell's recent expansion had necessitated a rethink of how its space was deployed, and Von had been assigned a large cupboard, converted to living space only because it had a window. She knew she was lucky to have a room, even if all it contained were a desk, two chairs and a filing cabinet with drawers were rusted shut. Steve was still waiting for his, and took every opportunity to point out that the Chief Super's office could be converted into two, or even three, rooms.

She was poring over a pile of documents, her pasta and tuna bake cooling on her lap. 'Jesus, Steve, I had no idea the Jack in the Box murder case was this big.'

Steve finished his Coke. 'I did warn you.'

'Okay, let's go through it. There were three boys killed: Gilly McIlvanny, Charlo Heggarty, and Liam Mahoney.'

He crushed the can and lobbed it into the bin. 'Irish.'

'They came over from Dublin. Hung out at the Iron Duke, in Soho.'

Soho. The word held different meanings for different people, but to a police officer, it meant only one thing: in the West End, and within walking distance of the theatre district, Soho had been the centre of London's sex industry for over two hundred years. Von was old enough to remember the prostitutes packing the streets, and the cards in private windows and phone boxes advertising French lessons. Although the streets were largely cleared of prostitution by the 1950s, it thrived behind closed doors, fronted by the clip joints and massage parlours which sprang up a decade later. Since the eighties, there'd been a degree of tightening-up of licensing, but the unregulated selling of sex, by both men and women, was still widespread.

Von took a forkful of pasta. 'It was the Duke's landlord who identified the boys' bodies. Suggests they were well known there.'

'Aye, the Duke's a popular place for picking up rent boys. The entire street's full of sex clubs and knocking shops.' Steve handed her a photo. 'This is Gilly McIlvanny, the first one. Gilly's short for Gilead. He was sixteen.'

The photo, taken from the waist up, was of a thin boy in a smart brown school blazer, cream shirt and striped tie. Gilly McIlvanny had wide blue eyes and a smile so big that Von could feel its warmth through the paper. A mop of red hair topped a face covered in large odd-shaped freckles.

'And this was taken after he died.' Steve handed her another photograph. 'You might want to stop eating.'

Von felt her stomach lurch as she stared at the white face, with its lidless pulpy eyes. 'Address in London?' she said quietly.

'Lived in squats. And that's where he was killed, a squat in the Covent Garden area, round the corner from the tube station.'

'Not a place you'd expect to find a squat.'

'The area's been redeveloped long since but, in 1985, the place was riddled with derelict buildings. Gilly's was used by several boys. His attacker blinded him with a piece of glass, then used it on the Jack in the Box. Here's a close-up of the doll.'

She studied the photograph. 'It's the same model as the one in Quincey's room. So how was Gilly strangled?'

'With string. Look at this enlargement. You can see it still round his neck.' He winced. 'Christ, those eyes.'

'Who found the body?'

'Another rent boy and his client. The next day. Gilly was lying in front of a mirror with his pants down. The client took fright and ran off but the rent boy called the police.'

Von picked at her tuna bake, no longer hungry. 'Did they find anything useful?'

'The place was dusted and several sets of prints, mainly partials, were found. But the doll had been wiped clean. The post-mortem showed Gilly had been penetrated anally. No semen, though. And no condom was found, except ones that were weeks old.'

She ran a hand over her face. 'Okay, victim number two.'

'Charlo Heggarty. This photo was supplied by his boyfriend, Jimmy Porteous. Porteous was also his pimp. Charlo was the only one of the boys to work through one.'

Charlo Heggarty stared out sullenly, his dark hair swept back from his forehead in a silky pony-tail. His features were delicate, the nose small and thin, the mouth almost invisible. He wore black goth-style clothes, studded with razor-blades and pieces of metal.

'Jesus, Steve, they're so young.'

'Charlo lived with Porteous. Took his clients back to their flat.'

'Where was Porteous when it happened?'

'Out of town with a cast-iron alibi. He discovered Charlo's body a week later.'

'A week?' She glanced up sharply. 'None of the neighbours noticed a smell?'

'If they did, they didn't report it. Porteous found Charlo fully clothed, but with his trousers and pants down, like Gilly. He was lying in front of the bedroom mirror. No condom was found. The killer had used Charlo's belt for the strangling, and left it round his neck. The doll's and Charlo's eyes were scratched with the kitchen knife.'

'Let me guess.' She threw the rest of the pasta bake into the bin. 'No prints on the doll or the knife.'

'Except for Porteous's. He stated he'd touched them when he arrived.'

'What was his alibi?'

'He was in a VD clinic. The clinic corroborates it.'

So the killer's pattern was already emerging. He'd been careful not to leave behind any trace of himself. But why had he brought a doll? She pressed the heels of her palms into her eyes. 'And the third boy?'

'Liam Mahoney. Found in the disabled lavvie round the corner from Tottenham Court Road tube station. It's used extensively for cottaging. In the morning, the attendant saw the door ajar and looked in.' He riffled through the report. 'Similar details. Liam had had anal sex. Pants left down. No condom. The killer used string. No fingerprints on the doll. The blinding was done with a dirty pocket knife. May have been Liam's.'

Von stared at the photograph of the limp body lying on its side in an attitude of abandonment, the black curls not quite hiding the port-wine stain on the cheek. 'Was there a mirror?'

'Not inside the cubicle. The basins were outside and they did have mirrors.' Steve looked up. 'You think the mirrors are significant?'

'They may be. So, the last one, the one who survived?'

'Manny Newman. According to his statement, he was picked up at the Duke. They went to Manny's place, a warehouse nearby. After sex, the man throttled him and blinded him with Manny's razor.'

'In that order?' she said quickly. 'Strangling and then blinding?'

'Aye, he was certain about the order.'

'Could he give a description?'

'His attacker's hair was cropped. He was neither tall nor short. And average build.'

'Eyes?'

'Surprisingly, nothing about the eyes.'

'Not that surprising, Steve. Manny had just lost his, so perhaps the interviewer was being sensitive. Do we know the attacker's age?'

'Early to mid twenties.'

'That would make him in his late thirties, or even forty, now.'

'He wore jeans and a t-shirt. And a black leather jacket and gloves.'

'If it's the same man, then he intended to kill Manny because he killed the others. So why did he bungle it? They usually get better at it, not worse.'

'DCI Harrower thought it was because they'd been surprised by the security guard. Manny heard his voice just before he blacked out.'

'I don't get it. Why blind the boys after they're dead?' She ran her hands through her hair. 'Did the security guard see anyone?'

'He was on his rounds, heard a noise and looked in. But the attacker had gone by then. The rest you can guess. No fingerprints, and no condom. The doll was scratched and covered with Manny's blood. His attack was particularly vicious.'

'Where is he now?'

'No address. He was in hospital when the case went cold. Here's a photo taken before the attack, supplied by his mother.'

'What a beautiful boy,' she murmured.

'Aye.'

'So what about CCTV? Were there cameras near the scenes of the murders?'

'There's a note to say that Harrower looked through CCTV

footage but found nothing conclusive.'

'Around the Duke, then?'

'There don't seem to be cameras there.'

'A pub that's frequented by male prostitutes? In Soho?' She stared at him. 'I don't believe it.' After a silence, she said, 'So, do you think there's a link between these attacks and Quincey's murder?'

'We can't rule it out. Strangling, blinding. And the doll with the mutilated eyes.'

'Don't forget the play. Max Quincey told me that Jack in the Box is opening next Tuesday. He was in London in 1985 when the play ran then.' She nodded at the report. 'Is he mentioned?'

Steve flicked through the file. His expression changed. 'I don't think you want to know this.' He hesitated. 'Max Quincey was Harrower's prime suspect. The word prime is unnecessary here, he was his only suspect. The Chief Super's brother,' he added.

'Forget about that,' she snapped. 'It's not relevant to the investigation.'

'Sorry, boss.'

'Was Quincey charged?' she said quietly, regretting her outburst.

'His prints were taken, but there was no match for any found at the crime scenes. So, no, he wasn't charged. Also, Manny was played a recording of Quincey's voice, and didn't recognise it.'

'That's not always reliable. Anything else in the file?'

'Interview transcriptions, and newspaper cuttings.'

'Let's have a butcher's.' She flicked through the cuttings. 'I can understand now how I heard about this in the States. The whole world and his dog were covering this case.' She tapped a piece of yellowing newsprint. 'There's even an article by Kenny. He interviewed Quincey. Says here that Quincey was the play's director.'

'I thought you said he was an actor.'

'That's how he began, but he was director in 1985. And he was directing the production that opens next week.' She closed the file. 'We need to move quickly, Steve. If the rent boys' killer has started killing again, we can't assume that Max Quincey will be the only victim. Set up a team meeting for later this afternoon. If we can drag Danni away from her students, better still.'

'And now, boss? The landlady?'

'The landlady.'

The photo of Manny Newman had fallen to the floor. She reached for it and smoothed it flat on the desk, gazing at the uncertain smile and warm eyes, full of expression. Slowly, she ran a finger over the suntanned cheeks with their bloom of youth. Without a word, she replaced the photograph in the file.

The door opened a crack and a suspicious eye stared out.

Von smiled. If she could put the landlady at her ease, the interview was likely to be productive. 'Mrs Deacon?' she said. 'We met this morning. I'm Detective Chief Inspector Valenti, and this is Detective Inspector English.'

The door opened wider. 'That's as may be, but I need to see some identification.' The woman spoke in a strong East-End accent.

Von had seen this behaviour before from members of the public who felt it their duty to give the police a hard time. She studied the openly hostile face, and held up her card, nodding to Steve to do the same.

The woman peered myopically, taking her time reading the print and scrutinising the photographs. 'My brother ain't here,' she said finally.

'It's you we've come to see, Mrs Deacon.'

'Very well.' She ran a hand lightly over her lacquered bronze hair, built up in a beehive. 'Better come in then.'

It was now afternoon, but she was still dressed in her nightgown, a pink flannelette, reaching to her ankles, creased but spotless. Over it was a knee-length blue chenille dressing gown which she clutched at the neck nervously. Her hands were distorted with arthritis.

The sitting room smelt of oil-fired central heating and Johnson's polish. The five occasional tables were covered in linen cloths so long that, not only did they drop to the ground, they were arranged in tasteful folds over the carpet. A glass cabinet packed full of miniature teapots stood against the wall. In front of it was the sofa, upholstered in a shiny dark material, with shinier darker patches on the arms. Every inch of space on the walls was covered with reproductions of Hogarth's engravings: the rest of 'A Harlot's Progress', and others which Von couldn't identify.

Mrs Deacon motioned to the armchairs. 'You may as well sit down. Would you like some tea?' she added in a voice that encouraged the answer, no.

'We've just had lunch,' said Steve. 'But thank you.'

'Mrs Deacon, I expect you know why we're here,' said Von.

Tears welled up in the woman's eyes. She fumbled in her pocket and produced a crumpled handkerchief. 'Mr Quincey,' she whispered, dabbing at her face.

Von waited till she'd got herself under control. 'We need to establish certain facts, Mrs Deacon. Can you tell us, as accurately as you can, when you discovered Mr Quincey's body?'

Mrs Deacon blew her nose loudly. 'Can't be precise but it was about seven o'clock. That's when I get up. I popped outside to buy the morning paper.'

'In your night clothes?' said Steve, surprise in his voice.

Her hand flew to her neck. 'The newsagents is just round the corner.'

Von shot Steve a warning look. 'And then?' she said.

'I happened to glance up at Mr Quincey's window. I'd noticed yesterday that the curtains were drawn, see. All day. It made me wonder.'

'Was the window open?'

'Never is. Got a broken hinge.' She sniffed loudly. 'I went upstairs and knocked on his door. When there was no reply, I went inside.'

'So the door was unlocked?'

She nodded. 'And that was when I saw poor Mr Quincey. It was terrible, him lying there like that. It made me come over all dizzy. I closed the door and came downstairs and called the police. I didn't touch nothing. I know how important it is not to disturb a crime scene.'

'Was anything missing?' Von said, wondering how anyone could tell in the mess they found in the room. But her mother had been a landlady before she married, and Von knew that landladies can be extraordinarily observant.

'Didn't look,' Mrs Deacon was saying. 'Soon as I saw the body, I came away. The clothes on the floor, though, that wasn't like Mr Quincey. He was neater than that.' Her eyes widened. 'Was he robbed, then?'

'We don't know, Mrs Deacon.'

'And you didn't go into the bathroom?' said Steve.

'I've just said I haven't. Why are you asking?'

He looked up from his notebook. 'We noticed the mirror was broken, and wondered whether the killer might have done it.'

'It's been like that for years. You can't get good tradesmen round here for love nor money,' she added defensively.

'Do you know whether anyone entered the room either before or after you discovered Mr Quincey's body?' said Von.

'They could have. As I said, the room was unlocked. I didn't see no-one, but I was out for part of yesterday.'

'Yesterday was Wednesday. What about the day before? Did you see the curtains drawn then?'

'Can't say that I did, but then, I didn't look. I saw Mr Quincey at breakfast on the Tuesday. That was the last time I laid eyes on him.' The tears again.

'Did Mr Quincey always take breakfast here?' Von said gently.

Mrs Deacon drew the dressing gown more tightly to her neck. 'Course he did. I do a good breakfast, I do. Best in this street. And you can write that down,' she nodded to Steve.

'So, weren't you suspicious when you didn't see him at breakfast yesterday? Wednesday?'

'Well, he occasionally has' – she stiffened – 'overnight guests. When that happens, they don't come down to breakfast.'

'Could you describe any of them?'

'Don't see them. But I hear them come in.' She smiled craftily. 'After all these years as a landlady, I can tell how many feet are climbing the steps without having to see. And whether they're men or women.' She settled herself into the sofa. 'Mr Quincey was a *beau viveur*, as those Frenchies say. But that's what you'd expect. He was an important man. Always entertaining visitors.'

'Did he have visitors on Tuesday evening?'

'Can't say. Was out myself at the bingo. Left at about five and didn't get back till eleven.'

'How often did Mr Quincey have overnight guests?' said Steve.

Mrs Deacon pulled the gown to her throat. 'Often enough, him being such a good-looking feller. Mind you, overnight guests are against the house rules. But I usually let my tenants off provided they're quiet.'

So Max Quincey received guests in his room. Nothing unusual about that. 'Do you have a signing-in book?' Von said suddenly.

'Don't need one. My tenants come and go as they please, with or without guests.'

'So had Mr Quincey been lodging with you long?'

'He arrived on September 1st. It was a Friday. I remember because my brother was visiting. He always pops in on a Friday. He helped Mr Quincey with his luggage.'

It was time for the question Von always dreaded asking. The answer could set them chasing their tails. 'Mrs Deacon, can you think of anyone who might have wanted to kill him?'

'Everyone liked him.' Her voice became agitated. 'He was a proper gentleman, he was. Always treated me like a lady. And he was a good tenant. Paid his rent on time every month. In cash. And he was never late.'

Every month? She's just told us that Quincey arrived on September 1st. That's only a fortnight ago.

Von looked at Steve. He shook his head to indicate he had no further questions. She got to her feet and handed Mrs Deacon a card.

'You've been very helpful. If you think of anything, please get in touch.' She paused. 'How long have you had this establishment, Mrs Deacon?'

The woman lifted her eyes from the card. 'Twenty-three years, this coming month. Why do you ask?'

'Do you keep records of your lodgers?'

A note of caution crept into the voice. 'Course I do. Keep everything for the Revenue, don't I?'

'Had Mr Quincey ever rented from you before?' Von said softly.

'No,' came the quick reply. 'First time I clapped eyes on him was that Friday my brother was here.'

'What about when the play ran in 1985?'

'I don't remember anything about that.'

'But you know which play I'm talking about, don't you, Mrs Deacon?'

A haunted look came into the woman's eyes. 'I remember the killings. Who wouldn't? I mean, it was all over the papers, wasn't it?' She turned her body so that Von couldn't see her face.

'Thank you, Mrs Deacon. We'll let ourselves out.'

As they left the building, the sun slipped from behind a cloud, painting the brick walls with light. A man on roller skates sailed past, executing a rapid turn on one leg.

'She's hiding something,' Steve said, when they were settled in the Toyota. 'You saw how she came over all shifty when you mentioned the old murders.' He turned the car round. 'So is she in the frame?'

'Because the first person to discover the body is the prime suspect?' Von smiled. 'I'd put down good money that there'll be no end of people who'll vouch she was at the bingo the night Quincey was murdered.'

He switched on the radio and the sounds of 'Lady Hear Me Tonight' filled the car.

'Can you turn that down, please?'

'Not a fan of Modjo, boss?' he said, reaching for the volume control.

'Never heard of him.' She gazed out of the window. The autumn wind was rising, blowing dead leaves and litter into swirls.

'So what have we learnt from Mrs Deacon?' he said.

'That Quincey was a *bon viveur*.'

'As those Frenchies say. And he was a proper gentleman.'

She lifted an eyebrow. 'Not many of those around.'

'No, boss.'

'But Mrs Deacon was lying about one thing.'

'Only one?'

She turned to face him. 'September 1st wasn't the first time she met Quincey. She knew him from before.'

Chapter 5

Back in the incident room, they found that house-to-house had revealed nothing, the other landladies had neither seen nor heard a thing, and none of the taxi drivers had been round by Mrs Deacon's on the night Max Quincey was murdered. Mrs Deacon's payphone had been out of action for weeks, and there was nothing yet from Quincey's mobile.

A big fat zero, and more or less what Von had expected. Rapid nil returns came at the start of most murder investigations. She rubbed her forehead. 'Okay, everyone, DI English and I have been looking through the Jack in the Box murders case file. There appear to be strong similarities with Max Quincey's. We're going to review the old case to see if we can find anything that'll help us catch his killer.'

'Ma'am, are you thinking that whoever killed Max Quincey is also the Jack in the Box murderer?' The speaker, a milky-complexioned girl called Zoë, was the only female detective sergeant at Clerkenwell.

'All I'm saying is that there may be a link between the cases. Finding that link may help us find Quincey's killer.' Von opened the file. 'There were four victims. The first was—'

Everyone sprang to their feet. The Chief Super had entered the room.

He spoke quietly. 'If I could have a word, Yvonne? In my office.'

'Of course, sir.' She turned to Steve. 'Carry on, Steve.'

In the office, the Chief Super motioned her to a chair. He remained standing. He was shaking visibly, his eyes blazing. 'What in God's name do you think you're doing?'

She hesitated. 'What is this about, sir?'

'I understand you've requested the file from 1985.'

'The Jack in the Box murders. That's right.'

'Well, you can take it from me you're wasting your time. To say nothing of tax-payers' money. That case has absolutely no relevance to the murder of my brother.'

'I beg to differ. The modus operandi is too similar. I simply can't ignore it.'

'It's a copycat killing. Nothing more.' He passed a trembling hand over his forehead. 'The play comes back to London and some psycho decides it'll be fun to kill my brother the same way.'

'Even if that were so, sir, I still need to know what happened in 1985.' She looked him full in the face. 'I'd be failing in my duty if I ignored the Jack in the Box murders. We both know that.'

For an instant, she saw hatred in his eyes, but she kept her gaze steady. 'Of course, you're right,' he said. 'I was just hoping to keep my brother's name out of' – he waved a hand dismissively – 'all that.' He collapsed into his chair. 'So where are you with your investigation?'

'The crime scene has been compromised. Your brother's body lay in an unlocked room for at least a day, so anything Forensics find may have been deposited after death.'

'Not an auspicious start. Has the profiler come up with anything?'

'Nothing definite. What we need to do is interview friends, and–' she paused. 'Family. Sometime soon, I'll have to ask you some questions.'

'You may as well do that now. Take your notebook out. Do it properly.'

She caught the expression in his eyes. *The bastard. I haven't prepared for this. And he knows it.*

'Tell me about your brother, sir.' She opened her notebook. 'What kind of man was he?'

'I didn't know him well. Not since we went our separate ways.'

'And when was that?'

'College. I left home first. I'm older.'

'Which college did your brother attend?'

'Sydney Sussex. Cambridge.'

'Was that your college too?' she said, knowing the answer but wanting to hear him say it.

He smiled bitterly. 'I went to a red-brick university.'

'Did you visit him at Cambridge?'

'Once or twice. I was in the Force by then, and too busy with my career.'

'What did he study?'

'Nothing sensible.' He snorted. 'Philosophy.' He swivelled in the chair to face the window. 'Cambridge was where he developed his love of acting. He joined Footlights. Loved it so much he went on to become an actor. I've no idea whether he was any good. He gave it up after a few years and went into directing.'

'Was he popular at Cambridge?'

'Very.' He turned and looked hard at her. 'Too popular, you could say.'

She frowned. 'I don't understand you, sir.'

'He formed certain friendships.' He hesitated. 'With others in the college.'

'Is Sidney Sussex a male college?'

'It was when my brother was there.'

The silence lengthened, but she didn't intend to be the one to break it.

'You see, Yvonne, my brother was experimenting. That's what he told me, and I believed him.'

'What happened after he left Cambridge?'

'He married shortly after he took his MA. But it didn't last.' A vein pulsed in his temple. 'His wife discovered him in bed with their neighbour's teenage son.'

'And did your brother come out?' she said, after a pause.

'If you mean did he broadcast his homosexuality, then the answer's no. But nor did he hide it. After his divorce, I saw even less of him. Until a few weeks ago, when he rang me out of the blue and told me he'd be coming back to London to direct his play.'

'What was your reaction?'

'Hard to say. In an odd way, I was proud of him.' A wistful expression came into his eyes. 'He was, after all, leading exactly the sort of life he'd always wanted, doing what he loved.'

'Were you envious?'

The expression vanished. 'Of course not,' he said, contempt in his voice.

'We've not been able to establish a permanent address for your brother. Did he own a house?'

'He had nothing material. No house. No car. He lived out of a suitcase.'

She thought of the Chief Super's London flat, with its silk wallpaper and French furniture. The two men couldn't have been more different.

'Can you tell me anything about his friends, sir?'

'I don't know who they were. As I said, I rarely visited him at Sydney. When I did, he took care to, how shall I put it, shield me from them. Nor can I tell you who his current friends are.' He corrected himself. 'Were.'

'Have you any idea who might have wanted to kill him?'

'None.'

She wondered how far to go, but the Chief Super would have read the old case file. 'Sir, are you aware that your brother was DCI Harrower's prime suspect for the Jack in the Box murders?'

'Only because Harrower thought he was gay, Yvonne. Tom Harrower was looking for a gay man because the victims were all male prostitutes, and the only survivor admitted to having sex with his attacker. But he found no material evidence it was my brother.' He dismissed the idea with a shrug. 'London is full of gays.'

'So why did he single out your brother?'

'It was the play. The dolls were the link to the play, and from there to my brother. Not only were the dolls left behind at the crime scenes, the period of the killings coincided almost exactly with the play's run. Read the file. It's all there.' He ran a hand over his eyes. 'I'm not convinced of my brother's homosexuality, Yvonne. He liked women.'

She was tempted to point out that even homosexuals have female friends, but she'd get nothing useful if she antagonised him. 'Were you involved in the investigation?' she said.

'Good God, no. Conflict of interest.'

She hesitated. But she'd have to ask, he'd be expecting the question. 'Could your brother have murdered those boys?'

'My brother was not a killer, Yvonne.'

Jesus, if I could only have a pound for every time I've heard that. She closed the notebook. 'Thank you, sir. If you can think of anything else that's relevant, please let me know.'

'There's one question you haven't asked.'

She looked into the slack face with its deep-set eyes. 'Where were you on the evening of Tuesday, September 12th?' she said.

The answer came back quickly. 'At my club, Boodle's.'

'Thank you.' She got to her feet. 'Sir, the press—'

'I'll handle the press.' He inclined his head. 'In consultation with you, of course. I've arranged a conference for first thing tomorrow. Please be there.'

She was about to suggest there might be a conflict of interest, but his expression silenced her.

Von paused in the corridor, glancing at her watch. 4.45pm. Not worth calling Kenny. He'd understand, being late was an occupational hazard for both of them. And Steve would have brought the others up to speed. It would be a wasted opportunity not to press on.

She walked briskly into the incident room, ignoring the looks of sympathy. She handed Steve her notebook. 'My interview with the victim's brother. The main thing I've learnt is that Max Quincey developed a taste for boys.'

'We've just found that in the file, boss. Several of those interviewed referred to him as "a queer who liked young boys". Max admitted he frequently had sex with boys, although he claimed he'd never met any of the victims.'

Then what the hell was the Chief Super playing at? He'd have read the file. How could he doubt his brother's homosexuality if Max admitted to sex with boys? The man was in denial...'So what else have we got?' she said wearily.

Steve jerked his head at the wall. 'We've written it up.'

The wall looked like a plan for a military campaign. At the centre was a London street map. 'Take me through it, Steve. I need cheering up.'

He jiggled the coins in his pocket. 'The first thing to note is the spread of dates. In 1985, Jack in the Box opened on October 2nd, and finished on October 27th. So, more or less the whole month of October.'

'And the attacks?'

'Gilly McIlvanny on October 5th, Charlo Heggarty on the 9th, and Liam Mahoney on the 11th. The final victim, Manny

Newman, was attacked on October 25th. That's two days before the play folded.'

'So no murders before the play's run started, and none after it ended,' she said thoughtfully. 'Okay, how did Harrower proceed?'

'He started at the Iron Duke, which is where the victims found their clients, but that led nowhere. The Jack in the Box dolls at the crime scenes made him think the murderer had seen the play, so he scoured the lists of credit card names. It was a dead end.'

'It could have been someone who hadn't gone to the play, ma'am,' Larry said. 'Half of London must have seen the dolls. There were posters everywhere. The plastic bags they were sold in carried their picture. There were even adverts in the newspapers.'

'That's a good point,' she said, keen to encourage comments from the others. 'And what conclusion did Harrower come to about the mutilations of both the boys and the dolls?'

'There's nothing in the report, boss. If the DCI came to a conclusion, he didn't record it.'

Von had met Tom Harrower only once, at a police awards ceremony. His vacant stare, sulky mouth, and nasal voice had reminded her of a schoolboy. When she'd steered the conversation to the latest developments in psychology, it was clear from the way he listened with a polite sneer on his face that he put little stock in behavioural science.

'One of his team suggested the killer might have been a member of the play's *cast*,' Steve was saying. 'But the DCI rejected that hypothesis.' He turned to the wall. 'You need to look at the street map to see why.'

The Garrimont, the theatre where the play was running, was at the Piccadilly Circus end of Shaftesbury Avenue, and was circled in red. Four green squares were marked on the map.

'These squares show the locations of the bodies, boss. I've recorded the time of death underneath. Gilly McIlvanny's is estimated as between 9.00pm and 10.00pm. His squat is just over half a mile from the Garrimont. Jimmy Porteous's house is much further away, across the river in the Borough. His boy, Charlo, has a recorded TOD of between 10.00pm and 11.00pm. The gents' lavatory where Liam was attacked is not far from Tottenham Court Road tube. His TOD is between 2.00am and 3.00am. The most accurate time, of course, is Manny's. His warehouse is further up Tottenham Court Road behind the shops. He was attacked just before the security guard found him at 1.00am.'

'What time did the play end?'

'We don't know for sure. All we could find is a reference in DCI Harrower's report that the play was over by the time Manny and Liam were attacked in the early hours, but not over when Gilly and Charlo were killed. As DCI Harrower assumed the same Mr X was responsible for all the attacks, he concluded it couldn't be a cast member, as no-one could leave the Garrimont, pick up Gilly and Charlo, have sex, attack them and then get back in time for curtain call.'

'That's fine as far as it goes,' she said impatiently, 'but what about the interval? Do we know when it was and how long?'

'We don't, but how long are intervals? Half an hour, tops. Yet look where Jimmy Porteous's house is. South of the river. Charlo died between 10.00pm and 11.00pm. The play would have been into its second half by then.'

'Too many ifs, buts, and maybes. We need to get a handle on the timings. Let's see if we can track down a programme from 1985.' She examined the map. 'What about the director? Is he around once the play starts?'

'I've got Max Quincey's statement,' Zoë said, leafing through her file. She handed Von a sheet. 'He claimed he always stood in the wings throughout performances. Problem is that the stage manager and staff said they were so used to his presence they could neither confirm nor deny it. It didn't help that they were interviewed several days after the first two murders.'

'And the two late attacks? Manny's and Liam's? Did Quincey have an alibi?'

'He claimed he was alone in his digs. You'll note, ma'am,' Zoë added wryly, 'that in 1985 he lodged with Mrs Deacon.'

'Did he indeed? She told us the first time she saw Quincey was two weeks ago.'

Larry was playing with his mouse mat, a slight frown on his face. 'You've been unusually quiet,' Von said to him. 'What's your take on this?'

He cleared his throat as though he'd been caught napping. 'Max Quincey was arrested but not charged.' He tossed the mat aside. 'Maybe the fact he was a suspect was enough to seal his fate. Maybe Quincey was murdered out of revenge by someone who *thought* he'd killed the rent boys.'

Von smiled encouragingly. He was thinking along the right lines, searching for a motive. 'You're saying the co-incidence of the *play's* return could be nothing more than the co-incidence of *Max Quincey's* return?' she said.

'Quincey's arrest in 1985 was widely covered. Everyone knew he was the prime suspect.'

'But who knew he was returning to London this month?' Zoë said quietly.

'His brother,' said Von. 'And everyone who attended the National Gallery reception last Saturday.'

'The posters advertising Jack in the Box are all over the underground,' someone chipped in. 'It's billed as "The Play Of The Year 2000". Quincey's name is everywhere.'

Steve rubbed his face. 'I don't get it. Who would want to revenge themselves on a group of rent boys?'

'And why?' Von said. 'It's a possible motive, though, and we can't afford to ignore it.' She paced the floor. 'Right, find out what you can about the boys. Start at the Iron Duke. Show photos of them, Quincey as well. There might be someone still there from 1985. While you're in Soho, double-check the CCTV. I can't believe there's none in that area.' She stared at the photographs of the rent boys, pinned up on the incident wall. 'Manny Newman is still alive. Find out where he's living. Okay, there's more to be squeezed from the old case, but that's it for tonight. Before you leave, I need to tell you there's a press conference first thing tomorrow.'

There were groans from every part of the room. Zoë caught her eye. 'Ma'am, after this story leaks, there'll be no end of crank calls.'

'It can't be helped. Draft in more clerical to deal with them.'

The detectives left, some singly, most in groups. Their excited voices reached her from the hall. They'd be off to a pub to talk over the case, and possibly her handling of it. She smiled. It was how she'd behaved as a junior detective, always thinking she knew better than her superiors. She should join them, try to get to know them better, but she wanted to get home. Kenny might call round.

Steve hovered at the door. 'You staying late, boss?'

'Just going. Don't wait for me.'

He opened his mouth, then shut it again. 'Night, then.'

She stood looking at the photo of Manny Newman, the tousled brown hair, the freshness of his cheeks, the light in his eyes. He'd been in his teens at the time of the attack. Still a child. She ran her fingertips over his eyes, feeling her heart clench. Then she fetched her coat, switched off the lights, and left.

Chapter 6

As she turned the key in the lock, Von knew that Kenny was in. It was that pungent blend of Chinese food and stale cigarette smoke that settled like fog in her flat whenever he chose to visit. In the early days, he'd visited every night. She was barely through the door, when he'd be pushing himself at her, grabbing at her breasts, his mouth seeking hers. They never reached the bedroom, making love as soon as their clothes were off. Depending on what they wore, it could be the hall, the kitchen, or the sitting room. Lately, he'd been visiting less often. And it was weeks since they'd made love. Instead, they had sex.

The deep voice came from the sitting room. 'That you, Von?'

She dropped her bag onto a chair. *Jesus, he asks that every time. Who the hell else is it likely to be?*

The kitchen was depressingly the same: piles of dishes were balanced under the still-dripping tap, and discarded cartons of take-away food littered the working surface. He might at least have cleared up. But then, this wasn't his flat. They'd taken the decision to keep separate households. Just in case.

She'd met him not long after she started working at Clerkenwell. The press officer warned her that a Kenny Downley was coming to interview her, the first female DCI at the nick. She and Kenny hit it off straightaway. He'd just started working for The Guardian. A step up from The Mirror, he said, means I get to interview big shots and not just the small fry. She laughed at his jokes, most of which were against himself, and accepted his suggestion they have a drink after work. Two days later, he took her out to dinner but, instead of trying to get her into bed, he left after seeing her home. The following morning, flowers arrived with a note saying how much he'd enjoyed her company. She was flattered, and thought her run of bad luck with men had come to an end.

After a few months, Kenny hinted at moving in, but she wasn't ready. They had their first real row, made worse by her inability to explain her reticence. He took it personally and disappeared for several days. She was surprised at how much it had affected her. But he returned, grudgingly accepting it might be wiser to keep their separate flats. Her concession was to suggest they exchange keys, convincing him it was almost the same as cohabiting. After they made love, and he fell asleep, she asked herself why she was unwilling to share her life fully with him, why she was unwilling to share her life with anyone. Was it simply because she'd lose control of it? But how much control did people have over their lives anyway?

She opened a cupboard packed with tins past their sell-by date, then closed it again. 'Have you eaten?' she shouted through the kitchen door.

'I stopped off at the Pearl. I had mine a couple of hours ago. Yours is warming.'

She peered inside the oven. Mongolian beef and egg fried rice: the speciality of the Pearl of Hong Kong. What he always brought her. She'd given up asking for something different.

She was piling food onto a plate when he came into the kitchen. 'I meant to ring,' she said. 'I'm sorry.'

He smiled, the creases round his eyes deepening. 'Don't apologise. I know how it is.'

'It's a new case, and I had to get it started.'

'Forget it.' He reached into the fridge.

'I thought you said you were going to lay off beer. You'll

never get rid of that belly otherwise.'

'You wouldn't love me skinny, believe me.' He held up a bottle. 'You drinking?'

'I'll have wine. There's some open next to the sink.' She picked up the plate. 'You couldn't bring it in, could you?' she said over her shoulder.

The sitting room was the largest room in the flat. It had a high ceiling and elaborate coving, and could have been furnished elegantly had Von not bought too much of the wrong kind of furniture at a local auction. The sofa and easy chairs fought for space amongst the general clutter of small tables, Pink Floyd CDs, and piles of police magazines and forensic journals on loan from The Vulture. Cheap IKEA rugs had been thrown onto the patterned carpet, and the walls were hung with scenes from a Moorish harem, left behind by the previous owners. She hadn't made time to replace either the pictures or the sixties-style wallpaper. After ten years in the flat, she probably never would.

Kenny sank into an armchair. 'So, a new case.' He lifted a hand as though to ward off an objection. 'Don't worry, I won't pry. And anything you tell me won't leave this room. I haven't forgotten our rules.'

'You never do,' she said softly. She surprised herself by adding, 'That's why I love you.'

'Is there anything about the case you *can* tell me?' he said, filling her wine glass.

'Remember the man we met at the National Gallery? The Chief Super's brother?' She blew on the food to cool it. 'He's been murdered.'

His arm jerked, causing him to spill wine on the carpet. 'God, I'm sorry, love. I'll get that stain out.' He fetched a cloth from the kitchen and mopped up the spill. 'His brother, was it?' he said, not looking up.

'Max Quincey. It's a pity you didn't talk to him. I noticed you didn't stay long after the Chief Super came over.'

'And you know why that is. Remember the thrashing he gave me after that article?'

Kenny, hoping to get the inside track on the work of the drugs squad, had interviewed the Chief Super as part of a series entitled 'Man of Today'. The piece was flattering enough, and cast Richard Quincey in as favourable a light as possible. The Guardian's editor, however, who'd had a previous run-in with Richard Quincey, changed the title at the last minute (without Kenny's knowledge) to 'Man of Yesterday'. The Chief Super had been livid and had taken his anger out on Kenny.

'What made you leave in such a hurry?' she said, chewing on a piece of beef. 'Your readers would have loved Max Quincey.'

'I'd arranged to meet someone, this hot story I'm working on. After weeks of running round in circles, I've finally managed to get a lead.'

'Must be good, I've hardly seen you. Did you get enough out of the reception to write your piece?'

'Pretty much. These events are all the same. I got a list of the attendees, I can wing the rest.' He handed her the glass of wine. 'So, what did this Max Quincey have to say?'

'He wanted to know what it's like being a detective. Amazing the romantic notion the public have about solving crime.'

'And did he tell you why he'd decided to come back to London? I mean, specifically?'

She lifted her eyes to his. 'That's a strange question to ask.'

He smiled his crooked smile, where one corner of the mouth lifted. 'Can't help being a journalist, I suppose.'

'Now that he's a murder victim, I bet you wish you'd stayed and interviewed him.'

He took a swig of beer. He set the bottle down, then picked it up again. 'So how did he die? Are you able to tell me?'

'It'll come out tomorrow at the press conference. He was strangled.'

He ran a hand across his face. 'Jesus.'

'You behave as though you knew him,' she said softly.

He looked up so sharply, she heard the bones in his neck crack. 'I've never met him,' he said.

'Haven't you?'

'I'd have remembered someone like that. You saw how he dressed.'

She kept her voice steady. 'Maybe he didn't dress like that fifteen years ago when you interviewed him.'

The beer bottle stopped halfway to Kenny's mouth. 'Fifteen years ago? I would have been in the army.'

'It was 1985, you were out of the army by then. Max Quincey was here, directing a play. He was the prime suspect in a murder case, and you interviewed him.'

'I don't remember. You sure it was me?'

'I saw an article written by you in the case file.'

A defensive note crept into his voice. 'It was a long time ago. I can't remember everyone I interviewed that far back.'

'But you would have remembered this particular case.' She stirred the rice with her fork. 'The Jack in the Box murders.'

He slammed the bottle down. 'Well I don't. Look, love, this isn't your interview room, and I'm not one of your suspects, so stop giving me the third degree, all right?' He snatched up the bottle and took a vicious gulp.

She was surprised by his outburst. 'Sorry, Kenny. Old habits die hard.'

They sat in silence, she eating her supper, and he drinking steadily.

'I'm going away for a few days,' he said suddenly.

She put down her fork. 'Again?'

'Can't afford not to. I've had a tip-off that may lead to

something big.'

There was a time when she'd have been annoyed that Kenny's work now came before his private life. Yet, could she really blame him? Her own work had always come before hers. He'd once complained that police work was like a drug. And he'd been right. The business of policing was her daily fix. Specially the business of murder.

'Shall we try to stay in touch this time?' she said wearily.

'Love, it's you who never phones, not me.' His eyes wandered over her body. 'So, are we going to bed, or what?' He reached across and ran a hand over her breasts. 'There's something about crisp white shirts concealing a double-D cup that always makes me go hard.'

She gazed into his eyes, her pulse racing. 'Come on, then.'

Afterwards, she lay thinking about their conversation. Had Kenny forgotten he knew Max Quincey, or was that a fabrication? It troubled her to think he might have lied. If he had, it marked a milestone in their relationship, after which there would be no turning back. Although she dealt on a daily basis with habitual liars, she couldn't decide about Kenny. She watched him sleep, his receding hair tousled, the dark tattoo running down the side of his neck and over his shoulder. She ran a finger across his three-day-old stubble, silver in the weak light. Then she tucked the duvet around him and switched off the bedside light.

Something woke her. He was shaking her gently. Grey light was seeping through the curtains. She groped for the clock on the bedside cabinet and brought it to her face, squinting at the luminous dial. His hand was moving over her breasts, sliding down her body and between her legs.

She turned towards him sleepily. *Jesus, why do men have to have erections at six in the morning?*

Chapter 7

The first press conference of any murder investigation was always well attended and, in anticipation of the turnout, the station had been scoured for chairs. Even the Chief Super had given up his, for once without a fuss. It was 9.00am, and the conference room was packed.

Richard Quincey was sitting behind a table, Von next to him. Before them were the massed ranks of the press. Representatives from at least two television stations were crammed with their equipment into the front two rows. It was as she'd feared: the case had aroused the public's interest. And she'd put down good money it wasn't because the victim was the brother of a high-ranking policeman, but because the way he'd been killed was similar to that of the Jack in the Box murders.

'That's all I'm able to tell you,' the Chief Super was saying. 'Now, are there any questions?' he added, with exaggerated politeness.

'Do you think there's a link between the killing of Max Quincey and the 1985 Jack in the Box murders?'

The speaker was Arabella Carrington, the crime reporter for the Daily Mail. She was young and ambitious, and she let you know it. Her trademark panda eyes and hair curling down her back made every head turn whenever she entered a room. Von's mouth tightened. They'd locked horns before, and Von rarely emerged victorious. Arabella was quick-witted, always several steps ahead, and Von had learnt the hard way that arguing with her was like trying to nail fluff to the wall. She'd never understood what had lured Arabella to journalism. She would have earned far more as a barrister.

'We're ruling nothing out at this stage,' the Chief Super said. 'DCI Valenti is examining that case for possible connections.'

'Is the DCI *reopening* the old case?' a man at the back asked.

Von opened her mouth to speak, but was cut off by the Chief Super. 'We're doing nothing of the sort.'

'Why not?'

'We haven't the manpower to waste on cold cases.'

'*Waste*?' Arabella said with a quick smile. 'Do you use that word, Chief Superintendent, because the victims were male prostitutes?'

'That's a preposterous suggestion. We treat all our victims with equal respect.'

Von had seen this before. The Chief Super lost control of the situation too easily. She could never understand why a man of his experience gave consideration to every question or comment, instead of side-stepping, as a politician would, or simply refusing to answer. If she'd had the nerve, she'd have suggested he go on one of the Met's training courses.

Arabella pushed a stray lock of hair behind her ear. '*Equal* respect? But some are more equal than others, Chief Superintendent? Isn't that it?' she added coyly.

'Miss Carrington,' Von said, not giving the Chief Super the chance to reply, 'the senior investigating officer put a huge effort into trying to solve that case, but there was simply no hard forensic evidence. Cases of that nature are almost impossible to solve after such a long period of time. However, if we do find a material link to the Jack in the Box murders, we will re-open the case.' She raised her hand, and the hubbub died down. 'But I'm sure you'll understand that the bulk of our effort must go into this current investigation.'

Arabella raised a perfectly waxed eyebrow. 'Because he's the Chief Superintendent's brother?'

Von looked directly at her. 'Because he's a member of the public, like yourself. I'm sure the readers of the Daily Mail will be relieved to hear that.' She addressed the room. 'We're asking for every assistance from the public. If anyone was near the scene of the crime on the evening of September 12th, we urge them to come forward.'

'And can you tell us, Chief Inspector, whether Max Quincey picked up rent boys?' Arabella said, smirking.

A ripple of interest ran through the room.

'I won't answer questions like that.'

'Could he have been killed because he was a homosexual?'

'No comment.'

'Is that why you're not answering my questions?'

'No comment.'

'Is that no comment on he was killed by a homosexual, or no comment on no comment?'

'It's just no comment.' Von gathered up her papers. 'Now, you must excuse us, we've a murder investigation to run. Press releases will be issued from this office in the usual way.'

She rose, ignoring the cries of protest, and left the room, the Chief Super following.

In the corridor, he rounded on her. 'Do that again, Yvonne, and you'll be out of the force so quickly, you won't know what's hit you.'

'Excuse me, sir?'

He thrust his face into hers. 'Don't ever take over from me like that again.'

'I thought it the best course of action.'

'Did you? I didn't.'

She drew her head back to escape the reek of his after-shave. 'It wasn't my intention to undermine you, sir.'

'It didn't look that way to me,' he said, his voice measured. 'I thought I made it clear I'd be the one handling the press.'

'And you did, sir. Admirably. But questions of detail should be left to me.'

His lip curled, and he marched away.

She watched him go. *Wanker. That's the last time I'm bailing you out.*

'Dr Mittelberg's arrived, ma'am. She's in your office.'

Von nodded her thanks and left the incident room.

Danni was sitting in Von's chair, swivelling round in circles. She was wearing one of her couture suits, the kind Von wished she could wear but her bust was too large. Danni's hair was loose today, falling in waves over her shoulders. She wore little make-up, just a lick of gloss on her lips and indigo-coloured mascara, which enhanced the blueness of her eyes. Von sometimes wondered what the male academics at the university made of their colleague. Not only was her appearance stunning, she was at the top of her game. Von had seen the looks of envy laced with sexual desire that crossed the faces of Danni's colleagues whenever she attended her lectures on criminal psychology. But Danni's tastes didn't run to academics. An expert horsewoman, her weekends were spent riding on her father's estate, and few of the lecturers would have guessed the nature of the extra services she required of the stable boys.

'So how did it go?' Danni said. 'Judging by your face, not brilliantly.'

Von sat down heavily. 'Jesus, Danni, there are days when I can't understand the Chief Super. I save his bacon and he gives me a drubbing.'

Danni crossed her legs, displaying an expanse of smooth white thigh. 'You'll never get into the masons now, you've been wasting your time practising that funny handshake.' She regarded Von with an expression of affection. 'Look, I wouldn't worry too much. I've seen the Chief Super in action before and I put it down to repressive potty training. Forget about his antiquated behaviour, he's really not worth expending emotional energy over.'

'And that cow, Arabella Carrington. I swear, one of these days I'll forget myself and chin her.'

'That'll fast-track you to the end of your blossoming career. Incidentally, I'm sorry I wasn't there. I had a book-signing.'

'Ah, yes, "Dissection of a Mind". How's it selling?'

'Fantastically.'

Von reached over to the inner window and pulled down the blind into the corridor, catching the look of disappointment on a constable's face. Danni's appearance always caused a stir; the moment she sashayed into the police station, all conversation stopped.

Danni flicked back her hair. 'Talking of dissection, when's the autopsy?'

'This afternoon. Coming?'

'I'm lecturing. Term's just started.' She paused. 'So, I looked through the old case last night. The guy who ran it, Chief Superintendent Harrower—'

'Chief Inspector. He retired as DCI. Jack in the Box was his last case.'

'Whatever. There are some significant questions he seems not to have asked.' She shuffled through her notes. 'The blindings, first of all. The sole survivor, Manny, says he was blinded *after* he was strangled. I'm assuming the others were too. Normally, an opportunistic killer doesn't blind after he kills. He high-tails it pronto.'

'We wondered about that.'

'Initially, I thought he blinded the boys to make sure they couldn't identify him, in case he botched the strangling. Do you remember the Stryker case?'

Von's mouth twisted. 'Who could forget?'

'He told the police that he hadn't intended to kill them. All he wanted was to see the fear in their eyes. He stopped the strangling before they died, then revived them, even had a conversation with them. With some, he repeated the strangulation. But my point is this: eventually, he blinded them all so they couldn't identify him.'

'So what are you saying?'

'Look at the dead boys, Von.' Danni held out the photo of Gilly McIlvanny. 'This one in particular. There's no way whoever killed him botched it. He knew this boy was dead.'

Gilly's face swam before her eyes. She looked away quickly. 'So what sort of a person blinds a corpse?'

'One that's deeply disturbed. And there's something else. In every case, he used a mirror. Manny stated he took care to move the mirror so he could watch himself.'

'That's not unusual.'

'Not for sex. But I'm not convinced he used the mirror to watch himself having sex.'

'What then? To watch himself killing?'

'That's not unusual either, Von. I don't need to remind you of the cases where the killers have recorded themselves.'

'Liam's body was found in a disabled lavatory. The cubicle didn't have a mirror.'

'Look at this schematic, though. If he opened the door, he'd see himself in the mirror above the basins. A bit risky, but the time of death was between 2.00am and 3.00am. It would have been quiet.'

Von pushed her hands through her hair. 'And mutilating the dolls?'

'The doll is an integral part of the process.' Danni sighed heavily. 'I just don't know why.'

'And Max Quincey? I know there was no evidence, but could he have killed the boys?'

'Impossible to say without further information.'

'Then here's another question,' Von said impatiently. 'Could the killer of the boys also have killed Quincey?'

'It's a completely different pattern of behaviour.'

'Come on, Danni, there are similarities.'

'Quincey was strangled. His eyes were slashed. As were those of the doll. Okay, I give you that. But look at the boys' faces. Their eyes were hacked so badly they lost their eyelids. And yet you had to point out to me that Quincey's eyes had been cut. There's also the mirror. There wasn't one in Quincey's room. The only mirror was in the bathroom and it couldn't be seen from the bed, even with the bathroom door open.'

Von played with her pen. 'Bottom line, Danni, what was the state of mind of the rent boys' attacker?'

She hesitated. 'This might sound strange, but I'd say, self-loathing.'

'Yet he watched himself.'

'Not unusual for someone who loathes himself.'

'And Quincey's killer?'

'Hard to say. But I'm sure of one thing.' She placed her hands flat on the desk. 'The profile of the killer in the two cases is completely different. You're looking for two separate people.'

'We're looking for a Mr X *and* a Mr Y? Look, could Mr X have evolved into Mr Y? Or becomes Mr Y when the conditions are right?'

'Like Jekyll and Hyde?' She shook her head slowly, her eyes steady. 'Not a chance in hell.' It was that look of defiance that Von disliked: Danni knew her expertise gave her the upper hand in the argument.

'Have you ever been wrong, Danni?'

If Von had expected her to bristle, she was mistaken. 'Of

course.' Danni smiled, inclining her head. 'But so have you.'

Von threw down the pen and stared out of the window. Maybe the Chief Super was right, and she was wasting her time on the Jack in the Box murders.

'Not necessarily, boss,' said Steve, tucking into a Cornish pasty.

They were in the Drunken Duck, having lunch. Although the Clerkenwell area was full of Italian cafés, which Steve preferred, Von always steered him to the Duck. It was a cheerful pub whose trademark was a giant castor-oil plant in the corner. The décor hadn't changed since the seventies, yet despite the dinginess the place was frequented by the young and upwardly mobile who worked in nearby offices. Steve was generally wary of discussing police work in public places, but the alcoves in the Duck afforded almost complete privacy.

'What do you mean, not necessarily?' said Von.

'The clue to Quincey's murder may still lie in the old case.'

'Tell that to the Chief Super when he sacks me.'

He wiped crumbs from his mouth. 'Two different people, eh? And she'd put money on it? Easy for her to say. As the daughter of a millionaire, she's got plenty to splash around.'

'Don't be like that, Steve.' Von smiled. 'Money isn't the cure for everything.'

'It's the cure for being poor,' he said with feeling. He nodded at her empty glass. 'We've time for another wee swallie.'

'We won't get served, you know what this place is like at lunch time.' She studied him. 'Can you manage as you are?'

'What do you mean?'

She chose her words carefully. 'I know you need to be plastered before you can face a cutting room.'

'Thanks for that.' He got to his feet. 'Let's go,' he said stiffly.

'The cause of death is asphyxia due to ligature strangulation.' Sir

Bernard peered over the rim of his spectacles. 'Haemorrhaging in the inner ear is a clear signature.' He indicated the red welt on the corpse's neck. 'Whatever did that was smooth, consistent with the tie we found. There are no fingermarks on the skin, so he wasn't manually strangled and the tie wrapped round his neck afterwards.'

'How quick would it have been, Sir Bernard?' Von said. She was sweating under the lights in the windowless room.

'With this type of strangulation, the constriction has to be held even after loss of consciousness. I'd say ten to fifteen seconds before he fell unconscious.'

'Was the attacker left or right-handed?'

'He would have had to use both hands, therefore I can't tell.' Sir Bernard peeled off his gloves. 'I've yet to analyse the internal organs but at first glance there's nothing unusual for a man of his age. The state of the lungs is consistent with his being a heavy smoker. And I can now give you a more accurate time of death: between 8.00pm and 10.00pm.'

'And the eyes?'

He smiled faintly. 'I was wondering when we'd get round to that. They've been pricked with something sharp. Not a needle. Something wider. A scalpel, perhaps, or a small knife. The incision in the cornea was quite clean, so not a knife with a serrated edge.'

'How much strength would you need?'

'A quick stabbing motion with something sharp would puncture the eye.' He regarded her coolly. 'I see where you're going with this. All it needs is a determined jab from someone with moderate strength so, yes, a woman could have done it.' He motioned to the corpse's face. 'The eyelids were intact so the eyes were open when they were pierced. Quite a neat job. If it was a scalpel, you might be looking for a surgeon.' He inclined his head. 'Like myself.'

'Not the result of a frenzied attack, then.'

'The cut was deep enough to pierce both humours, but the weapon didn't reach as far as the retina. I've seen some attacks which were so bad that the eye socket was damaged. This is nothing like that.'

Then Danni was right. There *was* a significant difference between Quincey's attack and those of the rent boys. 'Did he have sex before he died, Sir Bernard?'

'He did.'

'Anally?'

'He wasn't penetrated anally. There was no semen in his mouth, but there were traces on his penis, so he ejaculated before he was killed. And he wore a condom.'

'We didn't find any.'

'Pity. In the absence of the condom I can't tell whether he penetrated his partner anally, vaginally, or orally. But the lab should be able to identify the brand of condom from the chemicals on his skin.' He pulled off his robes. 'There were traces of sweat residue on his body, but I'm not sure how much DNA we'll extract.' Like most pathologists she had worked with, Sir Bernard liked to stray onto her patch. 'I don't need to remind you, Chief Inspector, that if the person he had sex with was his killer, any DNA the killer deposited as sweat will be contaminated with Quincey's own. It may be virtually useless in a court of law.'

No, you don't need to remind me. 'And the report will arrive when?'

'The preliminary findings should be ready early next week.' He peered over her shoulder, as though looking for someone. 'Your partner lasted a little longer this time, Chief Inspector. It was a full fifteen minutes before he went green.' He lowered his voice, although he and Von were the only ones in the room. 'We have a little sweepstake going, my staff and I. We estimate how long DI English will last after the first incision. The person who gets closest wins.'

He looked up at the first-floor observation window. A group of people were standing grinning. One of them gave him the thumbs-up sign.

'I believe it's me again,' he said gleefully. 'I have an unfair advantage, of course. I know what causes your DI to faint, so I can time things accordingly. At fifty pounds a throw, it's a nice little setup.'

She recalled her last sight of Steve, gagging, rushing from the room. And they'd all been waiting for it. She glowered at the observation window. *Bastards. All of you.*

'Now, I must go, Chief Inspector. It's Friday and I'm off to the opera with the Commissioner. I trust you know your way out.'

After he'd gone, she stared at Quincey's remains. The ultimate degradation: Max Quincey was a piece of flesh on a butcher's slab, his organs laid aside, the top of his head sawn off, his brains packing the scales. Sir Bernard was off to the opera with the Commissioner, leaving a junior to reassemble the corpse.

She moved closer, ignoring the sharp odour nipping at her nostrils, and peered into the ruined eyes.

'Come on,' she murmured, as if the dead man could hear. 'Speak to me. Give me something.'

Steve was sitting in the Drunken Duck, nursing his soda water. He was looking into the glass as though it held something interesting. His complexion was like cheese. 'Sorry about that, boss.'

'Forget it.' Von sat down next to him. 'Did you barf in the taxi?' she said gently.

'I did it in the lavvie.' He rubbed his arm. 'Did the wee shite win the sweepstake, then?'

'You know about that?'

'Everyone knows.'

She wanted to take his mind off the autopsy. 'I'm thinking of going to see the Millennium Dome.' She nudged him playfully. 'Have you taken your barmaid yet?' She knew Steve had his pick of women, but Annie MacMullen, a woman that Steve had described as having a tidy body, was the girl he came back to. 'I take it you're still seeing her.'

'Annie? Only just.' He shifted in his seat. 'I took her to the ballet at Covent Garden. Thought I'd try something different. Turned out it really wasn't her thing. Wasn't mine, either. A waste of time and money all round.'

'Which ballet?'

'Swan Lake.'

She sipped at her vodka. 'What was it about?'

'A white swan, black swan, bad guy, and a corps de ballet.'

'Like a murder investigation but without the two swans.'

He downed his soda. 'Can I get you another drink before I go?'

'You get on, Steve. I'll see you tomorrow.'

She watched him push his way through the crowded pub. A night out with Annie would take his mind off the post-mortem. She wondered idly how far on they were in their relationship. Few women could resist Steve, Annie would have had him in bed by now. Her thoughts wandered back to the early morning: Kenny's fingers between her legs, the bed warmed by their lovemaking. She pulled the phone from her bag and called him. It went straight to voicemail. Strange. Journalists were like policemen, they always kept their phones on. Why had Kenny switched his off?

Chapter 8

'Look, I know it's first thing in the morning, but can I see some evidence you're still alive?' Von surveyed the room, which reeked of stale beer. All of them, Steve included, looked as though they'd had a wild night. She, on the other hand, had spent her time catching up on paperwork. It gave her the moral authority to be bitchy. 'So, who's first?' she barked.

Steve glanced up from his papers. 'We've been in touch with Boodle's, boss. The Chief Super was there throughout the evening of September 12th. He arrived just before 7.00pm and left at 11.30.'

And they'll tell him I checked. 'So, he has an alibi,' she said.

'Also, we've got Quincey's phone records now,' he continued. He waited till everyone looked at him. 'Max got a call on his mobile the night he was killed. It was made from the Garrimont, the theatre manager's office, to be precise.'

'What time was this?' Von said.

'Shortly after 6.00pm.'

'Do we know the manager's name?'

'Christine Horowitz.'

A phone call taken by the victim on the night he was killed might not be significant, but, as with everything, it would have to be chased up.

'And we've been back to the boarding houses,' said Zoë. She threw Steve a smile as if to apologise for trumping him. 'The landlady at number seventeen told me Max came to London often. He was back earlier this year.'

'Was he now?' Von said, narrowing her eyes. 'I bet I know where he was staying. Okay, get over to Mrs Deacon's. I want the precise dates Max was in London.'

'Do we pull her in for obstruction, ma'am?'

'Nah, if every copper did that, the nicks would be bursting.'

Zoë scanned her notes. 'Mrs Deacon's other tenants saw nothing suspicious on the night he was killed, but few have alibis. They say they only knew Max to talk to.'

'He must have had friends somewhere. We need to find them.' She ran her hands through her hair. 'So, any leads on Manny Newman's whereabouts?'

'His last known was his mother's address, but she couldn't tell us where he is now,' said Zoë.

'Couldn't or wouldn't?'

'She's off her face most of the time, ma'am. She's a user. We've drawn a blank.'

'Not quite. Manny's blind. That means he's probably supported by the state. Try social services. And what did you come up with on the other rent boys?' She caught the look that passed across the room. 'Okay, let's have it.'

'Zoë and I went to the Duke, ma'am,' said a detective. He glanced at Zoë for confirmation. 'But it's like we were lepers. Everyone clammed up the moment we began asking questions. Some of the regulars are old enough to remember the murders but they had sudden cases of amnesia. As soon as the photos of the boys came out, we got the cold shoulder.'

'Did you ask them about Max?'

'Same story. No-one recognised him.'

'The landlord knows more than he's letting on,' said Zoë. 'Dickie Womack. He's been there for years.'

'As far back as 1985?'

'Even further.'

'And is there any CCTV?'

'Zoë and I did a thorough recce,' said the detective. 'There's nothing within several streets of the Duke.'

'With the sex trade in that area?' She stared at him till he looked away. Something wasn't right. Every square inch of Soho was bristling with cameras, so why wasn't the Duke? 'Okay, keep digging. Try the other places frequented by the boys, but don't turn up anywhere mob-handed. It's softly, softly.' She nodded at Larry. 'You've not been to the Duke. Get yourself down there, but don't let them know you're a copper.'

He smirked. 'Sure thing, ma'am.'

'Right, it's high time we talked to Quincey's work mates, starting with the theatre manager. Someone get hold of a list of the cast and crew for the current production of Jack in the Box.'

Larry held up a yellow leaflet. 'No need. I've got a programme.'

She looked at him enquiringly. 'Going to see it?'

'The whole nick has bought tickets, ma'am.'

The Garrimont was on Shaftesbury Avenue, the heart of London's West End theatre district. It stood on the opposite side of the street to the Trocadero, but nearer Piccadilly Circus. A four-storeyed Victorian building, it was faced with Portland stone and crowned with a small cupola. It had never been profitable, and had come close to being earmarked for redevelopment after the war, but a former actor who remembered his days treading the boards had bought it for an undisclosed sum. Although the theatre had been saved, few funds were available for its upkeep, and its steady decline began. The entrance, once a forest of white columns, was reinforced with concrete blocks, and the rich mahogany doors had been replaced with steel-framed glass.

'Bit of a dive,' said Steve, pulling at the door. 'Couldn't see Swan Lake performed here.'

A grand staircase swept up from the foyer into darkness. There were doors on either side, and a flight of steps leading to the basement. The carpet, which had originally been red, was faded and starting to fray, and the all-pervading smell was a blend of floral room spray and carpet cleaner.

A woman in a superbly tailored red suit was standing at the foot of the staircase, an anxious look on her face. Seeing them, she smiled hesitantly, then came forward, hand extended.

Steve's jaw dropped. 'Ding dong,' he said, under his breath.

'Miss Horowitz?' said Von. 'I'm Detective Chief Inspector Valenti. This is Detective Inspector English.'

The woman shook hands. 'Please, we don't stand on ceremony here. Everyone calls me Chrissie.'

'And I'm Steve,' he said, grasping her hand firmly.

Her gaze lingered on his face. Von noticed he seemed reluctant to relinquish his hold.

'I thought I'd better come and scoop you up,' Chrissie said. 'This is a real rabbit warren. You need to lay a trail of coloured beads if you want to find your way back from anywhere.' Her laugh was full-throated and confident. 'Shall we go to my office?' Without waiting for a reply, she turned and disappeared through a door.

They followed her down the cramped corridors.

Von glanced at Steve. 'You okay?' she murmured. 'You look as though you're having difficulty breathing.'

'Wow, boss, I hadn't expected such a goddess.'

She smiled mischievously. 'She's taller than you, Steve.'

'Only because she's wearing heels.'

With or without heels, Chrissie Horowitz was tall for a woman. Von, who had never been able to wear stilettos, admired the effortless way she walked without slipping. Her skirt was tight over her narrow hips, the length just the right side of elegant, and her jacket, reaching to the edge of the skirt, was cut to accommodate her large bust. Von made a mental note to find out where she shopped. Chrissie's appearance seemed at odds with the general shabbiness of the building, and Von wondered if all theatre managers were as glamorous.

Chrissie stopped outside a door and fumbled with her keys. 'Do come in. I've sent for coffee.'

The small dark office was made darker by the low ceiling. Whatever wallpaper had been pasted up had long since been covered in paint, presumably in an attempt to brighten the room, which held nothing but a cluttered desk, several chairs, and stacks of cardboard boxes.

Chrissie arranged herself behind the desk. Von and Steve took the chairs opposite.

'Miss Horowitz—,' Von began.

Chrissie raised a hand, smiling. 'Chrissie.'

'Chrissie. I expect you know why we're here.'

'I'm assuming it's about poor Maxie. I've already had the press snooping around, sniffing for a story. But what could I tell them?'

'We're hoping you can tell us something that will help us catch his killer. How long did you know Max?'

Chrissie ran her hands down her thighs. 'Less than three weeks. I'd corresponded with him about the forthcoming show, of course, but I didn't actually meet him till he arrived in London.'

'Can you remember the date?' Steve said, writing.

'It would have been' – she opened a large book bound in green leather – 'September 1st. A Friday. We had a drink in the evening and ran through some work-related matters.'

Von felt Steve glance in her direction. He was thinking the same. *A drink in the evening? That was quick off the mark...* 'What sort of a man was Max Quincey?' she said.

'Oh, enormous fun. He had a wicked sense of humour. We

hit it off straight away, it was impossible not to like him.'

'Someone found it possible.'

'Well, he wasn't in the first flush of youth. By the time you reach his age, you'll have made enemies. Specially in the acting business.'

'More so than in any other business?' said Steve.

Chrissie crossed her legs, pulling her hem down, but not before Von had seen a brown birthmark, the shape and size of a butterfly, partly hidden under the stocking top. 'Do you know much about the world of the theatre, Steve?' Chrissie said.

'Only from the viewpoint of a paying customer,' he smiled.

'It can be vicious. More vicious than you can imagine. Everyone hates everyone else.' She nodded, her face serious. 'If Maxie had enemies that were prepared to kill him, that's where you'll find them.'

'You've painted a bleak picture,' said Von. 'Didn't he have any friends at all?'

'The people you need to ask are those who've worked with him over the years. I can give you the names and addresses of the Quincey Players. Many of them go back a long way.'

There was a knock at the door. 'Coffee,' she said, getting to her feet.

A small dumpy woman in an overall and cream lace-ups stood beside a trolley, glaring from behind huge glasses. 'The muffins is all finished,' she declared with an air of self-importance.

'Thank you, Mrs Marks,' said Chrissie. 'I'll take over from here.' She handed round the coffee, brushing Steve's shoulder with her breast. Von looked away, smirking, as he nearly dropped his cup.

Chrissie tossed back her blonde mane, and resumed her seat. 'Mrs Marks is our general factotum. She insists we use the title Mrs, even though she's never married. She refers to herself as an undiscovered treasure. So, where were we?'

'Tell me about the crew,' Von said over the rim of her cup.

'The Quincey Players do have staff who tour with them. The lady who works in costumes is one. But most of the crew stay permanently with the Garrimont.'

'Could you compile a list, please? Who works at the Garrimont and who was travelling with Max?'

'Easily done,' Chrissie said smoothly. She tapped away at the computer keyboard.

'I take it you're continuing with the play, even without a director,' Von said, watching her type.

'You know the old cliché – the show must go on. The cast know the play so well they can perform it with their eyes shut. And ticket sales have rocketed since Maxie died. I hate to hear myself say it, but his murder has been excellent for business. Which reminds me.' She reached into a drawer. 'Let me give you these. Two tickets for tomorrow night. With my compliments,' she added, looking at Steve.

'Tuesday's performance?' Von said, taking the tickets.

'I never give out anything but opening night. It's unlucky.'

The printer behind them suddenly spewed out sheets of paper, which fell to the floor. As Chrissie bent to gather them, displaying her cleavage, Steve leant over so far that he nearly fell off his chair. Von lifted her cup to hide her smile.

Then she saw it on the windowsill. 'I notice you have a Jack in the Box, Chrissie.'

'For luck.' Chrissie smiled. 'Actors are a superstitious lot. As soon as they arrived this morning, I sent one out to all the cast and crew. The manufacturer left it a bit late, they've been on order for weeks.'

'The same manufacturer you used when the play ran before?' said Steve.

'I believe so, Steve. Maxie sent me their address.' She handed the sheets to Von. 'I've included home addresses.'

'And your number, in case we need to reach you?'

'My card.' She handed one to each of them. 'It has all my numbers, including my home landline.' This last piece of information was directed at Steve.

Von glanced at the card before dropping it onto her lap. 'Were any of the Quincey Players here in 1985, Chrissie?'

'Heavens, I've no idea, I've not been here long myself. I wasn't even in London then.' She ran a finger round the rim of her cup. 'Why are you asking about 1985?'

'Have you heard of the Jack in the Box murders?'

'Who hasn't?' she breathed.

'So you'll know what happened to those boys. Do you think it's a co-incidence that someone from the 1985 production has been murdered in the same way? And just when the play is running again in London?'

'You know, I really haven't thought about it.' Her expression cleared. 'Wait, I do remember now,' she said triumphantly. 'You asked who was here from 1985. Michael Gillanders. He told me he was the only member of Jack in the Box who was in the old production.'

Von felt Steve turn in her direction. *He's spotted it too, the nifty change of subject.* 'Do you have a cast list for the 1985 production as well?' she said.

'I don't keep records, not from fifteen years ago. There was a huge throw-out before I arrived. You've seen how small this office is. We keep only the bare minimum.'

Von looked at the tickets. 'I notice it's an 8.00pm start. Is that usual?'

'The Garrimont plays have always started at eight. The interval's at nine and we aim to be finished by eleven.'

'How long have you been at the Garrimont, Chrissie?'

'Four years. It was the job that brought me here.' She gave

a self-deprecating smile. 'Would you believe I'd never been to London before?' Her manner became brisk and she stood up, smoothing the back of her skirt. 'I'll do my best to unearth an old cast list, although I can't promise. Now, is there anything else? It's just that opening night is tomorrow, and—'

'Where were you on the night of Tuesday, September 12th?'

She looked bewildered. 'The 12th?' she said, sinking back into the chair. 'I think I was here, in my office.'

'Alone?'

She stared at Von. 'Yes.'

'Between what times?'

'Why are you asking me this?'

'It's part of a line of questioning.' Von nodded at the green book. 'Perhaps you'd like to consult your diary.'

'I don't write that sort of thing down. I think I was here from about seven onwards. It may have been earlier. I can't remember, exactly.'

'Could someone have been in your office without your knowledge?'

'Only Mrs Marks, but she's away by four.'

'What were you doing?' said Steve.

'If you must know, I was looking through the expenses for the Quincey Players' summer tour.'

'If I've understood you correctly, you had nothing to do with that tour,' Von said.

'I'm good with figures, and Maxie isn't. He asked me to run my eye over them.'

'Someone phoned Max Quincey from this office at 6.10pm on the night he was murdered.'

A look of relief crossed her face. 'Yes, that was me. I found a discrepancy in the accounts, and called Maxie. He came over and we went through them together.'

'Why didn't you tell us this earlier?'

'I'm sorry,' she said sheepishly. 'I forgot.'

Steve's voice was friendly. 'A strange thing to forget, that you asked a man who has just been murdered to come over.'

'You've been firing all these questions at me, I was confused. Maxie arrived, we looked at the ledger, and he left.'

'And that would have been when?' said Von.

She frowned. 'About 7.30pm. After he left I stayed and caught up on paperwork.'

Von nodded at the ancient PC on the desk. 'Did you use your computer?'

'When I said paperwork, I meant paperwork. I've only just started getting everything computerised.'

'What sort of paperwork?'

'Letters mainly. We're running an appeal. The theatre's losing money hand over fist.' She motioned to the pile on her desk. 'Correspondence with benefactors. Take a look, if you like.'

'Did you ever visit Max Quincey at his digs, Chrissie?' Von said, watching her closely.

'Never. Why would I?'

'You said you got on well. It's not an unreasonable question.'

She sneered. 'Getting past that shrew of a landlady is a major hurdle, and not one I'm prepared to tackle.'

'You've met her, then?'

'I've told you I haven't.'

'I'm wondering how you know she's a shrew.'

'Maxie told me about her. Now, if there's nothing else, I really do have to get on.'

'You've been most helpful, Chrissie. Perhaps you could take us to the front entrance? Unfortunately, we didn't leave a trail of coloured beads.'

She got to her feet, smiling warmly. 'This way.'

In the foyer, Von said, 'If you can think of anything else that might help us, Chrissie, please do get in touch.'

'I will.' She turned to Steve. 'Goodbye, Steve.' She threw him a final lingering glance before making for the stairs.

Von was studying Steve over the top of a super-sized sandwich, one of the Drunken Duck's specialities.

'We'd have got the truth if I'd left you alone with her,' she said.

'I don't know what you mean, boss.'

'Don't give me that look. I could see what was going on, *Steve*.'

'Och, she's not my type. All fur coat and nae knickers, that one.'

She smiled. 'I thought blondes *were* your type. What colour hair does Annie have?'

'Dark.' He looked away. 'Like yours.'

She laid her sandwich on the plate, and wiped her fingers. 'Okay, let's review where we are. So far, the last sighting of Max Quincey was by Chrissie Horowitz, an hour or so before he was killed. She mentioned someone called Gillanders, who was in the original production. The name rings a bell.'

'He's one of Mrs Deacon's lodgers.'

'He's next on our list, then.'

'Where the hell's my scampi and chips?' Steve muttered. 'Can I have some of your sandwich? My stomach thinks my throat's been cut.'

She pushed the plate towards him. 'Here, have the rest.'

'That phone call Chrissie made just after six was interesting, boss. We had to worm that out of her.'

'Ah, but it's not the only interesting phone call made the day Max died.' She pulled a sheaf of papers from her bag. 'I've been looking through his mobile records. Just after 10.00am, Max made a call to Directory Enquiries. It was the last call he ever made from his mobile, and I'm sure it's significant.' She scanned the pages. 'But look, look at this, Steve. Chrissie Horowitz phoned him, not just after 6.00pm on the 12th, but several times since he arrived on September 1st.' She drew out Chrissie's business card. 'And he's been phoning her mobile and office number too. They were in touch almost every other day. Apart from the calls he made to Andolini's Pizza Palace and the Jaipur Indian Takeaway on Pentonville Road, most of his calls involved Chrissie.'

'That's a hell of a lot of errors in his ledgers,' Steve said with his mouth full.

'Yeah, I didn't buy that story any more than you did.'

'You know what was the final nail in the coffin? The shrew of a landlady she claimed not to have met.'

The scampi arrived. Von sneaked a chip and chewed it thoughtfully. 'All the phone calls between them were a couple of minutes long.'

'They were setting up meetings.'

'Okay, let's assume Chrissie did visit Max at his digs. She knows he's been murdered and lies about visiting him. A natural reaction.'

'But we've no reason to think she killed him. Where's the motive?'

'Why would she visit him in the first place, Steve? They weren't having sex, Max was gay.'

'So why the endless phone calls? What was going on between them?'

'Just friends? Having drinks together?'

He looked doubtful.

She took another chip. 'Even if we discovered she'd been in his room, what of it? It's circumstantial evidence. We need to find the man he had sex with.'

'Or the boy.' He opened the jar of tomato sauce.

'The report from Forensics should be waiting at the nick.' She glanced at the plate of scampi. 'Come on, shove that into your pocket and let's go.'

'But I've ordered rhubarb crumble,' he said in a stricken voice.

'Forget it. That report may provide us with our motive. And, once we have it, we'll be able to put our knickers on the outside.'

He looked at her appreciatively. 'You first, boss.'

As they hailed a cab, Von thought about their interview with Chrissie Horowitz. Chrissie had been economical with the truth, to put it mildly. It seemed an unlikely pairing but she was definitely involved with Max Quincey. Were they in a scam together? Serious enough to have got him killed? And, if so, was she next?

Chapter 9

Still no Forensics?' Von brought her hand down hard on the table. 'So get on to them. Use some initiative.'

'We've rung them several times, ma'am,' one of the detectives said unhappily. 'The report won't be ready till tomorrow at the earliest.'

'Call them first thing.' She turned to the room. 'Right, there's something we need to chase up. Quincey made a call to Directory Enquiries the morning of the day he was killed. Did anyone check whether he was put straight through?'

'I did,' Zoë said. 'There's no record of Directory Enquiries connecting him.'

'It couldn't have been to get Chrissie's number, boss. Both hers were stored in his mobile. If he phoned Directory Enquiries, it was to get another number.'

Von massaged her temples. 'Yet he made no other calls from his mobile that day. To all intents and purposes he was incommunicado till he was killed.'

'The press have been asking to see you, ma'am,' Zoë said. 'They want a statement from the senior investigating. I referred them to the Chief Super, as you requested.'

Larry looked up. 'Talking of press releases, some nutter came in to confess to the Jack in the Box murders.'

'You're sure he was a nutter?' Von said quickly.

He grinned. 'He would have been seven in 1985, ma'am.'

This was par for the course. Every murder investigation had

its quota of crank calls. 'Okay, Steve and I are going hunting,' she said. 'Michael Gillanders knew Max Quincey in '85. That makes him number one on my list of most-wanted.'

Steve steered the Toyota out of the station car park. Late afternoon light shone half-heartedly over the rooftops as they turned into Farringdon Road, and there was a taste of rain in the air.

'I could have had that rhubarb crumble after all, boss.'

'Stop acting like a big girl,' Von said good-naturedly. 'I'll buy you dinner some time.'

He smiled. 'Best offer I've had all day.'

'Don't give me that. Chrissie Horowitz's home phone number was the best offer you've had all day.'

'Boss!'

She glanced at him. He was trying his best to look shocked, but failing.

The young man was removing Jack in the Box dolls from a large crate and stacking them on the tables in the foyer. 'I'm afraid he's not here,' he said. 'Have you tried his digs?'

Von was having difficulty concealing her irritation. 'There was no reply from his digs. As you're opening tomorrow, I assumed he'd be here rehearsing.'

'Not him. He's always telling us he knows the part like the back of his hand.'

Brilliant. Gillanders has gone to ground. And Steve isn't letting me forget his rhubarb crumble.

'You could try Rose Manning,' the young man was saying. 'Wardrobe mistress. She might know where he is.'

'Where can we find her?'

'In the costumes room, giving the clothes a final press.' He motioned towards the stairs. 'The ceiling's a bit low down there, so watch yourselves.'

The dimly lit costumes room, deep in the basement, was the size of a small warehouse. Von peered through the gloom. There seemed to be nothing but long racks of clothes. The strong smell of mothballs, mingled with cigarette smoke, hung in the air.

Steve nudged her. 'Boss. See this?'

Inside the door, illuminated by the light from the corridor, was a cluster of large packing cases.

She bent over them. 'Yes, the knots. They look like the ones round Max's wrists.'

'Can I help you?' The voice was harsh, grating.

'We're looking for Rose Manning,' she said, straightening quickly.

'I'm Rose,' the disembodied voice said. 'And who may you be?'

She spoke into the darkness. 'Police officers.'

From the back of the room, a tall thin woman emerged. She came slowly towards them, pushing through the racks and sending up faint clouds of dust. She stopped under a hanging lamp. Her hair was short, coloured with henna, and so badly permed it was like wire. The light from the lamp filtered through it, transforming it into a three-dimensional orange halo.

'I'll need to see some identification. Hold on, I'll put the main lights on.' A defensive note crept into the woman's voice. 'I've been told to save on electricity.'

She reached behind Von and flicked a switch, flooding the room with strong white light. As she stepped past, Von caught the sickly smell of cheap perfume. Carnation, an old woman's scent.

'As I said, some identification, please.' The woman leant against the wall and brought a cigarette to her lips. Her nails were long and sharp, and painted in a blood-red varnish.

She gave their warrant cards only a cursory glance. Her clear blue eyes bored into Von's. Her face was a smoker's, heavily lined, the skin sallow. Like many women in her fifties she'd applied too much powder, and it had settled into her wrinkles and on the hairs above her lip. Her finely-plucked eyebrows had been pencilled in perfect arches, giving her a look of constant surprise.

'Mrs Manning,' Von said, 'we're looking for Michael Gillanders.'

'It's Miss.'

'One of the workmen told us you might know where we can find him.'

Rose dropped the cigarette and stubbed it out with her toe. 'I've no idea why he said that, I'm sure. I'm not his keeper.'

Jesus, how hard is it to give a straight answer? 'Do you know where he's likely to be?'

'This is about poor Mr Quincey, isn't it?' She closed her eyes and tears coursed down her face, leaving wet lines in her powdered cheeks. 'I'm sorry, I need to sit down. Come through to my work area, I've some chairs there.' She turned away, clutching at her pearls.

The back of the warehouse was like a small sitting room, with a sofa, a table, and two wooden chairs. Against the wall was an ancient foot-operated Singer sewing machine and, beside it, an ironing board. An industrial-strength iron sat at the side, steaming gently. The presence of an ancient Grundig television set in the corner, and a bottle of Harvey's Bristol Cream on the table, bore testament to the fact that not all Rose Manning's working hours were spent working.

Rose sank into the sofa and wiped her eyes with a patterned handkerchief. 'Mr Quincey was such a lovely man, a real gentleman.'

'How well did you know him?' said Von.

'We go back a long way, we do. I knew Mr Quincey since he first came to this theatre, long before he formed the

Quincey Players.' There was pride in her voice. 'I worked here permanently then. In charge of all this. My empire, it was. They used to say the Garrimont had the best wardrobe mistress in London.' She tapped the side of her head. 'I had a system. I could find a costume in less than fifteen seconds flat, I could.'

She disappeared into the labyrinth of clothes, returning a few seconds later with a long black dress. She laid it on the table lovingly. 'Bombazine. From our production of Lady Windermere's Fan. You don't see it much these days.' She nodded towards the clothes lying on the ironing board. 'But that's my stuff now. And what's in those packing cases. I was about to start pressing the costumes when you arrived,' she added in a pained voice.

'We'll try not to keep you long, Miss Manning. So, when did you first meet Mr Quincey?'

'Lord, now you're asking. When the play ran here first.'

'Jack in the Box?'

'Can't remember the year, though.'

''85.'

'If you say so,' she sniffed.

She seemed disinclined to continue, more from apathy than a genuine reticence to talk about the past. 'Mr Quincey was the director, wasn't he?' Von prompted.

A light came into her eyes. 'After the play ended he set up the business and went on the road. He asked me to leave the Garrimont and join him.' Her expression softened. 'Rosie, he said, you're the best. I can't do it without you. That's what he called me, Rosie. Course I went. I mean, I couldn't leave him in the lurch, could I?'

'You were here as wardrobe mistress in 1985?' said Steve.

'I've just said so, haven't I?'

'Then you'll remember the Jack in the Box murders,' Von said quietly.

Her hands flew to her chest and she clutched at the rope of pearls. 'Those boys,' she breathed. 'Of course I remember.'

'Max Quincey was a suspect.'

'He never did it, he was innocent. He couldn't have killed those boys. He didn't have a harmful bone in his body.' Her voice broke. 'It was a vicious slander, that's what it was. A wicked thing to say.'

'Why do you think he was a suspect, Miss Manning?'

'He was fingered, that's what he was,' she spat out. 'He was seen at the Duke, talking to young boys. And he always had a doll with him.' She nodded towards the sewing machine. Beside it, on the floor, stood a Jack in the Box, already popped. 'I asked him why he carried them around. Good for luck, Rosie, and good for business, he used to say. He was trying to publicise the show, you see. Lord knows, he didn't need to. After the first murder we were sold out, right to the last day, we were.' She smoothed her skirt, running her fingers over the pleats. 'Everyone knew he liked little boys. But that wasn't his fault, it's the way he was made. That detective, what was his name, Harrington, he didn't like men who did, well, you know what I mean. Anyway, he had to drop the charges in the end. No evidence, you see.' She jabbed a finger at Von. 'That boy that survived, he listened to a tape of Mr Quincey's voice. Said it definitely wasn't him.'

Von was impressed. If Rose could recall details like this after fifteen years, she had an excellent memory. 'Who else was here back then, Miss Manning, that's still here now?'

'Just myself and Mr Quincey.'

'Miss Horowitz told us Michael Gillanders was also here.'

'What would she know, she wasn't around then. But she happens to be right. Michael Gillanders *was* in the play when it first ran. A minor part.' Her mouth twisted into an expression of distaste. 'If you ask me, he should have stayed with it. His acting skills leave a lot to be desired. Mr Mediocrity, that's who he is. Can't understand why Mr Quincey gave him the star role, Jack the Lad.'

'Jack the Lad?' said Steve.

She fixed him with her steely gaze. 'The name of the character. I take it you don't know the play.'

'We've got tickets for opening night,' said Von. 'So what sort of a person is Michael Gillanders?' She smiled conspiratorially, hoping Rose would take her into her confidence. 'Apart from being a bad actor.'

Rose sighed heavily. 'I really can't think why Mr Quincey ever took him on tour. I asked him once and he said, Keep your friends close, Rosie, but your enemies closer. Says it all.'

'No love lost between them, then?' said Steve.

She threw her head back and laughed. As she drew in her breath, the laugh turned into a hacking cough. 'No-one likes Gillanders,' she wheezed, 'specially the cast. Don't take my word for it, ask them. He's always trying to spike their performances. Makes him look so much better, you see. But then, if you can't act…' She wiped her eyes. 'Gillanders told me once he wanted to be in films, in a Hollywood movie. You wouldn't believe he fancies himself as a great romantic lead. I could just see it now: From Here to Obscurity.'

Von ran a hand across her mouth, trying not to laugh. She didn't dare look at Steve.

'Mr Quincey got lots of placings on the tour, he did,' Rose was saying. 'We went all over Britain. And the cast loved him. He was a brilliant director.' Her eyes were glistening. 'I used to sneak in and watch the rehearsals. Mr Quincey never directed from the seats. He stood on the stage, close to the actors. I can see him now, in his cashmere shawl. He'd wear it hanging from his elbows, like a lady's wrap. He had such style. The actors were like his family, he once told me. He gave them so much support whenever Gillanders was doing his thing.'

'Doing his thing?' said Steve.

'Ruining their performances, I've just told you.' She glared at him. 'Do keep up. You're not half as quick as she is,' she said, indicating Von.

'Why do you think Michael Gillanders stayed with the Players, Miss Manning?' Von said. 'From what you've told us, he didn't seem happy.'

'He wanted to take over running the Quincey Players and get all the money for himself. That was his big ambition. Plain for all to see, it was.'

'Do you think he could have harmed Mr Quincey?'

'Course he could,' she said, almost to herself. She dropped her voice to a whisper. 'Yes, I think he could have done him.'

'But why wait till now?' said Steve. 'Why wait fifteen years?'

Her jaw dropped. 'Where *did* they find you? Look, I'd have thought that was obvious.'

'Not to me,' he said, smiling faintly.

'Gillanders would be a suspect, wouldn't he, if he did it on the tour. Better to wait till they were back here.' She took his silence for incomprehension. 'There'd be loads of people to come under suspicion, wouldn't there? Half the regulars at the Duke, I should imagine. That Detective Harriman really didn't do his job there either, did he?'

'Why the Duke?' said Von.

'They didn't like Mr Quincey. That landlord was always giving him the eye. That's why—' She stopped, as though she'd said too much.

'That's why what?' Von said quickly.

She hesitated. 'That's why he kept himself to himself.'

She's lying. She was going to say something else. But Von knew better than to persist when someone clammed up. There were other ways of obtaining information. She decided to change tack. 'Miss Manning, did you ever visit Max Quincey in his lodgings?'

Rose drew herself up. 'Our relationship' – she accented the word – 'was strictly professional. An unmarried lady would never visit a gentleman in his rooms.'

'Even one who's gay?' said Steve.

She stiffened. 'Whatever his persuasion, he was still a single gentleman.'

Von jerked her head towards the back of the room. 'You said those packing cases travel with you. The knots look complicated. Did you tie them?'

She seemed mildly surprised. 'Zack Lazarus showed us all how to tie them years ago. He's the lighting manager. Good at knots, he is. It looks difficult but it's easy once you know how.'

'Why not use simple knots?'

'They can come undone. No use when you're on tour. Costumes are expensive.' She stared fixedly at the clothes waiting to be pressed.

Von took the hint. She handed Rose a card. 'Please do contact me if there's anything else you'd like to tell us.'

At the door, Rose gripped her arm. 'The papers said that Mr Quincey had been strangled.' She brought her face so close that Von could smell her sour smoker's breath. 'And that he'd been blinded. The doll too.'

'That's right, Miss Manning,' Von said softly.

She brought her hands to her chest, fingering the pearls, her nails like drops of blood against the pale jumper. 'Lord, I don't know what the world is coming to, I'm sure I don't. Such a wicked place.' She turned away. 'Wicked, wicked.'

In the foyer, Von and Steve watched the men remove the last of the dolls from the crates.

'I have to say it, boss, but Max Quincey could certainly

charm the ladies. Whatever his sexual orientation.'

'Maybe, but if I see another woman in tears over him, I'll be reaching for the sick bag.'

They left the building and walked towards the Toyota, parked a couple of blocks away.

'I see those dolls everywhere now,' Von said.

'Aye, and after opening night, London will be heaving with them.'

'Even the wardrobe mistress had one.'

'She was something else, wasn't she? Pity her name doesn't match her appearance.'

She tapped him lightly on the forearm. 'That's bitchy, Steve.'

'My mother had a twinset just like that, in a colour she referred to as heather mixture. And she wore American Tan tights.'

She watched a cyclist mount the pavement to get ahead of the slow-moving traffic. 'Interesting that Rose seems to have adored Max Quincey enough to give up her empire at the Garrimont and take to the road with him. Not an easy life.'

'Fine when you're young, but she isn't. How old would you say?'

'Pushing retirement.' She held up her warrant card as the cyclist approached. With a rapid motion, he swerved back onto the road and disappeared into the distance.

'So, in her early forties, when the rent boys' murders took place.'

'Did you see how she buttoned it when I pressed her about the Duke? And what do you make of Gillanders wanting to run the Quincey Players?'

'I don't buy it, boss. If Gillanders decided to kill Quincey and take over the Players, he wouldn't have waited this long.'

'People can be patient.'

They reached the Toyota. Steve started the engine and they

moved away at a crawl. The cyclist, several cars ahead, was weaving in and out of the traffic.

'Steve, have you noticed that everyone seems remarkably keen to tell us that Gillanders was around in 1985? What did Harrower have to say about him?'

'Gillanders had no alibi for the two late attacks on the rent boys. And as for the earlier attacks, the sergeant taking his statement scribbled in the margin that his character disappears early, so he could have left, killed them, then returned for lights up.'

'But no hard evidence?'

'That was the problem with the old case, boss. Everything was circumstantial.'

'Let's get back to the murder of Max Quincey.' She pulled a document from her bag. 'The floor plan of Mrs Deacon's shows Gillanders's room one floor down from Quincey's. Leaving aside there's no evidence Gillanders had murderous intent, he could easily have slipped into Quincey's room, stunned him, tied him up and strangled him.'

'And made it look like the old murders?'

'Nothing like throwing the filth off the scent.'

'What about the sex, though, boss? Quincey had sex before he died. Surely not with Gillanders.'

She shrugged. 'Quincey could have had sex with someone else, Gillanders heard him leave, then crept upstairs. Quincey would have been naked on the bed.'

'How can you be sure he had sex naked?'

She suppressed a smile. 'Do you have sex with your clothes on?'

'He'd have to get his timing spot on. He could have been seen by Quincey's lover coming down the stairs.'

'Come on, you saw how thin those floorboards are. Didn't you hear the creak on the steps?'

'You mean he'd have heard the guy pass by his room, and known that the rumpy-pumpy had ended?' He nodded. 'It's possible. Forensics might give us a lead.'

'Talking of which, if the report isn't at the nick first thing tomorrow, I'm sending you over. Don't give me the face. You know I can't send one of the others.'

'Why not?'

'Because they can't stand up to Sir Bernard. The last time I sent someone there, he came back a broken man.'

Steve pulled up at a red light. 'It's the smell of the place,' he said, closing his eyes.

'You don't need to go further than the secretary,' she said gently.

He smiled, his eyes still closed. 'Ah, Miranda.'

'I thought that might make a difference.'

Chapter 10

It was the morning of Tuesday, 19th September. Von was in her office with Danni.

'So, where's Steve?' said Danni, fingering the sick-looking plant on the desk.

'I sent him round to The Vulture's to fetch the report.'

Danni pulled a face. 'Rather him than me.'

'Rather him than anyone else. The Vulture's secretary has the hots for him.'

'Miranda? She can't have. She's a lesbian.'

Von pushed her hands through her hair. 'Oh well, I got that horribly wrong.'

Danni grinned. 'I'm sure Steve can handle himself. Anyway, you were telling me about this theatre manager.'

'There was no mistaking *her* signals. I thought Steve was going to trip over his tongue.'

'That sexy?'

'Personally I think she wore too much make-up. It was her voice, though. Reminded me of Marlene Dietrich. And she has these honey-coloured eyes with big lashes.' She smiled. 'What does it for Steve is that she's a blonde, the big-hair kind with layers and streaks.'

'You do surprise me.' Danni looked pointedly at Von's hair. 'His taste is in brunettes.'

She felt herself flushing. 'What do you mean?'

'I mean that if you ditched the semi-detached relationship

you have with that journalist, DI English would have your knickers off in a flash. Surely you've seen the way he looks at you, Von. Kenny's not making you happy, a blind man can see that.'

There was a time when she would have welcomed a chat about her personal life. But it was too late now. Her relationship with Kenny was in free fall, and she was watching powerless from the sidelines. He hadn't been in touch since the night she'd told him about her new case. He'd been away before, but this time was different. She thought about contacting his boss at The Guardian to find out what he was working on, but that seemed a step too far.

'Shall we get back to the business in hand?' she said, her voice measured.

Danni gave a brief nod. 'Fine, if that's what you want. You never take my advice when you need to.' She folded her arms, as if to signify that Von would come to regret it. 'So did this Horowitz woman give you anything?' she said.

'Here's the thing, Danni. The phone records show that she and Max were in constant communication from the day he arrived till the day he died. But when I asked her, she gave me a load of old cock about meeting up to go through his accounts. The two of them were up to something.'

Larry poked his head round the door. 'The forensic report's here, ma'am,' he said, staring at Danni's legs.

'Excellent. Get everyone into the incident room.' She smiled broadly. 'It's show time.'

'Let's go straight to the summary.' Von flicked to the back of the report and scanned the pages. 'First off, the bedside lamp had traces of Max's tissue. Means he was killed in his room. And the eyes were definitely cut after strangulation.'

'Like Manny Newman's,' Danni said thoughtfully. 'And

presumably the same with the other rent boys.'

'Nicotine in Max's bloodstream indicated he'd been smoking heavily. The ash and butt in the ashtray were found to be the brand, Hoyo de Monterrey, which has a distinctive aroma.'

'What the hell are Hoyo de Monterrey?' said Larry.

'Cigarillos, son,' said Steve.

Von frowned. 'Yet only Max's DNA was found in the saliva on the butt.'

'There was just the one butt,' Steve said, 'but that ashtray was too full for one cigarillo.'

'You think our Mr X was a smoker too, and took his butts with him?'

'We've seen that before, boss, killers who take their fag-ends away.'

'Good point.' She continued to scan the pages. 'From the internal penile swab, a sample of semen was recovered from the urethra. Normally semen is expelled by the passage of urine following ejaculation. It means he didn't urinate between having sex and being killed.'

'So, can we assume his attacker was the person he'd had sex with, ma'am?' said Larry.

'We can assume it's possible.'

'What about the DNA?' Danni said impatiently.

She skipped a couple of pages. 'No saliva on the penis, no foreign pubic hair on the body, nothing under the fingernails, the DNA on the toothbrush, towels, and dirty underwear was Max's. But here's something. The sweat on his skin had traces of someone else's.' Her expression hardened. 'Damn it. The DNA was contaminated with Max's to such an extent, it will prove impossible to find a match.' She felt like throwing the report against the wall. 'The DNA was our best chance,' she snapped. 'We can forget it.'

'We had this last time, boss. Mixed samples.'

'At least he can confirm the gender.' She paused. 'Male.'

'Hardly surprising for a gay man,' said Danni.

'As for fingerprints, Max's were everywhere. But there was nothing on the bedside lamp, nothing could be lifted from the tie, and the doll had been wiped clean.' She let out a breath. 'I'd hoped we'd be lucky with that.'

'Again, the same as with the rent boys,' said Danni. 'As I think you said yourself, Mr X wasn't panicked enough to flee the scene without covering his tracks. Pity, though. Even partials would have been better than nothing.'

'They rarely stand up in a court of law.' She'd never forgotten her first court case, thrown out because there were two fewer than the statutory sixteen points of identification. The defence pathologist was quick to point it out, defence counsel played on a possible miscarriage of justice, and she had to watch in silence as a man she knew to be guilty walked free.

'Here's something,' said Steve. 'Prints from the thumb, index and middle fingers of both hands were found on the bathroom taps. They're good quality. And they're not Max's.' He smiled. 'Killers who take their gloves off to wash their hands often forget to wipe the taps.'

'Before we get excited, remember that someone would have cleaned in there. The prints might be theirs.' She continued to read. 'There were no metal traces on the doll's eyes. Not surprising. The eyes are resin, so they're softer.'

'I take it the knife's not turned up?' Danni glanced around. 'Okay, ignore that, I can tell by your faces.'

'They found hairs,' said Zoë, excitement in her voice. 'Only Max's on the hairbrush, but there were foreign hairs in the room. No follicles, and no viable DNA could be extracted from the shafts, but the hair was dyed and otherwise chemically treated.'

'Where exactly were the hairs?' Von said, peering over Zoë's shoulder.

'Several on the bed, and some on an armchair. Sir Bernard has given the lengths. Average is about ten inches.'

'Colour?'

'Blond.'

'So, blond and not short.' She glanced at Steve. 'The only person, so far, who matches that description, and who Max knew, is Chrissie Horowitz.'

'But Max was gay, boss. He can't have had sex with Chrissie.'

'She may have visited him and sat on the bed. Those prints on the taps may be hers. We need to get her photo to Mrs Deacon and see if she recognises Chrissie as having visited him. We know Mrs Deacon has been keeping things from us, so this time let's lean hard.'

'Chrissie did say she'd never been to his digs, ma'am,' said Larry.

'People lie, Larry. Learn to factor that into your analysis.' She turned back to the report. 'Contents of Max's gut: anchovies, cheese, tomatoes, bread dough.'

'Pizza, boss.'

'Max's last meal was at lunchtime, according to Sir Bernard. And that's all we have so far.' She looked up. 'Right, we have three pieces of evidence: sweat that was deposited by a man, long blond hairs, and someone else's fingerprints on the taps. Danni, anything to add?'

'Three things.' Danni spoke in the precise way Von had heard her use when lecturing. 'First, Max's eyes were stabbed, but not otherwise damaged. If you look at page ten, you'll see a close-up of his doll's eyes. They were scraped only lightly. Max's injuries are mere scratches compared with the rent boys' blindings, which were done with great savagery, as were the mutilations of the dolls.' She paused, looking round the room. 'Secondly, Manny Newman stated that *he* was penetrated, but not his client. The pattern of anal bruising, and the absence of semen round their penises, indicates that was also true of the other boys. But in Max's case it was Max, the victim, who did the penetration.'

'How significant is that?' said Von.

'If he was killed by the man he had sex with, then very.'

'And the third thing?'

'The victims in 1985 were young rent boys. Max wasn't.' She hesitated. 'There's one final thing I need to say. In 1985, there were only four attacks. The killer was hardly trying for the Guinness Book of Records. Serial killers usually continue till they die or get caught, and they continue killing even if they move from the area.'

Danni had a point. One of Von's earliest cases had involved a serial who killed nearly twenty people across the length and breadth of Britain before he was apprehended. 'Harrower didn't see that MO anywhere else, Danni.'

'Then it may not have been a serial killer. Something could have linked the victims, and the link was broken when the last rent boy died. I keep coming back to it: Max's case is different from that of the boys. You're looking for two different killers.' She glanced at the wall clock. 'Sorry, but I have to go. Call me when you need me again.'

Larry leapt to his feet to open the door, nearly colliding with the constable coming in.

'A Chrissie Horowitz is on the phone, ma'am,' the constable said. 'Michael Gillanders has arrived at the Garrimont.'

Von jumped up. 'This is our cue, Steve.'

As they left the building, she looked at him sideways. 'How did you get on with Miranda?'

He puffed out his cheeks. 'She's playing hard to get, boss.'

Von was drumming her fingers on the arm rest. They were sitting in a traffic jam on High Holborn, listening to the cacophony of car horns.

'We'll be stuck in this gridlock for ages,' she said impatiently. 'I told you we shouldn't have come this way.'

'Sorry, boss. I thought it was the quickest route.'

'When is Red Ken going to do something about this congestion?'

Ken Livingstone had been elected to the office of Mayor of London just a few months before, with nearly sixty per cent of the vote. He was the only directly-elected mayor in the country, and everyone was waiting to see what he would do first. Sorting out London's traffic problems didn't seem to be top of his agenda, and Von wasn't sure it had even been put on the list.

'So the blond hairs in the room were long,' she said, more to herself. 'Despite what Chrissie told us, I'm convinced she visited Max in his room. But we shouldn't lose sight of the possibility they belong to a man.'

Steve was looking thoughtful. 'Aye, a man with long dyed blond hair.'

'Bet you a tenner Michael Gillanders has long dyed blond hair.'

'Was there a photo of him in the case file?' he said suspiciously.

'No.'

'In that case, done.' With horns blaring, he made a fast turn into Shaftesbury Avenue. The man behind the wheel of a large delivery truck bearing down on them gave him the finger.

'Always interesting driving with you, Steve,' Von said breathlessly. 'Next time, we'll walk.'

Chrissie Horowitz was in the foyer talking to the workmen. They were wearing identical t-shirts today, white, imprinted with a picture of a Jack in the Box doll.

She broke into a smile when she saw Von and Steve. 'You got my message, then. Rose told me you'd been looking for Michael Gillanders. He's preparing for the final rehearsal.' She turned to the man Von recognised as having directed them to the costumes room. 'Dexter, can you be a darling and take these officers to the dressing rooms?'

'It was thoughtful of you to call us, Chrissie,' said Von. 'I realise you're opening tonight. We'll try not to keep Mr Gillanders long.'

'I wouldn't worry about that. The rehearsal doesn't start till after lunch.' The corners of her mouth twitched. 'Mr Gillanders needs at least two hours to prepare himself. Mentally and physically.'

The dressing rooms were on the ground floor, on the other side of the building from the manager's office. The end door was stencilled with a large gold star. Music pulsed from behind it. Edith Piaf was singing 'Milord'.

'Michael Gillanders,' Dexter said, indicating the name on the door.

Von glanced back down the corridor. 'And we find our way back how?'

'Ask Himself to page me.' He looked curiously at her. 'Are you going to read him his rights?'

'We can't discuss that with you, Dexter.'

He grinned and left.

She waited until he'd disappeared, then knocked loudly.

'He won't hear you through that racket,' Steve said. He gripped the handle and pushed the door open.

Her first thought was that the room had been ransacked. Clothes lay scattered over the furniture and across the floor. A rack stuffed full of brightly-coloured costumes took up the length of one wall, opposite a large painted wooden chest, its top drawer gaping. A Jack in the Box, already popped, stood on the dressing table.

The source of the music was a Roberts radio cassette recorder, sitting amongst the clutter of jars and brushes. Steve marched over and switched it off. Edith Piaf died in mid-note.

Something stirred in one of the armchairs. A man in a light blue suit, pink shirt and red and black paisley cravat had been sitting so well camouflaged against the riot of colour, that neither Steve nor Von had seen him. He rose, pulling his hand quickly out of his flies. He zipped them up and thrust a handkerchief into his pocket.

His red face was twitching with rage. 'Get out. I said no interruptions. Who the hell are you, anyway?' His manner changed, and he said more quietly, 'Are you press?'

'Not even close,' said Von, studying his cravat. 'Police officers.'

His eyes narrowed. 'You're a strippergram, aren't you? So who's paying you?' He slammed his fist on the dressing table, making the jars rattle. 'I demand to know whose idea this is.'

She held up her warrant card. He leant forward and peered at it, screwing up his eyes.

'You can check us out with Clerkenwell Police Station,' she said patiently.

He straightened. 'You a copper too?' he said to Steve.

'Detective Inspector English,' said Steve.

'Well, what do you want? I'm in my costume, so you'd better make it quick. Rehearsal starts in a couple of minutes.'

'It doesn't start for a couple of hours,' she said. 'Are you Michael Gillanders?'

'What if I am?'

'We'd like to ask you some questions.'

'About?'

'The murder of Max Quincey.' She smiled warmly. 'May we sit down?'

'If you like, but there's not much I can tell you.'

'Why don't you let me be the judge of that?'

She wriggled into the armchair. Steve perched on the edge of the dresser, avoiding the spilt powder.

Gillanders hesitated, then sank slowly into his chair. He pulled a packet of cigarillos from his jacket and lit up, drawing slowly. Leaning back, he ran a hand over his hair. It was fine and silky, falling to his shoulders. And it was blond, with the beginnings of a bald patch.

Von, whose experience of actors was limited to her brief encounter with Max Quincey, studied him with interest. He seemed ill at ease, constantly glancing at his watch and smoothing down his clothes. His actions reminded her of a junky whose fix is long overdue. She wondered if all actors were as highly strung.

'So you're a detective,' Gillanders said, glaring at her.

'Does it show?'

His eyes travelled down her body. 'Now that I see you close up, I'm afraid it does.'

Highly strung, and rude with it. 'Mr Gillanders, how well did you know Max Quincey?'

He blew smoke through his nostrils, flaring them, the action accentuating his pinched features. 'We worked together. We didn't socialise, if that's what you're suggesting.'

'Why not?' said Steve. 'Max Quincey seemed a popular sort of man.'

'That pederast? Popular? You're jesting.' He dragged on his cigarillo, staring fixedly at Von's chest.

'We're not jesting,' she said. 'We're investigating his murder.'

'You can take it from me that no-one in this theatre liked Quincey.' He continued to stare at her chest.

She kept her voice level. 'Mr Gillanders, why are you talking to my breasts? Do you think they'll talk back to you?'

His head shot up. He looked away, flustered.

'So when did you meet Max?' she said.

'It feels like since before the dawn of man, but it would have been when Jack in the Box ran here in the eighties.'

'And were you in that production?' Steve said, writing.

'Not the lead, which I'm playing now, of course. I was the detective's assistant.' He smirked. 'A bit like yourself.'

Steve continued to write, not taking the bait.

'What made you go on the road with the Quincey Players?' Von said.

'Max offered me a job.' Gillanders wiped ash off his trousers. 'Jobs don't grow on trees in this business.'

'And you've been with the Quincey Players ever since?'

'Fraid so. I see myself doing Hamlet or Lear, eventually. The Quincey Players are merely a stepping stone.'

'But nothing better came along?' Steve said, his lips curving into a smile. 'In fifteen years, no-one from the RSC came knocking at your door?'

Gillanders threw him a look of loathing. 'Despite all appearances to the contrary, Max wasn't a bad manager. We had no shortage of bookings, and we performed a wide variety of plays.' He puffed slowly at his cigarillo. 'He ran the Players well, I have to give him that.'

'And how much are the Players worth?' said Steve.

'No idea,' Gillanders said lazily. 'But we did well enough we got hefty Christmas bonuses. Not many touring companies can boast that.'

'What will happen to the Quincey Players now?' said Von.

'Someone will take it over,' he said cautiously.

'Any name spring to mind?'

'I really can't say.'

'You hadn't thought of running it yourself?' she said, watching him.

He inclined his head. 'If I'm asked to help out as director, of course I'll step into the breach. I wouldn't want the Players to go under.'

He seemed to be holding something back. It was time to hit him in a different place. 'I notice you're lodging with Mrs Deacon, as was Max Quincey,' she said. 'A coincidence?'

'What are you insinuating?'

'It's a simple question.'

'Then here's a simple answer. Max arranged the accommodation. If you want to know why we ended up in the same boarding house, you'll have to ask him.' He smiled faintly. 'But you can't, can you?'

She kept her eyes on his. 'Where were you on the evening of September 12th, Mr Gillanders?'

'Ah, straight for the jugular. I went to the cinema, the Odeon at Leicester Square.'

'What did you see?'

'The Watcher. With Keanu Reeves.'

'What was it about?'

His smile mocked her. 'A serial killer.'

'Did you pay by credit card?'

'Cash.'

'Anyone corroborate that?'

'The man who took it could.'

'Did you go with anyone?'

'I went alone.'

'What time did the film start?'

'About seven. I can't remember exactly.'

'Did you eat before or after the film?'

'I ate before.'

'In Leicester Square?'

'I bought a kebab from a stall, and walked around the Square eating it.'

'It was a cold night for eating outside,' said Steve, not looking up.

Gillanders regarded him through a veil of smoke. 'That's not my recollection.'

'Can you think of anyone who would want to harm Max Quincey?' said Von.

'What an extraordinary question.'

'Would you mind answering it?'

'Most of the cast and crew, for starters. Max was a brutal taskmaster. Never satisfied with anything less than perfection.'

'But that was his job, wasn't it? Directing?'

'You didn't hear the tittle-tattle after rehearsals. The cast were on the point of mutiny. It was all I could do to calm them down – they look up to me as an older brother figure – but they nearly walked out.' He drew on the cigarillo. 'Nothing was right as far as Max was concerned. People standing too far forward, then too far back. Lighting all wrong. Max didn't raise his voice, you understand. He used sarcasm. He belittled. It's not how I would manage a team of actors.'

'Miss Manning seemed to suggest it was the other way round,' said Steve. 'It was Max who was popular and you who weren't.'

'Piffle. What would that hag know? Always downstairs in her little troglodyte cave. She rarely surfaces to join the world of men.' An ugly gleam came into his eyes. 'She's in hormone hell most of the time.'

'Did Max pick the cast for the play?' said Von.

'Max?' He laughed unpleasantly. 'He couldn't pick his nose. He left that to me. He had a say, though. Insisted on sitting in on the auditions.'

She glanced at his receding hairline. 'How old are you, Mr Gillanders?'

'A gentleman never tells.' His gaze was steady. 'And a lady

never asks.'

'You see, I'm wondering how old you were in 1985, when Jack in the Box ran here first.'

His eyes flickered, but he said nothing.

Interesting how they all become cagey when I talk about the old play. 'Answer the question please,' she said. When there was no reply, she added, 'We can do this down at the police station, if you prefer.'

'Ah yes, the old your-place-or-mine routine.' He pulled on the cigarillo. 'I'll be forty in December. That would make me twenty-five in 1985.'

'Twenty-four,' said Steve. 'You were twenty-four when Jack in the Box ran in the October.'

Gillanders regarded him under half-closed lids. 'A mathematical genius,' he lisped.

'Do you remember the Jack in the Box murders, Mr Gillanders?' Von said.

He glanced at the doll on the table, then looked away quickly.

Yes, he remembers. 'Well?' she said, when the silence had gone on too long.

He ran a hand over his eyes. 'What happened to those boys was terrible,' he said in a whisper.

'Did you know Max Quincey was a suspect?'

'Everyone knew. The police were all over the theatre. We saw him arrested.'

'Do you think he was involved in those murders?'

'Oh, without a doubt.'

'The police found no evidence,' she said, her eyes on his.

'Give me some credit. Please. Absence of evidence isn't evidence of absence.'

'Is there any evidence for your statement?'

'If there were, he'd have been locked up.' He pressed the

remains of his cigarillo into a pot of cold cream. 'You didn't know him. He had a vicious streak.' He smiled nastily. 'Max never could hold his liquor. A glass of Glenmorangie and he'd slur you his life history.' He drew a cigarillo from the packet and ran a fingernail over it. 'He was the worst kind of child, the kind that pulls wings off flies. You'd think you'd regret your childhood brutalities, but he didn't.'

'Brutalities that continued into adulthood?'

'Who knows what goes through a queer's mind? His bumboys were young and vulnerable. He liked them that way. I'm sure if they'd had wings, he'd have pulled them off.' He put the cigarillo to his lips and snapped open the lighter. 'I've no doubt he did them all.' He blew smoke to the ceiling. 'Now, is there anything else? It's just that—'

'What is your sexual orientation, Mr Gillanders?'

He stared at her, then laughed crudely. 'Oh, I love sex. But not with boys. I'm a red-blooded male.' He glanced at her breasts. 'Chrissie Horowitz can corroborate that.'

'I thought a gentleman never tells.'

'Hoist with your own petard. Your next question was going to be about evidence of my sexual orientation. Well, there it is. Ask the lady.' He looked at a spot behind Von. 'Yes, I could tell Chrissie Horowitz was up for it the moment I clapped eyes on her. It was only a matter of time before she invited me into her office, and I had my hand up her skirt.' He winked. 'I always check out the engine before giving it a service.'

Von got to her feet, trying to keep the distaste from her face. 'I think we're finished here, Mr Gillanders. Could you page Dexter and tell him we'll meet him at the end of the corridor?' She paused at the door. 'I notice you have a Jack in the Box.'

'We all have one,' he said carelessly. 'It's for luck.'

'Well then, good luck with tonight's performance.'

He froze, the cigarillo partway to his lips. His expression

changed to one of dismay.

'You should have said, break a leg, boss. That's why he looked so horrified.'

'I know. I couldn't resist it. It was the way he boasted he'd had sex with Chrissie Horowitz that did it,' she added with contempt. 'What a prick.'

Steve looked amused. 'Aye, a true gentleman would never fuck and tell.' He opened the car door for her.

As they moved away, her mobile rang. She glanced at the display. 'I need to take this, Steve.'

'No problem.'

She clamped the phone to her ear and turned away. 'Kenny? Where are you?'

The voice was faint. 'In the British Library, researching my story.'

'How's it going? When will I see you?'

'Possibly this evening.' He sounded excited. 'My contact is brilliant, love. I'm getting the scoop of the century.'

'That's great. But listen, I'll be home late. Steve and I are going to see this play, Jack in the Box.'

There was an edge of suspicion to the voice. 'Jack in the Box?'

Damn it. Just what I need. He's going to sulk because I'm with Steve. 'It's part of our investigation, Kenny.' She felt Steve glance in her direction.

'If you say so.'

She was annoyed she had to explain herself. 'Try to get back this evening, will you?'

'Not much point if you're going to be out, is there?' He rang off.

'Jesus,' she muttered, snapping the phone shut.

After a pause, Steve said, 'What do you reckon, then, boss?

About our Mr Gillanders?'

'You can keep him.'

'I meant could he be our Mr X?'

'Too early to tell.'

'You were right about Gillanders and the long blond hair, though. And it looked dyed.' He smiled ruefully. 'I owe you a tenner.'

'Buy me a sandwich at the nick.'

'Do you reckon that tan was real?'

'You could see the streaks under his chin.' She grimaced. 'It was his voice I couldn't stand, as though he'd swallowed a mouthful of oil. Must be my working-class upbringing.'

Steve massaged his neck. 'Bottom line, is Gillanders in the frame?'

'We need to check his alibi. Let's pull the CCTV from Leicester Square.' She thought back to the interview. 'Did you notice the brand of cigarillos he smokes?'

'Hoyo de Monterrey. I'd recognise that smell anywhere.'

'Maybe he and Max were chummier than he made out.'

'Could be they chatted and smoked together in Max's room.'

'Tempting to cast him as a suspect, Steve, but there's no real motive.' She hesitated. 'Except possibly the money angle.'

'Surely the Quincey Players aren't worth that much?'

'It's not how much they're worth but how much Gillanders believes they're worth. He might think Max was sitting on a nice little nest egg.'

'I'll check him for priors, boss. Maybe we'll strike lucky.'

But she had stopped listening. Her mind was back at her conversation with Kenny. Kenny, who'd told her he was phoning from the British Library. With faint sounds of laughter and music and clinking glasses in the background.

Chapter 11

Later that day, Steve put his head round Von's door.

'I've been trawling through the Police National Computer, boss. Gillanders is clean as a whistle.' He leant against the door jamb, smiling lazily. 'And before you say anything, yes, I'm sure. I know you don't trust computers, but I do.'

'After all that carry on about the millennium bug?'

'It didn't hit the PNC,' he said patiently.

'And the ILOVEYOU virus earlier this year?'

'Nor that.'

She let it go. She would never win the argument about computers. Like many people not brought up on them, she both hated and feared them, even though she knew they had become a necessary part of policing.

'Okay, so Gillanders has no priors,' she said. 'Where do we go from here?'

'I was thinking about the Quincey Players and how much they're worth. We didn't find the Players' books at Max's. We could ask Chrissie this evening if she still has them.'

'It can wait till tomorrow. Tonight's her grand opening, we don't need to spoil it for her.'

He slipped his hands into his trouser pockets. 'Talking of which, shall I pick you up at yours?'

'We could meet at the theatre.'

'You don't fancy a wee bevvie beforehand?'

She registered the disappointment in his voice. 'Not a bad

idea,' she said. 'We could rendezvous at that fancy wine bar two blocks up from the Garrimont.'

He looked at his feet. 'You know, boss, it would be easier if I just called for you.'

She knew he wanted to be in charge of the evening. 'You're right, Steve. Seven at mine?' She pulled the tickets from her bag. 'Here, why don't you look after these?'

The doorbell rang at seven on the dot.

'Hold on, Steve,' Von shouted, putting the final touches of Fauve Fuchsia to her lips. There was no need to hurry. She knew Steve would wait patiently, he was the waiting kind.

As she opened the door, the wind blew against her face, lifting the ends of her silk scarf.

Steve was standing gazing at the street. He turned at the sound. 'Wow, boss, I've never seen you with your hair up.'

'And I'm still on duty. You should see me on a non-work night.' She nodded at his silver Nissan Primera. 'You're not driving, are you? There's nowhere to park on Shaftesbury Avenue.'

'Good thinking, boss,' he said hastily. 'I'll call a cab.'

She smiled to herself. She recognised this behaviour from her teens. The sensible thing would have been either to come by tube or take a taxi to her flat. But by bringing his car, Steve would have to return with her at the end of the evening to fetch it.

'Kenny home tonight?' said Steve.

Von sipped at her vodka tonic. 'He said he might be. But that can mean anything with Kenny.'

He gazed into his malt, saying nothing.

They were sitting in a dark wine bar on Shaftesbury Avenue. Von was surprised to find it half empty. The drinkers nursing their cocktails seemed to be serious types, dressed for the theatre. It was the type of watering hole she shunned, preferring bright noisy pubs, but it had been Steve's choice. He behaved as though he knew the place, and she wondered idly whether he brought Annie here.

'Okay, let's get back to business,' she said. 'We need to check timings in the play. That's entrances and exits. If we both do it, we won't miss any.'

He brandished his notebook. 'And I've brought a pencil torch. So, we do all the characters?'

'All six.' She scrutinised the programme. 'In order of appearance, we have a wife, a postwoman, a detective, his assistant, Jack the Lad, and the husband.' She glanced up. 'Did you say you'd seen this play before?'

'I was in Glasgow in eighty-five. It never came that far north.'

'Then listen carefully as there'll be a little test at the end.' She read from the text. 'Millie and Sebastian Davenshawe, a happily married couple, are living their dream in rural Berkshire. However, Sebastian's many absences as an MP to Westminster soon cause Millie to find solace in the capable arms of Jack Forrester. But, where Jack is concerned, all is not what it seems. While declaring undying love to Millie, Jack is also declaring undying love to Sandra, Annabelle, Jeanette, Marie, and Veronica.'

'That's more than six characters, boss.'

'They're not all in the play. Must be noises off.' She continued to read. 'Jack juggles his love affairs, keeping his many mistresses sweet with tokens of affection. But when the arrival of his latest gift, a Jack in the Box doll, coincides with the arrival of Scotland Yard, Millie realises that Jack is less of a Lover and more of a Lad. Follow his antics as he tries not only to escape the long arm of the law, but also the wrath of his various mistresses.'

'There's a joke in there somewhere.'

'Now, when it comes to timings, I'm particularly interested in the detective's assistant, the role Gillanders played in 1985.'

He scratched his chin. 'You know, I've been thinking about it and Gillanders doesn't strike me as a killer. Unpleasant, yes, but not a killer.'

'I'm ruling nothing out. We're dealing with actors, Steve. And liars.' She nudged him lightly. 'Lose your faith in human nature.'

'Yes, boss.'

Chrissie Horowitz, resplendent in a silver-sequinned sheath dress, a glass of champagne in one hand and a cigarette holder in the other, was in the foyer chatting with a large group of guests. She was clearly on the lookout for someone, turning to the front door whenever it opened.

Seeing Von and Steve, she excused herself and came over. 'I'm so glad you could make it,' she said, clasping Steve's hand. 'Let me take you to the hospitality suite.' She smiled at Von. 'We've oodles of champagne and it all has to be drunk.'

'I expect you're sold out,' said Von, as they passed a table loaded high with Jack in the Box dolls.

'We are.' There was pride in her voice. 'Standing room only.'

'Are you expecting to sell all these?'

'This is the first time the dolls have been on sale to the public. They don't go into the shops till tomorrow. All these will vanish tonight. Even people who aren't seeing the play will come in and buy.' She smiled over her shoulder. 'And this pile is nothing. You should see the storeroom.'

The hospitality suite was a large oval room with gilded columns and fading gold brocade curtains. A poorly executed decorating job had caused the plaster to fall off the ceiling and the yellow paint to flake off the walls. Despite this, the atmosphere was one of old-world charm. The room was heaving with guests.

'The canapés will be here shortly.' Chrissie beckoned to a waiter holding a tray of glasses.

Von took a flute. The champagne was so chilled that the glass had turned misty. She took a sip. It was good quality. Whatever the Garrimont's financial problems, Chrissie wasn't stinting on opening night.

Dexter came over and whispered into Chrissie's ear.

'I'm afraid I need to go,' she said. 'I'm doing poor old Maxie's job and I have to get to the wings. We're about to start.' She smiled at Steve. 'Enjoy the performance. And do come back after the show to meet the cast.'

Dexter seemed reluctant to leave. 'May I say how ravishing you look, Chief Inspector?' He lifted Von's hand and kissed it, his eyes on hers. With a nod to Steve, he followed Chrissie out of the suite.

'Bit of a chancer,' muttered Steve. 'I doubt his balls have dropped yet.'

Von took his arm. 'Come on, there's the bell. Five minutes to curtain up.'

'But we haven't had the canapés yet,' he said in an anguished voice.

Chrissie had done them proud: their seats were in the front row of the grand balcony. Below was the vastness of the stalls, sprawling towards the stage.

'This was a marvel in its day, Steve,' Von said. She had a fear of heights and kept her eyes directed upwards. 'I used to come here as a child to see the Christmas panto.'

Steve was fingering the threadbare red velvet. 'I'm not surprised they're running an appeal. The upholstery's falling to pieces.'

'Most London theatres are past their best, but everything

here's just that bit too worn.' She studied the ceiling. The chandelier suspended from the cusp of the arch was dingy with dust. The few lights that still worked glowed weakly. 'It was grand once. See those gilded cherubs.'

'Aye, if you like that sort of thing. Bit over the top for my tastes.'

'You're not telling me you don't get this kind of opulence in Glasgow.'

'Not the part I came from. The paint peeling off the walls is a familiar sight, though. At least it's not damp.'

Chrissie walked onto the stage. She held up a hand, and the conversations died away. 'Ladies and gentlemen,' she said, 'as you know, the director, Max Quincey, is unable to be with us today.'

'That's the understatement of the year,' Steve said under his breath.

'But I'm sure he'll be with us in spirit. Maxie was a great inspiration to us all, both cast and crew. His first, his greatest love, was the theatre. He worked selflessly to ensure that not only did he never let us down, he never let his audience down. I'd therefore like to dedicate to Max Quincey, this opening-night performance of the play he made his own: Jack in the Box. Thank you.'

To thunderous applause, and a few wolf whistles, Chrissie swept off the stage.

'Nice touch, boss. Let's hope the actors are up to it.'

The lights dimmed, but not enough that they couldn't see to write. Von glanced at Steve. He looked as surprised as she was.

To the strains of Tom Jones singing 'Sex Bomb', the curtain went up. The stage was designed as a split set, bedroom at one end and living room-cum-kitchenette at the other. There were several places to hide, the hallmark of a bedroom farce.

The music faded away, and a slim woman in a pink chiffon

nightie and matching dressing gown floated onto the stage. She went into the bedroom and sat in front of the dresser, combing her hair.

'The wife, Millie. Character Number One,' whispered Steve. He peered at his watch, and wrote in the notebook.

A minute later the doorbell rang. It was the postwoman, delivering a parcel for Millie. They bantered about the weather being unpredictable, like men. She left, and Millie carried the parcel into the living room, unwrapping it as she went. A frisson ran through the audience as they saw what it was.

Millie held up the gilt-edged card and read to the audience. 'To Millie, from your ever-loving Jack.' She lifted the lid and the doll sprang out with its cry, 'Jack-jack! Jack-jack!' Even from the balcony, Von could see it was identical to the doll in Max Quincey's room.

The doorbell rang again and the detective and his assistant arrived, asking to interview the husband. They left when they discovered he was not at home. But the moment Millie closed the door, the living room window opened and Michael Gillanders, instantly recognisable by his blue suit and paisley cravat, climbed in. It soon transpired that Jack was a bank robber who was dispersing his loot, hidden inside the dolls, prior to laundering it. While Millie was making coffee in the kitchen, he rang his various mistresses telling them he was sending them presents. The timing of his one-sided conversations with the women was superb and, despite her dislike of Gillanders, Von found herself admiring his acting.

Jack stayed the night with Millie. The transition between night and day was effected by the hands of the large wall clock moving rapidly round to 8.00am. The detective arrived while Jack and Millie were still in bed. Jack scrambled to his feet and hid inside the wardrobe.

'He's come without the assistant, boss,' whispered Steve,

scribbling. He glanced at her. 'You're not writing.'

'Sorry, I've been watching Gillanders.'

The detective told Millie he was looking, not for her husband, but for Jack. As Gillanders poked his head out of the wardrobe, a look of shock on his face, the curtain came down on the first half.

'Brilliant,' said Von.

'Was it?' said Steve petulantly. 'I was too busy writing to notice.'

'Oh, don't be like that. You've a much better eye for detail,' she added guiltily. 'Come on, let's get a drink.'

The foyer was packed with people queuing to buy the Jack in the Box dolls. Dexter and his mates, clearly harassed, were stuffing them into plastic bags and thrusting them at the buyers. Von caught his eye and gave him a sympathetic look. He grinned and held out a doll, lifting his eyebrows questioningly. She shook her head.

'Not buying, boss?'

'A bit steep at £49.99.'

'Aye. And I'll bet good money they'll be a one-month wonder. After the show's run is over, they'll be consigned to attics.'

'I thought you said they became collectors' items.'

'And the collectors have thousands in their attics.'

The crush at the bar was so great, they took their drinks into the corridor.

'Did you notice something odd?' she said, sipping. 'Once the lighting dimmed, it didn't change. It was the same level all the way through.'

'I've seen that technique before. They sometimes use music.'

'There was music only at the start.'

He took a swig of beer. 'Maybe it'll all happen in the second half. That's when the action takes place.'

'What action?'

'You've never seen this type of play before, boss?'

'I rarely go to the theatre.'

The creases round his eyes deepened. 'Then I won't spoil it for you.' His expression changed suddenly. 'Hey, isn't that Kenny?'

She spun round in time to see a man in a dark jacket slip out of the corridor. 'Hold this,' she said, thrusting the glass into Steve's hand. 'I'll be back in a minute.'

In the foyer, she scanned the area rapidly.

He was standing lolling in the queue for the dolls, his weight on one leg.

She clutched his arm. 'Kenny!'

The man turned, and she realised her mistake. 'I'm so sorry,' she breathed. 'I thought you were someone else.'

He smiled suggestively. 'I'm sorry I'm not,' he murmured.

She released his arm. Reluctantly, she returned to Steve.

'It wasn't him,' she said.

'Sorry I got your hopes up, boss.' He handed her the glass. 'We're not going to this reception afterwards, are we?'

'All the cast will be there. I want to see what sort of a dynamic there is. With luck, we'll learn something useful about Max.' She sipped her vodka. 'Anyway, I thought you wanted your canapés.'

They stood with their drinks until the bell. 'First bell, boss.' He jotted the time in his notebook. '9.15pm on the dot. The interval's twenty minutes.'

They returned to the balcony. After the second bell, the curtain rose suddenly, catching out some of the dawdlers.

Millie and the detective were standing where they'd been at the close of the first half. Jack was nowhere to be seen. While Millie busied herself in the kitchen, the detective took the opportunity to snoop around the bedroom. He found Jack hiding in the wardrobe.

Then the fun began. Unwilling to confess she had a lover, Millie introduced Jack as her husband. But then Sebastian arrived unexpectedly. Spinning him a yarn to explain the presence of the detective, Millie persuaded him to hide in a large blanket box, telling the detective that the mystery caller was a debt collector, arrived to extort money from her husband. Fearful that he himself might be taken for Sebastian, the detective hid under the bed. The rest of the play was a wild romp consisting of disguises, chases, and near-miss discoveries. Eventually, however, the game was up. The detective (now minus his clothes and wearing Millie's dressing gown) realised he'd been duped, and Jack was apprehended. Sebastian, seeing the doll in the bedroom, concluded Millie must have a secret lover. In the final scene, when Sebastian said to the detective (still wearing Millie's clothes), 'Well, if it wasn't you in my wife's bedroom last night, who was it?', the doll popped out of its box and screeched, 'Jack-jack! Jack-jack!' The audience shrieked with laughter. Jack the Lad, suitably crestfallen, lifted the doll, unscrewed the base, and a large wad of banknotes fell out.

As the curtain came down to 'Sex Bomb', deafening applause filled the auditorium. The curtain rose and the six actors came onto the stage. Michael Gillanders, still in pink chiffon, clasped his colleagues' hands and bowed deeply.

'It was good,' said Von.

'Aye, can't deny it. Specially the lass who played Millie. I may bring Annie tomorrow night and actually watch it.'

'You think it's Annie's thing?' she said, her eyes still on Gillanders.

'After Swan Lake, anything would be her thing.' He handed Von her bag. 'You were right about the lighting, though. And the music. It came on only at the start and end.'

As they left their seats, she peered up the raked auditorium to the lighting box. For a second, she thought she saw a head bob inside.

'You go on to the reception, Steve. I'll catch you there.'

'Where are you going?'

'To poke around upstairs.'

'Shouldn't I come with you?'

'I won't be long. I need you at the reception.' She patted his arm. 'Try to draw the cast out. But don't introduce yourself as a copper. Socialise. Drink a lot.'

'At this rate I'll turn into an alkie.'

She threw him an affectionate look. 'What's the problem? You're a Scotsman.'

She made her way up the rows to a door at the back. The sign on it read: Staff Only. The door would lead either out of the auditorium, or into a cupboard. She glanced around quickly, then leant against it, turning the handle. The door opened onto a short corridor with a flight of stairs at either end. From the sound of voices and laughter, she guessed that the stairs to the left led to the foyer. She turned right.

As she reached the end of the corridor, she saw the door with the word, Lighting, in faded red paint. She knocked gently. There was no reply. She gripped the handle and twisted firmly. The door was locked.

The stairs descended into darkness. She pulled a torch from her bag and started down, switching it on when it became too dim to see. The last few steps ended abruptly at a fire door. She played the beam over it, examining it closely. It was a door that opened from the inside, but needed a key to come in from the street. There was no sign of an alarm, so she pushed it open and poked her head out. The side alley was littered with styrofoam cups and half-eaten burgers. The stench of urine hit her nostrils.

She shut the door and made her way up the stairs slowly, doing the calculation. From the lighting box, it would take a minute to reach the alley. And less than five minutes to Shaftesbury Avenue and Piccadilly Circus. And from the tube station, to the rest of London.

She was so deep in thought that she didn't see him.

He was standing at the top of the stairs, his bulk eclipsing the light from the ceiling lamp. Her torch was shining directly into his eyes. She switched it off quickly.

'Who the devil are you?' The voice was gruff.

She retrieved her card. 'Detective Chief Inspector Valenti.'

'Where's your warrant?'

'This is my warrant card.' She continued to walk up the stairs.

'I mean your warrant to search this place. I know the law.'

'I don't need one. I'm here at the invitation of the manager.'

'Not in this corridor, you're not.'

She reached the top of the stairs and stood so she could see him. He was short for a man, and solidly built, like a bulldog. His head was closely shaven. Although his complexion was not spotty, his face was scarred with childhood eczema. She put him in his late thirties.

'Are you Zack Lazarus?' she said.

He looked surprised. 'How did you know my name?'

'Rose Manning mentioned you'd helped her with her knots.'

'You've been speaking to Rose about me?'

'We interviewed her as part of our enquiries.' When there was no response, she added, 'We're conducting an investigation into the murder of Max Quincey.'

'Saw that in the papers.' After a pause, he said, 'Best thing that ever happened, if you ask me.'

'I will ask you, Mr Lazarus. But not here and now.' She nodded towards the corridor. 'I take it that leads straight down to the foyer?'

'Yeah. Three flights.'

'Thank you. Good night, then.'

She walked down the corridor, resisting the urge to look back. She knew he'd be watching.

Chapter 12

The foyer was swarming – even more people seemed to want to buy the dolls now that they'd seen the play – and Von had to push her way through the corridor into the hospitality suite. She stood on tip-toe, searching the room.

Steve was near the drinks tables, talking to the actress who'd played Millie. She'd changed into a little black dress and wound her hair into a knot which sat at the nape of her neck. Steve seemed to be enjoying himself. He was leaning into her, his face close to hers.

He glanced up and, seeing Von approach, beckoned to her. 'Over here, boss,' he shouted above the noise.

Von wriggled through the throng, knocking someone's glass and showering liquid over his dinner jacket. 'Sorry,' she said, cringing, 'I have a habit of doing that.'

The man muttered a curse and, excusing himself to his companions, made for the door.

Steve was smiling broadly. 'Boss, meet Jools Lamberton. Jools, my boss, Von Valenti.'

Good boy, he's remembered. Only names. No mention of what we are. 'Pleased to meet you, Jools,' she said.

'Likewise, darling.' Jools's eyes were a vacant blue under her false lashes. She hadn't removed her stage make-up, a mistake as it made her look more tired than glamorous.

'From now on I'll only ever be able to see you as Millie Davenshawe,' Von simpered. 'That part was made for you.' She waited until she had the woman's full attention, or as much of it as she ever granted to anyone. 'But you're too young to have played it when it first ran.'

Jools looked puzzled.

'In 1985,' Von said.

'Oh no, did it really run then?' She drew her brows together, caking her make-up into fine lines. 'Bother. It's bad luck to star in anything other than a new play. The way Max talked, I'd assumed tonight was the world premiere.'

'Max Quincey?'

She turned her glass in her hands. 'Such a lovely man. I thought so, anyway.'

'You sound as though there were people who didn't.'

'Well someone killed him.' She smiled maliciously. 'The police haven't a scooby. They probably think it was one of the cast. But, between you and me, none of the men here has two balls to rub together. And they're so brainless, they wouldn't know how to murder anyone.' She leant forward conspiratorially. 'No, I have a *theory*.'

'Do tell,' Von said, making a show of being riveted.

'A debt collector killed him.'

She struggled to keep the disappointment from her voice. 'Like in the play?'

'Sounds a bit of a co-incidence, but everyone knew Max was in hock.'

'But didn't he own the Quincey Players?'

'Well, not outright,' Jools said, sounding unsure. 'I think he owned it jointly with that brother of his. He's some big detective or other. An Inspector.'

'Gosh, did Max tell you that?'

'He confided to me once that his brother had provided the start-up money. That would have meant he part owned it, wouldn't it? And it must have been the lion's share.'

'Might he just have put up the money and left Max to it?' said Steve.

'Oh, come on, I know all about detectives. I've read the novels. They're down there with tax inspectors and traffic wardens. They're always either on the take or running some sort of racket.' She gulped the last of her champagne. 'Anyway, enough of this. Tell me more about yourself, Von. What's it like being a taxidermist?'

As Von opened her mouth to speak, Jools shrieked, 'Oh, there's Michael.' She thrust her glass into Steve's hand. 'Sorry, darlings, got to go. Photo call and all that. But don't go away, this won't take long.'

They watched Jools stumble across the floor.

'A taxidermist?' said Von.

'She asked me what I did, and I had to say something.'

'And if Chrissie or Gillanders had come along?'

'I'd have rescued the situation,' he said confidently.

'Have you talked with anyone else, Steve, or was it just Jools?'

He seemed keen to change the subject. He motioned with his chin. 'Take a look at Gillanders. Have you ever seen such a get-up? I think I preferred him in pink chiffon.'

She peered through the melee. Michael Gillanders, sans nightie and in an ochre-coloured satin suit, was standing at the door. His black shirt was open to the waist, revealing hairless tanned skin. A gold chain hung round his neck. With him was the young man who'd played the detective's assistant. Gillanders was speaking to him earnestly.

'What do you think he's saying, boss?'

'He'll be telling the assistant how he played the part in 1985.'

Chrissie arrived with a tray of canapés. 'Ah, there you are. So tell me, what did you think of the show?'

'Marvellous,' said Von. 'So good that Steve's thinking of

seeing it again.'

'We're very lucky with the cast,' she said, watching Steve taking as many canapés as he could fit into his hand. 'Now, you'll really have to excuse me. I've been standing up for four hours. I need a long bath with expensive-smelling stuff in it. I now know what poor Maxie went through, night after night, standing in the wings making sure everything went smoothly. Any ideas I might have entertained of becoming a director have gone straight out of the window.' She signalled to a waiter, who took the empty tray. 'I'm really glad you enjoyed the performance. It would have meant so much to Maxie, knowing how his work has been appreciated.'

They watched her leave, moving effortlessly through the crowd, pausing to exchange the odd word with her guests.

'Okay, Steve, what do you think of Jools's theory that Max was killed by a debt collector?'

'Pish.'

'My sentiments too. A debt collector would have put a bullet in his head.'

'But the Chief Super underwriting the Players, boss?' He rubbed his cheek. 'That's something new.'

And something he neglected to disclose.

'So what does it tell us?' Steve said.

'It tells us that nothing in this case is what it seems.'

'I knew I should have stayed in Glasgow. Everything there is exactly what it seems.' He lowered his voice. 'So what did you find in your little recce upstairs?'

'A lighting box. And a flight of stairs leading down to a fire door, and an alley.' She looked meaningfully at him. 'Shaftesbury Avenue's at the other end.'

'Well?'

'Well, Sherlock, you yourself pointed out that the lighting didn't change, and there was music only at the start and end.'

'Sex Bomb.'

'It's the lighting manager who controls that.'

'Aye, boss. And so?'

'And so,' she said with exaggerated patience, 'once he's set the lighting level and played the music, the lighting manager isn't needed till right at the end. He could have sneaked down those stairs into the alley, and reached Piccadilly Circus station in a matter of minutes. We've been knocking ourselves out recording the timings – okay, *you've* been knocking yourself out recording the timings – and missed the simple fact that whoever killed the rent boys may not have been one of the cast, but a member of the crew.'

He scratched his chin thoughtfully. 'So did you find the lighting manager?'

'We spoke briefly. At some point we'll need to interview him properly.'

'Did he have long blond hair?'

'He didn't have any hair at all.'

The taxi drew up a little way from her flat. As Steve paid the driver, Von levered herself out of the car and stretched. She was dog-tired. What she needed was a lie-in. Fat chance.

Despite the lateness of the hour, the night was warm and there was a sharp smell in the air. She glanced up at the brooding sky. A thunderstorm was building.

They reached Steve's Nissan Primera. He paused, looking at the ground. 'I'll walk you to your door, boss.'

She hesitated. Kenny might be home, watching from the bedroom window. Oh, sod Kenny. She was growing tired of his pettiness. She slipped her arm through Steve's, and they strolled down the street, seeming in no hurry to get anywhere.

'What made you stay in Whitechapel, boss? Not that there's anything wrong with it,' he added hastily.

'Jack the Ripper country, you mean?'

'And the Elephant Man.'

'I like the fact it's working-class, Steve. It's what I am. As a girl, I played on these pavements. My Dad used to work in a pub in Commercial Road.'

'Your dad was a publican?' He rubbed the underside of his jaw. 'What did he think of you joining the Met, then?'

'I think he was just relieved I didn't end up on the streets like his sister. It was my Mum who pushed me, though, she wanted me to go to college. It was a while before she appreciated that joining the police was as good as.'

He laughed. 'Never heard that before. Most people think coppers are the lowest form of life. So where are your folks now? Still here?'

'Nah. Retired to a cottage in Yorkshire.' A cottage she and her brothers had helped them buy.

She'd been lucky with her parents, she knew that. They were devoted to each other, and had provided a loving home for herself and her brothers. Not for the first time, she appreciated how different her upbringing had been from Kenny's. His father had beaten up his mother so many times she was constantly in hospital. Kenny had been raised by his aunt, a decent God-fearing woman, who tried to instil her values into him. But her words had fallen on deaf ears. He left school early, and earned his living shifting hot goods for a friend. Finally, he joined the army. Where his aunt had failed, the army had been the making of him. When his time was up, he returned to live with his aunt and worked as editor for a church magazine. He was good at sniffing out stories. And good with words. When his aunt suggested he submit articles to a newspaper, he jumped at the chance. A short while later, he was taken on by The Mirror, and it was just a matter of time before he got a break and moved to The Guardian. But Kenny had always made his own luck.

They'd reached her flat, the ground floor of a terraced house conversion whose Victorian façade had been reconstructed after the damage suffered in the Blitz. She'd bought the flat before the area's property boom. Despite the influx of migrant groups, or perhaps because of it, Whitechapel was becoming the place to live and house prices were rising. The large number of Bangladeshis, in particular, were the reason so many Indian restaurants had opened.

She motioned to the building. 'I'd have preferred a top-floor flat. There's a cracking view from up there. The Royal London Hospital is just visible from the roof.'

He smiled. 'Handy.'

'And my brothers have their garage a couple of streets away.'

'Handier.'

She saw it before he did. The striped box, sitting on the steps. 'Someone's left me a present,' she said.

She reached over, but he gripped her hand. 'Don't touch it.' He removed a pair of latex gloves from his jacket.

'You think it's booby-trapped?' she said, laughing nervously.

He bent and popped the lid. The doll sprang out, screaming, 'Jack-jack! Jack-jack!'

'Christ Almighty.' He put himself between her and the doll. 'Don't look at it, boss.'

But it was too late. She pushed him aside and stared at the smeared eyes and the string round the neck, with its fancy knot. And the paper, taped to the doll, with the words 'DCI Valenti'.

She'd seen it many times before but it still surprised her, how blood looks black in the dark.

'I'm fine, Steve. Stop fussing.'

They were sitting on the sofa.

'You shouldn't be on your own, boss. Not tonight.'

'I'll be okay,' she said weakly. 'Kenny will be here soon.'

'Then I'll wait until he arrives.'

'I'd rather you took that thing to Forensics.'

'They're closed at this hour.'

'You know what I mean. Just take it away.' She glared at him. 'All right, if you're not going to obey a direct order, you can at least make me another drink.'

'You're cold.' He took her hands and rubbed them briskly.

She pulled them away and hauled herself off the sofa. 'Christ, why do I have to do everything myself?' She snatched the bottle of whisky from the sideboard. 'Do you want some?' she barked.

He looked at her in silence.

She returned to the sofa and poured.

'Why don't you let me do it, boss?'

'Why should I?'

'Because most of it's going on the carpet.'

She slammed the bottle down. 'Fine. You do it, then.'

'Look, your nerves are shot, you can't stay here. I'll take you down to the station.'

'Are you going to lock me up?'

'I didn't mean the cells. There's a bed there you can use.'

'I see what you're doing, Steve, and I appreciate your concern, but I'm staying here.'

'Then I'll sleep on the couch.'

He's not going to leave. Just my luck to have an awkward bugger for a partner. 'Right, I'll get the spare duvet,' she said. 'Now pour me that fucking drink.'

They sat on the sofa, wrapped in the double duvet, and drank whisky till the bottle was empty. Her eyes closed and her head fell onto his shoulder. Neither heard the front door open and close.

'What the hell's going on?'

At the sound of the voice, she woke with a start. She pushed the duvet away and struggled groggily off the sofa. 'Kenny, where have you been? I've been waiting ages for you.'

Kenny picked up the bottle. 'I can see how you've been waiting. Been having quite a party.'

Steve got to his feet. 'Look, I know how this must seem, but—'

'And you can bugger off, mate,' Kenny said, poking him in the chest.

'For God's sake, Kenny,' she said, grabbing his arm. 'I asked Steve to wait with me. Something horrible's happened. Someone left a Jack in the Box outside the flat. There's blood on the eyes, and string round its neck.'

He stared at her. 'Where is it?'

'In the boot of Steve's car. He's taking it to Forensics.'

'Can I see it?'

'I don't want it contaminated,' said Steve.

He nodded. 'I owe you an apology,' he said curtly.

'Forget it.' Steve turned to Von. 'I'll be on my way, boss.' He made for the door.

'Steve,' she called after him, 'wait.'

But the door had already closed.

She glowered at Kenny. 'He didn't deserve that.'

'I saw you both under the covers. So I jumped to the wrong conclusion. Can you blame me?'

'No, I suppose not.'

He sank onto the sofa and ran his hands over his face. 'So tell me about this doll. You said there was blood on the eyes.'

'Someone's trying to send me a message.'

'What have you been doing?'

'Asking a lot of questions about Max Quincey. And the Jack in the Box murders.'

A look of alarm crossed his face. 'Then it's a warning. Like that other time.'

'Someone wants me to drop the case, or change the direction it's taking.'

'And are you going to?' He was angry now.

'How long have we been seeing each other, Kenny? Four years? Five?' She smiled sadly. 'And you still don't know me.'

'Jesus, love, it's not worth it. Ask to be reassigned. The Chief Super will understand.'

'He's given me a final chance to redeem myself.' She took a deep breath. 'If I screw this up, I'm back to pounding the beat.'

'I told you ages ago you should have gone ex-directory.'

'Drop it, Kenny. It's late and I need to get to bed.' She hesitated. 'I don't want to be alone tonight.'

In the silence that followed, she wondered if he could guess what she was thinking. If anyone had asked her at that moment whether she wanted Steve or him, she wouldn't have been able to reply. She didn't know the answer herself.

She took his hand and led him into the bedroom.

Chapter 13

'So I want you to be vigilant,' Von was saying, 'and tell me if anything like this happens to you. Come to me even if you're just suspicious.'

The team was crowded around her. She read their expressions: most looked shocked, some were thoughtful, one or two avoided eye contact. She had no intention of telling them how shaken she'd been by the incident. The last thing she wanted was for them to pick up on her fear. 'Right, let's get to it. Today, we're back with the rent boys. Specifically who from the Garrimont had the opportunity to kill them. DI English?'

'I've got the timings up for the play,' Steve said, nodding towards the wall. 'Jack in the Box starts at 8.00pm, there's one interval between 9.00pm and 9.20pm, and curtain call is at 11.00pm. Chrissie Horowitz seemed to suggest it was the same in 1985, so we'll work on that assumption.'

She studied the street map pinned to the wall. 'Liam was killed between 2.00am and 3.00am, and Manny was attacked shortly before 1.00am. That's well after the play finished. If the attacker came from the Garrimont, then it could have been anyone.'

'Correct, boss. Therefore we need only concentrate on Gilly and Charlo. Let's take Gilly first. He was found in a squat in the Covent Garden area. From Piccadilly Circus, Covent Garden is just two stops on the Piccadilly line.'

'So, we're talking, what, fifteen, twenty, minutes to get from the Garrimont to the squat?'

'About that, assuming the underground was running properly, or running at all. Longer if he walked up Shaftesbury Avenue or cut across to Cranbourn Street.'

She tapped the wall. 'Gilly was killed between 9.00pm and 10.00pm. It rules out Jack, and the detective. They're both on stage the minute the curtain goes up on the second half. What about Sebastian, the husband?'

'He comes on at 9.40pm and stays on. He's a possible, but the timing makes it highly unlikely.'

'So, who's left?'

'The detective's assistant. He's on at 8.12pm and leaves at 8.18pm. Next time we see him is curtain call.'

'8.18pm would give him plenty of time to pick up Gilly, have sex, murder him and be back for 11.00pm.'

'Aye.'

'Right, let's move on to Charlo. He was found in his pimp's house.' She ran a finger across the map. 'Porteous lives in a council estate half a mile from Waterloo Road. To get to the Waterloo tube from Piccadilly Circus, it's three stops on the Bakerloo line.'

Steve nodded thoughtfully. 'And then, what, fifteen minutes to the flat at a brisk trot.'

'Charlo was killed between 10.00pm and 11.00pm, again ruling out Jack, the detective, and the husband.'

'But not the assistant, boss.'

'Right then. Of the cast, the detective's assistant is the only one who fits the bill.' She frowned. 'Why didn't Harrower follow it up?'

'There's no evidence he timed the entrances and exits. He may just have looked at when the play started and ended.'

'Who was the detective's assistant in 1985?' said Zoë.

'Michael Gillanders,' said Von. 'As an aside, he has dyed

shoulder-length blond hair.' She turned to Steve. 'On the subject of Gillanders, did you get anything out of Jools before I arrived?'

'Who's Jools, ma'am?'

'The wife in the play.'

'The wife was played by a man? I thought that died out with Shakespeare.'

'Jools is one of those names that can be a man's or a woman's, Einstein,' said Larry, grinning. He pushed Zoë playfully off the desk.

'To answer your question, boss, Jools told me nothing we didn't already know about Gillanders.'

'Okay, let's look at the Garrimont's crew next. There are two contenders who are the right age. Max Quincey is one. Zack Lazarus is the other.'

A constable stuck his head round the door. 'Forensics are on the phone, ma'am, asking you to come over.'

'That was quick.'

Steve looked at his feet. 'I asked them to make it a priority. I squared it with the Chief Super.'

'I'm grateful,' she said softly. She turned to the others. 'One last thing. Jools suggested Max's murder might be money-related. We need to find out what the Players are worth. I'll be back by mid-day and we'll review Max's case over lunch. You've been working hard so it's a Chinese take-away on me.' A take-away for nearly twenty people would set her back, but it would be worth it. She noted the looks of approval. 'Larry, can you phone the order through, please?'

His face brightened. 'What would you like, ma'am?'

She thought back to the last time she'd eaten Chinese. The previous Thursday, the evening she'd spent with Kenny. 'Anything except Mongolian beef and egg fried rice.'

They were approaching Lambeth Bridge. The previous night's thunderstorm hadn't succeeded in clearing the air; the sky was heavy with clouds, and a mild rain was falling, misting the car's windows. A helicopter buzzed low overhead, drowning out the sounds of the late morning traffic.

Steve was staring silently ahead.

'I've often wondered who made the decision to site the Metropolitan Police Laboratory across from the Archbishop's Park,' Von said lightly. When there was no response, she added, 'You're very quiet, Steve.'

'I haven't had a chance to speak to you since last night.' He glanced at her. 'How are you?'

'Tired. I couldn't sleep.'

'Me neither. I was at work at 6.00am.'

'Explains why Forensics were so quick off the mark. What did the Chief Super say when you told him?'

'He sounded sympathetic, and agreed to my request for fast-tracking. He wasn't his usual self.'

She didn't answer immediately. 'The problem is, he can't bury his brother. Max Quincey will have to stay in the freezer.'

'Aye, I've never understood why the accused has the right to an independent post-mortem.'

'We've no prime suspect, Steve, let alone an accused.' She ran her hands through her hair. 'We've made no progress at all.'

'We need to take prints and a hair sample from Gillanders. I know the evidence is circumstantial – dyed blond hair, smokes the same cigarillos as Max, was the detective's assistant in 1985.'

'If only to establish him as being in Max's room, we should do it. But if there's no match on his hair, then we're looking for another blond man.'

'Or boy, boss.'

They were on Lambeth Road, pulling up outside a wide concrete and glass structure.

'Yes, or boy. Quincey liked them young.'

Miranda Avery was sitting at her desk, filing her nails. A plump pretty woman, not much taller than Von, she was employed by Sir Bernard primarily to ensure he was not disturbed. Many tried, but few succeeded in getting past her. Von was one of the exceptions.

Miranda sat up as Von and Steve entered. 'I'll tell Sir Bernard you're here,' she said, smiling at Von. 'He's been expecting you.'

'Thank you, Miranda.'

She spoke briefly into the phone, then replaced the receiver. 'You both know the way.'

Whenever Von entered Sir Bernard's office, she had the impression she was in someone's drawing room. The walls were patterned with the spines of leather books, and oriental rugs covered the floor. A jet of flowers stood on the mantelpiece, the sweet scent reaching them across the expanse of the room.

Sir Bernard was sitting behind a carved oak desk, a gift from a grateful student. Seeing them, he got to his feet.

'Thank you for fast-tracking this one, Sir Bernard,' Von said.

His rheumy eyes moved over her face. 'How are you taking this, Chief Inspector?'

Good Lord, he actually sounds concerned. 'It comes with the turf,' she said. 'It's not the first time.'

He nodded sympathetically, then motioned to the scallop-edged coffee table.

'You may keep this report.' He opened a file, even though she knew he could quote the contents verbatim. Sir Bernard's memory was legendary. At a police function, with over fifty guests attending, she'd seen him successfully accept a bet that he could memorise and recite the list of attendees in under five minutes.

'There were no prints and nothing we could use for DNA,'

he said, pushing his spectacles further up his nose, 'either on the doll or on the box. We took the whole thing apart in case a hair had lodged inside. There was no fluff even. The doll looked new.'

'It was bought earlier that evening,' said Steve.

'And you know this how?' Sir Bernard said tartly.

'Opening night was yesterday. The dolls were on sale only in the theatre.'

Sir Bernard addressed himself to Von. 'The string, too, had nothing we could use for DNA. Someone's been very careful.'

'Is it possible to get prints off string?' she said.

'Sometimes we can lift partials off certain types of plastic, but not this kind. The knot was complicated. It was identical to those in the ties round Max Quincey's wrists.' He looked at her over the rim of his spectacles. 'Could that be significant?'

'It would be if the press releases hadn't described the knots in detail.'

'That was careless.'

She was tempted to tell him it was the Chief Super who'd released that information without consulting her. But she said nothing. The Chief Super was a personal friend of Sir Bernard's, and she wasn't convinced that her comments wouldn't make their way back to him.

'And the blood, Sir Bernard?' said Steve.

'Not human, you'll be relieved to hear. It was chicken blood. We found fragments of chicken liver.'

'Which you can buy in any supermarket.'

'If you say so, Inspector,' he said in a matter-of-fact way.

She got heavily to her feet. It had been a wasted journey. 'Thank you for your time, Sir Bernard.'

He bowed his head. 'Glad to be of assistance.'

In the Toyota, Steve voiced her thoughts. 'Pity the press coverage described the knots in the ties.'

'I sometimes wonder where the Chief Super was when brains were being handed out.'

'Anyone who reads the papers could have left that doll,' he said angrily.

She watched the buildings speed by. *No, not anyone. Someone who wants me to give up the case. But which case? Max Quincey's? Or that of the rent boys?*

Von was stuffing crispy duck into her mouth. 'You say Mrs Deacon cleans the rooms herself?'

'Every Tuesday morning, ma'am.' Zoë thumbed through her notebook. 'That includes wiping down the bathroom taps.'

'If Quincey was killed on a Tuesday evening, then the prints on those taps were deposited between morning cleaning, and that evening.'

'We took Mrs Deacon's fingerprints to eliminate hers.'

'And how did she respond?'

'With outrage, ma'am.'

Von smiled, wiping her hands on a napkin. 'Good work, everyone.' She reached across the desk for the carton of chow mein. 'So how are we on the finances?'

'This Jools person was right,' Zoë said. 'Max Quincey was heavily in debt.'

'How much did he owe?' Von said, stuffing noodles into her mouth.

'More than the third world. On his credit card, it's in excess of £50,000.'

'How much?' She nearly choked. 'What the hell has he been buying? Let me see the statements.'

'They go back several years, ma'am.'

She examined the sheets. 'Nothing out of the ordinary, just living expenses he's let mount up. He pays back little more than the minimum monthly on his card.'

'What was his income?' said Steve.

'He paid himself a small salary as director of the Quincey Players, sir. Obviously not enough to cover his living expenses.'

'Have you found out yet what the Players are worth?' Von said, wiping her chin.

Zoë shook her head. 'We asked Chrissie about the books but she said Max had left them with his accountant.'

'Name?'

'Max never told her, ma'am.'

'If the Quincey Players are worth a small fortune, we might have our motive. And it might be Max's brother who gains now he's died.'

'We've also been looking at Mrs Deacon's records, going back as far as she has them, which is eight years. She records names, the rent, and the date it's paid.' Zoë smiled in mock innocence. 'Sounds like the model landlady.'

'And do her records confirm Max Quincey was a frequent visitor to London?'

'They do, and he stayed at hers each time. But, although we pressed her, she couldn't tell us what his business was.'

'Except that it was none of ours,' Larry chipped in.

Von leafed through the sheets. 'So, a couple of visits a year, on average. But why the hell was he returning to London?'

'To visit his brother, boss?'

'I intend to ask him. Anyway, Larry, what have you been up to?'

'I've been in under cover.' He bit into a fortune cookie. 'Deep cover.'

She smiled. 'Fancy yourself as double-oh-seven?'

'Double-oh-idiot, more likely,' said Zoë.

Larry threw the cookie wrapper, but she ducked without lifting her eyes from her food. She raised her middle finger, prompting guffaws from across the room.

'Come on, Larry, thrall us,' Von said.

'Okay, so I went to the Iron Duke masquerading as a stockbroker. Made some tentative enquiries about the rent boys. The three Irish boys definitely knew each other. Came over from Dublin together.' He swallowed the rest of the cookie. 'Only one of the regulars gave up anything. Even then, I had to get him totally rat-arsed before he'd talk. We were quite chummy by the end.'

'And you stayed totally stone-cold sober,' said Steve.

'Well, I had the odd pint, sir,' he said, poker-faced. 'It would have looked odd otherwise. Anyway, the Irish boys were well known at the Duke, happy lads, always arsing around. To hear this guy talk, they almost lived there. Every Christmas, the regulars had a whip-round and bought them presents. There was a big karaoke party. Gilly would sing Irish ballads, unaccompanied. Had a voice like a songbird. When he sang "The Sunshine of Your Smile", the old lags would start crying into their beer. This regular told me that sometimes they came with' – he looked uneasy – 'Charlo's nigger boyfriend.'

'Jimmy Porteous,' said Steve.

'The boys had nothing steady. When they did work, they tried to get jobs they could do together. They sometimes painted houses for the council.'

'What about Manny?' said Von.

'He flipped burgers during the day, but this regular didn't know where. Manny seemed to keep himself to himself.'

'Not pally with the Irish boys?'

'Neither with them, nor much with anyone, ma'am. That's why most of this guy's talk was about Gilly and the others.' He paused. 'Get this, though. He let slip that the Irish lads were into something. But when I pressed him, he buttoned it pretty quickly. I got nothing more out of the old bugger after that.'

'Into something?' Von said softly. 'No indication what?'

He shook his head. 'The landlord looked at me strangely when he saw me huddled with this guy. He may have suspected I'm a copper.'

'Surely not with that ponytail,' Steve said, smiling.

'I also tried round by the river and Manny's warehouse.'

'Did you get anything more?' said Von.

'Only offers of blow jobs, ma'am.'

She massaged the base of her spine. 'Harrower may have missed something. He assumed the rent boys' killings were random. But maybe not. Didn't Danni say their deaths might be linked?'

'A gangland execution, boss, made to look like a sex attack?'

'Yes, they may have been killed to order.' She dropped her chopsticks into the carton. 'Right, let's get back to Max's murder. It's time to get those prints and hair samples. We'll start with Chrissie Horowitz. I want her here, at the station. And someone ring Danni.'

'Should we bring Gillanders in as well, boss?'

'I don't want them bumping into each other. We'll do him later.'

Zoë had the phone to her ear. 'Ma'am, Dr Mittelberg can be here at three.'

Von turned to Steve. 'Enough time for you to sprint over to the Garrimont and pick up Chrissie. Take Zoë.'

'You're not coming?'

Her mouth tightened. 'I want a word with the Chief Super.'

'Sit down, Yvonne.' Richard Quincey stared at her impassively. 'I take it you've come to give me a progress report.'

'I've come to ask about your brother's financial affairs, sir.' Without waiting for a reply, she said, 'Can you tell me how your brother started up the Quincey Players?'

'I provided the start-up costs. It's no secret.'

No, but you still didn't think to tell me. 'Are you co-owner?' she said.

'I didn't want anything to do with it. I signed the cheque and my brother took it from there.'

'Have you any idea how much it's worth now?'

He hesitated. 'None.'

He's lying. 'Did you know your brother was in debt?' she said.

'I'm sure he had the same cash-flow problems as the rest of us.' He frowned. 'What are you driving at?'

'Just that his problem was less of a flow and more of a flood. And always in the same direction.' She pushed a sheaf of papers across. 'Here are his bank and card statements. He was spending money he didn't have.'

Quincey scrutinised the pages, his frown deepening. He dropped them on the desk. 'I really had no idea.'

He's such a bad liar. Like every Chief Super I've ever known.

'The sale of the Quincey Players will pay off these debts, Yvonne.'

'So you know, sir, that the business can cover them?'

'I'm assuming it can.' His voice was hard. 'Don't try to trick me. I don't like it.'

'Do you have the name of your brother's accountant?'

'Why would I?'

'I thought you might have given him the name of yours.'

'Well I haven't. You can get my accountant's name from my secretary. Check with him directly. Now, is there anything else?'

Oh, yes, I'm only just getting started. 'What do you know of your brother's movements after he formed the Quincey Players?'

'I've already told you, my brother and I hardly saw each other after university.'

'And you told me your brother hadn't been back to London

for several years.'

His tone was icy. 'Your point is?'

'You're unaware, then, that your brother visited London many times since 1985, the last being earlier this year?'

A look of bewilderment came into his eyes. 'He came to London?' he said, half to himself. He picked up a paper clip and opened it out. 'I didn't know that. But then there's no reason why he should want to visit me, after all this time.'

At last, he's telling the truth. 'And your brother had no family other than yourself?'

'Our mother is still alive. But Max had no children.'

'Your brother's statements show nothing in the way of regular payments to his ex-wife. Was there any agreement for spousal support?'

'Max left her the house. The split was final in that respect.' He stirred, as if from a dream. 'Mention of my mother has reminded me. I'm due to pick her up at Euston in less than an hour. She's arriving for the memorial service tomorrow afternoon.'

'I'll be there, sir.'

'I would arrive early,' he said, rising. 'All of my brother's theatre friends will be coming.'

She nodded. *And possibly his murderer.*

Chapter 14

'So I'm finally going to meet Steve's hot-knickered goddess,' said Danni. 'Do you want me to come in, or just observe?'

'Observe,' said Von, leaning back in the chair. 'Steve will be questioning her and I'll be outside, listening to your running commentary.'

'And what are you looking for?'

'She's lied to us about how much contact she's had with Max Quincey. I'm convinced the two of them were up to something. I want to find out what.'

Danni was silent for a moment. 'You've got dark circles under your eyes, Von. Burning the candle at both ends?'

'At one end.' She rotated her shoulders. 'We're nowhere near making a collar. The problem is motive.'

'And who stood to inherit on Max's death?'

'We've not found a will so it'll be his mother as next-of-kin. But I think we've finally hit on something. The Quincey Players may be worth a mint, and there may be a co-owner. I thought at first that it's the Chief Super, but he says no.'

'And now you're thinking it's Chrissie who's co-owner?'

'Max visited London several times in the last fifteen years, and it might have been to see her. She claimed their chumminess was all about looking through the Players' books. And maybe it was,' she added softly.

There was a knock at the door, and Larry entered.

'Chrissie Horowitz is being printed, ma'am,' he said, looking at Danni.

'Thanks. Can you ask DI English to come in for a minute?'

'Yes, ma'am.' He glanced at Danni's legs as he closed the door.

Steve entered, grinning when he saw Danni. 'Glad you could tear yourself away from your students, Dr Mittelberg. It's nice to see that not all academics sit on their jacksis all day.' He ignore Danni's playful V-sign, and switched his attention to Von. 'We going in, boss?'

'You are. I'm going to be sitting on my jacksi with Danni, observing through the window.'

'So how do you want me to play it?'

'Robustly. Lay off the charm, which she'll be expecting. If she's rattled, she's more likely to give something away.' She leant forward. 'I want to know what she and Max have been up to. All this guff about meeting for drinks and helping with the figures may have been intended to throw us off the scent.'

'The scent?'

'About who really co-owns the Quincey Players.'

'Sorry, boss. Still lost.'

'It may be Chrissie herself.'

His face cleared. 'Ah.'

'And take Zoë.'

'The strawberry blonde?' said Danni. 'That'd be enough to make any woman's self-assurance evaporate.'

'Use interview room three, Steve. And don't forget to ask for a sample of her hair.'

'She may refuse.'

'Ask nicely. If she wants to know why, then tell her.'

'Got it, boss.'

'You still haven't told me why I've been fingerprinted, Steve.' Chrissie Horowitz rested her clasped hands on the table, the tips smudged with black ink. 'Am I a suspect in your murder case? Should I contact my solicitor?'

'Only if you think you need one,' Steve said easily. 'But this won't take long, Miss Horowitz. We just want to clear a few things up.'

'So why have I been fingerprinted?'

'We've not been able to identify all the prints in Max Quincey's room. We've taken yours to eliminate them.'

She ran her fingers over the corners of her mouth, as though checking her lipstick. 'But I told you I've not been in his room.'

He smiled. 'Just routine. We'd also like a sample of your hair,' he added, matter-of-factly.

'Whatever for?'

'We found blond hairs in the room.'

She smoothed her brows lightly. 'How many times do I have to tell you I didn't visit Maxie in his digs?'

'Max may have accidentally picked up some of your hairs on his coat, and deposited them in his room.'

'Very well.'

Zoë held out a small plastic bag. Chrissie rummaged through her Jane Shilton handbag and produced a small mirror. She held it close to her face and, with great care, plucked four hairs from her fringe. 'Is that enough?' she said, dropping them into the bag.

'That's fine,' said Zoë, sealing the plastic.

'What are you hoping to get from her hair?' Danni said.

'The blond hairs in Max's room were dyed or streaked, like Chrissie's. If her sample can place her there beyond shadow of a doubt, she may crack when presented with the evidence.'

Chrissie sat back and crossed her legs. She was wearing stockings with seams, and stilettos even higher than Danni's. 'Is there anything else I can help you with, Steve?' she said suggestively.

'Come on Steve,' Von muttered. 'Go for the jugular.'

'I'll come to the point, Miss Horowitz.' He put down his pen. 'We believe you're co-owner of the Quincey Players.'

'Not true,' said Chrissie, startled.

'That's unsettled her,' said Danni. 'See how she's smoothing her skirt under the table? She can hardly keep still.'

Steve brought his face close to Chrissie's. 'You and Max were involved in something and I intend to find out what. We have Max's phone records and we know how many times you were ringing each other. Why were you meeting him, Miss Horowitz? What were you into?'

A note of panic crept into Chrissie's voice. 'What do you mean, into?'

'I'm talking about a scam. Why was the Garrimont really in debt?'

She stared, speechless.

He leant back and folded his arms. 'Here's what I think's been going on. You and Max were skimming the theatre's profits. You had one book for the tax man and another at the back of the filing cabinet. The Quincey Players were going from strength to strength, at the expense of the Garrimont.'

She looked about to choke with indignation. 'How dare you suggest that. I've been working day and night trying to keep that place going. Audit the Garrimont's accounts, if you don't believe me. It's been losing money for years, since long before Maxie came back to London.'

'Max Quincey was a frequent visitor to Mrs Deacon's, even during the time the Players were touring. Did you really only meet him for the first time this month? Or did you know him from way back?'

'Of course I only met him this month...' Her voice drifted away.

'Is she lying?' said Von.

Danni frowned. 'Hard to tell. If she is, she should give up theatre management and go on the stage.'

'We will be checking the Garrimont's accounts,' Steve was saying, 'and the state of your own finances.'

Chrissie pawed in her bag. 'Knock yourself out. I've nothing to hide.' She threw down her cheque book and credit card. 'Do you want me to call my bank manager?'

'That won't be necessary. This is all we need.' He nodded to Zoë, who wrote down the account numbers.

'Now, are you letting me leave, or do I call my solicitor?'

'I think we're finished for now.' He got to his feet. 'Thank you, Miss Horowitz. If we need to speak to you again, we'll know where to find you.'

She rose, giving her skirt a final smooth down.

He stopped her at the door. 'One last thing. If we find you've lied to us, we'll charge you with obstruction. Understand?'

She lifted her chin. 'Everything I've told you is the truth.'

Von watched her flounce out of the room. *But has she told the truth, the whole truth and nothing but the truth?*

'What do you reckon, Danni?' said Steve.

Danni was perched on the edge of Von's desk. 'She's jaw-droppingly sexy and she knows it. All that running of her fingers over her brows, that checking of make-up, she's more than usually conscious of her appearance. The way she softened her expression and leant into Steve means she knows the effect she has on men.' She nodded towards Zoë. 'Clever move having the detective sergeant there. But if you're asking me whether she was telling porkies, I'd say, probably not.'

'Could she be an expert liar?' said Von.

'She could have fooled us, yes.' Danni picked up the paperweight, a life-sized plaster skull, and balanced it in her hand. 'She's not short of money. Those were Jimmy Choos she was wearing. What do theatre managers earn? Not enough to buy designer shoes, I'm guessing.'

'We'll find out soon enough, but all we may have achieved is the means by which we eliminate her.' Von ran her hands over her face. 'Even if Forensics come up with a match on her hair, it will confirm she was in Max's room, but it's not proof of murder.'

'We need a firm motive before we tackle her again, boss, or she'll bring a claim of harassment.'

'What about this Gillanders character?' said Danni. 'Is he still a possible?'

'He's next on the list.'

Danni peered into the skull's eye sockets. 'And are you still chasing the Jack in the Box murderer?'

'It passes the time,' Von said with irony.

'Have you reinterviewed the surviving rent boy?'

'Can't find him.'

'We've just tracked him down, ma'am,' Zoë said quickly.

'Well, halle–bloody–luja.' She glared at the girl. 'So why are you telling me only now? And what took you so long?'

'Manny Newman changed his name when he left hospital. He's known as Frankie Lowry.'

Chapter 15

Rain battered against the windscreen as Von and Steve drove across London.

'You sure we shouldn't leave this till tomorrow, boss? North Peckham isn't a place I like to be in after the sun goes down.'

'Manny's likely to be out during the day.' She threw him a quizzical look. 'You're from Glasgow. I thought you Scots were made of strong stuff.'

'There are parts of Glasgow I wouldn't like to be in after the sun goes down.'

She peered through the window trying to make out the streets. Sodden litter was piling up in the gutter. Someone had left a grease-stained armchair at the side of the road. She doubted it would stay there long. 'God, this rain is something else. How much further?'

'Twenty fathoms. Just as well we can't see much of the landscape.'

'Looks all right to me. Anyway, I hear the place is being redeveloped. Isn't that greenery over there?'

'Burgess Park, we're nearly at Manny's. I wonder how long this regeneration's been going on. There are still old council estates here.'

'It's going to take time, Steve. But why did they relocate him here? Not the most salubrious of areas.'

'Probably couldn't afford to put him anywhere else.' After a pause, he said, 'Is Kenny home tonight?'

'I've not been able to reach him. He's switched off his phone.'

'Boss—'

'I'll be all right, Steve.' She ran a hand along the upholstery. 'To tell the truth, I'm more nervous about meeting Manny.'

He glanced at her in surprise. 'You've interviewed plenty of victims of crime before.'

'This is different. Manny may not want to talk to us.'

'It'll be fine, boss. You're good at putting people at their ease.'

They pulled up at the kerb. The door to the end house opened and a woman in a blue uniform appeared, holding a newspaper over her head. When she saw them, she paused at the porch.

'Police officers,' Von said, struggling with the golf umbrella. She held up her warrant card. 'Is Frankie Lowry in?'

The woman frowned. 'He in some sort of trouble?' she said in a ringing voice.

'We just want to ask a few questions.'

'That's what you all say. Then it leads to tears. The door's open, but shout who you are, otherwise you'll frighten him. He hasn't had a visit from the filth since it happened.' She looked them up and down. 'Be sure to close the door securely, mind. And wipe your feet.'

'Charming,' said Steve, loudly enough that she'd hear.

She pushed past them and climbed into a white van, leaving the disintegrating newspaper on the pavement. After several goes at starting, she drove off in a haze of blue exhaust.

Manny's maisonette stood in a large council estate. Two things distinguished it from the others in the street: as the end house it had something resembling a garden, and it was in a worse decorative condition, with paint peeling away and a window broken, the glass stuck together with brown tape. On closer inspection, the garden was a square of roughly-applied concrete. Rubbish of every kind had been thrown in – food cartons, empty bottles, blackened banana skins. And syringes.

They ran to the door. It gave onto a small vestibule. On the right-hand wall hung a heavy woollen coat and two waterproof jackets. A foldable white stick dangled from a peg.

Von shook the umbrella outside before hanging it up. 'Frankie Lowry?' she shouted into the house. 'I'm Detective Chief Inspector Valenti. Could I have a word?'

'You'd better come in,' came a voice from inside. 'I expected you yesterday.'

She glanced enquiringly at Steve. He shrugged as if to say, 'Don't look at me'.

'Where are you?' she shouted.

'The living room. Come into the hall. It's the door on the left.'

The narrow hallway was empty except for a crate of beer bottles pushed against the far wall. A flight of stairs disappeared into the shadows.

The door on the left stood ajar. She pushed it gently.

The living room was open plan, converted from a sitting room and a kitchen. A smell of curry lingered in the air. To her right were the kitchen surfaces, an oven, fridge, and washing machine. To the left, a large sofa and a table littered with papers. The sash windows were streaked with dirt, the frayed curtains held back with frayed curtain ties. A sudden gust of wind rattled the panes, stirring the dead wasp on the sill.

Beside the window, a young man sat in a Parker Knoll wing chair. He was dressed in jeans and a green sweat shirt, worn and creased, but clean. On his feet were suede boots with heavy-duty soles.

'Please take a seat. Anywhere you like.' He turned his head in her direction. 'DCI Valenti, you said? Who's your pal? A man, from the sound of it.' He laughed humourlessly. 'Surprised? I can tell by the way he walks.'

'Detective Inspector English,' said Steve. 'We're from Clerkenwell Police Station.'

'You're Scottish, west coast accent.'

'Aye, Glasgow.'

'So, a DI *and* a DCI? I'd better offer you some refreshment, then. To tell the truth, I just expected a sergeant like last time.'

'Mr Lowry,' Von began, but stopped as he got to his feet.

'Call me Frankie.' His tone was friendly, and she felt her nervousness evaporate. 'Would you like tea or coffee?' he said.

'Coffee. White, no sugar.'

'Same for your DI?'

'Please,' said Steve.

He walked confidently to the kitchen, skirting the table as though he could see it.

'May I help?' she said, bracing herself for a rebuttal.

'If you don't mind.' He reached for the jar of Nescafé, pulled off the lid, and fumbled inside for the scoop. He spooned powder into a mug, holding it by the rim and guiding the scoop carefully. 'Could you fill the kettle, please? The milk's in the fridge.' He pulled a face. 'Hope it's not gone off. I left the door open this morning by mistake.'

She ran the water, watching his fingers grope over the plates and bowls. As he slid mugs towards the Nescafé jar, his arm knocked against a glass. It fell to the floor, and rolled towards her. She bent to retrieve it.

'Everything here's unbreakable,' he said. 'The wonders of technology, eh?'

As they waited for the kettle to boil, she took her first close look at him. Fifteen years after the attack, he was unrecognisable from the photograph. The short brown hair was long and tangled, although it smelt newly-washed. The cheeky smile was gone, and the suntanned skin was covered in blackheads. Over the bridge of his nose and across his temples was a deep white scar. But it was the glass eyes that held her. Lidless, they stared unblinkingly. She felt her heart bang against her ribs. *He knows I'm watching him.*

The kettle switched itself off. 'Do you take milk?' she said.

He nodded, his face turned towards hers. 'I've no biscuits, I'm afraid. The price I pay for help from the social is that Mrs Mannion scoffs my jammie dodgers. Do you mind carrying yours?'

He walked unerringly back to the Parker Knoll. 'So I take it you've come about the attack,' he said, settling himself.

Von sat down next to Steve. 'How did you know, Frankie?' she said.

'What do you mean, How did you know, Frankie?' he said, mimicking her tone. 'I was the one who rang the police. But you haven't been here before, I'd have remembered that perfume.' He cupped his hands round the mug. 'Where the hell's Clerkenwell, anyway? It's not the local nick.'

'We're north of the river,' said Steve. 'Borough of Islington.'

'I'm pleased to hear it's being properly attended to. And not before time. I'd almost given up waiting.' He brought the mug to his lips. 'You going to pull them in, then? I know who they are although, obviously, I can't give you a physical description. But I'd remember the voices. Can you do a police line-up with voices?'

'Frankie, what attack are you talking about?' Von said in exasperation.

'Haven't you been briefed? The last attack. Same as the others. I was pushed over in the street, and my cane was stolen. It's the third time that's happened. It's always at the bus-stop.' A note of anxiety crept into his voice. 'I need to use the bus to get to college.'

'We haven't come to discuss that,' she said softly.

'No? Then why the hell have you come?'

She took a deep breath. 'We've come to talk to Manny Newman.'

Steve sprang from the sofa and lifted the mug from Manny's hands. 'Let me take that, son. You're spilling it over your jeans.'

Manny was shaking uncontrollably. 'How did you find me?' he said in a whisper. 'I've changed my name.' He gripped the chair, rocking back and forth.

'We're police officers,' she said gently.

'Who else knows where I am?'

'Just my staff, and they're not telling anyone.' She hadn't expected such a violent reaction. 'Breathe deeply, Manny. I'm sorry we've given you such a shock.'

'Were you followed?'

'No, we weren't.'

'So, why have you come?' he wailed. 'What do you want?'

'To talk to you about what happened in 1985.'

He stopped rocking. 'The Jack in the Box murders.' There was fear in his voice now. 'He's done it again, hasn't he? I knew he'd come back. Knew he'd want to finish what he started. He's afraid I'll finger him, that's what it is. He meant to do me like he did the others. And now he's going to.'

'Manny—'

'You've led him here, haven't you?' He was rocking again. 'He'll be waiting outside.'

'There's no-one outside,' said Steve. 'We weren't followed.'

'You're sure about that?'

'Aye, son.'

He sat still, and turned his face towards them. His tone changed to one of anger. 'All right, then. Get it over with. Ask me your questions.'

'We can come back another time if it's easier,' Von said.

'Do it now.'

She hesitated. This wasn't how she'd wanted to do it. But

they were here now. 'What do you remember about your attack, Manny?'

He chuckled. 'I don't believe this. Police officers, and you haven't read the file? I gave my statement before, and I'm not going over it again just because you can't be bothered to do your homework.'

'We've read your statement, but there are things that aren't clear. Can you remember back to the night of the attack?'

'What a stupid question. You really think I'd forget that?'

'Tell us about your attacker, Manny.'

After a silence, he said quietly, 'His eyes are what I remember best. It's what drew me.'

'So he didn't approach you?' said Steve.

'Can't remember that particular detail.' His head bobbed as he spoke. 'Anyway, who really approaches who, in the game? You do this little dance, see? You catch their eye. Or they catch yours. Then it's a longer look, or maybe a smile. That's how we did it in the Duke. Different on the street, of course, people are more direct. But in a pub you have to be careful.'

'Can you remember what colour his eyes were?' Von said.

'Now you're asking. It's the expression I remember, not the colour. Could have been brown or hazel.'

'Not blue?'

'Could have been blue. Who notices the colour of people's eyes?' He tapped his right eye with a fingernail and laughed softly. 'Mine are brown. They were blue before.' He shrugged. 'No-one asked me what I wanted.'

'You stated you'd seen your attacker before. So what was he like, Manny? Lively? Quiet?'

'He was like everyone else. Sometimes lively, sometimes quiet. Mid-twenties, maybe. I could be wrong, never was very good at guessing men's ages.' He paused. 'All right, now it's your turn. I'm saying no more till you tell me why you're asking these questions.'

She felt her heart contract. *No-one's told him...* 'There's been another murder, with some similarities to the Jack in the Boxes.'

He clutched at the chair. 'So, I was right. He's done it again.'

'It may be someone else.'

'Copying the old murders for a lark?'

'It happens.'

He seemed to be digesting the information. 'So who snuffed it? Another kid from the Duke?'

'An older man. Max Quincey.'

'Never heard the name.'

'You heard a tape of his voice,' she said slowly. 'He was the prime suspect in the Jack in the Box murders.'

'The one who was arrested?'

'He was never charged. There was no material evidence.' She hesitated, but she had to ask the question. It was why they were here. 'Manny, are you absolutely sure it wasn't his voice on the tape?'

'Am I absolutely sure? No, I'm not absolutely sure, either about the voice or how old he was. I was pestered so much by that old plod, he almost camped beside my bed, that I said what he wanted to hear just to get him to go.' He slumped back. 'All I wanted was the coppers to leave me alone, see? I've thought since that maybe if I'd paid more attention they'd have got him.'

'Don't blame yourself, Manny. So, there was only the one tape played to you?'

'Only one.' He turned his head towards her, something he must have learnt in therapy. 'Was this Quincey guy a regular at the Duke?'

'He seemed to be.'

'Then that's where you need to go,' he said angrily. 'Talk to Dickie, if he's still there.'

'Dickie Womack? The landlord? Yes, he's still there.'

'He'll tell you what was going on.'

'Why don't you tell us, son?' Steve said.

'I never found out. And I wouldn't want to know. I kept my head down.' He laughed harshly. 'In more ways than one. I was good at blow jobs.'

'Were you often in the Duke?' Von said.

'Every day. Picked up my punters there.'

'Even after you heard what had happened to the other boys?'

'Had to, didn't I? Needed the money,' he said bitterly. 'And you never think it's going to happen to you.' He rested his head against the chair back. 'But you're curious about the sex, aren't you? Did the earth move? Well, I did it for the money, not for the sex.'

'Did your attacker use a name?' she said anxiously.

'Can't remember. If he did, it would have meant nothing. No-one ever tells anyone their real name. I always asked my punters what name they wanted to call me by. Sometimes they used a girl's name.' He grinned. 'There are some really screwed-up people out there.'

'How well did you know the Irish boys? Gilly and the others?'

'Christ Almighty, give me some credit. Do you think I'd keep company with that bunch of Fenians? I kept away from them. They were always involved in some racket or other.' He rocked back and forth again. 'That's why they were killed. They knew what was going on at the Duke.'

She glanced at Steve. This confirmed what Larry had learnt when he went undercover.

'And you really have no idea?' said Steve.

'I've said so, haven't I?'

'Then why do you think you were attacked?'

'I went to the Duke to pick up punters. I was there sometimes when Gilly and Liam were around. Maybe he saw me and thought I was in with them.' There was an edge to his voice. 'Murderers can make mistakes, can't they?'

'And all this time you've been worried he'll come back?' Von said, suddenly close to tears.

'Wouldn't you? Each time I go out, I ask myself, is he going to be there? Is he round the corner? Is he at the bus-stop? Whenever I'm shoved around by those low-lifes from the estate, I wonder if he's with them and this is going to be it.' He shook his head slowly. 'I know I've been lucky. It was only because Pete heard us that I'm still alive.'

'The security guard?' she said, brushing at her eyes.

'He used to look out for me. Told no-one I dossed at the back. He was a good mate. Wish he was living with me now.'

'Your mother's still in London. Why aren't you living with her?'

'You are joking, aren't you? She's a druggie. She's the reason I left home.'

Von glanced at the table. 'I see you've learnt Braille,' she said encouragingly.

He straightened his shoulders. 'I go to college now,' he said, pride in his voice. 'Been there for three years. I have tapes and everything.'

'What have you been studying?'

'Sociology. I'm getting good grades.' He flushed slightly. 'I have a girlfriend. Met her at ballroom dancing classes.'

Von pictured him dancing, stumbling against the other couples. But perhaps not. He'd walked confidently enough across the room. Maybe the blind develop a sense of the objects around them. 'Have you made many friends at college?' she said.

'I'm not good at that. Never was. Even on the game, I never had friends.' His head drooped. 'What we all wanted was a friend, just one punter who'd protect us and treat us nicely. Set us up.'

'What about regulars?' she said quietly. 'Did you have anyone who asked just for you?'

He fell silent.

It's impossible to tell what he's thinking because of the eyes. With a jolt, she realised why they looked familiar. *They're identical to the doll's...*

'There was this guy,' he said. 'He was different.'

'A client?'

'We never did it. He just sat and smiled. Paying for the pleasure of my company, he used to say. Liked to stroke my hand.' He snorted. 'Said I should quit the game and do something else. I knew he must have picked up other boys, so I didn't put much store by what he said. It's only now I've come to realise he was probably my only friend. This might sound strange, but I was gutted when he stopped coming.'

'When was this?'

'Shortly before it happened.'

'How long did he come to the Duke?'

'Not long. Two or three weeks.'

She glanced sideways at Steve. He caught the movement, and shook his head slightly. This couldn't be the rent boys' killer, they hadn't had sex.

But, still, the information might give them a lead. 'What did he look like?' she said.

'Heavy build.'

'Tall?'

'Never really found out. He was always sitting when I arrived, and he was still sitting when I left to find a punter. And before you ask, no, I don't remember the colour of his eyes. He had bad skin, though.'

'How old?'

'As I said, I've never been good at men's ages. Older than me, but not by much. In his twenties.'

'Would you recognise this man's voice?'

'After fifteen years?' He sneered. 'What do you think?'

'Maybe you'd recognise the touch of his hand,' she said softly.

For one heart-stopping moment, she thought he was going to cry. She nudged Steve, who nodded. They got to their feet.

'You've been very helpful, Manny.' She laid a gentle hand on his shoulder. 'We'll leave you to get on with your studies.'

He clutched her arm. 'You will catch him, won't you?'

'I give you my word,' she said, her heart twisting inside her.

He released her. 'You can't promise that, neither you nor your pal. That's lovely perfume you're wearing, by the way. Paris, isn't it? My girlfriend uses it.' He sat back. 'I bet you're gorgeous. You know your pal is sweet on you, don't you? It's amazing what you see when you're blind.'

She resisted the urge to throw her arms round him. 'We'll let ourselves out,' she said, her voice choking.

They walked to the Toyota in silence. It had stopped raining, and the roof tiles gleamed in the early evening light.

'Well, that didn't go too badly, boss.'

'Oh, shut up,' she said, tears stinging her eyes.

Von was sprawled on the sofa, sipping wine. A half-drunk bottle and the remains of a boxed pizza lay on the table. She was thinking about Manny. Her heart ached. Poor lad, getting pushed about like that. She knew the Superintendent at his local nick, maybe she could do something about getting a uniform to patrol the area around the bus stop. She'd learnt something from the visit, though: if Manny was right about not recognising the voice on the tape, Max Quincey was still in the frame for the Jack in the Box murders. She pushed her hands through her hair. Christ, she was no further forward with solving any of the murders.

She sat up. Something Manny had mentioned stuck in her mind. The man who'd stroked his hand. Who was this well-built man who paid just to sit with Manny? Something niggled. He'd come to see him when the play was running, then stopped two or three weeks later. How long did the play run? A month, then they went on the road.

And the Iron Duke. *That's where you need to go. Talk to Dickie.* The Duke. Again. Her breath came out in a rush. She'd made an error of judgement sending her detectives in. If the regulars were closing up like limpets, she'd need a cooling-off period before trying again. Problem was, they'd smell a copper a mile off. So, she wouldn't send in a copper. She'd send Tubby. It wasn't his patch, so he wouldn't be known, and he was good at gaining people's trust. But she had to do it soon. If she didn't take something to the Chief Super, he'd bring someone in over her head. She was that close to being kicked off the murder squad, this time for good.

She poured the last of the wine, then phoned Kenny's flat. His answer-machine came on. She listened to his voice, remembering how they'd laughed when he recorded the message. The answer-machine had been an early Christmas present because he was hopeless at staying in touch.

'Kenny,' she said, 'I can't get you on your mobile so I'm phoning here. If you're home tonight, please give me a call. Even if it's late.'

She dropped the phone into her bag, and sank back against the cushions. The image of Manny's face with it dead glass eyes floated before her. She replayed their conversation, remembering the pleasure in his voice when he'd told them he was a student, and his anxiety about getting to college. His mother wouldn't know anything about him, how he'd turned his life around. *She's a druggie. She's the reason I left home.* Couldn't he forgive her? Parents forgave their children everything. So why couldn't children forgive their parents?

She thought of her own child, a child she hadn't seen in years. These days, no-one batted an eyelid when children were born out of wedlock, but it hadn't been like that for her; teenage pregnancies, although depressingly common, could ruin a girl's chances then. Strangely, her parents had been neither angry nor disappointed. Her mother had strenuously encouraged her to keep the baby although the idea of an abortion had never entered Von's mind. Fortunately for the baby, she had an extended family. Even Von's brothers had rallied round. She smiled as she remembered her daughter as an infant, the head of downy hair, the warm milky breath, and the tiny fists she made whenever she cried. Von had loved her so much that it ached...

She tottered to her feet and stumbled into the bedroom. The blanket box stood in the corner, buried under a pile of forgotten ironing. She swept the clothes to the floor, then knelt and lifted back the lid. The scent of old roses drifted out, wrapping itself round her, awakening slumbering memories. She burrowed under the sheets. At the bottom, she found what she was looking for.

She laid the shoe box on the floor. The pink satin ribbon was knotted loosely in a huge bow, flattened by the weight of linen. She untied the knot, set the lid aside, and parted the thin tissue paper. With trembling hands, she removed the baby shawl and buried her face in it. Maybe she imagined it because she wanted to, or maybe it was still there, faint but distinctive, that marvellous caramel smell that babies have. She set the shawl aside and, heedless of the tears now streaming down her face, she lifted the tiny shoes and baby rattle and brought them to her lips.

Chapter 16

'Still not sure why we're here,' said Steve.

'To see the lighting manager,' Von said, with exaggerated politeness.

'But there's no evidence he even knew Max Quincey.'

She threw him an amused look. 'True, but if we thought that way we'd never interview anyone, would we?'

'So where's his office? How are we going to find it in this maze of corridors?'

'I phoned ahead.'

On cue, Dexter appeared. He was dressed in a t-shirt stamped with the words 'Body of a God, Pity it's Buddha'.

'Nice to see you, Chief Inspector,' he said. 'You too, Inspector English,' he added quickly.

'So we're good to go?' she said.

Dexter cracked his knuckles. 'Zack is still in the lighting box.'

'You didn't warn him we were coming?'

'I've followed your instructions to the letter.' He smiled dreamily. 'Shall I take you up?'

'I think I know the way. Those stairs?'

'Third floor, follow the corridor round. His is the last door on the right. I'll be around in case you need me.' With a small bow, he left.

'Polite young man,' she said, as they made for the stairs. 'Don't you think, Steve?'

'I've always found him gormless-looking. What's all this cloak and dagger stuff? I've followed your instructions to the letter,' he added in the tone of an undertaker.

'I want to surprise Lazarus. Corner him in his den.'

'Put him off his guard, eh?' He rubbed his cheek. 'In Glasgow, that tactic often landed me with a shiner.'

'Isn't that part of the fun of being a detective?' She glanced at the wall. 'Okay, here's the corridor.'

'This place is dark and poky, and everywhere looks the same.'

'I've cracked it, Steve. It's the pictures. Along here, we have Monet.'

'Impressive, boss,' he breathed.

They stopped outside the lighting manager's room. She recognised it from opening night. She was about to knock, when the door opened, leaving her with her hand in the air. Zack Lazarus stood in front of her.

'Mr Lazarus, we'd like to speak to you.'

'You're police,' he said calmly. 'I remember you.'

'Detective Chief Inspector Valenti.' She indicated Steve. 'Detective Inspector English. Can we come in?'

'I'm working.'

She stepped past him. 'As it happens, so are we.'

In front of her was a wide glass window through which she could see the auditorium and the stage. A small console was fixed to the table, the switches labelled. On the floor was a rusty toolbox, its lid thrown back to reveal a jumble of screwdrivers, spanners, and wrenches. A faint smell of oil hung in the air, reminding her of her brothers' garage.

There was hardly enough room for three people. A Jack in the Box was sitting on the only chair. They'd have to do this standing.

Lazarus closed the door. 'There's nothing I can tell you,' he said without preamble.

She smiled prettily. 'You don't know what I'm going to ask.'

'Max Quincey. You told me before.'

'And you said his murder was the best thing that could have happened. Why was that, Mr Lazarus?'

'You know why. He was a queer.'

'That's a justification for murder?' she said, feigning surprise.

''Tis in my book.'

'Where were you on the night of Tuesday, September 12th?'

He drew his shoulders back, glowering at her.

'Please answer my question, Mr Lazarus.'

He continued to say nothing.

'You've got ten seconds,' she said softly, 'or we take you down to the nick.'

Steve took a step forward. Lazarus frowned, throwing him a glance. 'Okay, then. A Tuesday? Can't remember.'

'Not visiting Max Quincey in his digs?' she said.

'Don't even know where he lives.' He nodded at the equipment. 'I was probably here, trying to get all this ready.'

'In the evening?'

'Best time, no-one's around a week before opening night. In the day, there are rehearsals, and the theatre's also booked out for schools who need a stage. Chrissie's idea, a way to make money. Been very successful.' He nodded. 'Got a business head on her shoulders. God knows, we need someone to turn this place around.'

'Do you work the lights when the schools use the place?'

'Sometimes.'

'I couldn't help noticing that the lighting didn't dim when I was here on opening night.'

He flushed. 'Still trying to get it working.' He avoided her eyes, as though ashamed of his lack of expertise.

'What's the problem?'

'System's so antiquated that dimming and brightening isn't

safe. Whole place needs rewiring. Chrissie's promised it's the first thing we'll do when the funds come in. In the meantime, I have to do what I can with this.' He indicated the console. 'I'm trying a workaround, but I haven't succeeded.'

'What do you do in this room while the play's actually running?' she said, examining the console.

'Keep an eye out that nothing fuses.'

'And if it does?'

'I spring into action.'

She studied his face. 'How well did you know Max Quincey?'

'As well as anyone else,' he said caustically.

'But you weren't a member of the Quincey Players.'

'I'm employed by the Garrimont. Chrissie Horowitz is my boss, not Quincey.'

She glanced through the window. 'You've been working with him for, what, three weeks?'

'About that,' he said warily.

'But, apart from this season, you've never seen him before.' She made it sound like a statement. It was a tactic which sometimes got results.

He sneered. 'Is this what the Old Bill call entrapment? Look, you know I was here the last time the play was running, when Max Quincey was director. Ergo, I've seen him before.'

He's no fool. I'll have to tread carefully. 'So what was your relationship like with Max Quincey that first time?'

'He wasn't my boss then, either. Always been the theatre manager.'

'But you would have worked with him,' said Steve. 'He would have given you directions about when to dim, when to use spotlights, and so on.'

'He may have. Can't remember.'

'Try, Mr Lazarus,' Von said.

He sighed loudly. 'We had several meetings about the

lighting. He lost it and bawled me out.'

'Over what?'

'The system was just as crap then as it is now.' He hesitated. 'When he arrived a couple of weeks ago, he gave me a flea in my ear that it still hadn't been fixed. As if it were all my fault. So we had to do it the way we did before. I set up the lighting at the start of the play and then leave it.'

'And that's how it was done the last time?'

'Exactly the same.'

'You didn't like Max Quincey, did you, Mr Lazarus?' she said suddenly. 'I don't mean to work with, I mean personally.'

'He was the worst kind of faggot. Rolled in shit, like a dog.'

'Meaning?' said Steve.

'Don't you understand plain English? Perhaps you should go back to Jockland.' He spoke through clenched teeth. 'There are different kinds of queers. Some that like their own kind. And others that prey on young boys.'

'And which kind was Max Quincey?' said Von.

'You know which kind. You know what I'm talking about. Those young lads.'

She resisted the urge to step backwards. 'The rent boys?'

He was shouting into her face now. 'The Jack in the Box murders, by God.'

'Let's talk about those murders, then,' she said, pulling a file from her bag. 'In your statement, you said you'd no alibi for the murder of Liam Mahoney, or for the attack on Manny Newman. Those attacks took place after the play had ended. You claim you went for a drink after work, then straight home. No-one at the bar could remember seeing you.'

'Doesn't mean anything,' he spat out. 'If it did, that old copper would have done something about it.'

'The other two murders took place while the play was running. If the lighting level didn't change, you'd have had nothing to do.'

He thrust his face into hers. 'What are you insinuating?'

'You could have slipped out at any time,' she said, drawing back her head to escape the reek of sweat.

The anger drained from his voice. 'You think I did those boys.'

'Well, in your language, weren't they queers?'

The temper was back. 'I've no idea. Not all lads who go on the game are homosexuals. They're victims of a system and a society that refuses to help them. Victims to pond life like Quincey.'

'Which is why he deserved to die.'

'Spot on. And I'll tell you another thing. There'd be no end of people lining up to do it.'

'People like yourself?' she said softly.

'Oh no, you don't catch me that easily.' His eyes drilled into hers. 'Go to the Iron Duke. That's where you'll find Quincey's killer. And I hope you give him a medal.'

'Why the Iron Duke?'

He seemed unsure of himself. 'It's where the boys hung out.'

'Have you ever been there?'

He looked away. 'No.'

Gotcha. Now you're lying. 'One final thing, Mr Lazarus. We'd like you to come down to Clerkenwell Police Station.'

'What the hell for?'

'To take your fingerprints.'

'I didn't kill him,' he said, his voice flat.

She smiled. 'Then you've nothing to worry about. There's a constable waiting outside. It won't take long, and we'll bring you straight back.'

He let out a long breath, and reached for his jacket.

'Has your hair always been that length, Mr Lazarus?'

'It's been short for years.'

'You didn't have it cut recently?'

'No, why do you ask?'

'Just a line of questioning. Shall we go?'

On the pavement, they watched Lazarus drive away with the constable. Dexter appeared, hurrying down the steps.

'I'm so sorry, Chief Inspector, but I can't find Michael Gillanders anywhere. He may have gone home to change.'

'For the performance?'

'For the memorial service. We're all going. Chrissie is insisting.'

'Thanks anyway, Dexter.' She squeezed his arm. 'You're a brick.'

He grinned, then gave a brief nod and left.

Steve watched him go. 'I didn't take much to Lazarus, if I'm honest. That holier-than-thou attitude stuck in my craw.'

'Really? I quite liked him.'

'Is he in the frame for Quincey's murder, though? Or the murder of the rent boys?'

'Difficult to tell. He could have done Quincey. But he doesn't fit the profile for the boys.'

Steve gave a thoughtful nod. 'Unless he's putting on an act.'

'Either way, Lazarus knows more than he's letting on.'

'Couldn't we say that about everyone we've interviewed, boss?'

'Sadly, yes.'

Chapter 17

Steve was watching Von. She was standing at the wooden-framed office mirror, adjusting her scarf.

'Do I have to go, boss? It'll be heaving with Max's poncey friends.'

She looked at his reflection. 'Who else might attend a memorial service for a murdered man, Steve?'

'Aye, right enough.' He paused. 'The murderer.'

The service was in Kensington, at St Mary Abbots, an impressive Victorian Gothic church boasting the tallest spire in London. Von could still remember seeing on television the thousands of votive candles lit to commemorate the Princess of Wales, possibly the church's most famous parishioner.

The building was already packed, despite their early arrival. The altar under the five stained-glass windows was a mass of lilies, starkly white against the heavy stone. From her position at the back, Von could smell the sweet spicy scent.

'Better split up, Steve. You take the left and I'll sit here. Keep your eyes peeled for anything unusual.' She squeezed herself into the back row.

Richard Quincey was sitting at the front, his shoulders straight. Beside him was a small woman in a fur coat and velour cloche hat. A few rows behind, the cast and crew of the Garrimont were spread across several pews. Chrissie Horowitz, in a black suit, was wearing a hat so enormous that the people on either side had to lean away. Behind her was Michael Gillanders in a black woollen coat, with Dexter on one side, and the actor who played the detective's assistant on the other. Jools, the detective, and the actress who'd played the postwoman were sitting behind them. Rose Manning, wearing a brown coat, was kneeling at the back, her orange hair springing out from under her black beret. Her head was bent, and she was clutching a string of pink rosary beads.

Von scanned the congregation, suddenly struck by the realisation that the person who'd left the blood-smeared doll outside her flat was likely to be present. And also knew that she'd be there. The thought chilled her.

The service began with 'The King Of Love My Shepherd Is'. She knew the words, so was able to keep her eyes on the congregation. Richard Quincey didn't sing, but kept an arm round his mother.

It was as the minister was starting his eulogy that they heard the commotion. Turning, Von caught sight of Arabella Carrington. She hadn't seen the Daily Mail's crime reporter since the Chief Super's press conference, but she remembered their little sparring match. Arabella stopped briefly at the door, then made for the nave, her silver ankle boots ringing on the flagstones. With her was a man holding a Canon digital camera.

The duty policeman sprang forward and gripped her arm. 'You can't come in here, madam. This is a private service.'

'Let go of me,' she snapped. 'You've no right to detain us.'

Von slipped out of the pew. 'He has every right, Miss Carrington. You and your companion will have to leave.'

'Chief Inspector Valenti.' Arabella's eyes slid down Von's black trouser suit. 'So, Richard Quincey has marshalled his big guns. Well, we're not leaving, and you can't make us.' She nodded to the photographer who'd been watching the scene calmly.

As he lifted the Canon, Von stepped forward smartly and

snatched it from his hands. She opened the case and removed the memory card. Smiling at Arabella, she let it drop to the floor and splintered it under her heel. 'Oops, sorry about that,' she said.

Arabella went purple. 'You did that deliberately,' she said, not bothering to keep her voice down. 'You've destroyed private property.'

Von, in turn, let her eyes run down Arabella's suit. It was shocking pink with tiny white dots. *The stupid cow hasn't even bothered to dress appropriately.* 'Send the bill to Clerkenwell CID, Miss Carrington,' she said quietly. 'Now, if you don't mind, we're in the middle of a service.'

She nodded to the constable, who'd kept his grip on Arabella's arm. He marched to the door, dragging her behind him. The photographer followed. As he passed Von, he gave her a sly wink.

She resumed her seat. From the pew in front, a woman wearing a black Paddington Bear hat turned to face her.

'She'll think twice before she does that again,' Mrs Deacon said, with a look of satisfaction.

But Von wasn't listening. She was looking at the frail elderly woman in the fur coat and cloche hat, standing in the nave staring at her, eyes brimming with unshed tears.

The service was over and people were leaving. Most went by the back, but some were pushing through the door at the side of the altar.

Steve joined Von. 'What was that rammy about, boss?'

'Gatecrashers. Arabella Carrington and one of her hobbits.'

'They don't give up. What were they expecting? People are grieving.'

'The Chief Super's not been lavish with his press releases. And when he is, he says the wrong things.' Her eyes wandered over the congregation. 'Did you see anything of interest, Steve?'

'Loads of people I didn't know, but no-one who behaved suspiciously.'

'Let's get back to the nick, then.'

They were nearly through the door when she caught sight of him. He was in a black coat, standing in front of the altar, listening to the minister. He nodded, in apparent agreement at what was being said. A minute later, he disappeared behind the display of lilies. He would have heard the altercation at the back and seen her. Yet he'd made no attempt to find her afterwards. She was surprised she hadn't picked him out earlier. But that was understandable. She didn't know Kenny owned a black coat.

As Von and Steve entered the incident room, everyone leapt to their feet.

'I want to tell her,' said Larry, grinning. 'Hold the front page, ma'am,' he added, before the others could speak, 'the Quincey Players are "The Quincey Players Limited".'

'A *registered* company?' Von said in surprise.

'We couldn't find the books so Zoë contacted Companies House. There are two partners. Max Quincey was one of them.'

'Let me guess,' she said, smiling craftily. 'The other is Richard Quincey.'

'The other is Michael Gillanders,' said Zoë.

Michael Gillanders. The last name she had expected. She let out a breath. 'Okay, Zoë, give me the bottom line.'

'The Players were set up in 1985 with £20,000 provided by Richard Quincey. Gillanders didn't put in anything.'

'And Max made him a partner? For nothing?'

'The devil's in the detail, ma'am. The Quincey Players is essentially an investment company. Gillanders made all the investment decisions. Max was just a sleeping partner.'

'How much is the company worth now?'

'In excess of £500,000.' Her statement silenced the room. 'And here's the crucial clause. On the death of either partner, the surviving partner inherits the company in its entirety.'

Von's mind was racing. 'If we're looking for a motive for Gillanders to murder Max, this is a perfect worked example. He can now get his hands on half a million.' She frowned. 'Max was a partner in a successful company, so how come he was in so much debt?'

'He couldn't use the Player's funds, ma'am, or offer the company as surety for a bank loan, not without consent from Gillanders. I suspect the Players were to provide for him and Gillanders in their old age. Nothing was ever withdrawn.'

'There's something else,' Larry said. 'We've had a closer look at Max's bank statements. Every so often, money comes into his account as cash. Always a few hundred at a time.'

'Regular deposits?'

'No. Nor is it the same amount each time. But it's been going on for the last fifteen years.'

'Could his brother be helping him out?' Steve said.

'If he is, I'd be surprised if he gives him cash,' said Von. 'He's more likely to pay by cheque or bank transfer.'

'Not if he wants to keep it quiet, ma'am,' said Zoë.

'If it's coming out of his account, it can be audited and he'll know that.' *Which is why he won't lie to me when I ask him.* 'But Michael Gillanders, a partner. I'd have guessed it was Chrissie before I guessed it was him.'

'There's nothing equivalent coming out of her account,' said Zoë, 'so Max wasn't getting the cash from her. Her bank manager told us there's nothing unusual or irregular in her finances.'

Von paced the floor. 'If Chrissie was in a scam with Max, she may not have put the cash through her account. She may have laundered it.' She slammed her hand against the wall. 'Chrissie was up to something with him. Something she's hidden well.'

'The Garrimont's books are kosher too, ma'am,' Zoë said quietly.

'And Gillanders?' said Steve. 'He'll be back at the theatre.'

'We now have our first solid motive for the murder of Max Quincey. I think it's high time we had another chat with the gentleman. Bring him in.'

'If he protests?'

'Caution him.'

Chapter 18

'He's in room two, ma'am,' the constable said.

Von looked up from her desk. 'And DI English?'

'Waiting for you there.'

Steve was outside the interview room, watching Michael Gillanders through the glass. He straightened as Von approached.

'Any trouble?' she said.

'He complained all the way to the car. I thought he was going to do a runner so I had to strongarm him. I tried to be discreet but Rose Manning heard the rumpus and came to the foyer to investigate.' He looked at his feet. 'She saw me cuff him and caution him. It'll be all round the theatre by now.'

'Can't be helped,' she said sympathetically. 'Let's go.'

As they entered, Gillanders rose abruptly. 'I really must protest,' he blurted.

She nodded to the constable, who stepped back. 'Please sit down, Mr Gillanders,' she said. 'And stay seated.' She switched on the recorder. 'Interview commencing at 5.45pm, Thursday, 21st September, 2000. Officers present are Detective Chief Inspector Yvonne Valenti, and Detective Inspector Steven English.' She turned to Gillanders. 'Would you like your solicitor here, Mr Gillanders?'

'How long will that take?'

'Depends how far he has to travel.'

He sighed theatrically. 'Then let's just get on with it.'

'For the tape, Mr Gillanders has waived his right to a solicitor. He is interviewed under caution, on tape, and without his solicitor present.' She opened her file. 'Mr Gillanders, you are a co-director of the Quincey Players Limited. Is that correct?' She watched the passage of emotions on his face. 'Please answer the question. For the tape, Mr Gillanders nodded.' She paused. 'Why didn't you tell us this before?'

'Why should I? It can't possibly have any relevance to Max's murder.'

She kept her tone professional. 'On Max Quincey's death, you became sole owner of a company worth over £500,000 which you can now liquidate in its entirety, something you couldn't do when Max Quincey was alive. And you say there's no relevance?'

'You're not suggesting I'd kill Max for £500,000?'

'It's been done before.'

'What pathetic people you deal with. I wouldn't be a copper for any money.' He pulled out a packet of Hoyo de Monterrey. 'May I smoke?'

'You may not.'

He shrugged, and threw the packet onto the table. 'Is this all you've got, Chief Inspector? It's just that the show—'

'Mr Gillanders, I put it to you that you killed Max Quincey. You had motive and you had opportunity. You waited until the play, Jack in the Box, was running in London again and deliberately chose that period to murder him using the same modus operandi as in the Jack in the Box murders of 1985. You knew those murders were unsolved and you wanted us to believe that the man who killed those boys, also killed Max Quincey.'

He swallowed hard. 'I told you where I was when Max was murdered. At the Odeon in Leicester Square.'

'You were nowhere near Leicester Square, Mr Gillanders.

You were in your room at Mrs Deacon's. It happens to be directly beneath Max Quincey's. You heard Max Quincey's lover leaving his room, and you waited till he passed through your corridor and downstairs. Then you crept up to Max's room, struck him with the bedside lamp, tied him to the bedframe and strangled him. To throw us off the scent and make us think we were looking for the Jack in the Box murderer, you slashed his eyes and did the same to the doll.'

The colour left his face. 'That's a vicious lie.'

She nodded at the packet of cigarillos. 'That's the same brand Max Quincey smoked. A co-incidence? I think not. There are, after all, hundreds of brands. Did you visit Max Quincey in his room, Mr Gillanders?' She brought her face close to his. 'Did you sit with him, trying to drum up the courage to kill him, calming your nerves by smoking?'

'You're clutching at straws, Chief Inspector. I detect the whiff of desperation.'

'There's another facet we should explore. Perhaps Max Quincey wasn't your first victim. In the 1985 production of Jack in the Box, you took the role of the detective's assistant.'

'Where's this going?' he said slowly.

'It was a role which allowed you to leave the stage twenty minutes after the play had started. That gave you ample time to slip away from the Garrimont, murder Gilly McIlvanny and Charlo Heggarty, and return in time for curtain call.' She clasped her hands loosely on the table. 'What do you say to that, Mr Gillanders?'

He was staring at her, his eyes wild. He seemed to be having difficulty breathing.

She made her voice deliberately harsh. 'Did you also murder Liam Mahoney and attack Manny Newman?'

'By God, you're wrong about this. All of it.'

'According to your statement, you had no alibi for those two attacks.'

He was shaking with rage now. 'That doesn't mean I murdered them. Why in God's name would I?'

'You tell me, Mr Gillanders.'

'I didn't know them. I didn't know anything about them,' he shouted. 'They were forced onto the streets, poor devils.' His voice broke, and tears trickled down his cheeks. He pulled a brightly-coloured handkerchief from his pocket. 'Where's your evidence for these preposterous allegations?' he said, his hands trembling.

He knows we've got nothing. She waited until he'd finished wiping his face. 'We'd like your fingerprints and a sample of hair.'

'To eliminate me from your enquiries, I suppose,' he said listlessly, pocketing the handkerchief. 'And if I refuse?'

'We can get a court order.'

'And if we do it now?'

'We'll get them to Forensics today. If you've nothing to worry about, it will put you in the clear.'

He looked at her hopefully. 'If I agree, you'll let me go now?'

'A car will take you back to the theatre.'

'Then for goodness' sake, let's get on with it.' His eyes held hers. 'You're looking in the wrong place, Chief Inspector.'

'Where should I be looking?'

'The Iron Duke. Where else?'

'Why the Iron Duke?'

He looked bewildered. 'Because it's where the boys worked, of course.'

After a silence, she said, 'Interview terminated at 6.15pm.' She switched off the machine, and nodded to the constable. He ushered Gillanders out.

'Worth a try, boss. Sometimes they're jolted into confessing.' Steve jerked his head at Gillanders's chair. 'I didn't think he'd break down like that, though. Could he have been acting?'

'This time, I don't think so. He didn't behave like a guilty man. That state of shock came from somewhere else.'

'Aye, it was mention of the rent boys.'

'He was understandably rattled when we accused him of murdering Max, but he went to pieces when I started to talk about the boys.' She removed the tape and dropped it into a plastic bag. 'Can you make sure Danni hears this?'

'We have it now, boss. Prints, and hair. I'm betting Forensics will get a match.'

She looked at him. 'And I'm betting they won't.'

Von was lying on the sofa when Kenny arrived. She heard the key in the lock, the heavy footsteps, the pause in the hall as he wiped his feet. Sounds she'd heard a hundred times before. And a hundred times before, she'd waited for him in eager anticipation. But this time was different.

'You're home, love,' he said cheerily. He threw his jacket onto the sofa and nuzzled her neck. 'If I'd known, I'd have brought a takeaway.'

'Why wouldn't I be here, Kenny? It's nearly midnight.'

'When you're deep in a case, you work late.' He fetched a beer from the kitchen, then flopped into an armchair.

She studied his face. 'So how deep in do you think I am?'

'I read the papers.'

'And what have you learnt from the press releases?'

'Just that you're no further forward in catching Max's killer.'

Interesting how he refers to him by his first name. As though he knew him. 'Did you think you'd learn more by going to his memorial service this afternoon?' she said. She felt rather than saw him freeze. 'Before you deny it, Kenny, let me save you the bother. I saw you there.'

He drank deeply from the bottle, his head tipped back.

'What were you doing? Sniffing for a story?' She was having difficulty keeping the anger from her voice. 'Did you think I wouldn't see you sneak out the back?'

'I didn't sneak out,' he said firmly. 'If I'd seen you, I'd have come over.'

'For Christ's sake, Kenny, the whole church saw my barney with Arabella Carrington.'

He played with the bottle, turning it in his hands. 'If you must know, I was hoping to get something for a story. A human interest angle.'

'The grieving mother?'

'That sort of thing.'

She swung her legs over the side of the sofa. 'You know our agreement, Kenny. We don't stomp on each other's patches.'

'The grieving mother is hardly your patch, love,' he said sarcastically.

'Why do you need that particular story? You've got this thing going with your contact. Or so you keep telling me.'

The muscles in his face tightened.

'It's all right,' she said, 'I'm not going to ask you about it.'

He hesitated. 'Look, I was out of order, I'll try and do it differently next time.'

'Not good enough. I want a sentence including the word, sorry.'

'I'm really sorry.'

She was determined to rub his face in it. 'And you won't do it again?'

'Jesus, if you're going to be like this,' he said, under his breath. He slammed the bottle down and picked up his jacket.

'Kenny, wait, I didn't mean it to come out like that.' She massaged her temples. 'I'm tired, that's all.'

He stopped at the door, and looked at her with disdain.

'We're getting nowhere fast and it's just a matter of time

before the Chief Super takes me off the case,' she said.

'You told me a murder investigation requires you to play the long game. Can't you tell that to the Chief Super?'

Everyone in the force knew of Richard Quincey's legendary impatience. And it got him results. He'd risen through the ranks because of it. But only a few knew that he didn't tolerate failure in his subordinates. The chance he'd given her to redeem herself was uncharacteristic, and she knew it was her last one. 'Not this time,' she said.

'Have you got a motive, yet?' he said, after a pause.

'There's no shortage of motives, almost anyone could have done it. But we've no real evidence and, without that, our hands are tied.' She looked up at him. He'd made no effort to move from the door. 'I'm still convinced there's a link with the old murders,' she said.

'The ones with the dolls?'

Why doesn't he call them the Jack in the Box murders? He's a journalist. He remembers details like that. 'The only lead we have is the pub in Soho, the Iron Duke,' she said. 'Do you know it?' she added quietly.

'I've heard of it, but I've never been there.' He motioned to the empty wine bottle. 'The wine's finished. You want some beer?'

She shook her head.

He returned to the armchair, and sat drinking quietly.

'Are you staying?' she said, after a while.

'Do you want me to?'

This was the first time he'd asked her that. Another milestone in their relationship.

'You know I do,' she said wearily.

He smiled his odd crooked smile. 'Sometimes I think I know you, love, and other times I realise I don't.'

In the bathroom, she slapped on her moisturiser, the part

of her beauty routine she never skipped, no matter how tired she was. As she worked the cream into her skin, she watched in the mirror while he brushed his teeth. He was telling her about the research he'd been doing. He had a habit of speaking as he moved the brush up and down, something which had endeared him to her once, but which she now found irritating. Maybe he found her habits equally irritating.

Afterwards, she lay in his arms, panting. She had to admit that, after all this time, he was still good in bed. She turned to face the wall, pulling the sheet over herself. She doubted he could say the same about her. Perhaps that was why she was smelling perfume on him, a perfume she didn't wear.

Chapter 19

Richard Quincey was reading in his office.

'I need a word, sir.'

'Come in, Yvonne.' He took off his glasses. 'What the hell happened at the church yesterday?' He spoke quietly, but his voice carried an undercurrent of menace.

'Arabella Carrington and her photographer barged in and wanted to take photographs.'

'Why didn't you leave the constable to deal with it? You realise the minister had to halt the service.'

She knew the policeman, a tired nervous man whose wife had recently left him. She'd seen him at the supermarket, struggling with a screaming toddler and a trolley full of shopping. 'We dealt with it together, sir.'

Quincey regarded her from under bushy brows. 'I understand you destroyed the camera's memory card. Carrington has already lodged a complaint.' He threw down the newspaper. 'And there's this.'

It was a copy of the day's Daily Mail. The front page carried an account of the memorial service, which seemed to consist entirely of interviews with some of the congregation. Arabella must have lurked in the bushes and pounced. Von could see now that it had been an error of judgement not letting her have her way: instead of photographs, there was a cartoon showing the Chief Super as a sleeping bulldog, with herself and Steve as yapping terriers running round him in diminishing circles. The resemblance to Steve was particularly striking. She knew Steve wouldn't give it a second glance, nor did it bother her, but the Chief Super had always been sensitive to how he was portrayed in the media.

She passed the paper back. 'Despicable, sir.'

'So what are you here for? I'm assuming you've disturbed me to tell me you've made a breakthrough.' His voice was laced with sarcasm. 'I hope so. Your performance lately hasn't exactly been blowing my skirt up.'

'It's about the state of your brother's finances.'

'I thought we'd been through all that,' he said testily.

'Your brother formed the Quincey Players as a private limited company. Did you know?' When he said nothing, she added, 'The company is currently worth half a million pounds. Your brother and Michael Gillanders were sole equal partners. Gillanders now owns it outright. We may have our prime suspect.'

If he was surprised, his face didn't betray it. He continued to stare at her.

'You knew none of this, sir?' she said, puzzled by his silence.

'I've told you before, Yvonne, I knew nothing about my brother's affairs.'

'I'm wondering why you didn't become a partner yourself. It seems the natural thing to do, given that you provided the start-up costs.'

'Must we go over old ground?' he said impatiently. 'I wanted my brother to run his own business.'

She chose her words carefully, not wanting to antagonise him. 'Over the last fifteen years, your brother has been making cash deposits into his bank account. A few hundred at a time. It's not yet clear where this money's been coming from.'

She had his attention. 'Are you suggesting I've been giving it to him?' he said.

'Not suggesting, sir,' she said, smiling faintly, 'just asking.'

'I've given him no money, other than the start-up costs. We both know that statement can be verified.' He busied himself in folding the newspaper. 'So, how are you proceeding?'

'We pulled Gillanders in for formal questioning. He denied killing your brother. We have no material evidence against him.'

He turned his pitiless gaze on her. 'Then for Heaven's sake, Chief Inspector, carry on and find it.'

He stopped her at the door. 'I heard about that business with the doll. The one left outside your flat.'

'It's not putting me off my stride,' she said quietly.

'Stride?' He snorted. 'More like baby steps.'

Well, fuck you very much for asking, sir.

It was 11.20am and he was late. As usual. But there was no point fretting. Tubby Wainwright kept his own time. Over the rim of her mug, Von cast an eye around the Euston Road caff, wondering what the customers would think if they knew she was a detective waiting for her snout.

There were three other people there: a middle-aged couple who sat a few tables away, the woman speaking in bored tones to the man, who kept his eyes glued to his newspaper, and the mousy-haired waitress. She'd left the counter and was clearing away the remains of the fat breakfasts, stacking the plates noisily. Although it was still morning, she moved with the same lethargy that Von remembered from her own summer jobs waiting tables. Von had eaten in this caff when she was training – it did the best mutton pie in London – but it had downsized considerably since. The décor was the same, though: the custard-yellow walls still sweated grease and the strip lights still flickered. The other things unchanged were the smell of chip fat, and the artery-clogging menu. And the tea was always scalding.

It wouldn't have been her first choice of meeting place, but Tubby would have no other. And she was the one asking the favour.

She'd positioned herself so she could see the door. Ten minutes later, a short man with a shock of red hair and John Lennon glasses arrived.

He gave no indication he'd seen her, just sauntered to the counter, his red-and-gold cowboy boots clicking on the lino. He brought a mug to her table. Still not meeting her eye, he reached for the sugar bowl and all but emptied it into his tea.

She knew the routine. Tubby wouldn't even acknowledge her existence until she did it. She rose and went to the counter. A minute later, she returned with a large plate piled high with cream cakes and set it down in front of him.

'Hello, Chief Inspector,' he murmured. 'Long time, no see.'

He took a chocolate éclair from the pile and bit into it. Cream oozed from the sides and dripped onto the table. She watched him eat. He wouldn't be hurried. And he was worth the wait.

He'd been her grass for longer than she could remember. He was one hundred percent dependable and, since the death of the wheel man for a London gang who'd turned Queen's evidence (but not before he'd made a pile of money that would start a bank) she used no-one else.

She'd been a detective sergeant when she met him. It was her first collar. He'd been selling ladies' watches on Oxford Street, watches which had disappeared the day before from a large department store. She'd bought one, then returned the following day when he was selling brassieres. She complained the watch wasn't working and she'd have the law on him unless he got her a replacement. His watery blue eyes, huge behind the spectacles, stared helplessly at her. He'd get one if she came back later that day, he said. She waited in a nearby alley till he passed, then shadowed him to the store, nodding at the house detective as she followed him in. Tubby was good – he knew how to work it so the theft was hidden from the cameras – and she found herself grudgingly admiring his expertise. As he stepped out onto the pavement, she arrested him. In the dock, he kept the jury in stitches, chronicling his exploits. When asked if he'd stolen the watches, he replied, I never stole them, My Lord, I just liberated them from captivity.

She was waiting for him on his release. She'd taken him to this caff. And she'd made him a deal. That was several years ago. He'd been in prison only once since, for robbing a bank. His undoing was that he knew the clerk. When he saw how terrified she was, he lifted his hood and whispered, 'It's all right, Ellie, it's only me'.

Tubby had finished the cakes. He belched lightly, and loosened the bottom two buttons of the striped waistcoat he'd bought on the Portobello Road. A smile of contentment spread over his spotty face.

'You've lost weight, Tubby,' she said affectionately. 'Spanish cuisine not agreeing with you?'

'Too rich, by far. Though there are some fish and chip shops and Irish pubs now.' He slurped his tea. 'So, what's your pleasure, Von?'

'I've a job for you.'

He waved a soft white hand. 'If it's like the last one—'

'This is nothing like that. I want you to do some fishing for me.'

'That's what you said last time.'

She lowered her voice. 'Have you heard of the Iron Duke?'

'Course I have. He won some war, didn't he?'

'I mean the pub.'

'In that case, no.'

'It's in Soho.' She pushed a piece of paper across. 'Here's the address. I want you to have a good sniff around.'

He gazed at her, his eyes swimming behind the lenses. 'What smell are you expecting to find?'

'Do you remember the Jack in the Box murders?'

'When was it?'

'1985.'

'I was on the Costa del Sol in the eighties. Enjoying the sun with me mates.'

'You stayed straight that long?' she said, blowing on her tea.

He shifted in the chair, lowering his eyes. 'I did a few jobs, just to keep my hand in, like.'

'Fleecing the Spaniards?'

He looked up, scandalised. 'Von, I swear. I never touched the locals. People who do that give honest thieves a bad name. No, I only fleeced the tourists.'

'I'm not interested.' She leant forward. 'But this job is important. I'm running a murder investigation and all roads lead to the Duke.'

'Murder?' His eyes narrowed.

She hesitated. Her sergeants had got nowhere showing their hand and she doubted she and Steve could succeed where they'd failed. Tubby was now her only hope. But, if he was to play the innocent successfully, the less he knew about Max Quincey the better.

'I want you to find out what's going on there,' she said. 'All I can tell you is there's some kind of scam. I need to know what it is, and who's controlling it. It may be long running, going back at least fifteen years.'

He arched his eyebrows. 'Drugs?'

She didn't recall mention of drugs in Harrower's file, but the area was notorious for it. 'It may be something bigger.'

'Bigger? How much bigger?'

'No idea. I've nothing to go on.'

He scratched between his legs. 'When do you need this by?'

'Yesterday. But I'm prepared to wait if that's what it takes.'

The silence lengthened.

'So, do we have a deal?' she said. 'Okay, I'll take that lame grin as a yes. Now, let me get you more tea.'

She returned from the counter and placed the mug in front of him, drawing her head back to escape the smell of rancid fat from his hair.

'Ta very much, Chief Inspector.' He lifted the mug and, with a practised movement, withdrew the notes she'd left underneath. 'I'll be in touch.'

Von and Steve were in her office, finishing the greasy specials from the station's canteen.

'The Duke seems to be the key to this whole thing,' she said, wiping coleslaw off her fingers. 'I let the genie out of the bottle when I sent the others in. It was a bad mistake, Steve.'

'You think your snout will succeed where they failed?'

'If anyone can do it, he can.'

Steve rubbed his neck. 'I've never been able to get anywhere with snouts. The last one was a disaster. He wore his wire outside his clothes.'

'Ever tried seasoned criminals? When I engaged mine, I didn't realise how ahead of the curve I was.' She took a sip of coffee. 'Talking of the Duke, there's someone else who might shed light on what's going on there.'

'Charlo's pimp, Jimmy Porteous?'

'Larry said Porteous would sometimes go to the Duke with his boys. Maybe he still does. He's the last living link to Manny and the others.' She considered Steve's half-eaten pork pie, lying in its wrapping. 'You're obviously not hungry. Let's go.'

He stared at the pie. 'Now?'

Von had always felt at home in the Borough. On her days off, she'd shop in Borough Market, combing the stalls looking for her brothers who often helped out their mates in return for the odd box of fruit or cut of meat. Like much of London's East End, the Borough had been badly damaged during the Blitz. The terraced streets had vanished, as had the theatres and music halls. It was one of the oldest parts of London and, as with other areas earmarked for development, it was a mix of office blocks, expensive residential areas, and run-down council estates.

It was in one of these run-down estates that Jimmy Porteous lived, on the fifth floor of a high-rise block of flats.

Unwilling to leave the Toyota unattended, Von instructed Larry to stay at the wheel. She and Steve climbed the stairs carefully, stepping over refuse and trying not to brush against the walls. They reached the fifth floor, and paused to get their breath. The temperature had dropped, and the wind was stiffening, snatching up leaves and litter and hurling them into the air. She peered over the balcony, wondering how Larry would cope with the unwelcome attention he was attracting. He'd opened the car door and was talking to a group of teenagers, one of whom was showing more than usual interest in the Toyota's paintwork.

'I imagine this part of London's a bit like Glasgow,' she said.

Steve was a pro at this game. 'Glasgow's not nearly as up-market.' They exchanged smiles.

She turned her attention to Porteous's door. When there was no reply to her knock, she hammered with her fist.

'Why not try the bell, boss?'

'It's broken.'

He examined the hinge. 'So is the door.' He put his shoulder against it and forced it open.

'Jimmy Porteous?' she shouted.

'In here,' came a voice from inside.

They stepped into the tiny hallway. Her first instinct was to cover her mouth and nose. 'God, Steve, what a stink.'

'Reminds me of home. That heady mix of damp plaster and stale cabbage.'

'Where are you, Mr Porteous?'

'In the kitchen. Through the lounge.'

'He's taking a risk, letting in strangers,' Steve said, following her.

'Look around you. What is there to steal?'

The lounge had once been a pleasant room, its centrepiece the gas fire with tiled surround, but it had been allowed to fall into decay. A thin film of dust covered the surfaces, the foam sofa had split across the back, and the striped orange curtains were faded and in tatters.

She stepped over the empty food cartons and Coke cans, trying to find a place for her feet. As she brushed against a box, something sleek and black ran across the room.

The door to the kitchen was open. A middle-aged man, his black hair flecked with grey, was standing on a chair, relieving himself into the sink. He was wearing a black shirt and crumpled blue and white pyjama bottoms. On his feet were felt slippers that had once been red.

He turned, still urinating, and grinned, revealing badly-discoloured teeth. 'The loo's blocked,' he said, shaking himself. 'You've caught me at a bad time. I was just getting dressed.'

He stepped off the chair and held his hands under the tap. With a rapid motion, he ran them over his face.

'Sorry about that,' he said, wiping his forehead with the bottom of his shirt. 'I don't expect guests at this time of day.' His eyes slid over her body, lingering at her breasts. He tilted his head, a calculation in the eyes. 'I take it you want a boy. You after a threesome?'

'We're police,' she said, showing him her warrant card. 'Are you Jimmy Porteous?'

He wiped his mouth with his knuckles, barely glancing at the card.

'Relax, Mr Porteous. We're just after some information.' She gave this time to sink in. 'You lived with Charlo Heggarty, I understand.'

For an instant, an expression of hopelessness appeared on his face. 'Is that a question?'

'We know you lived with him, it's in your statement,' she said in a friendly tone. She was keen not to upset him. 'Have you heard of Max Quincey?'

'Can't say I have,' he said guardedly.

'He was arrested for Charlo's murder, but released without charge.'

'Why are you talking about Charlo after all this time? Have you caught the prick, then? Is it this Max guy?'

'Max Quincey has been found murdered in the same way as Charlo.'

He came close enough that she could smell him. It was an oily sweaty smell, but she didn't flinch. 'The same way?' he said.

'We think the two murders are related. We're hoping you can help us catch Quincey's killer.' She paused for effect. 'And Charlo's.'

He said nothing, but a veil came down over his eyes.

'Are you a male prostitute, Mr Porteous?'

'Me?' He shook his head.

'Do you still pimp boys?' she said, smiling.

'I'm not telling you anything.'

'Please answer the Chief Inspector,' said Steve.

'I don't have to.' He looked from one to the other. 'I know my rights, so piss off.'

It was time to take off the gloves. 'Listen to me, Mr Porteous,' she said, 'this isn't good cop, bad cop. This is a woman having her period and perfectly within *her* rights to drag your arse down to the nick. So what's it to be? Do you answer my questions here or from a police cell?'

Her change of mood unsettled him. 'Okay, yes, I run boys.'

'Now we're getting somewhere.' She glanced around. There was nowhere to sit in the kitchen. 'Shall we go into the lounge?'

He nodded silently.

Remembering the rat, she took the armchair furthest from the sofa. Steve sat at the table. Porteous sprawled on the sofa, oblivious that his flies were gaping.

'Mr Porteous, I'd like you to take a look at this photograph,' she said. 'It's Max Quincey. I think you've seen him before.'

'The ponce with the fancy clothes. Yeah, I've seen him,' he said in a bored tone.

'How well did you know him?'

'I didn't. I just saw him at the Duke. He was always there.'

'What was he doing?'

'Picking up boys. Same as the other punters.'

'When was this?'

'Years ago.'

'Around the time of the Jack in the Box murders?'

He nodded, watching her.

'Did Max Quincey ever come here?'

'Here? No, he never came here.' He said it as though she'd insulted him.

'Tell me about the boys, Jimmy, the ones killed at the same time as Charlo. I'm trying to build up a picture of what they were like.' When there was no response, she added, 'You do remember who they were?'

'I remember.' He bit his lip. 'There was Liam,' he said, half to himself. 'Dark hair. Never could keep it combed.' He lifted a hand to his face. 'Had a stain here.'

She nodded encouragingly. So far, the description was

accurate.

'Always in demand, he was. One look at him would send the punters wild, even with the mark on his skin. It was the expression in his eyes. Cheeky like. Made a shedload of money on the game, he did. Bought himself a posh coat. Went right down to the ground. Liam. Never knew his last name.' He smiled, as though at some secret. 'Then there was Gilly. We called him Gilly McIlly. Red hair. Great pal of Charlo's. Always larking about, the two of them were. From the same part of Dublin. Liam was quieter. I used to wonder why the other boys bothered with him. I asked Charlo once.'

'What did he say?' Steve pressed, when Porteous seemed disinclined to continue.

He looked up, as though surprised to see them still there. 'He said they all looked out for each other, simple as that. You see, they hadn't intended to go on the game. No-one does. I mean, what kid dreams of being a rent boy? No, they wanted to find jobs in London. Proper jobs. Brought money with them, to get themselves started, like. But it ran out sooner than they thought. Much sooner.' His expression softened. 'They had no idea what it costs just to exist in London.'

He fetched tobacco and matches from the mantelpiece, and rolled a cigarette. 'I picked up Charlo for myself,' he said matter-of-factly. 'Met him at the Duke. Brought him here.' He struck a match. The loose strands of tobacco flared as they caught. He inhaled deeply, then dropped the spent match on the carpet. 'Took a shine to him, I did. Told him he could stop with me if he liked. It was safer for him than on the street, so he was happy enough. At least he had a proper bed, not like some.' His eyes focussed on the tip of his cigarette. 'I let him bring his punters here. He did it mainly with straight couples who wanted threesomes. A good boy, was Charlo. And clean. Always washing himself. Used to keep the flat spotless.' He glanced around. 'I've let the place go a bit.'

'What did the boys do when they weren't with their clients?' said Von.

'Working, or looking for it. Sometimes they'd get things, you know, from the Jobcentre, like.' He shrugged. 'When that dried up, it was back to the Duke. Best place for punters. They'd get a drink, and sit and wait. I'd go with them, usually.'

'Did you stay with them when they were with their clients?'

'Sometimes.' He tapped the cigarette, flicking ash onto the floor. 'They felt safer when they knew I was round the corner. I only took a small cut of the takings.'

'Did you love Charlo?' she said gently.

'Love him?' A look of tenderness appeared on his face. 'Sure, I loved him. And he loved me back.' His mouth twisted into a cruel smile. 'It's not easy living on the estate when you're like me. I still get banana skins in my face, and people making monkey noises. Charlo hated that. He'd have a go at them, he would. Got himself a couple of nasty shiners on account of it.' There was a hint of pride in his voice. 'If that isn't love, I don't know what is.' He ground the remains of the cigarette into the carpet. 'I've never forgiven myself for not being here. You know, when it all went down. After Gilly was killed, I knew he wouldn't be the only one.'

She felt the blood pounding in her ears. 'How did you know, Jimmy?'

He stared at his slippers as though they belonged to someone else. 'They were up to something. All of them. And they were in deep.'

Her heartbeat quickened. Could this be the break they were looking for? 'Something at the Duke?'

'Sure, at the Duke,' he said impatiently. 'Where else? And I'll tell you something for nowt. It's still going on. I didn't want to know the details, I told Charlo to keep me out of it.' His voice hardened. 'He was using, although he never did it here. But I could tell. Got the sweats now and again, he did.'

'Drugs?'

'Smack, if you want to be precise.'

'Was he selling?'

'Like I said, they all were. Every last man.'

'Everyone at the Duke?' Steve said in astonishment.

'Everyone at the Duke knows something,' Porteous said with a self-mocking smile. 'They either deal, or they know who's dealing.'

She stared at him. *Everyone at the Duke.* My God, this was huge. No wonder they'd zipped it when her guys went nosing around. She could see Steve was thinking the same: Why had it been allowed to go on for so long?

Porteous was watching her. 'I see what you're thinking, but you'll get nothing out of them. They've learnt how to keep quiet over the years.'

'How many years? From the time of the murders?'

'Way before.'

Her mind was in a whirl. So it predated even the Jack in the Boxes. A thought struck her. 'Manny Newman wasn't involved, was he?'

'The Jew boy?' he said with indifference. 'He wasn't in on it.'

'Charlo and the boys knew him, though.'

'They'd see him at the Duke. To chat to, like. They weren't best mates.' He played with the tassel on his pyjamas. 'Manny was a loner. Sat on his own, didn't want company. Just waited for a punter, then went out. Had his own place to kip.'

'And you're sure he didn't deal?' she said, praying he'd give her the answer she wanted.

'I'll tell you how I know.' He scratched behind his ear. 'It was around New Years. A big haul of dust must have come in because the boys were flush with cash. That's how I knew, see.

Charlo had a whole pile of notes and he could never have made that much on the game.' He nodded at the television in the corner. 'Bought me that in the sales. Late Christmas present. Anyway, we went down to the Duke for a drink. Manny was there, in the snug. Some geezer went up to him and tried to slip him some dust, to sell on, like. Manny went spare, threw it back in his face. The packet split and it went everywhere.' He laughed mirthlessly. 'The look on the geezer's face. Everyone saw. Manny wasn't too popular after that. Charlo told me it was on account of Manny's mum that he wouldn't deal. She was so far gone that World War Three could have broken out and she'd never have noticed.'

'Were drugs passed around so openly?'

'Course not.' He picked a strand of tobacco from his teeth. 'Most of them were so good, you'd never know how they did it.'

'Was Max Quincey into drugs?' she said, after a pause.

'He came to the Duke for boys, nothing else.' He sneered. 'I doubt he could tell smack from baby food.'

'Did you ever see Max pick up any of the Irish lads? Or Manny Newman? Please think carefully.'

'Can't say that I did. But my memory's not what it was.'

'I appreciate you telling us all this, Jimmy. Just one more question. When Charlo was killed, did you inform the police about the drug dealing?'

He almost spat out the words. 'Didn't want to know, did he?'

'Who?'

'Him. The copper that ran the murder enquiry.'

'DCI Harrower?'

'Yeah, I think that were his name. I tried to tell him that's why Charlo and the others were killed but he just nodded as though I were telling him about my summer holidays. He didn't write any of it down.' His expression dissolved into one of despair. 'At least you're listening. That's why I'm sticking my neck out, saying all this. I want you to nail the piece of shit who killed my Charlo. I was the one who found him. Lying there. His lovely dreamy eyes gone.' The words were barely audible. 'And you say he's done it again?'

'He may have, Jimmy,' she said softly.

'You have to catch him.' He crossed himself. 'And, God help me, I hope he burns in hell.' Tears slid down his face. He wiped his nose with the back of his hand, smearing snot over his lip.

She got to her feet. 'Thank you, Jimmy.' She held out a card. 'Please get in touch if you think of anything else.'

He ignored her, hugging himself as though he were suddenly cold.

She laid the card on the table. 'We'll let ourselves out.'

They reached the Toyota just in time.

Three youths were kicking Larry, who was rolling around on the tarmac, shielding his head with his hands. Steve grabbed the nearest boy by the hair and wheeled him round, pulling his arm up his back. The boy squealed in pain. As Steve snapped on the cuffs, the larger of the boy's companions rushed at Von. She held her ground and tried to block his punch, but his fist glanced off her cheekbone. Ignoring the pain, she moved in swiftly and drove her knee hard into his groin. The youth howled and dropped like a stone. He rocked in the foetal position, snivelling, his hands thrust between his legs. The third boy assimilated the situation, and promptly ran off.

She pulled out her cuffs and turned the boy over. 'Don't rub them, sunshine,' she said, securing his wrists. 'Count them.'

Larry dragged himself to his feet. He collapsed against the car, breathing deeply.

'Good of you to take one for the team, Larry,' she said. 'You all right?'

'Just a few bruised ribs, ma'am,' he gasped. 'You'll have to show me that manoeuvre some time.' He managed a smile. 'It's not in the manual.'

Steve was bundling the boys into the car. 'Watch it,' the tall one yelled. 'I nearly hit my head.'

'It's all right, son.' He pushed him in. 'The car's insured.'

Chapter 20

Steve was watching Von trying to get coffee from the machine in the hall. It offered the usual choice of tea, chocolate, and several types of coffee, but the only thing worth drinking was the americano.

'Aye, boss, a pimp with a heart.'

'Most of the ones I've come across beat up their lads, not take care of them,' Von said, pressing buttons at random.

'So what do you reckon? The Irish lads were involved in a heroin ring, got too close, and were killed? Danni said their murders might be linked.'

'I don't buy heroin as the link, Steve. It doesn't explain why Manny was attacked.' She banged the side of the machine and five paper cups fell onto the floor. Hot liquid flowed into the waste reservoir. 'God, why is everything in this nick broken? Oh come on, let's leave it.' She strode away towards her office.

He nearly had to run to keep up. 'Manny could have been attacked because the killer assumed he was in on it.'

'But you heard Porteous describe Manny's reaction when he was offered heroin. Everyone saw the stuff flying.' She flopped into her chair. 'No, if the boys were all attacked for the same reason, it wasn't the drug angle.'

'Heroin, though, boss. Drugs and prostitution are usually linked. How come we didn't clock it before?'

'Because the others found zippo. But was there really nothing in Harrower's report? Porteous said he told him about the drugs, and Harrower showed no interest.' She rubbed her temples. 'Let's take another look at the old case notes.'

He took the file from the shelf and leafed through it. 'There's a throwaway comment here that traces of heroin were found on the crime scene dolls.'

'Then why wasn't the drugs squad swarming over the place?' she said impatiently. 'I don't get it. They send in dogs and everything.'

He was browsing through the file, looking at pages at random. 'Pity Harrower isn't still around. He passed away not long after he retired.'

'Maybe there's someone else in the drugs squad we could talk to.' She nodded at the file. 'Who else is in there?'

He flicked to the list of names. 'Simon Hensbury.'

Her voice softened. 'My old governor.'

'According to this, he was Harrower's boss on the case back then.' Steve glanced up. 'Bit younger than Harrower, if I remember. I met him on my inspector's course. Something of a talking textbook.'

She smiled. 'That's him in course tutor mode. He was a good governor, though.'

'Do you see much of him now?'

'Hardly.'

'Went early, didn't he? To the Costa del Sol?'

'He's back. Got tired of running into people he put away.'

'Shall I ask him to come in?'

'He won't come to the nick.' She tapped the biro against her teeth. 'I'll call him. He owes me dinner.'

Steve looked at her with interest. 'Owes you, boss?'

She put the biro down. 'Steve, there's something we need to make clear to the others. I want everyone quiet about the drug angle for now. I don't intend to tell the Chief Super yet.'

'You sure about that?' he said uneasily.

She knew what he'd be thinking: not only was keeping your superior officer in the dark a bad idea, it was a disciplinary offence. If he found out, the Chief Super wouldn't hesitate to haul her over the coals. 'I'm not having the drugs squad taking over,' she said firmly.

He opened his mouth to speak, but stopped when he saw Danni at the door.

Danni glanced from Von to Steve, and Von wondered how much she'd heard. But she'd discovered years before that Danni's discretion could be relied upon.

'Is this a good time?' Danni said. 'I was on my way home and thought you'd like my analysis of your interview with Michael Gillanders.'

Von smiled. 'I'd offer you coffee Danni, but the machine is kaput.'

'No problem, I'm over-caffeinated as it is.'

Steve gave her his chair, and lolled against the wall.

'So, what's the bottom line?' said Von.

Danni pulled out her notebook. 'Cool customer, to begin with. Most people would have found your line of questioning intimidating. Not Gillanders, he held his own. You touched a nerve only when you suggested he might have killed the boys.'

'Could he be the Mr X who killed Max Quincey?'

'My best offer is, possibly.'

'And the rent boys?'

'He's definitely not the Mr Y who killed them.'

'Still thinking it's two separate people?'

'Aren't you?' When Von said nothing, she added, 'So, any leads?'

'Only one,' Von said. 'The Iron Duke.'

'Thought you'd drawn a blank.'

'Where my officers failed, others might succeed.'

'A snout?' Danni nodded. 'And if he fails?'

'Damn it, I'll go there myself.'

'Undercover?' Danni said, her eyes sparkling.

'It'll have to be. They spotted the coppers I sent in and closed ranks.' She stood up, wanting to bring the interview to a close. She was tired, and Kenny might be home. 'I won't keep you, Danni. And thanks.'

Danni remained seated. 'Actually, I was hoping to entice you out for a spot of supper.' She looked up at Steve. 'You too, of course.'

He smiled warmly. 'I've made other plans.'

'Ah, the beautiful barmaid. You two still together?'

He hesitated. 'Sometimes.' He turned to Von. 'I'll see you, boss.'

They watched him go.

'What's this about, Danni? You don't usually include Steve in your invitations.'

'I'd hoped to do a spot of matchmaking. I was intending to leave the restaurant early.'

'You're not still banging on about Steve and me.'

'Fetch your coat, Von.'

The large glittering restaurant was Friday-night busy and every table was taken. Blonde waitresses in gold livery, the hallmark of the restaurant, fussed over the guests.

'Don't know why you've chosen this place,' Danni said. 'I don't eat in hotel restaurants.'

'This is one of the top hotels in Kensington,' Von said. 'Anyway, I'm hoping to see someone.'

'Not Kenny, surely. This doesn't look like his type of watering hole.'

'Last time I was here, I had dinner with Simon Hensbury.'

Danni smiled, her eyes a cat's. 'You think your old Guv will be here tonight?'

'If he's in London, this is where he eats.' She sipped at her mineral water. 'It's not only his type of watering hole, it's his only watering hole. He's allowed to smoke in this restaurant.'

'Are you hoping to bed him again?'

'I want to talk to him about the Jack in the Box murders. He was Harrower's boss at the time.'

'You didn't answer my question.'

She studied the menu. 'The fish looks good.'

'There's something you're not telling me, Von.'

'Kenny's having an affair.'

When the silence had gone on too long, she glanced up. Danni was watching her calmly.

'You don't seem surprised,' Von said.

'I've seen this coming.'

'Then why haven't I?'

'You're trained to look for different sorts of clues.' Danni played with her fork, running her fingers over the tines. 'So what made you suspect the affair?'

It seemed a betrayal to discuss her failing relationship with anyone, even another woman. But she needed to talk to someone, and Danni was the closest she had to a female friend. 'I smelt a perfume on him that I don't use,' she said finally.

'And you think that falling into bed with Simon Hensbury would be getting your own back.'

'I'm not intending to fall into bed with Simon Hensbury,' she said testily.

Danni looked past her. 'Is that him? With the Chief Super?'

She swung round. Richard Quincey and a tall broad-shouldered man had entered the room. They were deep in conversation, and continued talking as a waitress led them to a table by the window. Von's eyes remained on Quincey's companion. The blood sang in her ears as she watched the familiar movements, how he waited till Quincey sat down before pulling his own chair out, how he patted his pockets feeling for cigarettes.

'I can see the attraction,' Danni said. 'He's sexier in a way even the Chief Super isn't. But the Chief Super's queered your pitch by coming with Hensbury. Are you still going to try to talk to him?'

She buried her face in the menu. 'I'll do it at the end of the meal. As though I've just spotted him.'

'Too late. He's coming over.'

Simon Hensbury was making his way towards them.

Her heart clenched as she looked into the familiar blue-grey eyes. She drank in every detail: the hair falling over his forehead, the lines in his face, the slight bump in his nose. And the smile creeping onto his lips.

'Von,' he said, his eyes roaming over her face. He laid a hand on her shoulder. 'I haven't seen you for such a long time.'

His voice was as she remembered it, rich and deep. She tried to think of a suitable reply but words failed her. It was the effect he always had when she saw him after an absence.

'So, how are you?' he said. Without waiting for a reply, he turned, his hand still on her shoulder, and appraised Danni quickly.

Von made the introductions. 'Sir, I see you're with Chief Superintendent Quincey,' she added hesitantly. 'I don't want to disturb your dinner.'

He turned back to her, frowning. 'Dreadful business about his brother. Just as that play's returned too.' He dropped his voice. 'And Richard told me about the doll outside your flat. Just ghastly.'

This was her opportunity and she had no intention of wasting it. 'I'd like to pick your brains about that old case. Could I give you a call next week?'

'Let me give you my card.' He reached into his jacket pocket, the light reflecting off his signet ring. 'Richard and I have a lot to catch up on, but do come over before you leave.' His eyes ran quickly down Danni's body. 'Delighted to have met you, Dr Mittelberg.' He walked away, holding his shoulders straight.

'Wow, he's even sexier close up,' murmured Danni. 'What was he like?'

'Outstanding.'

'I meant in bed, not as a governor.'

'So did I.'

Danni's lips curved into a smile. 'Married?'

'Occasionally.'

'Married now?'

'No idea.'

The waitress arrived, took their order, and left.

'I notice you keep looking over my shoulder,' Von said, staring hard at the table. 'What are you seeing?'

Danni brought the glass of Chablis to her lips. 'They go back a long way. It's the body language, the way they're easy with each other. That's rare for professional men of their rank.' She glanced at Von. 'Has the Chief Super ever mentioned his friendship with Hensbury?'

'He wouldn't, he took over from Simon at Clerkenwell.'

'Now they're talking about you,' Danni said into her glass. 'They've turned in this direction.'

She kept her eyes on the tablecloth. 'You sure it's not you they're talking about?'

'You're the common denominator so it's natural they'd be discussing you.'

'Discussing my progress on the case, you mean. Or rather, the lack of it,' she added caustically.

Danni laid a friendly hand on her arm. 'Forget it and enjoy your meal. It's Friday. Haven't you got the day off tomorrow?' She glanced up. 'Ah, here's the turbot.'

As they ate, Von filled Danni in on her more recent discoveries, including the drugs scam at the Duke.

Danni blew on her coffee. 'Take care, Von. Police who break up drug rings often end up dead. Maybe that's why Harrower fought shy of it.'

'I didn't become a copper so I could hide behind my warrant card. When things get tough, that's when you have to step up.' She risked a glance behind her. Simon was listening intently to the Chief Super. 'What do you feel like doing now, Danni? Shall we get a nightcap at the bar?'

'You don't want to get back to Kenny?'

'His mobile's switched off again. I've left him a message I may be late.'

Danni drew back her chair. 'We should bid the gentlemen goodbye.'

Von led the way to their table. As they approached, the men got to their feet. The Chief Super looked none too pleased at the intrusion.

She glanced at the full ashtray in front of him. 'Evening, sir,' she nodded cheerfully. Turning to Simon, she said, 'It's been good seeing you again.' She paused. 'We're just leaving.'

His eyes were steady. 'So soon?'

'We're having a nightcap at the bar,' Danni said when Von didn't reply. 'It's been a pleasure,' she added, smiling.

As they walked towards the door, Von could feel the men's eyes boring into her back.

'What on earth were they smoking?' Danni said, once they were outside. 'Whatever it was, it was horrible. Sweet and sickly.'

'Cigarillos. I recognise the smell. It's a brand called Hoyo de Monterrey.'

'Hold on. Max Quincey smoked those.'

She lowered her voice. 'They'd finished smoking by the time we got there. From where you were sitting, could you see which one of them had the cigarillos?'

'They were both smoking.' Danni pulled a face. 'But I think it was the Chief Super who offered his packet to Simon. Why do you ask?'

'No particular reason.'

They found the bar and were about to order drinks, when Von felt an arm slide round her waist.

Simon's face was close to hers. 'Richard has just left, Von. If you want that chat, now is as good a time as any.' He turned to Danni, letting his eyes rest on hers. 'Provided, of course, that Dr Mittelberg doesn't mind.'

Von was about to reply that she'd call him the following week, when Danni said, 'Of course I don't mind.' She gathered up her bag. 'I'll catch you next week, Von,' she said, making sure Simon couldn't see the wink.

'I do hope you don't mind my breaking up your evening,' Simon said, watching Danni leave, 'but Richard has filled me in on the case. I'd like to offer my help, it's what old friends are for.'

'Sir—'

'Simon. I'm no longer your governor. Why don't we take that table in the corner?' He smiled. 'Still drinking vodka and tonic?'

She was flattered he remembered. But he'd always been good with details. His arm was still round her waist. He squeezed gently, then left to order the drinks.

He returned with her vodka and a glass of brandy. 'So, what would you like to ask me?' he said, settling himself beside her.

'I'm trying to get a handle on the Jack in the Box murders. DCI Harrower ran the case.' She chose her words carefully, conscious that Simon, as Harrower's boss, might think she was criticising him. 'I've uncovered inconsistencies in how he handled things.'

Simon raised a questioning eyebrow.

'We've interviewed someone who said the murdered boys were involved in a drug scam. You remember the details of the case?'

'I remember them well.' He brought the brandy to his lips. 'But Tom gave no hint to me of drug dealing at the Duke.'

She bent her face to her drink, hoping her expression hadn't given her away. She'd not mentioned the Duke to either Simon or the Chief Super. So, why had Simon brought it up? Had he jumped to this conclusion simply because the Duke was frequented by the boys? Or was there something he knew and wasn't telling her?

'I think I know why that was,' he was saying. 'Tom probably ignored it because he'd followed a false drugs trail once before, with disastrous consequences. Before your time, but it led to great embarrassment for him.' He smiled knowingly. 'Tom was old school, did everything by numbers. He'd be very careful to get hard evidence before pushing that sort of thing upstairs. And we both know how difficult it is to get drugs-related evidence.' He took a mouthful of liquid. 'I know there are things you can't tell me but, broadly speaking, how are you proceeding? Have you been fishing at the Duke?'

'We've found nothing.'

'A dead end? Maybe Tom was right, and your informants, wrong.'

'I've sent my snout in.'

He chuckled. 'Still using Tubby? I thought he'd gone to ground in Torremolinos. I've been on the lookout for him.'

'He's back in London, sir.'

He gave her a long look then, the kind he'd given her in the past, which made her feel like a sixteen-year-old. 'How are things with you, Von? I'm not talking about work.'

What could she tell him? He was the last person she could talk to about Kenny. She set down her glass. 'Never better,' she said.

He cupped her chin and lifted her face to his. As he looked deep into her eyes, something twisted inside her. After a long silence, he released her. 'Shall I get a room?' he murmured.

She didn't hesitate. 'Yes, sir.'

Chapter 21

'You've never been out of my thoughts,' Simon said, undoing the buttons of her blouse. 'We should have done this more than just the once.'

It had been three years before, as he was retiring. Probably the only time they could have done it, a working relationship would have been impossible otherwise. They'd been working late, a week before his retirement do. It was a huge send-off at the Dorchester with officers from every force in the country. He was clearing his desk, and she was finishing a report that could have waited till the following week. He suggested talking through her current case over a quick drink. They went to this same hotel, where dinner had followed the drink, her case forgotten. He seemed reluctant to let her leave, asking about her childhood, her family, questions he'd never asked in their years of working. She, usually unwilling to speak about her past, found herself desperate to tell him everything. He was a good listener, a quality which had earned him a reputation as one of the best detectives at the Met. They had a nightcap. Then he made the suggestion, using the same words: *Shall I get a room?* She'd never told Kenny. Why hurt him? It was only going to be this once.

Simon unzipped his fly and guided her hand inside. He slipped his fingers under the front of her bra, then ran them round to the back and unfastened the hooks expertly. He stepped back to look at her, the movement pulling her hand from his trousers.

Then he was grabbing at her, cupping her backside with both hands. His mouth closed on hers, the force of his body crushing her breasts, his erection stabbing her. As he pulled her towards the bed, she decided that there was no need to tell Kenny. It was only going to be this once.

She woke in the morning to see Simon in a bathrobe, towelling his hair. He dried it quickly, rubbing his head in short rough movements. She remembered this from before, how she'd been afraid to spoil the moment but he'd seen her in the mirror looking at him.

She sat up, pulling the sheet over her breasts.

'Good morning,' he said lazily. He came over and took her hand. 'I've ordered room service for you.'

'Only for me?' Her voice sounded strange to her ears.

'I've a plane to catch, and I still need to pack.'

Her reply was automatic, and she hoped it masked her disappointment. 'Business or pleasure?'

'Some business, but mainly pleasure.' He pulled away the bedclothes. 'But nothing as pleasurable as last night.'

Her eyes held his. If she could only detain him, she was confident they would make love again. 'Won't you at least stay for coffee?' she said.

He was kneading her breast. 'I can't tell you how tempting that offer is, but I really must go.' He pushed back her hair and kissed her neck.

She watched him dress, wondering what he did in his retirement. Perhaps old governors never retired. She knew so little about his private life. He had a villa in Spain, and a house in London, and who knew what business interests. Nothing to do with the force, she was sure. What little filtered into Clerkenwell had more to do with his appearances at his London club or at some society boxing event, sometimes accompanied by his latest wife.

He was knotting his tie when there was a knock at the door. She grabbed the bedclothes and pulled them up. A young man entered, wheeling a trolley.

Simon motioned to the window. 'Leave it there, please.' The man threw her a quick smile as he closed the door.

Simon brought the coffee to the bed.

Her heart was pounding. *Make the phone call. Take a later plane.*

He picked up the signet ring and worked it onto his left hand. His eyes didn't leave her face. 'I hope I'll see you again.' He made it sound like a question.

'Call me when you're back in town, sir,' she said, deeply disappointed.

He smiled, his eyes wandering over the outline of her body under the sheet. Then he picked up his coat and left.

She took a quick shower and slipped on the robe Simon had worn, wrapping it tightly round her body as though she could wrap him with it. She sat at the window, sipping coffee. She was in no hurry to leave. She had the day off and could spend it as she pleased. She could go swimming (the only exercise she took as her large bust made it difficult to do sports and gym routines). Or she could go shopping, squander money on clothes she didn't need, something she hadn't done for months. She glanced at the sober navy blue suit, lying where she'd let it drop. Maybe she should take Danni's advice and buy something red. She could call her and invite her along. Except that Danni's weekends were spent at her father's pile in Buckinghamshire, and she was unlikely to come to town just for shopping. No matter, she'd go on her own. Yes, a day at Harrods was what she needed.

Her shoulders sagged. She was fooling herself. What she

needed was Simon to come through the door and make love to her. She couldn't define what attracted her to certain men, but it was never the obvious, like good looks or athletic physique. Men like that who'd succeeded in slipping between her sheets had rarely lived up to the promise. Simon was an exception. He'd paid her the most attention in bed, and was highly skilled at sex. *I hope I'll see you again.* Her pulse quickened as she remembered his fingers, running like a breath along her skin.

Another exception, of course, was Kenny.

She felt the first prickle of guilt. Had he returned last night and found her gone? What would he have thought? She was working late? Sleeping at the nick? Sleeping with someone else? Strange how the guilt she felt now, when she was convinced he was cheating on her, was greater than it had been the first time she'd slept with Simon, when her relationship with Kenny was at its strongest. And why had she slept with Simon that first time, when she was all but living with another man? Was it just the anticipation of great sex? She'd never been sure. And somehow it hadn't seemed important, he was out of bounds, always married. Maybe that was part of the attraction, that she wouldn't have to commit.

She shredded the croissant and stuffed the pieces into her mouth. She ate quickly, out of habit, forgetting she didn't have to rush to the police station. She wasn't even hungry after the huge dinner. She always ate too much when she was with Danni.

Danni. The woman's words came creeping back: *I think it was the Chief Super who offered his packet to Simon.* A feeling of unease stole over her. The Chief Super smoked Hoyo de Monterrey. He'd read the Forensic report and seen the analysis of the contents of his brother's ashtray, but he'd not told her he smoked the same brand of cigarillos. Was that significant? Everything was significant until proven otherwise. Her old governor had told her that. Simon. She ran her fingers over the robe, remembering how her body had moved under his hands.

It was time to get herself across London.

In the bathroom, she stood before the mirror, brushing her teeth vigorously. The toothbrush was one of a pair, each in shrink-wrapped plastic. Unlike the tiny foldable toothbrushes supplied by most hotels, these were normal-sized with a wide handle. Simon's lay discarded on the shelf. She was about to throw it in the bin, when something stopped her. *I think it was the Chief Super who offered his packet to Simon.*

I think. Danni wasn't sure...

It seemed a betrayal, but she told herself it was a precaution, a routine piece of investigation, eliminating him from her enquiries. She was a copper, after all. This was what she did.

She removed a plastic bag from her handbag. Taking care not to touch Simon's toothbrush, she wrapped the bag round it, and sealed it shut.

Von let herself into the flat. 'Kenny? Are you home?' she shouted into the silence.

She'd rehearsed what she would tell him, to the evident amusement of the passengers on the tube who must have enjoyed her constantly changing facial expressions.

But there was no reply. She let out a breath. She was off the hook for now, she wouldn't have to lie. But still, the guilt came nibbling at the edges.

She changed into jeans and a sweater, then set about tidying the flat. She swept the newspapers and pizza boxes into a black bin bag, glanced at the pile of ironing in the kitchen, separating out the only items that needed pressing (her shirts for work), then loaded the washing machine, snagging the tights as she crammed them inside.

She was opening a tin of soup when she heard the key in the lock.

Kenny's head appeared round the door. 'Put that down, love, I'm taking you to lunch.' Like a conjurer, he brandished a huge bunch of yellow lilies from behind his back.

'Kenny!' She threw her arms round him, pressing her face against his neck. Suddenly, she stiffened and stepped back quickly.

'What's got into you? You look like you've just kissed a leper.'

She busied herself with the flowers. 'So, where are we going? Do I need to put on my glad rags?'

'How about the Al Sole di Napoli?'

The restaurant near Greek Street where he'd taken her on one of their first dates. She turned to face him. 'Why, Kenny? Why are we going out to lunch?'

'Why not?' He ran his thumb lightly down her arm. 'Aren't you curious to see the place? Remember what we did afterwards?' he added, smiling.

'I doubt we'll get a table at short notice.'

His smile faded. 'Look, love, if you don't want to go, just say. I've got plenty of things I need to do right now, and I—'

'Okay, what, precisely, do you need to do? What have you been doing these last couple of weeks?'

'I've told you what I've been doing,' he said slowly. 'Researching a story.'

'In the British Library?'

'Among other places.'

'Don't lie, Kenny,' she said, conscious of the strain in her voice. 'You're piss-poor at it. You haven't been working.'

He flushed. 'And you know this how?'

'You've been keeping your phone switched off. There isn't a journalist alive who does that.' She paused. 'Unless he's up to something and doesn't want to be contacted.'

'You know the trouble with you? You're always playing detective. It hasn't occurred to you there might be a simple

223

reason for my phone being off?'

'I'm listening.'

'It's been playing up.' The words were measured, as though he were speaking to a child. 'Phones do that from time to time.'

'You're lying.' She was shouting now. 'It's a badge of honour with you. All right then, so here it is. When you phoned from the British Library, I heard music and laughter. You were somewhere else, Kenny.' She poked him in the chest. 'Where was it? A pub? Al Sole di Napoli? Were you there with someone?'

'That's it, isn't it? You think I've been shagging my wick off. Well, I've been working, you dozy mare. Earning an honest crust. Not like you and your shitty little murder investigations.'

'What's her name?'

He turned away. 'Who?'

She kept her voice steady. 'The woman you're seeing.'

'I'm not seeing anyone,' he mumbled, his back to her.

Something inside her snapped. 'I can smell her on you. I smelt her when we went to bed and I can smell her now. I may be many things, Kenny, but I'm not stupid.'

He spun round, staring wildly. He opened his mouth, then closed it again.

'So I was right,' she said, with the calm of fury. 'What's her name?'

He started to move away but she gripped his arm. They stared at one another for what seemed like eternity.

'It's Georgie,' he said finally.

Her stomach convulsed in shock. Her legs gave way and she found herself on the floor. She struggled to catch her breath, knowing that if she lost control, she'd throw up. Unable to rise, she crawled to the wall and leant against it, seeing for an instant what Kenny would be seeing, a woman approaching middle age, hunched on the floor, her face bled white.

The effort of holding it together defeated her. 'Fuck you, you bastard,' she screamed. Hot tears ran down her cheeks. Pressing her head against her knees, she wept as though her heart would break.

He made no attempt to go to her. 'I love her, Von,' he said.

She heard his words through her sobbing, surprised at the strength of emotion behind them. She lifted her head and wiped her face with the back of her hand. 'And I suppose you're going to tell me she loves you.'

He avoided her eyes. 'I don't know. I don't think so.'

At least he's honest about something.

'How long has this been going on?' she said after a silence.

'A few months.'

The muscles of her throat tightened. *The bastard.*

He walked to the window. 'So, where do we go from here?'

'I'd have thought that was obvious,' she said, dragging herself to her feet. 'You love Georgie. End of.' She snatched up the bouquet ribbon and wound it viciously round a finger.

'There's something else.' His next words sliced through her. 'There's a baby on the way.'

'A baby!' Her heart contracted. *A baby. Oh, Christ…*She forced out the question. 'Is it yours?'

His silence was more eloquent than words. She turned her head away so he wouldn't see her face.

'Jesus, love, the last thing I wanted to do was hurt you.'

'Oh, spare me the clichés,' she shouted. She took a deep breath. 'You know something, Kenny? When it comes to being a bastard, you never let me down. Now get the fuck out of here before I do something we'll both regret.'

He made to move towards her but she backed away.

She waited till she'd heard the front door close, then collapsed into a chair. Her body felt as though the skin had been stripped from it.

I've seen this coming. Danni's words. Yet, if Danni had seen, then why hadn't she, the ace detective? She crushed the lilies in her hands, snapping the leaves off the stems. No, she was fooling herself, she'd seen the signs. It was over. Had been for months. She and Kenny had been going through the motions. She took the bottle of vodka from the fridge and poured herself a glass, drinking it neat the way she had when she was younger and her constitution could stand it. As the alcohol reached her knees, her anger drained away. What rankled was not that their relationship was over, but that he'd been betraying her for months. Maybe, subconsciously, she'd known all along and that was why she'd slept with Simon, to get her own back. Yet, was there any difference between Kenny's betrayal, and hers? Was a one-night stand, where she'd had fabulous sex with Simon, better or worse than Kenny's affair with a woman he said he loved, a woman now carrying his child? She threw the glass across the room, feeling a stab of satisfaction as she heard it shatter. That was the problem: she no longer knew.

Chapter 22

Von stared, incredulous. 'You're absolutely sure? There's no match for Gillanders on the bathroom-tap prints?'

Zoë lowered her gaze.

She glanced across the room. The other detectives were looking everywhere but at her.

'There's no match with Zack Lazarus or Chrissie, either.' The girl took a deep breath. 'We also tried cross-matching with what's on the PNC, but nothing came back.'

'The blond hairs, then?' she said, running a hand over her face.

'You might want to sit down for this one, ma'am. Forensics have checked the samples from both Chrissie and Gillanders. There's no match for either. They say the hair structure is entirely different.'

She sank into a chair. 'Fuck. We're right back where we started.'

'Pity there was no CCTV at Mrs Deacon's,' Steve said, sympathy in his eyes. 'We might have seen the bugger going in.'

'Talking of which, where are we on the footage from Leicester Square? The tapes arrived today. Did we find Gillanders going into the Odeon?'

'Larry's in the AV suite now, ma'am,' Zoë said. She exchanged an amused glance with Steve.

'You might want to take a look, boss.' He slipped his hands into his trouser pockets. 'It'll cheer you up.'

'Don't tell me you found him.'

'From the way the cameras are positioned, he could have gone into the Odeon unnoticed.'

'Did anyone check with the cinema staff? Show his photograph around?'

'All the usual things,' said Zoë. 'The cinema staff didn't recognise him but they said themselves they don't remember faces.'

'Brilliant.' She slammed her hand against the desk. 'Another inconclusive result. It's the first year of the new millennium, and we can't even establish whether someone went to the cinema.'

'Gillanders said he walked around Leicester Square, ma'am. Larry's going through the tapes from the surrounding streets.' She waited till Von looked at her. 'DI English is right. You really want to see this.'

Von hauled herself to her feet. 'Okay, let's see what Larry's got.'

Larry was sitting in the AV suite, his feet up and the remote in his hand, watching images on a large monitor.

'Show me the footage from September 12th,' she said.

'Nothing yet on Gillanders.' He grinned, fast forwarding. 'But this might amuse you, ma'am. It's a few blocks away from Leicester Square.'

She squinted at the screen, leaning forward for a better look.

A young couple rounded the corner into a deserted street. The man had an arm round the girl's waist, and was propelling her forward because her legs seemed incapable of functioning. At the end of the street, he stopped and propped her against the wall. As he shifted his weight, her head rolled forward, hitting him in the face. He cursed loudly and pushed her back. After a quick look around, he undid his belt. His zip undone, he yanked his trousers down and pulled up her skirt. The girl seemed barely conscious. He fumbled underneath and got her

228

knickers down to her knees. All of a sudden, he sprang back with a cry and stared at his trousers in an attitude of dismay. Released from his support, the girl slumped to the ground, oblivious. It was as he moved back that they saw what had happened: the girl had emptied her bladder. He pulled up his trousers and shook his left leg. With a final glance of disgust at the girl, who was snoring now, he limped away.

'You should sell tickets for that, Larry,' Von said, nodding. 'The Met could solve its underfunding problem.'

'We're going to call it "Don't Drink And Jive". Catchy, eh?'

The door opened suddenly and the Chief Super appeared. She and Larry sprang to their feet.

'A word, please, Yvonne.'

She sensed something in his voice that made her uneasy. 'Of course, sir,' she said quickly. She followed him out of the room.

He stopped at the end of the corridor. 'Where are we with the case?' he said, not bothering to keep his voice down.

This was a first, he'd never harangued her in a public place before. Briefly, she filled him in on the recent forensic results.

He nodded curtly. 'So are you saying this Michael Gillanders is no longer your prime suspect?'

'He's still my prime suspect, sir – the money angle can't be ignored – but we've no hard evidence he was in your brother's room.'

'We've nothing to feed the media, Yvonne.'

'Then tell them nothing,' she said impatiently. 'My staff have been inundated with crank calls. After the last press conference' – she was tempted to add, Which you held without telling me – 'we had a call from someone who claimed to have murdered your brother.'

'Did you follow it up?'

'It was a wasted effort. He couldn't have killed your brother. He was at his local A&E, being treated for substance abuse.'

She hesitated. 'Sir, have you been discussing the case with Chief Superintendent Hensbury?'

'Not in detail. Why do you ask?'

She thought quickly. 'He's offered his help.'

'Then take it. Simon is an experienced police officer. But he's gone back to Spain. You'll have to catch him when he's next here.' He drew his brows together. 'Look, have you examined opportunistic robbery as a motive?'

She stared at him in amazement. *Why is he back with robbery? We've been through this.* 'The landlady confirmed nothing was missing,' she said. 'What would a thief be after if he left behind your brother's wallet with his money and cards? And his mobile phone? You said yourself your brother owned nothing of value.'

'And you're still convinced there's a connection with those' – he rolled the word in his mouth before spitting it out – 'boys?'

'Aren't you?' she said, her dislike for him rising dangerously quickly.

'I hope you're not letting your feelings cloud your judgement.'

'That would be unprofessional, sir.'

'You know I'm not one for micro-managing, Yvonne, but I want to be kept more closely informed. Where do you intend to go from here?'

'I'm seeing my snout.'

'Whatever for?'

'He may uncover something about the boys that's relevant to the case.'

He snorted. 'I very much doubt that. And afterwards?'

'That depends on what he tells me,' she said, struggling to keep the anger from her voice.

'I'm not happy with the way you're handling this, Yvonne.' He brought his face close to hers. The menace in his eyes was unmistakable. 'Your grasp on this case is perilously close to slipping. Take care you don't slide with it.'

She froze. *Is he threatening me?* She took a step back, unable to tear her eyes from his, seeing a stranger.

He straightened, then strode away.

Her body went limp, and she slumped against the coffee machine. So why hadn't she told him? Why hadn't she simply said, There's a drug ring operating out of the Iron Duke and your brother was killed because he was mixed up in it. She knew why. It wasn't that she wanted the drugs squad kept out. It was because she was convinced there were things Richard Quincey was keeping from her. Although he had a cast-iron alibi for the time of Max's death, he could still have visited him in his lodgings. He could have smoked Hoyo de Monterrey cigarillos, and left to arrive at Boodle's by 7.00pm.

This time it was Von who was late. Tubby was already at the table, picking his nose. He hardly looked at her as she laid the cream cakes in front of him.

She stared, unbelieving. 'For God's sake, man, turn down the volume on that tie.'

'It's my Monday tie. I hate Mondays.' He looked at the cakes for a full minute before diving in.

She watched him eat. 'My meter's running, Tubby, so shall we get to it?'

'Not yourself today? You're usually so full of bonhomie.'

She stirred her tea viciously. 'You wouldn't be if you'd just been puréed.'

'Rather you than me. Here, have a cake.' He held out an éclair. 'On me.'

'I'm trying to give them up. So shall we cut the foreplay, Tubby? What did you find at the Duke?'

'Well, first of all, they made me feel about as welcome as a dose of the clap.' He held up a reproachful hand. 'I know what you're thinking, but it wasn't that. They didn't take me for a copper. No, it was on account of the way I was dressed.'

She smiled to herself. 'What's wrong with your clothes?'

'Not this. This is my Sunday best.' He cocked his head. 'Which I put on specially for you. No, I had on my working clothes. My long coat.'

'The one you wear when you expose yourself to schoolgirls?'

'Von, I swear. I don't do that no more.' He scooped up a blob of cream. 'Anyway, I thought it was going to be a spit-and-sawdust sort of place so I dressed to fit in. Some of my clothes, trousers in particular, had one or two stains. But the Duke turned out to be a swanky joint. The landlord told me they had a dress code.'

'A dress code? Is this a wind-up?'

'God's truth.'

'The landlord of a Soho pub threw you out because of your clothes?'

'Worse. Told me to behave myself. Must have thought I was some sort of rabble-rouser.' He examined the cakes, unable to decide between the iced puff and the cream horn. 'So, after a while I got talking. There's a regular there, a man with a tache.'

'Name?'

'Malkie. Sits in the snug. Turns out we have history.'

She sipped her tea. 'What kind of history?'

'We did time together a while back. Anyway, we had a natter about the good old days.'

'That must have been interesting.'

He licked cream off his fingers.

'Come on, Tubby, I can't take the suspense.'

'Well, we'd been chatting a while when he asked me if I was after making a bit. He looked me up and down while we were talking, see?'

She glanced at his clothes. 'Yes. I do.'

'Said there was good money to be made. Regular money. And I'm not talking serving behind the bar neither, he said.'

'And where was the landlord all this time?'

'Downstairs, changing the barrels. Anyway, Malkie told me he wouldn't talk at the Duke. Said he'd meet me in Soho Square. He left and, after a quick slash, I left too. He was as good as his word, waiting for me by that little black and white hut.' He wiped his fingers on his trousers, his eyes on hers. 'You were right, Von. It's drugs. But big drugs, bigger than anything I've ever seen, probably bigger than anything London's ever seen. Malkie asked if I wanted in. I said yes, as I reckoned you might want me to go back.' He played with the handle of his mug. 'But I'm not sure that I can.'

'What do you mean?' she said sharply.

'I'm frightened, Von, I don't mind admitting it.'

She laid a hand on his arm. 'I'm giving you a "Get Out Of Jail Free" card, Tubby. If you have to do a bit of dealing to dig deeper, then I'll make sure you're not prosecuted.'

'It's not prison I'm worried about.' He gripped the mug. 'Everyone knows the eleventh commandment: Thou shalt not grass. If I'm not careful I'll end up with my nuts removed with a cheese grater.'

'Getting caught has never worried you before. You're the best. You don't get found out.'

'Everyone gets found out eventually.' He ran a sweaty hand across his eyes. 'And that place, the atmosphere, there are eyes and ears everywhere. No wonder Malkie would only talk outside.'

'And Dickie's not in on it?' she said, searching his face.

'According to Malkie, he knows what's going on, but keeps his beak out. Can't do anything about it, he says, but he won't get involved.'

'So how does it work? The usual way?'

He lowered his voice to a whisper. 'The pure stuff comes in, gets cut, and redistributed into packets. The packets are given to the street dealers.'

'And Malkie deals?'

He nodded. 'He basically wanted to know if I'd be interested in dealing too. As he said, the supply's regular and the money's good.' He ran a finger around the plate, smearing the remnants of cream. 'There's a sort of layer cake with three layers. There's the bottom, where Malkie is, along with the other street sellers. The geezers above, the distributors, packet the stuff and hand it down. Malkie gets his always from the same bloke. All the street men work that way. Each one sticks to his distributor like shit to an army blanket.' He glanced around quickly. 'But above the distributors, there's someone who cuts the stuff. Uses quinine.'

'He's the guy at the top?' she breathed.

'He's only the number two. He's known as the Cutter. No-one knows his real name.'

This didn't surprise her. When it came to playing for high stakes, anonymity was the name of the game.

'How is the stuff sourced?' she said, after a pause.

'Above the Cutter there's the main man, sort of the icing on the cake. Mr Big. He gets the uncut stuff from abroad.'

'Did Malkie tell you anything about him?' she said, knowing the answer.

'No-one, and I mean no-one, knows his identity, because no-one ever sees him.' He let out a breath. 'Malkie said that, if you screw up, Mr Big makes it so you disappear fast. Doesn't tolerate any weakness in the system.'

'And it's Mr Big who goes back twenty years?'

'He began the whole operation. And controls it.'

Her mind was racing. This tallied with Jimmy Porteous's account of a long-standing ring, going back before 1985, a ring in which the three Irish boys had become involved. And perhaps died because of it. But what was Max Quincey's involvement? Porteous reckoned that Max wasn't dealing, yet he'd been seen at the Duke. Rose had told her Max hadn't been made welcome. *They didn't like Mr Quincey there. That landlord was always giving him the eye.* So why didn't they like him? Had he discovered something he shouldn't? Had he threatened to expose the whole thing unless he was paid? Had someone learnt about his blackmail and slipped a word into an unsympathetic ear?

'Malkie told me they need more street men,' Tubby was saying. 'Some of the guys are repackaging the stuff faster than you can fart. Everyone's been told to ask around. I said I was interested but had a few questions.' He glared at her defiantly. 'That's all I have, Von. If you want more, I'll have to go back, and it'll cost you. And not just the usual, this time. As I said, I don't like that place, it gives me the shivers.'

She punched him lightly on the arm. 'If you can get me names, you'll get a bonus. I want Mr Big or, at the least, his second-in-command.'

He hesitated. 'Cash in advance?'

'It's under the mug.'

Von and Steve were in the snug at the Drunken Duck. From their position in the corner, they could just see the ancient grandfather clock. It was missing its insides, and the hands were frozen at ten past seven. It was a common joke with the landlord that at least it told correct time twice a day, which was more than could be said for the other clocks in London.

Von rotated her shoulders. 'The long day closes, Steve. And, God, what a day it's been.'

'Aye, and it's only Monday.'

'My turn to get them in.' She nodded at his glass. 'Glenmorangie?' She caught the landlord's eye and gave their order.

'Are you thinking what I'm thinking, boss?' Steve said, studying her thoughtfully.

'Probably, but tell me anyway.'

'Max Quincey was in the ring at the Duke, and wormed his way up the chain.'

She looked at him in surprise. 'I wasn't thinking that, no.'

Their drinks arrived.

She sipped slowly. 'This ring has been running for years, Steve. Everyone we've spoken to says the regulars won't talk because they're in on it. We need to do something radical. There's only one person who might be willing to spill, someone who knows what's happening but won't get involved.'

'He's been quiet a long time.' He played with a beer mat. 'What makes you think he'll talk now?'

'I'll make him an offer he can't refuse.'

'Immunity?'

'The only offer I have. Somehow I don't think cash would do it. If he'd wanted money, he'd know how to get it.'

He paused before speaking. 'I know I've said it before, but don't you think we should contact the drugs squad? This *is* their patch.'

She set down her glass firmly. 'They screwed up my investigation last time. It's why I was thrown off the murder team.'

'You've never told me what happened,' he said cautiously.

What was there to tell? He knew the facts, that she and a female colleague had been staking out the house of a drug dealer wanted for triple murder, when members of the drugs squad blazed in. She'd alerted them of her intentions and requested they stay away till she'd made the arrest, but they'd ignored her, wanting to take the credit for the bust. In the ensuing shootout, her colleague had been killed. Von, too gutted to put up any resistance, had taken the rap. She studied Steve's face. No, he didn't want the facts, he wanted her to tell him how she felt. But she had no intentions of telling him that there wasn't a day when she didn't wake up, feeling she was to blame.

He tossed the beer mat aside. 'Don't you trust the drugs squad on this?'

'Sorry, I've run out of trust.'

'You've a pretty low opinion of them.'

'More like subterranean.'

He frowned. 'Okay, so how do we proceed?'

'Maybe the simplest solution is the best. I'll go there tomorrow.'

'Wouldn't it be better to wait and see what your snout comes up with?'

'There's no longer any time left for waiting.' After a silence, she nodded towards the bar. 'Is it me, Steve, or are you seeing these dolls everywhere?'

At the far end of the counter, a young man was sitting on a stool, playing with a Jack in the Box. He seemed to derive endless pleasure from pushing the doll into the box, then popping it again.

'Time to leave,' she said. 'Whenever I hear that screech, I feel like going outside and shooting myself.'

Chapter 23

The desk sergeant raised his head as Von arrived. 'Ma'am, they're paging you.'

'Someone's at work before I am?' she said.

'That must be a record, Chief Inspector,' he replied shyly.

She threw him a smile and made her way to the incident room.

As she entered, Steve waved the phone at her. 'Chrissie Horowitz is on for you, boss. She won't speak to anyone else. Sounds like she's going to throw a wobbler.'

She took the phone. 'Miss Horowitz? What can I do for you?'

'Oh, thank goodness you've arrived,' came the husky voice. 'It's Michael Gillanders. He's gone missing.'

'Missing? Are you sure?'

'He didn't show up for the Sunday performance. We had to use the understudy.' There was an edge of panic to her voice. 'He's never done this before. He's meticulous about his performances.'

'You've checked his lodgings?'

'I haven't, no.'

He's probably on a bender. I would be, if I had five hundred grand.

'If he's not here tomorrow, Wednesday, what should I do?' Chrissie was saying.

She tried to sound reassuring. 'Check his lodgings. There

may be a simple explanation for his non-appearance.'

'And if he's not there?'

'His understudy is going to get some valuable experience.' She regretted the words immediately. She could almost feel Chrissie freeze.

'Do you think he's done a bunk?'

'If he's not at his lodgings, call me and I'll get someone to check the hospitals.'

Horror in the voice now. 'You don't think he's dead?'

'If I thought that, Miss Horowitz, I'd be checking the mortuaries.'

A pause. 'Very well, I'll be in touch. Thank you.'

Steve was frowning. 'Don't tell me Gillanders has gone AWOL.'

'And he's our prime suspect. Brilliant.'

'Should we be worried?'

'Probably, but I can only worry about one thing at a time.' She reached for her coat. 'I'm going to the Duke.'

'It's 9.00am, boss. The pubs aren't open yet.'

'I'm going to the house.'

He began to protest but she cut him off. 'It's the obvious place, Steve. We won't be seen or overheard.' She picked up her bag. 'Mind the shop while I'm gone.'

The bell jangled deep in the house. A minute later, Von heard the shuffling of slippered feet, followed by the sound of bolts being drawn. A white-haired woman, bowed with age, opened the door a fraction.

'Mrs Womack?' Von said brightly. 'I'm here to see Dickie.'

Fear shrouded the woman's eyes. 'What about?'

She hesitated. The wrong reply, and the door would be slammed in her face. 'I've come about a job. I heard that Dickie is looking for bar help.'

The woman's face cleared and she opened the door further. 'One moment, please.' She turned away and Von saw the sharp curve in her spine. 'Dickie,' the woman yelled. 'Someone for you.' She disappeared, leaving the door wide.

Dickie lived off Soho Square, a tiny oasis of green in a desert of brick and stone. The pavement was lined with poplars. At this time of year, the trees were almost bare, their branches like dense webs. Von watched a man sweeping leaves into piles. He worked steadily, his brush making a loud swishing noise.

A short while later, a tall gaunt man ambled down the corridor.

She held up her card. 'Is there somewhere private we can speak, Dickie?' She kept her voice low. 'Somewhere your mother won't overhear us?'

The man stiffened. 'What's this about?'

'I just want a confidential chat.'

'What do you mean, confidential?' he said, his eyes narrowing.

'I'm going to ask you some confidential questions, and you're going to give me some confidential answers.'

'If this is about serving after drinking-up time—'

'It isn't. Look, Dickie, I'm not here to give you grief, I'm just after some information.' She hoped he'd respond to the appeal in her voice. 'I don't want your mother to hear us and neither do you. Where can we go where we won't be overheard and you won't be recognised?'

A slow grin spread over his face. 'Wait here. I'll get my jacket.'

'It's years since I've been in a church,' Von said. 'I thought they were kept locked during the day.'

Dickie shrugged. 'Some are, some aren't. I took a guess with St Pats.'

'We'll be okay to talk here?'

'If you can't talk in a church, girl, where can you talk?'

They were in the confessional of St Patrick's Roman Catholic Church on Soho Square. The cubicle, a black wooden structure which reeked of body odour, seemed thrown together in a hurry, as though the builders had remembered it at the last minute. There was just enough room on the priest's side for two people.

She moved the heavy curtain and peered out. The church's interior was large and gloomy, incense hanging in the air like mist. The walls of the side chapels were stained with damp. Something gleamed on the altar; candlesticks, and a golden monstrance. The curved wall behind the altar was inscribed with the words, 'Sanctus, Sanctus, Sanctus' in grimy gold letters.

'Strange finding a Catholic church so close to Soho's sex shops,' she said. 'But conveniently near to where you live, Dickie. Do you come here to confess your sins?'

'I'm a Protestant.'

She smiled. 'Even so, it's nice and quiet. I should imagine it makes a change from the noise in the Duke.'

'You get used to working in a pub.' He was examining her warrant card. 'Valenti's an Italian name.'

'My grandparents were Italian.'

'I can tell by your looks, all that dark hair, and those eyes. But your skin's pale.'

'Not difficult in this climate.'

He motioned to her cheek. 'Your feller hit you?'

'Something like that. Looks worse than it is.' She knew that her bruise, however colourful, was nothing compared with what a Soho resident would see on a regular basis.

'Says here you're a DCI.' He handed back the card. 'You're a woman.'

'Last time I checked, anyway.'

'From where I'm sitting, you don't look the detective type.'

'Now I'm offended.'

He grinned. 'So, how can I help you, girl? Confidentially.'

'Call me Von.'

She considered how much to tell him. It was possible he was in it up to his neck, despite what Tubby and the others had told her. She doubted it somehow, he had the air of a man who kept on working because he had to. She decided honesty was the best policy. 'I'm running a murder investigation,' she said.

His eyebrows shot up. 'You?'

'I'm all grown up, Dickie, I even tie my shoelaces by myself.' She lowered her voice, unnecessary in the deserted church. 'Does the name Max Quincey mean anything to you?'

His breathing quickened. 'He was murdered. I read it in the papers, before you ask.'

'He was a customer of yours.'

'Was. Past tense.'

'Everything about him is now past tense, Dickie.' She played with the priest's missal, running a finger over the gilding. 'What was Max into?'

He gazed at her without blinking. 'I could tell you, girl, but it'll make you all hot and bothered.'

'I'll try to control myself.'

'Confidential?'

She nodded.

He licked his palm and slicked back his hair. 'He liked little boys.'

'Which he picked up at the Duke.' She held up a hand to stave off his protest. 'Before you deny it, I know what the Duke is, and I'm not here about that.'

'Okay, he picked them up there. But the Duke isn't your sleaze bar. We don't have a back room. The boys have to take their punters elsewhere.'

She studied his face. The skin was waxy with blotches around the mouth, the result of a poor diet. But his eyes were like her Dad's. They shone with humanity. 'How long have you been the landlord, Dickie?' she said.

'Since before you were born.'

'Flatterer.'

He grinned broadly.

'Ever had any trouble?' she said.

'I tell them to take it outside. Either that or sling it.' He laughed softly. 'Most folk just want to sit quietly and pickle their brains.'

'But Max wasn't like that?'

'He drank, singled out a boy, and left. His brain was rarely pickled.'

She flicked through the pages of the missal. 'Were there particular boys he preferred?'

'The younger the better.' He smiled thinly. 'That's how I remember him, after all this time. Haven't clapped eyes on him for years, but he's not a bloke you could forget. He dressed like a ponce, with fancy jackets and that, but mostly he came wearing that ridiculous pork-pie hat. And he liked to flash his cash.'

'Did he have much to flash?' she said carefully.

'Rolls of it, girl. Acting must be a lucrative profession is all I can say. I'm in the wrong job, that's for sure.' He leant forward. 'Max would find a boy, then settle on him like a fly on shit. Was none too discreet about it, either.' His lips twisted into a sneer. 'Always checking his meat and two veg, in case it weren't there no more. He was in the gents once, when I went in. Used to pee sitting down, like a woman. Didn't always lock the cubicle door.'

'Can you remember the boys who were around in 1985? It was when the play ran here first.'

He froze. 'Bugger me, that's too far back. My memory isn't

what it was.'

'Let me jog it. There were three Irish lads. You may not remember the names but I could describe them. One had a port-wine stain down his left cheek—'

He gripped her arm. 'You don't need to go on, I know the boys you mean. They were killed.'

'And mutilated.'

'I know, girl, I identified the bodies,' he said grimly.

'There was a fourth boy,' she said after a pause. 'But he survived.'

'So that's what this is about. You want to catch the Jack in the Box killer.'

'More than I want to catch Max's,' she said, surprising herself by the statement.

He smiled sadly. 'There weren't many who mourned for those boys. I was the only one from the Duke who went to the funerals.'

'Then help me catch their killer.' She laid her hand over his. 'Did you ever see Max with them?'

'Look, Von, Max was never without a boy. But as for which particular boy, I really can't remember. It was too long ago.'

'The lad who survived, Manny Newman, has made a fresh start.' She felt suddenly close to tears. 'He's learnt Braille and goes to college.'

'Ah, you've got kids of your own,' he said shrewdly. He seemed to be wrestling with his thoughts. 'Okay, girl, there are things I'm prepared to tell you. But so far you've been answering your own questions.'

'Let's start with the detective who investigated those murders.'

He snorted. 'Bit of a pansy.'

'DCI Harrower?'

'That were him.'

'In what way was he a pansy?'

'Gave up too easily.'

She tried a shot in the dark. 'He didn't give up. I think he was warned off.'

The shot found its mark. His expression changed. 'I knew this wasn't only about the murders. You've come about the dust.'

'I'm convinced they're related.' She searched his face. 'Was Max Quincey dealing, Dickie? I know those boys were.'

'I'm saying no more.' He started to get to his feet.

She grasped his arm and pulled him down.

'You're strong for a woman,' he said in surprise.

'Two older brothers. I developed muscles.'

He laughed. 'I like you, girl.'

'Likewise,' she said warmly. 'You remind me of my Dad.'

'Is that a compliment?'

'My Dad's a grand feller.'

He scratched under his chin. The veins in his hands were like cords. 'Look, I want to help you, but not with this. It's more than my life's worth.'

'I can give you protection.' She hesitated. 'That's more than Harrower offered, I'd be betting.'

'He couldn't. And you can't. If I say anything, I'll be dead.'

'Who are the distributors, Dickie?' she said, trying to keep the desperation from her voice.

'It's not the distributors you want, girl.'

'I want Mr Big.'

'Don't know who he is. No-one knows. No-one sees him except his mate, the one who cuts.'

'And this mate, have you ever seen *him*?'

'He never comes to the Duke.' A shadow crossed his face. 'But he's vicious, more vicious than you can imagine. I'd put money down it was him warned Harrower off. He's the only one with the clout. The distributors would never do it.'

'You know that for a fact?' she said, her heart pounding. 'Harrower was warned off?'

He grabbed her wrist. 'Will I be protected?'

'You have my word. Not just protection. You'll have immunity from prosecution.'

After a silence, he said, 'I heard them talking on the phone. Harrower had been snooping round, see, asking about the smack.' He ran the back of his hand across his mouth. 'I was down in the cellar, changing the barrels. Harrower was in the back room, on the phone. The floorboards are thin in that room and it's right above the cellar.'

'Did Harrower use this man's name?' she breathed.

'If he did, I didn't hear it. I came in part way through the conversation.' He brought his face close to hers. 'But there was no mistaking the terror in Harrower's voice. He begged this geezer to leave him and his family alone. Said he'd do whatever he wanted, including diverting his investigation away from the Duke.'

She looked away, hoping he hadn't seen the excitement in her eyes.

'Harrower said his daughter had a baby on the way,' he went on. 'He kept pleading with him not to touch her. After the call ended, I legged it back upstairs. Poor bloke looked as though he were going to collapse. I offered him a glass of water. He left the Duke and didn't come back. Never saw him again.' He hesitated. 'You don't know what happened to him? I mean, he was all right wasn't he? And his lass?'

'He retired after the case went cold. Died a while later, drowned in a fishing accident.'

'I felt sorry for him, he was just doing his job. I didn't mean it when I said he was a pansy.' He moved his legs carefully in the cramped space. 'Anyone would do the same if their family were in danger.'

So Harrower had been warned away from the Duke. Small wonder then that he'd ignored what Porteous told him about the drugs. Jesus, his family had been threatened. Her own warning, the mutilated doll left outside her flat, was tame in comparison. But who was this thug who'd threatened Harrower's daughter? 'Dickie, this guy on the phone, you say he was the second-in-command. Could he have been Mr Big?'

'Mr Big would never get involved directly. He's like fresh air. No-one sees him. No-one smells him.'

She looked at him with interest. 'How do you know so much about a man you've never met? He could walk into the Duke and you'd never know him.'

'Sure, he could. But stuff filters down, doesn't it? This mate of Big's talks to the distributors and they talk to the street men. And I listen, pretending I don't notice.' His eyes gleamed. 'It's pretending I don't notice that's kept me alive.'

'Could Max Quincey have been Mr Big?'

'Nah.'

'But you can't know for certain.'

He smiled mockingly. 'Did you ever meet Max Quincey?'

'Only briefly.' She smiled back, wanting him to see she agreed with him. 'I admit he's an unlikely candidate. Could he have been at the other end, then? Selling on the street?'

'If Max Quincey passed on packets of dust, I would have seen and I never did.'

She ran a hand through her hair. Always the same story. Whatever Max was guilty of, it wasn't dealing.

She fumbled in her bag and pulled out the programme for Jack in the Box. 'I want you to tell me whether you recognise any of these people, Dickie.' She pointed to the thumbnail of Gillanders. 'This is a recent photo. I don't have one from fifteen years ago.'

He peered at the programme. 'Never seen him.'

'Not even during the last couple of weeks?'

He held the sheet to his face. 'Absolutely sure. But it doesn't mean he's not involved. Some of the distributors meet their sellers outside. There are plenty of places around here for little clandestine meetings.'

She reached to take back the programme but he stopped her.

'Half a mo.' He tapped the photo of Zack Lazarus. 'I've seen *him*.'

'At the Duke?'

'A long time ago. Haven't seen him for ages.'

'What do you remember about him?'

'He came to see one of the boys. Always the same one, I forget which. Those eyes and that pockmarked skin are unmistakable. He sat with the boy. Didn't want to pick him up, mind. He bought him drinks and grub. Then left on his own.' He pointed at the sheet. 'And that one. She came in here too.'

Von stared, unbelieving. 'Rose Manning came here?'

'Never knew her name. But it's a face you'd not forget. She decked one of my customers with her handbag once for looking at her the wrong way. Used to sit near the door with her brandy and babycham. She'd size up the boys, pick one out, then leave with him.'

'She'd leave with a boy?' Von said in amazement.

'She was particular, like. Not just any boy.'

'What do you think she did with them?'

His mouth formed into a smile. 'Would have thought that was obvious. Some of the boys do it with women, too.'

Rose? Having sex with a rent boy? It beggared belief.

She pointed at the photo of Chrissie Horowitz. 'Did she ever come in? Take a good look, Dickie.'

'Ah, I'd remember a skirt like that,' he said approvingly. 'But, no, she's never come in, to my knowledge.' He tilted his head. 'You thinking there may be women in on the ring? Tends to be a boys' game, but some of the toms who work this area offer smack to their clients.'

'Could this man who cuts the stuff be a woman?'

'It's not impossible. I mean, these days women do the jobs men used to.' He grinned. 'Some of them even become detectives. Wasn't like that in my day.'

'When men were men?' she smiled coyly.

'And women were grateful.' He studied the photo of Chrissie. 'But there may be skirts in on it higher up. Even one as posh-looking as that.'

Higher up? So, Chrissie was a possible. Her mind was racing. And Rose and Zack frequented the Duke. Perhaps they were all part of the ring, the entire cast and crew of the Garrimont.

And maybe Max *had* been in on it, after all.

'Look, you did mean it, didn't you?' Dickie was saying. 'About protection. I've kept quiet all these years because I'm afraid of him. I have family too, my mother and three girls.'

She looked at him as though seeing him for the first time. 'You have my word.' She squeezed his arm. 'Thank you, Dickie. You've been extremely helpful.'

'I'll go out first,' he said, rising with difficulty in the cramped space. 'Maybe you could wait a bit? So we're not seen together?'

She handed him a card, and he left hurriedly.

In no mood to leave, she sat in the confessional, thinking through what he'd told her.

The footsteps were so soft, she didn't hear them approach. The curtain was drawn back gently. 'Do you want me to hear your confession, my child?' a voice said.

'Excuse me?' She looked up at the priest.

The man was smiling faintly. 'Do you want to confess your sins?'

'Father,' she said, getting heavily to her feet, 'how much time have you got?'

Chapter 24

In the Drunken Duck, as they were having lunch, Von updated Steve on her conversation with Dickie.

'You were away a long time, boss. I was worried.'

She picked at the congealing lasagne. 'Don't take this the wrong way, but he wouldn't have spoken if you'd been there.'

'You charmed him, then.'

'My Dad was a landlord, I know what presses their buttons.' She put her fork down. 'We've been barking up the wrong tree with Gillanders and the Quincey Players, Steve. I'm convinced now that the motive for Max Quincey's death is drug-related. The problem is, how, exactly.'

'You're not thinking he's Mr Big.'

'Whoever Big is, he's making big money. Max Quincey made small deposits into his bank account, and he was still heavily in debt. I don't think he's even the Cutter. But he may have been dealing, despite what everyone is telling me. It would account for that regular cash.'

'Rose, though,' Steve said, chewing his sandwich, 'now that was a surprise. I didn't know rent boys had sex with women. You learn something every day in this job, it's better than the Encyclopedia Britannica.'

Before she could reply, her mobile rang. She snapped it open and listened. Her expression changed. 'We're leaving, Steve.'

He looked at his half-eaten sandwich.

She hauled him to his feet. 'Take it with you.'

'What's the rush, boss?'

'It's the Garrimont.' She pushed the table aside. 'We have to get over there. Now!'

Chrissie was waiting in the foyer. Her face was ashen and she was trembling violently.

'Thank God you've come,' she moaned.

'Did anyone go into the costumes room, other than yourself?' Von said.

'Only the cleaner, Mrs Marks.' Chrissie swallowed hard. 'We didn't touch anything, and I made sure the door was relocked after I left.'

'What do you mean, relocked?'

'Mrs Marks found it locked.'

'Do you have the key?'

'Mrs Marks has it.'

Von instructed her constables to keep watch at all the building's exits, and she and Steve followed Chrissie to her office.

'We need your keys, please, Maureen,' Chrissie said, as they entered the room.

Mrs Marks's head shot up. She was sitting at the desk, her face flushed, sipping a golden-coloured liquid. She fumbled in her housecoat and produced a large bunch of keys. 'It's this one,' she said, indicating a blue Yale.

'Miss Horowitz, I need you to stay here,' said Von. 'You too, Mrs Marks. I'll have to question you both later.'

'Of course,' Chrissie murmured.

'Mrs Marks, where exactly—'

'At the far end. Where Miss Manning has her things.'

Back in the foyer, they pulled on their gloves and made their way downstairs.

Von examined the wooden frame. 'No sign of forced

entry.' She unlocked the door. As it opened, the familiar smell of carnation and mothballs hit her. But overlaid now with something sweeter.

Before her were the racks of clothes, facing her in the dark like an expectant crowd. Steve switched on the lights, flooding the room with a harsh brightness.

'Let's go round the side,' she said. 'If we disturb the clothes, we'll get dust over everything.'

'Aye, the forensics in here will be difficult enough as it is.'

They moved past the packing cases, and skirted the wall. The smell grew stronger.

They found Michael Gillanders beside the sofa. He was lying on his back, one hand gripping the upholstery. Beneath him was a partly-congealed puddle of blood, which had spread and seeped up into the material of the sofa. His hair was matted black, and his jacket, saturated with blood, had dried to a dull brown. His trousers were around his knees, revealing the tanned flesh of his thighs.

She examined the body. Sir Bernard would have no difficulty with this one: *Cause of death was a brain haemorrhage from a single blow to the back of the head.*

'Been dead a while, boss,' said Steve, squatting.

She stared into the sightless eyes. 'He was a no-show for his Sunday performance.'

'Killed the day before, then?'

'Chrissie would have told us if he'd missed Saturday's.' She straightened. 'From his colour, I'm guessing this happened after the Saturday show. He wore that blue suit and pink shirt in the play.'

'Looks like he was hit from behind, fell against the sofa and rolled off onto his back.'

She glanced around. It was all there, clothes, the television set. Even the bottle of sherry. But something was different. 'The iron's missing,' she said suddenly.

He jerked his head at the doll, still on the floor beside the sewing machine. 'Anything odd about the Jack in the Box?'

She noticed he made no effort to go over. She steeled herself, and peered into the grinning face. 'The eyes are untouched.'

'As are those of Gillanders. Looks like a straightforward murder.'

'There's no such thing.' She bit the inside of her lip. 'I've seen all I need. We'll leave the rest to Forensics. Come on, time to talk to the ladies.'

The women had been drinking heavily. A strong smell of whisky filled the room.

'Who has keys to the costumes room, apart from Mrs Marks?' Von said to no-one in particular.

Chrissie gulped her whisky. 'As far as I know, it's Rose Manning.'

'As far as you know?' When there was no reply she added, 'Surely, as theatre manager, you know who has keys and who hasn't.'

The woman pressed her fingers into her eyes, and sobbed loudly

She's not grieving for Gillanders. It's because she's lost her best actor. 'Look, Chrissie, I need you to focus,' Von said angrily. She was conscious Steve was staring at her.

Chrissie lowered her hands. 'I have a list of key holders somewhere,' she said, in a vague tone.

'Could you find it, please? An officer from Forensics will be here soon. He'll need to be taken to the basement. Do you think you can do that?'

'You're not staying?' Chrissie said, looking pleadingly at Steve.

'One of my sergeants is on his way,' Von said. 'He'll be taking your statements.' She glanced at the inch of whisky left in the bottle. *Assuming you're still capable of speaking.*

They were leaving the Garrimont, when a large black saloon drew up.

'Sir Bernard,' Von said cheerfully, 'we meet at the most inauspicious moments.'

'The nature of our métiers, is it not?' He smiled grimly and stepped past her into the theatre.

She watched him go. 'We'll need a search warrant, Steve. Then we're making a house call.'

Cathcart Street, in Kentish Town, was a row of two-storeyed, flat-roofed houses, with white frames round the doors and windows.

'Nice area,' said Von, signalling to Zoë to slow down. 'I've always fancied living in a cobbled street with trees. I bet these have back gardens.'

Steve was eyeing the houses. 'Aye, this place used to be solidly working-class, but loads of toffs are moving in now. And film stars.'

'I believe Karl Marx lived here somewhere,' Zoë said.

'Is that so?' Von said. 'Well, he wouldn't recognise the place now. You know this area, then?'

The girl's voice was noncommittal. 'It's the centre of London's pub rock scene.'

Von smiled to herself. This was as far as Zoë was prepared to go, but she'd told Von something she didn't know about her taste in music.

'I wonder why Rose doesn't bunk at Mrs Deacon's, boss, like the rest of the Quincey Players.'

'When she's in town, sir, she lives with her sister.'

They stopped outside a house distinguishable from its neighbours only by the brightness of the paintwork and the cleanliness of the windows. A weak sun dropped behind the roof, throwing the building into shadow. There was a sharp bite in the air.

Von rang the bell. After several minutes, the door opened a crack and Rose Manning peered out. Although it was late afternoon, she looked as though she had just left her bed: her hair was dishevelled and she was almost unrecognisable without her make-up, her pasty cheeks lined with tiny broken veins.

'We'd like to talk to you, Miss Manning,' said Von.

'What about?' came the suspicious voice.

'Something I'd rather not discuss in the street.'

The door opened wide, and Rose stood before them in shiny black slacks and a beige polo-neck. She stared at Zoë. 'Who's she?' she said.

'A police officer,' Von said patiently. 'She's going to search the house. I have a warrant that gives us the right.'

'As long as she doesn't make a mess. My sister will have a fit.'

Von glanced at Steve. Most people whose houses were about to be torn apart, kicked up a fuss. Rose seemed almost resigned. 'Where's your sister now, Miss Manning?' she said. She preferred not to have family witnessing what she was about to do.

'At work.' Rose stepped back to let them through. 'Better come in. We can use the parlour.'

The parlour was a typical woman's room, with silver frames on the mantelpiece and muslin curtains at the window. The dresser was crammed with garishly-painted Toby jugs. The furnishings, even the walls, seemed to exude the stench of carnation. *Her sister must use it too.* Von, almost overcome by the smell, tried not to breathe in too deeply.

She nodded to Zoë to search the house, and she and Steve took the sofa. Rose perched on the edge of the armchair, as though ready to make a dash for it.

'Miss Manning, when did you last see Mr Gillanders?'

Rose reached into her pocket and produced a packet of cigarettes. She lit one, hands shaking slightly. 'Can't say. Why do you ask?'

'He's been found dead.'

She said nothing, just stared, her cigarette in the air.

'His body was found in your costumes room.'

She had the manner of someone not interested in the conversation. But her eyes gave her away, moving restlessly from side to side.

'Why was Mr Gillanders in your room, Miss Manning?'

She blew smoke to the ceiling. 'The actors come in to have their costumes pressed.'

'Do they ever press their clothes themselves?' When there was no reply, Von added, 'Did Michael Gillanders come in for the Sunday performance?'

'Yes, as a matter of fact.'

'You're lying, Miss Manning. Michael Gillanders didn't perform on Sunday. There was an understudy.'

'I forget the days.' She waved her cigarette dismissively. 'Easy to get muddled up.'

She's such a bad liar. This isn't going to be difficult.

Zoë poked her head round the door. 'Ma'am, you need to see this,' she said urgently.

'Excuse me, Miss Manning.' Von followed her out.

'In the kitchen, ma'am.'

The door to the cupboard under the sink was open. Inside was a large steam iron.

'Take photos, Zoë, bag it, and take it to the nick. Ask Forensics to fast-track, if they can.'

The girl indicated the edge of the iron. 'Blood smears.'

She shook her head in disgust. 'What was she thinking, bringing the murder weapon to her sister's house?'

She marched back to the parlour. 'Miss Manning, you need

to accompany us to the police station.'

'I can't go like this,' Rose said, horrified. 'I need to put on my face.'

'You don't, Miss Manning.'

Rose glared at her, then slowly got to her feet.

Von switched on the recorder. 'Interview commencing at 6.15pm on Tuesday, 26th September, 2000. Officers present are Detective Chief Inspector Yvonne Valenti, and Detective Inspector Steven English.' She looked up at Rose. 'Would you like your solicitor here?'

'No,' came the sharp reply.

'For the tape, Miss Manning has waived her right to a solicitor. She is interviewed under caution, on tape, and without her solicitor present.'

Rose gulped her tea, regarding Von over the rim as though she were reading a shopping list.

'Miss Manning, were you in the costumes room on Saturday evening?'

'I had to press Jools's dressing gown.'

'She was there with you?'

'Course. Always watches me like a hawk, that one.'

Von glanced at her sheet. Both Mrs Marks and Chrissie had stated that, apart from Mrs Marks, the only person with a key to the costumes room was Rose.

'Mrs Marks arrived today and found the costumes room locked, Miss Manning. When she unlocked the door, she discovered the body of Michael Gillanders. Only two people could have locked that room. Mrs Marks herself, and you. What do you have to say?'

Rose removed a folded white handkerchief and dabbed her lips. 'It weren't me.'

'Who, then?'

'Must have been Mrs Marks, because it weren't me.'

'According to her statement, Mrs Marks cleans the costumes room only on a Tuesday. Michael Gillanders was alive on Saturday, because he performed in Jack in the Box. He was killed after that performance, and the door locked. You've just told us you were in the costumes room on Saturday.'

Rose returned the handkerchief to her pocket. 'If you say so.'

Von folded her arms. She knew she was skilled enough to wrap this up quickly. But she wanted more from Rose than a mere confession to murder.

'Mr Gillanders was killed by a blow to the head, Rose. The steam iron was missing from the costumes room. We found it in your sister's kitchen, under the sink.' She raised her voice. 'There were bloodstains on it. Forensics will prove it was Michael Gillanders's blood.'

'May I smoke?'

'You may not.' Von steepled her fingers. 'Rose, I put it to you that you killed Michael Gillanders, locked the door to the costumes room and hid the steam iron under the sink in your sister's kitchen. Even without the forensic evidence, I've enough to charge you.'

The woman lowered her head.

'Come on, Rose, you'll help yourself by admitting to it. It'll play well in court.'

She lifted her eyes. 'What do you mean?'

'The judge will direct the jury to be lenient.' When the silence had gone on too long, Von said, 'Did you kill Michael Gillanders?' She paused. 'For the tape, Rose Manning nodded her head.' She sat back. 'Why, Rose?'

'Because he deserved it, that's why. Your assistant arrested him – I saw him – and then you let him go. But I know he killed Mr Quincey.'

'Where's the evidence?'

'He couldn't stand him because he was a homo.'

'That's your evidence?' Von said, in mock surprise. 'The last time we spoke, you suggested Michael Gillanders killed Max Quincey so he could take over the Players. Now you're saying it's because he couldn't stand his homosexual activities. Which is it Rose?'

She glared, saying nothing.

Von chose her words carefully. 'It didn't bother you that Max Quincey was a homosexual, did it? He was a gentleman, after all.'

'The finest,' Rose said emphatically. She jabbed a finger. 'And I'll tell you another thing, you're no lady.'

It was time for the broadside. 'What was Max Quincey's business at the Iron Duke, Rose? I'm talking about the time of the Jack in the Box murders of 1985.'

It was as though Rose had been turned to stone. The colour left her face.

Bingo. I've got her... 'You said they didn't like Mr Quincey there, the landlord, in particular. But Max didn't always go to the Duke, did he?' she added softly. 'You occasionally found boys for him.'

Rose sucked in her breath, her lips trembling. Von nodded to Steve, who pushed over a lighter and a packet of Silk Cut.

Rose pounced on them and lit up greedily. 'He asked me to do it,' she said, her hands shaking.

'Did he tell you which boys to bring back?'

She drew on the cigarette, looking straight ahead. 'I knew the kind he liked. Young, and clean. I had to be picky.'

'Where did you bring them, Rose?'

'To the theatre. My costumes room.' She inhaled deeply. 'I put a sheet down.'

'Did you watch?'

She didn't answer immediately. 'Sometimes.'

'Did Max like you to watch?'

She spoke so quietly that Von had to strain to hear. 'Yes.'

'So, what was it? Blow jobs? Did he penetrate them?'

'I don't see that that's any of your business.'

'It's very much my business.'

She looked at the wall behind Von. 'He penetrated them. The boys were on their hands and knees.' She flicked ash onto the ground with a tap of her finger. 'If the boys wanted it, he'd give them orgasms. Using his hand. Some wanted that, you know,' she added defiantly.

'How long did this go on?'

'Till he was caught at it.'

'Who caught him, Rose?'

'Zack. He must have seen me bring the boy in.' She blew smoke through her nostrils. 'Mr Quincey liked them to wear make-up. Had to be done professionally, it did. Sometimes I'd do it for them, using greasepaint. Well, there was this young lad, all made up with red lipstick and the like. Zack came in as Mr Quincey was about to start. He just stared, then went over and wiped the make-up off. The boy was hollering to be paid so he paid him himself.'

'How did Zack behave? Was he angry?'

'More sad than angry, really. Anyway, after that, I took them to my sister's.' She stabbed out her cigarette. 'Beryl's a nurse, works shifts. But we had to stop. One of the neighbours told her and she raised merry hell.'

Von withdrew the photographs from the file, and laid them on the table. 'The suspect is being shown a series of photographs. Rose, do you recognise any of these as the boys you procured for Mr Quincey? Take your time.'

Rose pored over them. 'He was one,' she said, pointing to Gilly. 'A great favourite of Mr Quincey's, he was.' She tapped the photo of Charlo. 'And this one, I remember that collar round his neck. As for the others, I'm not sure.'

Von let her breath out slowly. So Max *had* known the Irish boys. And the Irish boys had been selling drugs. But she still needed to find evidence that Max was in the ring. 'Did you ever see Max give these boys anything?' she said. 'Presents? Anything at all?'

'Presents? He didn't even pay them. I handled all that.'

Von stared into the bloodshot eyes. *She's telling the truth. She knows nothing about the drugs.* 'Let's come now to how you killed Michael Gillanders, Rose. Just tell us in your own words.'

Rose lit another cigarette and smoked silently for a while. 'The actors come down before the performance if they want their costumes to get a final press, or there's something needs fixing. On Sunday afternoon, Michael Gillanders came in already wearing his. He did that sometimes. He'd take the suit off and stand there in his underwear while I ironed his clothes. He liked to taunt me, he did. Take a good look at what you're missing, Rose, he used to say. Not everyone has the good fortune to be hung like a donkey. This time he was especially nasty, said I must be missing my pederast friend. He undid his belt and started to pull his trousers down. I had the iron in my hand, and he was bending over. So I hit him.' She squashed out the cigarette, her face streaked with tears. 'He'd pushed me to the edge with his filthy remarks about Mr Quincey. Mr Quincey was such a lovely man. He'd never hurt a fly.' She rubbed at her eyes. 'I put the iron in my bag, locked the door as per usual, and went home.'

She seemed unaware of the enormity of what she'd done. Her tears were all for Max Quincey. Von almost felt sorry for her. 'You've killed a man, Rose. Do you know what the consequences will be?'

'The jury will understand why I did it,' she said defiantly. 'It was justice for Mr Quincey, a murdered man. It was a spur of the moment thing, unpremeditated, it was. They won't convict me.'

'I think you'll find you're wrong about that.'

'What do you mean?'

'You're going to prison, Rose.' She nearly added, *and for a very long time.*

Rose stared, her eyes blank. 'I knew today wasn't going to be a good day. My star sign said so.'

'Then let me read you your horoscope.' She took a deep breath. 'Rose Manning, I am charging you with the murder of Michael Gillanders.'

Before she could continue, Rose gave a groan and collapsed onto the table, scattering the photographs.

Danni was sitting in Von's office.

Von dropped the file on the desk, avoiding her eyes. *She wants to know whether I've slept with Simon. Well, she can whistle for it.* 'I take it you heard everything, Danni?'

Danni tucked her skirt under her thighs. 'Seems cut and dried.'

'Forensics will back it up but her confession clinches it. Though I thought she seemed a little too willing to confess.'

'She wants it off her conscience. It's a textbook case. She saw an opportunity, lost her head, and killed a man in the heat of the moment. She's no killer.'

'The jury won't see it that way. But we learnt something else, didn't we?' Von said, looking at Steve.

He rolled his eyes in mock exasperation, as he always did when she tested him. 'Aye, there's no doubt about it now. Max Quincey knew the boys who were killed.'

'And is Gillanders still your prime suspect?' Danni said to Von. 'If so, your job is done. You can't prosecute a dead man.'

'I'm shying away from Gillanders for any of the killings,

Max's included.' She chewed her lip. 'I think Max was killed because he was mixed up in that drug ring. The problem is that everyone I talk to tells me different. Jimmy Porteous, Dickie Womack, who had the opportunity to observe him many times at the Duke. And now Rose.' Her mind went back to the interview. 'But Rose finding his boys for him. And watching him with them.'

'An unlikely procuress.' Danni made an arch with her fingers. 'The picture I'm building of Max Quincey does him no favours. He used people, then discarded them when he no longer needed them. He knew Rose would do anything because she loved him, but he was indifferent to her feelings.'

'Do you think he was capable of love?' said Steve.

'Everyone is,' she said, as if Steve had insulted her. 'To get back to the drugs, how did the Chief Super react when you told him about the ring?'

'I'm keeping it from him for now,' Von said, playing with her pen.

'Why?'

'He'll bring the drugs squad in over my head. If I find evidence that brother Max was involved, one word from the Chief Super and they'll hush it up.'

'You really think he'd do that?'

I want a quick result, Yvonne. And I want a clean result. 'I wouldn't put anything past the Chief Super,' she said.

'But if you went to him with hard evidence, he couldn't ignore it.'

'He might still hand over to the drugs squad but, no, he couldn't ignore it. The problem is I've no hard evidence.'

'Then you need to find it.'

She struggled to hide her irritation. Danni had a habit of coming out with the obvious as though she'd thought of it herself.

'So what will you do?' said Danni.

'What all coppers do when they run out of leads. Go back to the beginning.'

Danni stared at her as though she'd told her Martians had landed.

Chapter 25

Zoë looked up from her desk. 'You're in early, ma'am.'

'I want another look at Max Quincey's effects,' Von said, unbuttoning her coat. 'If anyone asks for me, I'm in stores.'

The attendant, an elderly man with a white bush of hair and age spots on his face, led the way down the narrow corridor towards the back of the storeroom. Von disliked this room, with its cracked lino and smell of lavender polish. It was the type of room from which a quick exit was impossible, because whatever you wanted necessitated a tortuous journey through the maze of shelves and an equally tortuous journey back. Clerkenwell had such a large storeroom because it was shared between several police stations.

The attendant was fidgeting, clearly wanting to get back to his coffee and newspaper. 'It's all on this middle shelf, ma'am.'

'Thanks, Terry.' She smiled brightly. 'I'll call if I need you.'

'Yes, ma'am.' He handed her the list of contents, a plastic sheet, and a pair of latex gloves.

She waited till he'd gone, then drew on the gloves, and laid Quincey's bag on the sheet. Kneeling beside it, she removed the contents carefully. First to come out were the ties and cravats, including the blue and red Sydney Sussex tie that had strangled Max Quincey. Next were the Gieves and Hawkes clothes. She dug deeper, finding the ashtray, emptied and washed clean. She sifted through the items, mentally noting where in Max's room she'd seen them: the Jack in the Box doll, the mobile phone, the watch. At the bottom was the Parker pen and copy of The Guardian, dated September 12th, the day Max Quincey had died. She examined the items, all that was left of him, but they told her nothing she didn't already know.

She started to put everything back, pausing when she saw the pen and newspaper. When had Max bought The Guardian? First thing that Tuesday? Or had Mrs Deacon bought it for him? *Can't be precise but it was after seven. That's when I get up. I popped outside to buy the morning paper.* But later the same morning, just after 10.00am, Max had phoned Directory Enquiries. He hadn't been put through directly, and he hadn't used his mobile. That meant only one thing: unless he had an excellent memory for figures, whatever number he'd requested must have been written down. She turned the pen in her hand, remembering how it had lain on the newspaper. She opened The Guardian and examined it, poring over every inch. There was nothing. No writing. Not even doodles. She folded the paper the way she'd found it in the bag, the way it had lain on the table, the front page showing.

Slowly, she ran a finger across the paper. Was it her imagination, or was it less smooth in the margin? She fished in her bag for a soft pencil. With a glance down the corridor, she ran the tip gently over the paper. As if by magic, the imprint of a series of numbers appeared, numbers which someone had written down on something else, leaning heavily on The Guardian.

She stood under the light, and brought the page close to her face. The writing was large and clear, done hastily but with a flourish. She stared without seeing. Then she slid slowly down the wall in a shower of flaking paint, and squatted on the floor. She leant her head back, breathing with difficulty.

A phone number. One she recognised. She let the newspaper fall, and pressed the heels of her hands into her eyes. She sat in an attitude of hopelessness, praying there was an innocent explanation, telling herself it might even have been a wrong number, finally thinking of nothing.

A door slammed nearby, jolting her to her senses. She dragged herself to her feet. She'd have to destroy the paper. And quickly. She began to stuff it under her jacket, when the enormity of what she was doing hit her. What the fuck was she thinking? Tampering with police evidence was a crime. As a police officer, she'd get a custodial sentence. She replaced the paper and pen in the bag, thrusting them to the bottom. Anyone going through Max's effects would see the imprint, recognise it as a phone number, and conclude she hadn't acted on it. But that was a chance she'd have to take, she couldn't think about it now.

She was zipping the bag shut when her hand brushed against the doll. It sprang open with its cry of 'Jack-jack! Jack-jack!' She lifted it out and turned it over, examining it. It was identical to those she was seeing everywhere. No, not identical. Similar yet different. The green paint was flaking and scratched. Yes, that was it. It was worn, more worn than the dolls currently on sale at the Garrimont. *As soon as they arrived this morning, I sent one out to all the cast and crew.* Chrissie's words, spoken the day before she and Steve had gone to see the play. Nearly a week after Max had died.

Yet the doll in her hand had been taken from Max Quincey's room days before Chrissie's order had arrived from the manufacturer. There could be only one explanation. This wasn't one of the dolls made for the current production – this was an old doll, from 1985.

He was seen at the Duke, talking to young boys. And he always had a doll with him.

Adrenaline surged through her body. How could she have been so blind? Gripping the doll firmly, she untwisted the base.

It was stiff after years of disuse. She gave a sharp wrench and it came off, flying from her hand and clattering to the floor. She reached inside and pulled out the contents. Not a wad of money, as in the play, but something wrapped in yellow paper and secured with an elastic band.

She removed the band with fingers trembling with excitement. Inside the sheet were over a dozen small packets of white powder. She stared, light-headed, almost dizzy. *Good for luck, Rosie, and good for business.* She laughed softly. *Oh Max, Max, you crafty bugger. I've got you.*

Her heart pumping, she reassembled the doll and wrapped it in polythene. She put it carefully into her handbag.

She was returning Max's belongings to the shelf when she heard the sound. She paused, holding her breath. Soft footsteps. Someone had entered the storeroom.

'Is that you, Terry?' she shouted.

The footsteps stopped.

She felt a twinge of anxiety. If this was Terry, then why hadn't he answered? She dropped to her knees. The footsteps started up again. She sank back on her heels, straining to listen, trying to determine their location. The sound grew louder. Someone was walking, not down her corridor, but the one parallel to it. She peered through the rack, just in time to see a pair of legs in dark pinstripe trousers saunter by.

Her anxiety deepened. This wasn't the behaviour of someone with legitimate business. Officers were always accompanied by Terry, who was a stickler for protocol. And they conducted their business quickly in the airless echoing room. So what was this dawdler doing? Spying on her? Trying to find her? She scrambled silently to her feet, wanting nothing more now than to get out of there. If she kept to the wall, she'd eventually find Terry's desk. She crept away, alert to the possibility that the pinstripe might change direction. But the footsteps grew fainter. He was moving away.

A minute later, she arrived at the desk. Terry was nowhere to be seen. She picked up the visitor's book. Hers was the first, and only, signature that day.

'Can I help you, ma'am?'

She spun round. 'Jesus, Terry, you gave me a fright.'

He stared fixedly at the book in her hand. 'I'm sorry, ma'am.'

'Is there another way out of the storeroom?' she said, her voice low.

He indicated the fire exit behind her. Like all fire exits at Clerkenwell, it was alarmed. 'And there's a door at the back that leads to the main corridor. I don't have the keys, though.'

'You didn't see anyone come in without signing?'

'No-one comes in without signing. It's the rule.'

'But you weren't at your desk just now,' she said impatiently. 'Someone might have slipped in.'

He drew himself up. 'I'm allowed breaks to go to the lavatory, ma'am.'

'Of course you are, Terry, of course you are. I'm just saying that someone could have come in without your knowledge.'

'Then he'll have me to contend with when he comes out,' Terry said in a tone which was intended to close the conversation.

In the ensuing silence, she noticed that the footsteps had stopped. Perhaps the suit had overheard the conversation.

She dropped her voice to a whisper. 'I think there's someone in here who shouldn't be. When he comes out, make some excuse to detain him and ring me immediately, okay?'

'If there's someone in here who shouldn't be,' Terry said loudly, 'then I want to know about it.' Without waiting for a reply, he marched down the corridor.

Brilliant, Terry. Anyone in the room would have heard that. She had no option but to follow him.

They reached the door in the far wall. Before she could stop him, he grasped the knob firmly.

Oh, just great. Bang go the prints. She turned away to hide her frustration.

He pushed against the door. It opened smoothly onto a corridor.

'That's not right,' he muttered. 'It's meant to be locked.' He glared at her, as if this were somehow her fault. 'And how can I lock it without a key?'

'Willy can make you a copy,' she said, in exasperation.

His face brightened. 'It must have been him, ma'am, doing his rounds. He sometimes inspects the building, checking doors. Must have forgotten to lock this one after him.'

'It seems the most likely explanation.'

But, as she made her way towards the stairs, she knew it hadn't been the janitor. She knew Willy, a kindly man almost as old as Terry. He didn't wear pinstripe suits.

'This is the proof we need that, in 1985, Max Quincey was distributing drugs at the Duke.' Von was enjoying the expressions on their faces. 'He transported the packets in one of these dolls, and exchanged it for an empty one. It's probably how they all did it.' She paused for effect. 'And how they're doing it again now.'

The detectives were crowded around her, staring at the doll.

'We should have realised,' Steve said.

'It was the play. That's where he must have got the idea.'

'It would explain why no-one twigged. Everyone was carrying these dolls around.' He rubbed the back of his neck. 'Jack in the Box Fever.'

'The rent boys could easily remove the packets without being seen,' Zoë said thoughtfully. 'In the loo at the Duke, for example, or they could go round the back alleys. It would be straightforward to set up a simple exchange system. Much safer than slipping packets back and forth by hand.' She looked intently at Von. 'So should we start hauling in the dolls? The drugs squad should really be doing that.'

Von almost gabbled the words. 'I don't want them alerted yet.' She ignored the look of incomprehension on the girl's face. 'Let's get to work. There are questions we need answers to. For one, how did Max distribute the stuff during the fifteen years he was on the road? Those payments into his bank account have been continuing.'

'He must have had a partner, boss, one he knew well enough to entrust the business to. He may have double-crossed this guy and got killed for it. Those unidentified prints in the bathroom and that blond hair might be his.'

'Okay, but the prints aren't in the PNC, so it's someone we've never hauled in.' She pushed her hands through her hair. 'I keep coming back to Chrissie. Dickie didn't recognise her but it doesn't rule out the possibility she was in on it. It would explain the phone calls. The problem is that the fingerprints and blond hairs weren't hers.'

'Then there must have been three people in this marriage.'

She felt sick. That phone number on The Guardian. She knew the blond hair wasn't his. But could those prints be? Zoë was watching her carefully. She turned away, not wanting the girl to read her expression. If anyone could put two and two together, it was Zoë.

'We need Forensics to confirm the stuff is heroin,' Zoë said. 'We'll look like proper twats if it turns out to be talcum powder.'

That'll buy me some time. 'Get on to them. And, while you're at it, have the packets checked for prints. Let's pray that the dabs we find are Max's.'

Steve was staring at the doll. 'This is going to get the Chief Super into a bit of a lather.'

'I don't give a fuck about the Chief Super,' she shouted. In the shocked silence, she said, 'We'll wait for the fingerprint analysis before telling him. Otherwise he could say the drugs were planted by his brother's killer.' They were staring at her with puzzled expressions. 'I have to go. There's something urgent I need to do.' She almost ran out of the room.

In her office, she dialled his landline and his mobile, and left the same message. 'Kenny, it's vital I speak to you. Call me as soon as you get this.'

No apologies for their row. No entreaties. No endearments. Kenny had some serious explaining to do. He claimed he'd hardly known Max Quincey. So why had Max requested his landline number from Directory Enquiries on the day he'd been murdered?

Von was sitting with her head in her hands when there was a knock at the door.

'You all right, boss?' There was anxiety in Steve's voice. 'Can I get you a coffee?'

'I'm fine. Just tired.' She smiled weakly. 'We've made a breakthrough today. We're back on track for finding who killed the rent boys.'

He pulled out a chair. 'You mean, for finding who killed Max Quincey, don't you?' He searched her face. 'Sometimes I think the murder of the rent boys is the only case that interests you.'

Before she could reply, there was a quick knock and a detective poked his head round the door.

'We've brought in Zack Lazarus, ma'am. Shall we put him in one of the interview rooms?'

'Bring him here.'

Steve raised an enquiring eyebrow. 'We're seeing Lazarus again?'

'I'd like you to stay for this.'

Lazarus entered, bringing with him a whiff of sweat and machine oil. He looked bewildered.

'Please take a seat, Mr Lazarus,' she said, smiling kindly.

'What's this about?' He lowered his bulk into the chair. 'I'm not being charged, am I?'

'No, nothing like that. You might help me clear up something, that's all. I'd like you to cast your mind back to 1985, specifically the time of the Jack in the Box murders.'

He unbuttoned his jacket. 'You've asked me that before.'

'You've a good memory, Mr Lazarus. But so have I.' She motioned to her papers. 'And I have my notes to back it up. You told me you'd never been to the Iron Duke. But I have a witness who identified you.'

'He couldn't have.'

'He said you came to see one of the boys.' She watched his reaction closely. 'You paid for his food and drink. Sat with him, talked to him. Nothing wrong with that. I just want to know what it was all about.'

He clenched his fists, saying nothing. From across the desk she could feel the white heat of his anger.

'We've been speaking with Rose Manning. She's made a full confession.' She paused. 'About everything.'

His eyes bored into hers.

'We know that Max Quincey brought boys back to the Garrimont,' she continued. 'And we know about your intervention. Can you tell us about it?'

When he finally spoke, it was in a halting monotone. He seemed to be forcing the words out as though speaking were painful. 'When I was very young, my Dad left us. Mum married again. A man called Newman. Came with a kid of his own.' He shifted in the chair. 'Emmanuel. But everyone called him Manny.'

She felt Steve look at her, but she kept her eyes on Lazarus.

'I had no brothers or sisters. Neither did Manny. We hit it off from day one. Could say we became inseparable. And his dad was okay with me. Good to my Mum as well.' He picked at his nails. 'Thought we could be a proper family. But we never had any money and eventually my new dad did a runner. Didn't take Manny with him. Things went downhill after that. Mum couldn't cope, went on the vallies.' He stopped abruptly, as though he'd said too much.

'And Manny?'

'Heartbroken.' His voice caught on the word. 'Although she wasn't his real mum, I think he loved her more than I did. When he saw what she was doing to herself, he changed. Became bitter. Started to hate her. As if it were all her fault, which of course it wasn't. Anyway, it was just a matter of time before he left too.'

'How old would he have been?'

'About fourteen.' He ran a hand over his stubble. 'We lost touch. I left school as soon as I could. Helped a mate out with lighting work for some rock band's gig. Picked up more work and eventually moved to theatre lighting.' He shrugged. 'Been there ever since.'

'So how did you meet Manny again?' she said, when the silence had gone on too long.

'The play was running. It was my night off and I was out with some mates. We decided to go to the Duke for a drink. Come and look at the queens and bumboys, one of them said.' His voice grew hard. 'My mates went there a lot, for a lark. I wasn't too keen but I tagged along. Ignored them and sat quietly with my pint. And then he walked in. Hadn't changed. Except he was thinner, a lot thinner. But the eyes were the same. Eyes never change.'

'Did he recognise you?'

He shook his head. 'I'd put on some beef, and my face had filled out. Used to wear glasses but my rock-band friend suggested I try contacts. I thought Manny would recognise me on account of this' – he indicated the scarring on his face – 'but he didn't. Maybe he never noticed it when we were younger. Kids don't always see that sort of thing.'

'What was your reaction when he walked in?'

'Horrified. Could tell by the way he acted that he was on the game. My mates were nudging each other and giggling. I couldn't stand it. Made some excuse and left.'

'But you came back.'

He hesitated. 'The next morning. He wasn't there. The landlord said nights were best. Evening after, he came in again. I got him a drink.' He snorted. 'He thought I wanted sex. To keep him there, I gave him money. Bought him a burger. Don't know what he thought about it all, but he was happy just to talk.' He looked at his hands. 'I tried to persuade him to give it up. He just stared at me. We met a lot after that, but he always left to find someone.'

'Why didn't you tell him who you were?'

'I was afraid to. Thought he might be so ashamed, he'd run off and I'd never see him again.'

'Did he tell you about his clients?'

'I didn't ask. He knew I didn't approve.'

'And did you see Max Quincey at the Duke during that period?' she said, watching him closely.

'Many times. He just nodded at me and carried on doing whatever he was doing.'

'What was that?'

Lazarus scratched behind his ear. 'Depends. Sometimes he sat and drank. Sometimes he talked with people.'

'The regulars?'

'Regulars, the landlord. And the boys.'

'Did you ever see him with a Jack in the Box doll?'

He seemed surprised by the question. 'Hard to remember. But everyone had them. They were all over town.'

'And in the Duke?'

'Always a couple of dolls on the bar.'

'And after Manny was attacked, did you carry on going to the Duke?'

'Why would I?' He lowered his head. 'Never saw him again. The landlord told me he was taken into care.' He spoke slowly, an appeal in his voice. 'That's something, isn't it? He's being looked after.'

'Would you see him again if you knew where he was?' she said gently.

'Don't know. Doubt he'd want me to, I'd be a reminder of his old life.' He seemed to need confirmation, his eyes pleading with hers. 'He wouldn't want that, would he?'

Pity surged into her throat as she recalled the blind boy, and his pride in his new life. She remembered his words: *It's only now I've come to realise he was probably my only friend.* Maybe Zack was wrong.

'I hear Rose Manning is going to be charged with murder,' he was saying.

'She's confessed to killing Michael Gillanders.'

'No love lost between Rose and me, but you should know she's not had an easy life. Her parents live near my mother in Camden. Her mum's getting on and Rose is worried she'll have to give up work to look after her. Life's not given Rose anything.' He nodded. 'But she's tough.'

She's going to have to be, to survive in prison.

'Just wanted to put in a word for her, that's all.' He hesitated. 'Is there anything else? Or can I go?'

'There's nothing else. I'll have someone drive you back to the theatre.'

He gave a wry smile. 'The show must go on, eh?'

She held his gaze for a moment. 'Yes, Zack. The show must go on.'

Chapter 26

There was a crush at the Drunken Duck, and it was clear they weren't going to be served.

Von rarely waited more than five minutes for anything. She tugged at Steve's arm. 'Let's get a sandwich at the deli next door, and take it back to the nick.'

While Steve was ordering, her thoughts turned again to the dark-suited man in the storeroom. She'd checked the desk sergeant's log but, unsurprisingly for such an early hour, no-one had visited the station. It meant that the man she'd heard in the storeroom must work at Clerkenwell. Not only that, he had a key to the room's back door.

She checked her mobile for messages. Kenny hadn't tried to contact her. *Damn. Where the hell is he?* She could guess. *With Georgie.*

She was putting the phone away when it rang. 'DCI Valenti,' she said quickly.

The fear in Tubby's voice was unmistakeable. 'Von?'

'Where are you?'

'Not far from Euston. Can we meet in the caff?'

'Now?'

'Now.' He sounded desperate. 'Please come.'

'Hold on, I'll be there as soon as I can.' She snapped the phone shut. 'Change of plan, Steve. It's my snout. I'll see you at the nick.' She nodded at the sandwiches. 'You can have mine.'

He stared at the package. 'If I'd known, I'd have got beef.'

Tubby was sipping from a mug, his back to the wall, in the corner of the caff where he wasn't visible but could see anyone who came in. Von recognised this behaviour from his years with the gangs. *Poor tyke. He must really be frightened.*

She ordered tea but, when she started to choose the cakes, he waved her over.

'I can't eat, Von.' His hands were trembling. 'My nerves are shot.'

'What's happened?' she said, taking the seat opposite.

His eyes darted to the door. 'I'm being tailed.'

She frowned. If this were true, by meeting her here he was taking a huge risk. For them both.

'I've shaken him off for now.' He clutched at her arm. 'But he knows where I live.'

'You're sure?'

'Pretty sure.'

She murmured, 'Then we'll make this quick, and you can come back with me. So what have you got?'

'That name you were after. The Cutter.'

The Cutter! Her heart hammered in her chest. 'Who is he, Tubby?'

He tightened the grip on her arm. 'If I give you the name, will you make sure I get out of London? Permanently? It'll cost you, and you know how much.'

'I don't have that much on me, but I can get it,' she said quickly. It was a lie. She'd never get a large sum of money authorised at short notice. But she daren't say no, she was too close. If Tubby was this scared, he'd find some way to leg it to Spain where he'd disappear permanently, and she'd have lost everything.

'Meet me in our special place tonight, Von. 10.00pm. You can give me the money then.'

10.00pm. It would give her time to think up something. She

got to her feet but he pulled her down.

'Don't you want to know who it is?' he said in astonishment.

'I thought you'd need the money first.'

'I trust you. You've always been more than fair with me. I know you'll get the cash.' He brought his face close to hers. People turned to look at them, unlikely lovers meeting for a cup of tea and a quick snog in a greasy spoon. 'Max Quincey,' he breathed, so softly that at first she thought she'd said it herself.

She sat back, stunned. So, not only had Max been distributing, he'd been cutting the stuff as well. They'd been wrong about him. He must have laundered the big money and hidden it offshore, leaving just the pin money to go into his account. He'd outsmarted them. She stirred her tea, staring straight ahead. Other pieces of the jigsaw fell into place. The Cutter had threatened Harrower. As his prime suspect, Max would have known Harrower had turned his attention to the Duke as part of his investigation. Could Max have left word with someone there to contact him if the coppers came sniffing around? Could he have received the call, phoned Harrower, and threatened his family unless he backed off?

Tubby was looking at her strangely. 'Von?'

She switched her gaze back to him. 'Sorry, I was thinking.'

'You look weird when you're thinking.'

'So how did you get his name?'

'Told Malkie I wanted to know more before I agreed to come in, didn't I? He wouldn't say anything, he was too scared, but one of the other regulars must have overheard. Followed me out. Said he could tell me everything I wanted to know if I made it worth his while. I gave him what was left of your money.' Tubby gulped down his tea. 'He was the one told me who the Cutter was.'

'Did you get this regular's name?'

'Course not. And I wasn't going to ask him, neither. He

looks like Rocky Balboa.'

This was par for the course. In Tubby's world, people rarely told each other their real names. Malkie would have been baptised as someone else, if he'd been baptised at all.

'And no mention of who Mr Big might be?' she said, sifting the sugar in the bowl.

'Believe me, Von, no-one knows.'

Max would have known. As the person who cut the stuff, he would have got it from Mr Big. But Max was dead. The trail had come to an end.

Tubby picked up his copy of The News of the World. 'I have to go. You won't forget? Our special place, at ten?'

'I'll be there.' She hesitated. 'After tonight, we won't be meeting again. I just want to say—'

'We'll say our goodbyes later, Von.' He grinned, showing discoloured teeth. 'We'll see each other one last time.'

She felt a sudden shiver through her body. 'Come with me,' she blurted, grabbing his arm. 'I can take you to a safe house.'

'Got things to sort out. And one or two people to see.' He patted her hand. 'Don't worry. I've shaken him off. As long as I don't go back to my place, I'll be all right.'

She released him slowly. 'If you feel things are getting hot, Tubby, come into the nick and ask for me. Any time.'

Something passed across his face, a look of sadness. Then he pushed his chair back, and left.

She sat staring into her mug. So Max was the Cutter. They'd need to rethink. If Max had been so high up in this ring, then the motive for his killing was unlikely to be a simple double-cross. But his death had taken him out of the drug loop, and no-one would want that. All of them from the distributors to the street men were dependent on him. Mr Big would have to find someone else. He may well have done so already. She pushed the mug away. Damn it. They'd been so close. Max was the only one who'd known who Mr Big was. He was dead, and the information dead with him. Unless he'd left a clue somewhere.

She sat bolt upright. *Unless he'd left a clue somewhere.*

But Max *had* left a clue. A clue she'd found that morning on his newspaper.

'That's where I'm going, Steve.'

'I'll get my coat.'

'I'm going alone.'

'For God's sake, Von, if your snout thinks he's being followed, then it's not safe. Not safe for *you*.'

She smiled sadly. *He must be worried. He rarely calls me by my name.* 'If we go together, they'll know who we are,' she said. 'Look, I'll be careful. It's broad daylight.'

'We could go in undercover.' He looked at his feet. 'Pretend to be a couple.'

She did him the courtesy of taking the suggestion seriously. 'Don't be offended, Steve, but you've got the word copper printed on your forehead.' She waited until he'd lifted his eyes to hers. 'I won't be long. I have just one question to ask.'

'Whether he knew Max Quincey was the Cutter?'

'Got it in one.' She picked up her jacket. 'There's something you need to do while I'm out. Track down the Chief Super and get that money authorised.'

He rubbed the back of his neck. 'It won't be easy, you know how tight he is. Could you do it when you return?'

'No pun intended, but my currency's low with the Chief Super.'

He must have heard the anxiety in her voice. 'I'll do my best,' he said.

'And if Kenny calls at the nick, can you ensure he doesn't leave?'

'Okay. But why?'

'I've been trying to get in touch with him.' She wondered what to say. She wouldn't tell him till she had the proof. 'We had a row, Steve. He may come looking for me here.' Not quite the truth, but not a lie either. And men understood about rows.

His face cleared. 'Absolutely, boss.'

As Von stepped into the Iron Duke, all conversations stopped. She knew why they were staring. She'd been careful with her appearance, dressing the way she had a couple of years back when she'd gone undercover as a prostitute. She was wearing a skirt that could best be described as a long cummerbund, and a low-cut top, showing so much cleavage that any man she spoke to rarely lifted his eyes to her face. Better still, the bruise on her cheek had darkened.

She wobbled on her heels to the bar, and climbed onto a stool. Her feet were aching. She'd come by bus, not only because she didn't want to risk being seen in a car, but because driving down Soho's one-way streets was a nightmare.

She could have met Dickie at his house, or at St Pats, but she wanted to see the Duke. She found it easily enough near the street corner, wedged between a sex shop and a massage parlour. Above the tired façade was a board portraying Arthur Wellesley, the first Duke of Wellington, his right hand inside his jacket as was the custom for portraits. A few feet from the entrance, a woman selling The Big Issue was sitting leaning against the wall. Von bent to give her some coins. As she stepped back, her heels caught in the iron grille covering the delivery chute into the Duke's cellar.

The inside of the pub was surprisingly classy. The floor had been mopped, and the polished mirrors threw back such a perfect reflection that at first glance the room seemed twice its size. To one side was a platform with speakers and other equipment for karaoke night. There was a strong smell of malt.

She counted a dozen people, some in pairs, a few sitting separately, all nursing their drinks. Malkie and Rocky Balboa might be amongst them, but she didn't dare study anyone too closely.

On the counter was a Jack in the Box doll, already popped. Identical dolls were sitting on other tables.

Dickie was behind the counter, polishing glasses and hanging them from the tracks in the low ceiling. If he thought it strange a prostitute should enter a rent boys' bar, he gave no indication. He threw her the briefest glance. She remembered his words: *It's pretending I don't notice that's kept me alive.*

Good boy. Keep pretending.

'A vodka tonic, please, love,' she said, broadening her accent. She unzipped her jacket. 'Jesus, my feet are killing me.' She removed a shoe and, leaning over, massaged her toes, making sure everyone in the room had a good look at her breasts.

Dickie handed her the drink, barely looking at her.

'Can you tell me where the loo is, darling?' she said, after a while. 'If I don't pee soon, I'll go in my knickers.'

He continued to polish the glasses, motioning with his head to the door at the back of the room. 'End of the corridor, to your right.'

She followed the corridor to the ladies, and waited outside. A minute later, Dickie appeared. He hurried towards her, frowning.

She put a finger to her lips. With a furtive glance around, he took her arm and steered her towards the steps. The smell of yeast and malt grew stronger as they descended into the gloom.

'I'm the only one allowed in the cellar, so we should be okay,' he said. 'You're taking a hell of a risk coming here, girl.' He stared at her breasts and a slow grin spread across his face. 'But I have to say, your disguise is great.'

She smiled, moving closer so her breasts grazed his chest.

'I'm built for comfort, not speed.' She pulled a photo from her bag. 'Have you seen this man before?'

He gestured to her to keep her voice down, and held the photo up to the grille. 'That tattoo on his neck's unmistakable.'

The tattoo... She felt her legs give way. 'When was the last time?'

'A couple of days ago.'

'And at the time of the Jack in the Box murders?'

'Definitely then.' He paused. 'And many times since. He's a distributor.'

She was having difficulty breathing. 'You saw him pass packets to the boys?'

'I never saw.'

'Then how do you know?'

'I overheard one of the boys talking to him in the gents.' He pointed to the air vent high in the wall. 'Sound carries all over this building, girl. That's how I know things.'

'Did he meet with anyone in particular? Max Quincey, for example?'

He screwed up his eyes. 'Max Quincey? Gawd, now you're asking. Can't remember. It was too long ago. And Max hung around with loads of people.' His expression cleared. 'What I do remember is that he'd sometimes bring the boys presents.'

Presents...Her throat tightened. 'What kind of presents?'

'Clothes, mainly. Trendy stuff.'

'Didn't you think it odd? He wasn't a client.'

He shrugged. 'They were nice kids. And this guy seemed to have plenty to splash around.'

'Did he give the boys anything apart from clothes?' she said, knowing the answer.

'This might sound strange, but they seemed to like the dolls. There was talk they were becoming collectors' items. Once the shops began to run out, the dolls were traded by people who wanted to collect them.' He rubbed his cheek. 'This guy – what was his name? – yes, Robbie, he always had a doll with him.'

She felt faint. She leant against the wall and closed her eyes.

'You okay, girl?' he said, concern in his voice.

'I'm fine.' She straightened. 'One last thing, Dickie. I meant to ask before, but why is there no CCTV outside the Duke? Or on any of the streets nearby? The rest of Soho is bristling with cameras.'

'Dunno. There used to be cameras years ago, but they kept getting vandalised. I guess the council decided not to throw good money after bad.' He seemed nervous. 'Look, is this all you want to ask? It's just that changing over barrels doesn't take that long. People are going to start wondering what I've been doing.'

'What's the going rate for a blow job?'

He seemed alarmed. 'Twenty quid. Why?'

She took a twenty-pound note from her bag. 'When we go into the bar, just hand me this. People will stop wondering what you've been doing.'

Von was waiting on Oxford Street for the bus to take her to Clerkenwell. She shivered in her short skirt, feeling the cold suck of the wind. An ambulance screamed past, its siren drowning out the noise of the roadworks.

So now she had the proof. She stared at the photo of Kenny, remembering when she'd taken it. It had been high summer and they'd gone to Brighton. He hadn't realised she had the camera in her hand, and she'd captured that look of surprise close up. Close up enough also to capture the tattoos.

At the Duke, then, he was known as Robbie. His brother's name. Dickie's words sliced through her like a scalpel: *He's a distributor.* And had been for many years. All that time, Kenny would have been working with Max, getting his packets from him. *He's a distributor.* No wonder he'd quizzed her hard the night she told him Max had been murdered. When had he become involved? Was it when he interviewed Max at the time of the Jack in the Box murders? Or later. Perhaps he'd stumbled on the drug ring as part of some other investigation and saw it as too good an opportunity to pass up. Everything he'd told her had been a catalogue of lies. He'd even lied about going to the Duke: *I've heard of it, but I've never been there.*

What was going to happen to the ring now? Had Mr Big already found his new Cutter? Perhaps that was what Kenny had been up to these past few days. Trying to climb higher up the greasy pole.

She felt as if she were being squeezed in a vice. Could she suppress Dickie's evidence? Tip Kenny off? Give him a chance to leg it somewhere? And when the drugs squad came in to clean up the operation at the Duke, which they would eventually, would they uncover his involvement and her duplicity? The knot in her heart tightened. It hardly mattered. Either way, what future was there for them now?

The bus lurched into view. She tore the photo into tiny pieces and threw them into the gutter. As she climbed onto the platform, a gust of wind lifted them, scattering them high into the air.

Chapter 27

'He's late, boss.'

Von and Steve were waiting on the Thames Path at the southern end of Blackfriars Bridge. Little was visible in the dark other than the grey ribs on the underside of the bridge's arches, and the outline of St Paul's Cathedral dominating the skyline to the north. Von shivered, not daring to move in case she stepped into the foul-smelling water. As if recognising her predicament, the moon slid from behind a cloud and illuminated the river, revealing food cartons and other rubbish caught up in the rotting leaves that lapped back and forth in the scum. The cold penetrated her clothes and seeped into her bones, and not for the first time she asked herself why, of all the places in London, Tubby had chosen this spot for his special place.

'How will he react when he finds you've not got the money?' said Steve.

'I don't care. I'm taking him with me.'

'Kidnapping is a crime,' he said lightly.

'I'm in no mood for jokes, Steve.'

'Sorry.'

'What time is it?' she said after a while.

'A quarter past ten.'

She pulled her scarf around her face. 'He's never been late before. Something's happened.'

'Let's give it another fifteen minutes.' He paused. 'Did Kenny show up?'

'At home? There's nothing on my answer machine.'

'He'll phone eventually. He always does, doesn't he?'

Maybe not this time. She wondered whether Kenny suspected she was close to uncovering his drug involvement, or whether his lack of communication was simply because he'd left her. But she knew him too well. He wouldn't go without having it out. He'd want his big scene, his grand finale. He'd want closure.

Steve was fidgeting. 'When was the last time you—'

'Saturday lunchtime. I haven't seen or heard from him since.' She beat her arms in an effort to keep warm.

'Have you thought of contacting The Guardian? They might know what he's working on, and where he is.'

She was tempted to say she doubted he was still working for The Guardian. A time was coming when she'd either have to tell Steve everything, or keep quiet and go down with Kenny's sinking ship.

'What time is it?' she said again.

'Ten thirty.'

'He's not coming. Let's go.'

The Toyota was heading north across the bridge when Von said, 'Slow down a minute, Steve. This isn't the direction he'd be coming from. He operates north of the river, so he goes to Southwark tube and walks up Blackfriars Road.'

'Does he live around there?'

'He rents a house near the tube station, and he may have come directly from it. Either way, we won't find him here. So when we're off the bridge, turn the car round.'

'Boss, I don't think—'

'For God's sake, Steve, just do it.'

Five minutes later, they were heading back south.

'Would he think we'd wait this long?' said Steve. 'If he was held up, he'll be in touch again tomorrow, surely.'

'I don't think he was held up.' She was struggling against the growing feeling of dread. 'He would have called, he has my number.'

They drove to Southwark tube station but there was no sign of Tubby on Blackfriars Road.

She tapped Steve's arm. 'Stop here and park the car. We'll walk to his house.'

'What do you think's happened, boss?'

'He'll have gone back for his passport. He lives somewhere near Bear Lane, I'll know the place when I get there.'

They found Tubby in his doorway. She recognised the cowboy boots poking out from underneath the pile of rubbish. Whoever had killed him had made a poor job of concealing the body. The black bin bags had been tossed carelessly, and one had split and strewn its stinking contents across the pavement. In death, Tubby had merited less of anyone's time than he had in life.

She removed a torch from her pocket and pulled away the bags. Her stomach churned. Tubby's face was unrecognisable. The blood-clotted hair was plastered to the forehead, the spectacles missing, the swollen flesh a mass of cuts and bruises. Blood, which had coursed from the shattered nose, caked the mouth and chin.

Steve took her wrist gently and guided the beam down. The torchlight caught the glint of wire in Tubby's neck.

She straightened, groaning. 'This is my fault. I shouldn't have believed him when he told me he'd be okay. I shouldn't have let him out of my sight.'

Steve put an arm round her shoulders. 'You couldn't have known this is how he'd end up.'

Remorse surged through her. Why hadn't she taken him with her to the station? Why hadn't she insisted?

She remembered his words: *We'll say our goodbyes later, Von.*

She leant forward and stared into the broken face. 'Goodbye, Tubby,' she whispered.

Von ran a hand through her hair. 'I can't find the Chief Super.' She looked around the room wildly. Only Steve and Zoë were at their desks. 'Either of you know where he is?' she said.

'He left the station in a bit of a rush, ma'am,' Zoë said. 'We got a call from his mother's house to say he wouldn't be in. His mother's not herself.'

It wasn't like the Chief Super to put his private life first. After his wife had died, he'd taken only the day of the funeral off. His mother must be in a bad way for him to leave the station at such a critical time.

Zoë was watching her. 'Are you unwell, ma'am?' she said quietly.

'I'm fine. Where are the others?'

'At the crime scene.'

'Steve, can I see you in my office, please?'

He looked surprised. 'Sure, boss.'

In her office, she sat down heavily. 'Please close the door. And sit down.'

He smiled faintly. 'Why the cloak and dagger?'

'I have something to tell you,' she said, staring at the desk.

Her heart was hammering. But she couldn't dissemble any longer. She looked him in the eye and told him what she'd been concealing: finding Kenny's landline number on Max Quincey's Guardian, and learning from Dickie that Kenny was part of the drug ring.

He rose and went to the window. He rubbed his arm slowly.

'For God's sake, Steve, say something.'

He faced her. 'What do you intend to do?' His voice was calm. 'Are you asking me to keep quiet about this?'

'Of course not,' she said, confused. 'Kenny is now a suspect in the murder of Max Quincey. We have to act accordingly.'

'Why have you shared this with me and not the others?'

Jesus, he's determined not to make this easy. 'I don't know,' she said. 'I wanted you to understand why I did it. No, that's not why. I think I was hoping you might talk me out of it. I've been suppressing evidence. I know what the implications are.'

He sat down. 'You've hardly been suppressing evidence, Von. If you have, it was for all of twenty four hours. Less. You saw Dickie Womack yesterday afternoon.'

'But if I'd told you, then Tubby might still be alive,' she moaned.

'How do you make that out? You offered him immediate protection and he refused it. It was his choice.' He frowned. 'Are you thinking Kenny killed him, and if we'd pulled Kenny in yesterday, Tubby would still be alive?'

'The thought did cross my mind. Tubby was asking Malkie a hell of a lot of questions. Kenny may have got to hear from someone who was there.'

'I don't believe that. You told me once that, when it comes to extracting information discreetly, your snout is a pro. No, I think someone at the Duke has a loose tongue and it's that that's got Tubby killed.' He pushed his chair back. 'Come on. Everyone's out. Let's get it up on the board and fill the others in when they return. With luck, no-one will notice it's yesterday's news.'

'You're prepared to do that?' she said, gazing up at him.

His expression softened. 'There's nothing I've heard here today that two consenting detectives can't keep private.'

'We'll have to search Kenny's house,' she said quietly.

He saw her hesitation. 'You're not thinking of taking yourself off this case, are you?'

'Why would I?'

'Conflict of interest. He's your man, after all.'

She looked at him, saying nothing.

Chapter 28

Von turned the key and opened the door to Kenny's flat. As she and Steve stepped inside, the scent of freshly cut flowers touched her like a warm breath.

'Don't mean to pry, boss, but when was the last time you were here?'

'Can't remember. We've been meeting at mine.' She tried to sound professional, but the catch in her voice was unmistakable.

In the living room, the familiar bright IKEA furniture was tastefully rearranged and dotted with new scatter cushions. Not exactly Kenny's style. She noticed that the photos of herself, with and without Kenny, had been removed.

She fingered the carnations on the sideboard. They were lovingly arranged, unlike the flowers in her flat, thrown into a chipped vase and drooping now in stagnant water. 'Someone's been here recently.'

'Looks like it.' Steve ran a hand over the mantelpiece. 'Clean.'

'Amazing. He's not the type to dust.' *She's done it for him.*

He gazed out of the window. Kenny lived in Battersea, on London's south bank. Von had never thought it the most inspiring of districts, but he'd bought the flat to be close to his aunt. She'd passed away the previous year and, although Von had urged him to sell up and move nearer to Whitechapel, he'd refused, saying his roots were in Battersea.

'If he didn't live on the ground floor, boss, he'd have a cracking view of the Power Station and Chelsea Bridge.'

She knew what he was doing, trying to lighten her mood. But nothing was going to lighten her mood.

The bedroom was the largest room, with wall-to-wall wardrobes left behind by the previous lady owner. The king-sized bed, reflected in the wardrobe's mirrors, was unmade, the sheets thrown back. Von closed her eyes, seeing the two of them stumbling towards it, shedding their clothes. An odour rose from the bed. The mustiness of sex mingled with sweat.

'What's that smell, boss?'

'Perfume.' She turned to face him. 'Not mine.'

His eyes held hers. What was it she saw there? Pity? Hope? She looked away, unable to bear the expression on his face.

'I'm sorry, Von. I didn't know.'

'Neither did I till a couple of days ago.'

She slid open the wardrobe door. His clothes were hanging neatly. Her own were nowhere to be seen. She'd left a couple of good suits there. She pulled his jackets aside, searching, but he'd removed all trace of her. *The bastard. He's binned them.*

She was straightening his things when she found it near the back. A blouse which wasn't hers. Next to it was an Oscar de la Renta suit. And behind it, a negligee in champagne silk, with long thin straps. Her lips tightened. She closed the door before Steve could see the clothes.

He was jingling coins in his pockets. 'You think he's done a runner?' he said.

'Why would he? He doesn't know we're on to him.'

The kitchen was spotless. The dishes had been washed and neatly stacked, and the surfaces wiped down. She sneered inwardly. *Nothing like a woman's touch, eh, Kenny?*

Inside the fridge she found his beers, several microwaveable meals, and a bottle of champagne. She removed the food packages and examined them.

'Two of everything.' She threw them onto the kitchen table.

'Cosy.'

'You think he might be coming home for lunch?'

'When his fridge is full, he usually eats at home.'

He was clearly uncomfortable. 'Should we wait? We haven't exactly been invited in, although we've got a search warrant.'

Before she could reply, she heard the front door open and close. Her heart lurched with shock. *Oh, Jesus, she might be with him. Please let her not be. Please. Please...*

She heard him moving in the hall, hanging up his coat. Was it her imagination, or were there two sets of footsteps?

When he entered, he was alone.

He stopped short. 'Von,' he breathed. His eyes flicked to Steve, and his expression darkened. 'What the hell are you doing in my flat?'

'Hello, Kenny,' she said lightly. 'We'd like to talk to you. Take a seat.'

His shoulders sagged. 'Look, I get it, you've been trying to ring me. I'm sorry, I meant to call back, but—'

'We know everything.'

'What are you talking about?'

'Sit down,' she snapped.

He pulled out a chair, keeping his eyes on hers. She sat next to him. Steve took the seat on his other side.

He seemed composed. He turned his body away from Steve, cutting him out of the conversation. 'What's this about, love?' He tried a smile.

'We know about the drugs, Kenny. Or should I call you Robbie.'

If the statement shocked him, he gave no indication. 'You think I'm using?' He shook his head in mock amazement. 'Unbelievable.'

'Don't play games with me.'

'Games?'

'You've been distributing drugs at the Iron Duke.'

The statement found its mark. He drew in his breath sharply. 'That's a lie.'

'We have a witness who saw you. You're doing yourself no favours by denying it.'

'Who's the witness?' he said softly.

She ignored the question, holding to the promise she'd made to Dickie. 'A man was killed last night. Strangled with piano wire after he'd been beaten to a pulp. He'd been asking questions at the Duke.'

The colour bled from his face.

She noted it with satisfaction. *That's knocked him off balance.* 'You may be next, Kenny. I suggest you tell us what you know.' When he didn't answer, she said, 'For God's sake, you were working with Max Quincey. You're now a suspect in his murder.'

'I never murdered him.' He moistened his lips. 'You have to believe me. Whatever else I've done, I never killed anyone.'

She let her breath out slowly. 'Then, what *have* you done?'

'What's in it for me?'

'A jail sentence for drug dealing, for starters. Another for obstructing the police. What do you think, Kenny? I'm going to let you off the hook? For old times' sake?' She threw him a look of contempt. 'Start at the beginning. And work hard to convince me you didn't kill Max Quincey.'

He rubbed his hands over his face. 'I interviewed him in 1985. About the play, Jack in the Box.'

'I know that. Tell me something I don't.'

'It was the week before opening night. The town was buzzing with this new play, and I needed to do a piece. Max suggested we meet in the Duke.' He was silent for a moment. 'When I arrived, he was steaming. From the state of him, he'd been drinking since morning. I asked him a few questions but his mind wasn't on the interview. He was waiting for someone.'

'A boy?'

'That's what I assumed, I knew the Duke's reputation. And from the way Max dressed and behaved, I took him for a shirtlifter. Anyway, the boys came in.'

'Boys? Plural?'

'Three Irish boys.' He looked at his hands. 'I know who they were now, of course, they were the ones killed. They came up to us, joked about a bit, then Max bought them drinks. Eventually, they left.' He frowned. 'Except for one. He stayed behind with Max.'

'Which one?'

'Gilly McIlvanny. Didn't know his name then, but I got to know it later. After a while I realised I was getting nothing further out of Max so I got up to go. That's when I saw it. The doll.'

'Max had a doll?'

'They both did.' His eyes held hers. 'Max and Gilly were so into one another they didn't realise I hadn't left. I'd parked myself further away, near a crowd of city types, where I couldn't be seen. Gilly left his doll on the table and got up to fetch a drink. He returned and they chatted a few more minutes. Then he picked up Max's doll and went out to the corridor.'

'You're sure it was Max's doll?' she said, feeling her heartbeat quickening.

'Absolutely sure.' He paused. 'I had a choice. I could stay with Max, or follow Gilly. Whether I'd get a scoop depended on my decision. I followed Gilly. He'd gone to the gents. He was standing with his back to the door, too absorbed in what he was doing to notice someone had come in. He was taking the doll apart. He pulled out the packets. I must have made some sound because he looked up. He was terrified, poor lad, but I told him not to worry, I wasn't telling on him. He ran out.'

'And you ran to Max Quincey.'

'He was still there drinking on his own. I told him what I'd seen. He sobered up pretty quickly when I said I'd expose him if he didn't let me in.'

'You blackmailed him?' Steve said in mock surprise. 'The big story was forgotten?'

A gleam came into Kenny's eye. 'I knew the worth of the stuff in Max's doll, mate. But I wasn't greedy. I played it so it was a win-win. Quincey caved in readily enough. There's plenty to go around, he said in that posh voice of his.'

Steve looked thoughtful. 'He cut you in? Just like that? Wasn't he angry?'

'He seemed more resigned than anything else. If he'd not been drinking, he might have turned ugly. As I got to know him, I discovered his nasty streak when he was sober.'

'So how, specifically, did you work it?' said Von.

'Max would ring me when the dust came in, we'd take possession, then we'd divvy it into smaller packets.'

'And what was the Irish boys' role? They'd offer the dust to their clients?'

'Their clients, people in the street, anyone who'd buy. They were all Max's boys. The other distributors had their own.'

'And who were these other distributors?'

'No idea. There was this gentleman's agreement not to find out about each other. Better for security.'

She ran a hand through her hair. It had been too much to hope that Kenny could give her names. 'And how long did this happy state of affairs go on?' she said.

'Till Max got careless. He rang me when there was someone with him. This guy overheard everything, including my name. I heard him mumble something to Max. Well, Max and I had an almighty row. I told him he had to sort himself out. I made it a rule he shouldn't store my contact details anywhere.' He sneered. 'Max was hopeless at remembering numbers, but he managed to memorise my address. When he needed to ring, he got my landline from Directory Enquiries and phoned from a public place. As you know, my landline goes direct to my mobile.'

Clever. And it explains the imprint of Kenny's number on Max's Guardian.

'What about this guy who overheard?' she said. 'Who was he?'

'His name was Jonathan Moudry. Turned out he was another distributor. The three of us shared Max's boys. One of us would go to the Duke, sit with them, and pass the packets along in the dolls in exchange for dolls full of cash – the money was passed up the chain the same way. Jonathan was particularly good at it, blended right in. Profits rose sharply,' he added cynically. 'I went along with it, but I was none too happy.'

'Why not, if the money was good?' said Steve.

'Jonathan knew my name, and who I was.'

'So who was he, this Jonathan?' said Von.

He rubbed his chin. 'A good friend of Max's. He was an ordinary boy. I say boy, but he was in his early twenties.'

'Not a rent boy, then?' said Steve.

'Too old, mate. From something Max said, I thought he was trying to break into acting. Maybe that's why he latched onto Max.'

'Were they having sex?'

'If they were, it was just for the sex. They didn't behave like a couple.'

'What did he look like?' Von said impatiently. 'Long hair? Short hair? Come on, Kenny.'

'Short hair, couldn't tell the colour. There was nothing special about him.'

'So what happened when the boys were murdered?' Steve

said after a pause. 'That must have put a serious dent in your coffer.'

He shook his head slowly. 'You have no idea, mate. Max went to pieces before my eyes, first his boys being killed, then him under suspicion. He couldn't believe it was all disintegrating. Kept moaning about where he was going to get more boys. He needn't have worried, we soon found them.'

Max had been the prime suspect in the Jack in the Box murders. But this information of Kenny's was the final nail in the coffin of Harrower's theory. Max wouldn't have killed Gilly and the others: he needed them, without them he'd have no outlet for the smack.

'And when Max went on the road with the Quincey Players?' Von said.

'I did everything. He came up to town now and again, and did his bit. And got his cash. But, of course, the dolls had gone, so we had to be more careful. We'd hoped the play would go on forever like The Mousetrap and we could continue using the dolls. Such a pity it didn't.'

'We examined Max's finances, Kenny. He was heavily in debt. How come? Drug dealers are never that poor.'

He refused to meet her eyes. 'When Max wasn't in London, I didn't always split the cash down the middle.'

'So, no honour even among thieves?' When he didn't reply, she said, 'Tell me how you did the packaging.'

'Max had rented cheap office space. We weighed and divvied the dust there. There were scales, a press for sealing plastic bags, everything.'

'We didn't find a key amongst his effects.'

'The office has a keycode entry system.'

Steve was looking thoughtfully at her. 'Why didn't Forensics find any traces of smack on Max's clothes, boss?'

'I can answer that,' said Kenny. 'We wore jumpsuits. The

office has plumbing, and Max had a shower rigged up. We washed before putting our clothes back on.'

Steve pushed the pad across. 'I'll need the address, and the keycode.'

Von watched him write. 'What are you thinking, Kenny? Are you wondering whether distributing is worse than blackmail? Let me put you out of your misery. It is.'

He said nothing, just pushed the pad back.

'This Jonathan Moudry,' said Steve. 'What happened to him?'

'He left at about the time the play ended. As far as I know, he never surfaced again.'

'Was he from London?'

'There was a bit of the Geordie in there. That's all I can tell you.'

Von pushed her hands through her hair. 'Right, Kenny, wind to when the Quincey Players returned to London this month.'

'Max got in touch before he arrived. Told me the play was coming back and there'd be dolls again. We agreed to use them as before.'

'Tell me what happened on September 12th, the day Max was murdered.'

He hesitated. 'Max rang me first thing in the morning. Said a big shipment was coming in from the Cutter.'

She stared at him. Something wasn't right. Tubby had told her the Cutter was Max himself. 'Let me get this straight, Kenny, are you saying that Max didn't do the cutting?'

'Max? Cut?' he said, caustically. 'Where did you get that idea, love? Max wouldn't have a clue. You need to mix the precise concentration of quinine, otherwise the stuff's worthless. No, the Cutter was someone else.'

'You're absolutely sure Max wasn't mixing quinine in the rented office, perhaps when you weren't there?' Steve said, frowning.

Kenny looked at him with contempt. 'You think I'd get a detail like that wrong, bright boy? Give me some credit.'

So Tubby had been misinformed. Max wasn't the Cutter. Von pressed her fingers into her eyes. Was the whole operation at the Duke so shrouded in mystery that no-one knew who the Cutter was? Or had that piece of misinformation been deliberately supplied to throw Tubby off the scent? She lowered her hands. 'What else did Max say about the Cutter?'

'Just that they would be meeting at Max's digs.'

Max's digs... Her heart was beating so hard, she thought it would burst out of her chest. 'Later the same day? The twelfth?'

'He wasn't specific about the time but, yes, it was to be that afternoon.'

'Does that mean he didn't know? Or he just didn't tell you?'

'Max would know, love. The Cutter was always precise about the time of a meeting. And he never failed to turn up at the prearranged time. Never.'

She tried to keep the excitement from her face. The day Max had been killed, the Cutter had come to visit. This Cutter was the vicious thug that Dickie had said threatened Harrower's family, and almost certainly killed Tubby when he got too close. Could he also have killed Max?

'Wasn't it risky meeting at Mrs Deacon's?' Steve was saying.

'It was risky meeting the Cutter anywhere, mate. But when Max met him in his room, it was always Tuesday, after lunch. The place is dead then. Max told me that, after the landlady finishes her morning cleaning, she's out shopping. Comes home only briefly, to drop her bags. Then it's out for a meal with the girls, and off to bingo.' He smiled. 'He said she's regular as clockwork.'

I left at about five and didn't get back till eleven. Of course Max would know Mrs Deacon's routine. It meant he could meet the Cutter with impunity.

'How much stuff would the Cutter be bringing?' Von said.

'When he has dust to offload, it's a large amount. We have to have the dosh ready.'

'You must have had meetings with the Cutter too, when the Quincey Players were touring. Who was he, Kenny?' she said softly.

'I didn't know his name. He wanted to be called the Cutter, said we should address him as that. We never met for long. He handed over the package, counted the money, and left. We rarely talked.'

'Where did you meet?'

'Somewhere out of the way. Always a different place in a different part of London. And never during the day. He'd ring me. I had no way of contacting him.'

'Describe him,' she said, folding her arms.

'Like I said, it was dark, so I never got a good look at him. He wore a hood.'

'For heaven's sake, you must have seen something.'

'Tall, held himself erect. Might have been a military man once. I met plenty like him in the army.'

'Voice?'

'Well-spoken. Home counties accent.'

'Anything else? Come on, Kenny. Mannerisms?'

He ran a hand over his mouth. 'I was late once. When I arrived, he was smoking. Didn't smell like cigarettes.'

'Dope?' said Steve

'I'd recognise that. It was richer, like a top-grade tobacco.'

Her breath caught in her throat. *Cigarillos. Hoyo de Monterrey*. If the Cutter had visited Max that fateful Tuesday, they must have smoked cigarillos together. It would explain the large quantity of ash. 'Did you ever see his hair, Kenny? He can't have worn a hood every time.'

'He did. Either that, or headgear that covered his hair, like a ski hat.'

'No loose strands?'

He shook his head. 'And it was always at night.'

Just their bloody luck. Whoever the Cutter was, he was careful. They were dealing with a pro. A pro with blond hair.

'And where were you for the rest of that Tuesday?' she said.

'Max never rang me. And I never saw him again.'

'That's not what I asked.'

'I was with someone.' He looked at the table. 'I was with Georgie.'

She was conscious that Steve was staring at her. She kept her eyes on Kenny. 'All day?'

'And all night,' he added quietly.

'She'll provide your alibi, will she? When I put her on the stand?'

His mouth tightened. 'You're not dragging her into this, Von.'

'I have no choice. She'll have to testify.'

'You can't do that,' he said in a strangled voice.

'I can and I will.'

He threw her a look of loathing. 'This is so like you, love. Your fucking principles over everything else.'

'That's rich coming from you.' She spat out the words. 'A drug dealer.'

They glowered, like children daring one another to strike the first blow.

'So what did you do when Max didn't phone?' Steve said quickly.

He dragged his eyes from Von. 'I wasn't particularly worried. I assumed there'd been a hold-up and he'd get in touch eventually.' He paused. 'When Von told me he was dead, my first thought was that the Cutter had killed him. Max might have uncovered his identity and threatened him. Or double-crossed him over the money. I panicked. I thought I might be next. It was Max who'd introduced us, and it crossed my mind that the Cutter might be wanting to tie up loose ends. The following day, I went to Georgie's.'

'Your big tip-off,' Von said, remembering they'd had sex that night. 'And all the time, you were with Georgie. That's where you've been hiding.' Her voice was full of sarcasm. 'Behind a woman's skirts.'

He smiled his crooked smile, where a corner of his mouth lifted. 'I didn't always stop at hers. Sometimes we came here.'

'And what was your reaction when you learnt how Max had died?' said Steve. 'The mutilation, I mean.'

'I couldn't understand why he did it like that. I was convinced the guy was ex-army. They know how to do them properly.'

'I'll bet,' said Von. *Like he did Tubby.*

'I reckoned he wanted you to think it was the same guy who did the Jack in the Boxes. You'd be too busy chasing your tail to catch the real killer. Anyway, I went to Max's memorial. It was stupid – you saw me – but I thought he'd be there and I'd recognise the voice. If I could pinpoint him, it might give me some leverage.'

'Were you thinking of turning him in?' she said, astonished.

He avoided her eyes. 'I thought I'd let him know there was a letter to be opened in the event of my death. That sort of thing.'

She smiled thinly. 'You've been watching too much television, Kenny.'

'It was a waste of time, he wasn't there.' He played with the food packets, turning them over. 'There's something I have to tell you, Von. It was when I discovered you were getting close to the Duke. It was just a matter of time before you found out about me.' He looked at her pleadingly. 'I decided to put the frighteners on you. I went to the theatre and bought a doll.'

Opening night at the Garrimont. The man in the dark jacket. She closed her eyes. *Jesus, not you, Kenny, not you.*

'I was the one who left the doll outside your flat,' he said, his voice quivering.

He tried to take her hand, but she snatched it away.

'I did that stuff to it to warn you off. You know, with the knots and the blood. I should have known that you—'

'You bastard.' She sprang to her feet. 'You fucking piece of shit.'

She balled her hand into a fist and swung her arm. Kenny jerked his head back, but not quickly enough. Blood gushed from his nose. She took a step forward, bringing her fist back to strike again, but Steve threw his arms round her and pulled her away. She struggled briefly. He must have sensed her resignation because he released her. She collapsed into the chair with a low moan, and clamped her hands over her face.

Kenny was on his feet, blood dripping onto his shirt, but he made no attempt to staunch the flow. 'I deserved that,' he said, almost with satisfaction.

Steve shook a handkerchief from his pocket and threw it at him. 'Use this before you bleed to death.'

Kenny pressed the handkerchief to his nose. 'You always did have a great right hook, love.'

'Don't you dare make a joke out of it,' she said, through clenched teeth. A great sadness came over her suddenly, settling like a cloak. 'Why Kenny? Why did you do it? Is money so important?'

He lowered the handkerchief, letting the blood trickle over his mouth. 'You think I was doing it for myself. That's how it was to begin with, for sure.' His voice softened. 'Shall I tell you about Georgie? You deserve to know. Her mother had her when she was only sixteen. Abandoned her, left her parents to bring her up while she went and got on with her own life. But

Georgie grew into a beautiful, wonderful, woman. If you saw her now, Von, you'd understand how I fell in love. The money I stashed away over the last fifteen years went to her. All of it. I didn't keep a single penny.' He wiped the blood away, smearing his chin. 'I didn't mean for any of it to happen. I only wanted to help her. I tried hard not to love her.'

'Oh, Kenny,' Von said, tears spilling down her cheeks. She buried her head in her arms.

Steve moved away and gazed through the window, as though everything he ever wanted to know was out there. He traced a pattern on the pane, listening to the anguished sobs.

A moment later they heard the creak of the kitchen door.

Steve spun round.

'He's doing a runner!' Von yelled, jumping to her feet. 'Grab him, Steve!'

Steve bolted into the living room and hurled himself at Kenny. Kenny, easily the stronger of the two, landed a punch on his face that floored him.

Von dropped to her knees and took his face in her hands.

'For God's sake, never mind me,' he gasped. 'Go after him. Quickly. He's getting away.'

She heard the front door open and slam. She ran into the corridor and flung the door wide. On the steps, she looked frantically first in one direction, then the other.

But she was too late. Kenny had vanished.

Chapter 29

'We'll find him,' Steve said. 'He can't have gone far, we got it out quickly.'

Von looked up from her desk. 'Perhaps.' But she was less convinced.

The call had been put out for Kenny's arrest. Zoë had been dispatched with a group of officers to seal off the ports and airports. The detectives back from the scene of Tubby's murder had been sent to investigate the rented office, and the rest of the team had gone to search Kenny's flat. The Chief Super was still nursing his mother.

'Come on, Steve,' Von said weakly, 'buy a girl a drink.'

The corners of his eyes creased. 'You're sure this is a good time to start on the voddie?'

'Oh yes, this is an excellent time to start on the voddie.'

The Drunken Duck was empty. They were too late for lunch, but the barman, eying their bruises knowingly, made them cheese salad sandwiches.

'You up to talking about this?' Steve said, watching her picking out the salad onions.

'Look, I'm not weeping into a bucket over Kenny. What rankles most is that I've been a twenty-four-carat idiot. I usually am, where men are concerned,' she added bitterly.

'Boss—'

'Let's get on with the case, Steve.' She removed a piece of cheese and chewed slowly. 'If what Kenny said was true, Tubby was given wrong information about the Cutter. It wasn't Max Quincey.'

'Aye. And I take it we're ruling Kenny out as Max's killer.'

'Where's the motive?'

He smiled. 'Find the motive, and you find the murderer.'

'If Kenny killed Max for whatever reason, he wouldn't have mutilated him.' She offered Steve her sandwich. 'You want the rest? I'm not hungry.'

'So what do you think happened on the day Max died?' he said, taking half of the sandwich in one bite. 'We know the Cutter was meeting him in his room. We don't know the time, only that it was late afternoon,' he added with his mouth full.

'The landlady was out from 5.00pm. I'm betting the Cutter came shortly after, otherwise he'd risk running into her. And he strikes me as someone who doesn't take unnecessary chances.'

He set down the remains of the sandwich. 'You're giving me the look. What am I missing?'

'Think about it, Steve. One thing we didn't find in Max's room was a large package of heroin. The Cutter would have brought it, ready to be divvied.'

'Okay, so he must have come early enough for Max to leave his digs and get the heroin to his rented office. If the Cutter *did* kill Max, he must have returned some time that evening.'

'Here's the million-dollar question: why would the Cutter return to kill him? If that was his intention, he would have done it when he came earlier. The place was deserted after all.' She tapped the table. 'But the clincher is that he wouldn't have brought Max the package, whatever time he arrived. Why give heroin to a man you're about to kill?'

He looked blank.

'Regardless of the time he came,' she said patiently, 'the presence or absence of a package in Max's rented office will give us a clue as to the Cutter's objective.'

'Got it, boss. If there's no package, he intended to kill him.'

'If there's no package, he *may* have intended to kill him. But if there *is* a package, he definitely didn't. We should know soon enough, although if our guys don't get to that office before Kenny, then we're Donald Ducked.'

He wiped the crumbs from his mouth. 'If this package *is* in the office, we should find the Cutter's dabs all over it.'

'He'd have been careful to wear gloves. Remember the only prints we found in Max's room were on the taps. He was careless there.'

'What about Kenny's theory that the Cutter mutilated Max because he wanted us to think he was the Jack in the Box murderer?'

'Doesn't wash. That way of killing led us to the boys, and from them to the Duke and the drugs. Why would he lead us there?' She played with the salad onions, arranging them in a pattern. 'That mutilation is difficult to explain, whatever theory you formulate.'

He rubbed the back of his neck. 'I take it the Cutter's now our prime suspect.'

'Pity we don't have much of a description.'

'Other than an army man.'

She snorted. 'Kenny says that about everyone who stands up straight. One thing's for sure, though. We can definitely rule Max out as the Cutter. Kenny knew Max.'

'The Cutter seemed to have had a much more easy-going relationship with Max. He met Kenny at night, hooded, but he was willing to meet Max during the day at his lodgings. Suggests he knew him from before. That would tie in with him being Michael Gillanders.'

'Do you really see Gillanders masterminding all this, Steve? Okay, he had a good financial brain, but this sort of scam where huge numbers of people are involved doesn't strike me as his thing.'

'Gillanders smoked Hoyo de Monterrey.'

'But it wasn't Gillanders's hair we found in the room.'

'He could still have been there. He could have killed Max almost any time that Tuesday.'

'So whose hair was it?' she said in exasperation. 'If we could only put that one to bed.'

'Have you considered it might be this Jonathan Moudry's?'

'Kenny said he left London in '85.'

'Maybe he returned and resumed his relationship with Max. And Max kept quiet about it to Kenny.' A smile crept onto his lips. 'Maybe Moudry was the visitor Mrs Deacon was always hearing on the stairs.'

'Ah yes, Max, the *bon viveur*.' She scooped the onions into a pile. 'Perhaps they were having wild sex every day.'

'The kind where you tie each other up?' he said, raising an eyebrow. 'Moudry had short hair, according to Kenny, but he may have long blond hair now. Those unidentified prints on the taps might be his.'

She was silent for a while. 'You may be onto something. If we can't find Kenny, Moudry may be our best link to the identity of the Cutter. Moudry may have taken deliveries from him too. Okay, he only met him at night, but he might remember the voice. We have to find him first, though.'

'Geordie accent, boss. He'll be in his late thirties now. Not a rent boy, from what Kenny said. Strange we've only heard about Moudry now. And how come it's only Kenny who remembers him? Someone must have seen him with Max.'

'Dickie said Max hung around with loads of people. And Kenny did say there was nothing special about Moudry's appearance.' She reached for her bag. 'Moudry isn't a common name. Let's get back to the nick and run a background check. He may have some priors.'

He studied his glass. 'What if we find him, and it's his hair and dabs in Max's room, and he has a rock-solid alibi for the time Max was killed? We'll be right back where we started.'

'Moudry might still be able to give us the identity of the Cutter. Think positive, Steve.' Her lips twitched.

'What?'

'That's quite a shiner you're getting.'

He motioned to her cheek. 'Snap.'

Her expression softened. 'People are going to take us for an old married couple.'

'You cannot be serious!' Von's eyes were blazing. 'What do you mean? There's no office!'

Larry was looking uncomfortable. Amongst the junior staff, this behaviour was known as 'Ma'am's McEnroe Mode'.

'The address Kenny Downley gave us doesn't exist, ma'am. At least, not as rented premises.'

'So what was it?' said Steve.

'An old people's home, sir. We've got the dogs in there sniffing, just in case, but it's looking increasingly likely we'll find nothing.'

'Give me strength,' Von said under her breath.

'At least the old folks aren't complaining,' Larry said, trying a grin. 'They say they haven't had so much fun since matron's knicker elastic went.'

She turned away to hide her frustration. Kenny had outsmarted them. He must have known the minute he walked into that kitchen that he'd be doing a runner. He'd just been waiting for the right moment. It explained why he was so willing to talk. By now he'd have been to the office, taken the stash and disappeared. Finding the heroin might have provided them with a solid lead and, God knows, they needed one. She slammed her hand against the wall.

'Another thing, ma'am.' Larry lowered his voice. 'The drugs squad have been in touch. I think they've got wind that we're now investigating a ring.'

'How the hell did they find that out?' she said slowly.

'Not from us. We've been careful.'

'So what did you say to them?'

His eyes were steady. 'That this was still a murder investigation and if they thought otherwise they should get in touch with the Chief Super.'

'Initiative, Larry.' She nodded, smiling. 'Good work. And have you heard from the Chief Super?'

'No-one's been able to get hold of him, ma'am. His mother's phone goes straight to voicemail.'

Things could be worse. At least she could get on without having Richard Quincey breathing down her neck. But she'd expected him to ring in. He'd made it clear he intended to keep his finger on her pulse.

Larry handed her a file. 'The autopsy report on Michael Gillanders.'

'Anything surprising?'

He shook his head. 'The blood on the iron is his, ma'am, and the only prints are Rose Manning's.' He hesitated. 'Sir Bernard is autopsying Tubby tomorrow. He wondered if you and DI English would be there.'

She turned away, the tears welling. This was one autopsy she wouldn't be attending.

'And he apologised that the forensics on Max Quincey aren't through yet.'

She blinked back the tears. 'What forensics?'

'Something about chemical tests on the hair?'

'Pity he can't wave a magic wand and tell us whose it is.'

He was fidgeting. 'There's another thing, ma'am. We need Downley's prints so we can check them against those on the taps.' He looked at a point beyond her shoulder. 'We'd take something from his flat but we're not sure whose prints we'll find.'

They were all tiptoeing around her. By now, the whole nick knew, not only about Kenny's drug-dealing, but about Georgie. 'I'll bring something I know only he's touched,' she said. 'And tomorrow, let's see if we can find this Jonathan Moudry. He's the only lead we have left. For now, though, we'll call it a day.'

Steve hung back, busying himself tidying a desk that didn't need tidying.

'Not got a home to go to?' she said quietly.

He was looking everywhere but at her face. 'I'm thinking you shouldn't stay in your flat alone till we've caught Kenny. He may be dangerous.'

'He's hardly going to attack me.'

'You don't know that. It turned ugly back there.'

'Yes, I hit him, I seem to remember.'

'I meant—'

'I know what you meant, Steve.' She waited till he'd stopped what he was doing and looked at her. 'If anyone tries to force the front door, I'll climb out of the bedroom window.' She smiled brightly. 'The advantages of a ground-floor flat.'

He said nothing.

'You may think I don't know Kenny, but he wouldn't hurt me. Of that, I'm sure.'

'Let me stay with you, Von.'

'You can't.'

'Why not?' he said, a trace of anger in his voice.

It was a long time before she spoke. 'Because we both know what might happen.' She picked up her coat and walked past him to the door.

Von lay on the sofa, sipping wine, listening to 'Shine On You

Crazy Diamond'. Whenever she felt low, Pink Floyd was guaranteed to raise her spirits. God, she was tired. It was the worst kind of tiredness. Not the tiredness of physical exercise, or even of a satisfying day's work; it was like the lethargy after a long debilitating illness. They were still no nearer to finding Max's killer, or the killer of the rent boys. It was as though she'd stepped into quicksand: the more she struggled to make sense of things, the faster she sank to nowhere.

They were fooling themselves if they thought they'd ever find the Cutter. Or Kenny. Especially Kenny. He knew how to hide. He had a string of contacts from here to eternity. And many lived abroad. She'd got his details out to the ports and airports promptly, but that meant nothing. There were a dozen ways he could slip overseas without being detected. Would he be taking Georgie with him? Without a doubt. She was having his baby, wasn't she? His words still had the power to slice through her. *I tried hard not to love her.* Not hard enough, though, did you, Kenny?

She poured the last of the wine, and raised her glass. *Here's to you, Kenny and Georgie, wherever you are.* She wondered what Georgie would think if she knew that the designer clothes she stood up in had been bought with the proceeds of the heroin trade. Would Kenny have told her how he made all that money? Course not. *I didn't mean it to happen. I only wanted to help her.* The bastard. Tears stabbed at her eyes. If it took forever, she'd find him.

She rubbed her face hard. She was in danger of losing sight of the case. That was what mattered now; Kenny could wait. She considered the few options left to her. She could call the drugs squad and have them haul in everyone at the Duke. Tempting, but where would that get them? It would alert the Cutter and he'd melt into the darkness. Perhaps not, though. The Cutter had unfinished business. He'd marked her cards for certain; under torture, Tubby would have given up her name. If the Cutter had killed a copper's snout, he wouldn't stop at killing a copper. A part of her wanted him to bring it on, so she could look into his eyes.

There was something she'd forgotten, something she'd meant to do, but the bottle of Shiraz had waylaid her. Kenny's dabs. She dragged herself to the kitchen. The empty beer bottles were lined up beside the fridge, waiting to be taken to the bottle bank. She snapped on her latex gloves and lifted the one Kenny had used last.

She fished inside her handbag for the plastic bags which were, of course, at the bottom. It was a law of nature that everything she ever needed from that bag worked its way to the bottom. In a fit of impatience, she shook the contents onto the floor. The plastic bags fell out last. She wrapped the bottle carefully, pressing the plastic seal, and then placed it inside a carrier bag. She knelt to gather the rest of the items.

Something had fallen under the chair. She turned it over slowly and stared at it for a full minute. The slow poison of recognition seeped into her consciousness, followed immediately by the rush of comprehension.

She slumped onto the chair, and swallowed rapidly, trying not to be sick.

It was richer, like a top-grade tobacco. Hoyo de Monterrey. He was smoking it when he delivered the package to Kenny. And he'd been there at the restaurant, although Danni hadn't been able to tell which of them had the cigarillos. *They were both smoking.*

She'd discussed the case with him over a drink. She'd made no mention of the Duke, but he'd brought the subject up himself. *Tom gave no hint to me of drug dealing at the Duke.*

Worst of all, something for which she would never forgive herself, she'd led him to Tubby. *I've sent my snout in.* Tubby, whom he knew. *I thought he'd gone to ground in Torremolinos. I've been on the lookout for him.*

Her stomach felt tied in knots. She and her team had been careful to keep quiet about the heroin, so how had the drugs squad discovered she was investigating the Duke? He'd tipped them off. It was the only explanation. And with his contacts he could sidetrack or even close down her investigation, as he'd done when Harrower was the senior investigating.

She examined her reflection in the kitchen window as though seeing it for the first time. *He was tall, held himself erect. Well-spoken. Home counties accent.*

And he knew Max Quincey. Knew him well enough to visit him in his room, and sit smoking Hoyo de Monterrey. Knew him so well that he just had to wait for Max to lower his guard before he struck him on the head, stripped him naked, and strangled him.

Her head cleared. She knew what she had to do. This, after all, was why she'd become a copper. She stared at the plastic bag in her hand. Inside was the means by which she would bring Simon Hensbury down: his fingerprints were on the toothbrush.

Chapter 30

Von held up the bottle. 'A recent beer bottle, handled only by Kenny Downley. And possibly the factory that manufactured it. These come shrink-wrapped in packets of six.'

'Will your prints be on it, ma'am?' said Larry.

'Shouldn't be, but you've got my dabs, in case. You'll get a good set. When Kenny drinks, he holds a bottle not by the neck but further down, with all five fingers.' She was conscious Steve was watching her. 'So was there anything in Kenny's flat that might tell us where he is, Larry?'

He shook his head. 'No indication he was planning to go anywhere. Passport was in a drawer. It was the things he'd keep on his person – credit cards, mobile phone – which were missing.'

'No plane tickets, travel brochures?'

'And no letters of any sort.'

Who wrote letters these days? Kenny was like her, he used his mobile phone for everything. His contacts' details, and possibly the address of the rented office, would be on the phone card. He'd have destroyed it by now and bought a new one. He was way ahead of them.

'You pally with the fingerprint expert?' she said, smiling wearily at Larry. 'Can you get those prints done as a priority?'

'We knock a football around together occasionally.' He grinned. 'Anyway, Gerry owes me a favour, he stole my girlfriend.'

The young detective who was managing the scene of Tubby's murder was hovering at her elbow. 'We've been back to the street and done the usual but I'm not confident we'll uncover anything, ma'am.'

She drew herself up. 'Blood spatter?'

'No, and no pooling under the body. He was killed elsewhere.'

It was the worst-case scenario. The useful evidence would be at the site of Tubby's murder. 'Footprints? Tyre tracks?' she said, going through the list automatically.

'The area round the body looked too clean. I suspect the place has been swept.'

She gave him a knowing look. 'We're dealing with an expert.'

'The spectacles are missing. We searched everywhere, even in the bin bags. They might still be at the murder site.' He handed her an envelope. 'The photographs, ma'am,' he added gently.

They'd been taken at the crime scene later that same evening. In the strong light, the bruises on Tubby's face were washed to a sickly grey, the swollen eyelids flattened, the fiery hair bleached to a pale ginger. She felt the knot in her heart tighten. She'd wanted him to come to the station. For the first time, the thought struck her that he may not have been safe, even there. She felt a sudden rush of fear. Was she safe? Were any of them safe?

Steve was watching her. 'Whoever did this didn't make it difficult for us to find him, boss. They could have sunk the body out at sea. Would have been months or years before it turned up.'

'You think it was meant as a warning?'

His eyes were steady. 'Don't you?'

She said nothing. She pinned a photograph to the wall. 'Gather round, folks, and have a good look,' she said, raising her voice. 'This was taken at the mortuary under a different illumination. I've seen this type of bruising before. Tubby was beaten by someone wearing boxing gloves. But look here.' She ran a finger over the cheekbone. 'There are marks on the skin that haven't been made by a glove. They look like cuts.'

'The marks are only on the victim's right cheek,' Steve said. 'His assailant would have been standing in front of him, so it suggests he was left-handed.'

'Good point. Okay, I'll be at my desk. Can someone call me as soon as we know what the score is with Kenny's dabs?'

Steve followed her into the office and closed the door.

'Any problems last night, boss?'

She smiled. 'I didn't have to clamber out of the window in my pink and frillies.'

'But something's on your mind,' he said, after a pause.

Yes, there was something on her mind, but she was putting off telling him, waiting to see whether Kenny's prints matched those on Max's taps. Steve was expecting an answer. She didn't like lying but she had to say something. 'I'm worried about the backlash when the drugs squad discover we knew about the ring and didn't call them in.'

'The Chief Super will protect you.'

'Will he?'

He hesitated. 'Getting into people's bad books has never bothered you before.'

'This time I'll be in for more than just a ticking off. I'll be back to pulling people in for speeding and breaking up brawls on a Friday night.' She played with her pen. 'You know, Steve, the last time I saw the Chief Super, he threatened me. It's the first time I've seen him behave like that. He's always in complete control of himself.'

'The stress of his brother's death must be getting to him.' He ran a hand over his neck. 'It's not too late to tell him about the drug ring. You could contact him at his mother's house.' When she didn't reply, he added, 'Policing is one game where it's better to ask permission beforehand than forgiveness afterwards. Don't you think you should cover your back?'

She looked into his eyes. 'If I do, then I'll never find who killed the Irish boys.'

'You're like a dog with a bone when it comes to these rent boys. Anyone else would have given up by now.'

'Why should their lives be any less valuable than Max's? Anyway, the cases are linked,' she said in a tone intended to close the subject.

He leant across and took her hands, running his thumbs over them lightly. 'You don't think maybe your heart's ruling your head, boss? It's Max Quincey's murder we're here to solve.'

Before she could reply, the door opened. She pulled her hands away, but not before Larry had seen.

'Ma'am, Gerry's asking us to come into the IT room.'

'Kenny's prints?'

'He won't say.'

In the IT room, they crowded around the large workstation.

Gerry McNally, Clerkenwell's fingerprint expert, was peering at the monitor. 'These are Downley's prints, taken from the beer bottle.' He moved the mouse deftly. 'And here are the ones recovered from the victim's bathroom taps.'

They didn't need Gerry to point it out. The two sets couldn't have been more different.

'We've drawn a blank, Chief Inspector.'

They were waiting for her to speak.

'Gerry, could you give us a minute, please?' Her heart was thumping wildly. 'And can you clear the room, Steve? I want just the team.'

Gerry was used to being dismissed, and left without a word. Steve, who'd been studying the screen, turned and stared at her. She returned the stare without flinching. He walked to the corner and said something to the two men at the desk. With a shrug, they rose and left the room.

There was a tremor in her hands as she reached into her handbag and retrieved the plastic bag with the toothbrush. 'There are prints on this that may match those on the taps. How quickly can we get them lifted and onto the screen?'

'Are these Downley's?' said Larry. 'If so, we don't need them. The ones on the bottle are...' His voice tailed off as he saw her expression.

Steve's eyes were glued to the toothbrush. She felt her stomach churn. *He can see the hotel's name on the handle.*

His voice was cold. 'Whose prints are they, boss?'

'A man's.' She hesitated. 'A copper's.'

The silence in the room was absolute.

'How long will it take, Larry?' she said.

'Half an hour, ma'am. An hour, tops.'

'Get it done. I'll wait here.'

Steve was the last to go. 'I'll give them a hand,' he mumbled, getting to his feet.

She was about to call him back, but the door had shut behind him.

She closed her eyes. She knew what they'd be thinking. The number of circumstances in which a man's prints could get onto a hotel toothbrush were strictly limited. They would jump to the obvious conclusion. The correct conclusion. They would also wonder why ma'am had waited until now to present this piece of evidence, evidence which she'd been holding on to for nearly a week.

And Steve. What must he think? She'd kept quiet about finding Kenny's phone number on Max's Guardian. He'd baled her out then, smoothed it over, not asked awkward questions. She'd explained, he'd understood – Kenny was her partner and she'd stand by him. But this situation, this fling with Simon

Hensbury, wasn't something she could explain away. She'd cocked it up. Cocked it up royal.

She went into the corridor. Someone had put an 'Out of Order' sign on the coffee machine.

A young constable ambled past. 'There's another machine on the next floor up, ma'am. Last time I looked, it was still working.'

'Thanks,' she said, 'but what I need is something stronger.'

An hour later, they were back in the IT room. Gerry was absent.

'Show me what you've got,' said Von, her eyes on the screen.

With a few clicks of the mouse, Larry pulled up a number of images. 'Whoever used the toothbrush was left-handed. He made three near-perfect prints. Here they are, underneath the bathroom tap prints.' He hit a couple of keys. 'This software automates the rotation of each print, and changes the magnification accordingly. Then it superimposes the images. I'll do the thumb first.' A minute later, he said, 'And here are the index and middle fingers.'

Even before the images had stopped moving, she had her answer. She sat back, breathing with difficulty.

Steve's voice broke the silence. 'So, boss, can you tell us who these prints belong to?'

'Chief Superintendent Simon Hensbury.' Her voice sounded like someone else's. 'He was my old governor. Retired from Clerkenwell three years ago. I met him by chance last Friday. We spent the night together and in the morning he used this toothbrush.' She was conscious of their stares, but the time for embarrassment was past. 'I don't need to tell you the significance of this. These prints put Hensbury in Max Quincey's room on the day he died. That room was cleaned in the morning, so Hensbury must have visited Max in the afternoon or early evening. And the prints aren't the only piece of evidence.' Briefly, she went through the rest: the cigarillos, Kenny's description, Simon's mention of the Iron Duke, and that she'd told him Tubby was sniffing around there. 'I think Hensbury was the one who tipped off the drugs squad,' she said.

After an awkward pause, Larry said, 'Couldn't the Chief Super have told him about our investigations at the Duke, ma'am?'

'The Chief Super doesn't know. I've been keeping it from him till I was sure of the evidence.' She registered the shock on their faces. 'Dickie Womack told me DCI Harrower was warned off his investigations. I think the person who threatened him was Hensbury. He was Harrower's boss at the time.'

'I hate to say it, but this is all circumstantial,' said Larry. He locked his fingers together. 'It's not evidence that will hold up in court.'

'Which is why we need to find evidence that will. And we have to move quickly. Hensbury doesn't yet know we're on to him – Tubby told me Max was the Cutter, and that's what he would have given up under the beating – but it's only a matter of time.'

'You think Hensbury is that heavily involved?' Steve said, anxiety in his voice.

'I think Hensbury's the Cutter. He killed both Max Quincey and Tubby. Those are his prints in the bathroom, and he's left-handed, which is consistent with the marks on Tubby's cheek. He killed Max for reasons unknown, although I can think of any number of scenarios, but Tubby was killed because he got too close.' She dropped her voice. 'Hensbury is dangerous. He may not think twice about killing a copper. Any copper. Not just me.' She saw their disbelief turn to alarm.

'So how do we get him?' Steve said.

'No point examining his finances, he'll have covered his tracks. He's been doing this for years.' She pushed her hands through her hair. 'We need someone to identify him. That means getting hold of a distributor, they're the only people the Cutter deals with. Kenny might have been able to recognise the voice, but we've still to find him. Max, of course, isn't alive to testify. That leaves Jonathan Moudry. He's now top of our list of most-wanted.'

'There's also Mr Big,' a detective said. 'He knows the Cutter.' A look of longing came into his eyes. 'If we could only get him, that would be a scoop for this nick.'

'Nah, there's no Mr Big,' Larry said. 'Never has been. This Cutter and Mr Big are one and the same.' He fingered the mouse mat. 'Look, think about it. Everyone tells you there's a Mr Big, but no-one knows his name. No-one's seen him, heard his voice, knows anything about him. This Cutter has invented him to put the fear of God into everyone. What better ogre than one you've never seen? No wonder an almighty hush descends on the place when the coppers come around lifting stones. He's a shadow. And they're terrified of it.'

Steve rubbed the back of his neck. 'If it's true, the Cutter's kept the myth going for twenty years.' He stared at the monitor. 'What if we can't find anyone to finger Hensbury?'

'There's one other thing we could try.' She hesitated. 'I have his phone number.'

He dragged his eyes to hers. 'No point wearing a wire, boss, if you're going to be taking your clothes off.'

She looked away, unable to bear his unspoken accusation. 'We'll bug the hotel room,' she said.

'You're sure he'll come?'

She thought back to the Saturday morning, and Simon's parting words: *I hope I'll see you again.* 'He'll come,' she said.

'Let's do it, then.' He scraped the chair back, and left the room.

She watched him go. How quickly things could change.

If she'd suggested this yesterday, he'd have told her it was too dangerous.

It was lunchtime of the same day, and Von and Steve were in her office. He was sitting so he didn't have to look at her.

'I've left Hensbury a message asking him to call me,' she said, picking at her sandwich.

'Is he even in the country?'

'Let's assume he is. Tonight is too soon but tomorrow, Saturday, is a possible. We can get the place bugged today.'

'We'll need adjacent rooms,' he said quietly.

'Can I leave you to organise that?'

He nodded stiffly.

'And I'm cancelling all leave. We're getting too close.'

He said nothing. Nor did he look surprised.

The phone rang.

'Is that DCI Valenti?' came the voice at the other end.

'Miranda, what can I do for you?'

'Sir Bernard has finished the autopsy, Chief Inspector. He's wondering if you'd like to hear what he's found. Is now a good time?'

'Please tell Sir Bernard we're on our way.'

Steve eased the Toyota out of the station car park and turned into Farringdon Road.

The sky was clear except for a bank of cloud on the horizon. The wind had dropped and the mingled smells of petrol fumes and rotting leaves stank out the air. It was the end of September, but already people were wearing scarves and heavy coats.

'You're very quiet,' said Von.

'Got a lot to think about, boss.'

'You might slow down. You nearly hit that pedestrian.'

'Perhaps ma'am would prefer to drive,' he said smoothly.

'For God's sake, Steve, stop this now,' she muttered. 'We've got a murder case to solve.'

She stared at his profile but he wouldn't so much as glance at her. They continued in silence until they reached Lambeth Road.

Miranda ushered them into the office.

Sir Bernard was leafing through his papers. 'Good afternoon, Chief Inspector.' He inclined his head at Steve. 'Inspector English.' His eyes widened. 'Good heavens, you both look as though you've been in the wars.'

'We have,' Von said.

He didn't press them, just nodded slowly. He steered them to the coffee table.

'I'll get straight to the point,' he said, opening a file. 'The victim received a large number of blows to the head, resulting in severe damage to the optic nerves and traumatic brain injury.'

'How traumatic?' said Steve.

'Enough to cause massive intracranial haemorrhaging. One of the blows was fatal.'

'So he didn't die by strangulation?' she said.

'I suspect whoever was beating him simply went too far, found they couldn't revive him, and decided to make sure he was dead by strangling him.'

'Can you tell what he was beaten with?'

'His face was a mass of contusions. The condition of the skin and the nature of the bruising leads me to conclude that the attacker wore boxing gloves. Broken bones in his face might have suggested a knuckleduster but, apart from a smashed nose, there were none.' He peered over his spectacles. 'There are two further types of injury I need to draw your attention to. We found tiny pieces of glass embedded in one eye, consistent with spectacles shattering under a blow.'

Bile surged into her mouth, and she swallowed repeatedly.

'And there are cuts in the right cheek.' Sir Bernard removed a photograph from the file. 'They weren't made by someone wearing gloves. Nor were they made with a sharp implement, like a knife.'

'What then?' she said.

'Under magnification, they are more tears than cuts. The bruising is greater than that caused by a simple incision.' He frowned. 'It's difficult to say what could have done it. Something slightly pointed, perhaps, but definitely blunt.'

'Scissors?'

'Possibly.'

She glanced at Steve. 'Strange choice of implement, specially if you're extracting information.'

'Maybe it's all he had to hand, boss.'

'If you find the implement that did it, Chief Inspector, there'll be blood and tissue there, which I'm sure will further your investigation. There's one other thing I should tell you. Your friend hadn't long to live. The stomach cancer was well advanced.' He stopped, seeing her expression. 'Ah, you had no idea. I'm sorry,' he added more gently. 'His clothes were loose, suggesting his body weight was dropping.'

'Would he have known?' said Steve, after a glance at her face.

'There were scars on his body consistent with surgery.' Sir Bernard hesitated. 'I see this has come as a bit of a shock, Chief Inspector.'

'How long did he have?' she said, her voice shaking.

'Three months. Six at the outside.'

She was struggling to keep back the tears. 'Can you give us the time of death, Sir Bernard?'

He buried his face in his papers. 'The textbook answer is between 9.00pm and 10.00pm but, as he was found promptly, I can say with some certainty that it was nearer 10.00pm.'

'Had he been beaten over a long period of time?'

'From the nature of the contusions, I would say he sustained his injuries over several hours.'

If he'd been beaten that long, it wouldn't be because he'd withheld information: Tubby would have given it up after the first blow. Whoever did this did it because he wanted to. He wanted her to see what he was capable of. Steve was right, it was a warning. They were taunting her. *He* was taunting her. Simon. The killer…

'On another topic, Chief Inspector, we now have the toxicological results on the powder you sent us.'

Her mind was still on Tubby. 'Powder?' she said faintly.

'The packets in Max Quincey's doll, boss.'

'It was high grade heroin, mixed with quinine. Whoever did the mixing knew what he was doing. He added quinine so the proportion of heroin was just sufficient to give the user a high.' He smiled bleakly. 'A professional. You may be looking for someone with a biochemical background.'

Or a copper who's worked in the drugs squad. 'And the fingerprints?' she said.

'We found several on the packets and the paper they were wrapped in. They were Max Quincey's.'

She held her breath. 'Any others?'

'None that we could distinguish. His were the prevalent ones, deposited the most recently.'

She was aware of what was going through Sir Bernard's mind. He knew Max Quincey was the Chief Super's brother and that, at some stage, she was going to have to tell him that Max had been a drug dealer.

'I don't envy you, Chief Inspector,' he said quietly, watching her.

She looked him full in the face, intending him to read her expression. When the time came, she would have no hesitation in revealing to the Chief Super, and to the world, what sort of a man Max Quincey had been.

'Thank you, Sir Bernard,' she said, getting to her feet.

He stopped her at the door. 'One moment, Chief Inspector, I've just remembered.' He opened a drawer. 'It came in today. That blond hair from Max Quincey's room, there was something unusual about it. It's why it's taken us this long.'

Her heart was racing. 'Have you managed to extract DNA after all?'

'Not with the follicle missing. But the DNA is now immaterial. It wouldn't belong to whoever deposited that hair. You see, it's precisely because it's blond, that we nearly missed it. The hair is Asian.' He glanced down the page. 'Asian hair that's been dyed blond, and treated with the chemicals you use to make hair into high quality wigs.'

She stared at him. *A wig.* No wonder they hadn't found a match with Gillanders. Or Chrissie. Whoever had visited Max Quincey had worn a blond wig. 'If we found this wig, Sir Bernard, would you be able to say whether there's a match with the sample from Max's room?'

'Most certainly. The hair was dyed and chemically treated to create a glossy look. Everyone's hair responds differently to treatment, so the sample is unique.'

'Could it have been a toupee, instead of a wig?' Steve said.

'It could, although the hair was on the long side for a toupee. But some men may want to wear their hair long.'

Of course, it made sense. Simon had worn a blond hairpiece. Although it would have been quiet at Mrs Deacon's, he'd have disguised himself in case the street's landladies moved their lace curtains for a better look.

Sir Bernard was frowning. 'I'm sorry we couldn't send those results to you sooner, Chief Inspector. I hope it's not hampered your investigations.'

She knew he prided himself on getting information to the

police promptly. A delay such as this might have caused him sleepless nights. She smiled warmly. 'It's not hampered our investigations at all, Sir Bernard. Thank you. We'll let ourselves out.'

As they drove through London, Von said, 'What did you make of that?'

'The autopsy results?'

'Everything.'

'The wig or toupee is the most significant thing. From what I remember of Hensbury, his hair is dark, going grey. And short. A long blond wig would disguise him perfectly.'

'But?' she said, sensing doubt in his voice.

'It's circumstantial. As is his left-handedness.'

'We're back to getting an ID, then. We need to find Kenny and this Jonathan Moudry.'

They were nearing the police station. She gazed out of the window at the lunchtime traffic. Would she see Kenny again? Probably not. What surprised her was how much pain the thought gave her.

Chapter 31

'A wig?'

'Or a toupee, Larry.'

'It explains why we got no match with the lot at the Garrimont, ma'am. But who would wear a blond wig?'

'My bet's on Simon Hensbury.' She chewed her thumb. 'So has Zoë phoned in yet?'

'She's double-checked the airports and ferry ports.'

'The Tunnel?'

He nodded slowly. 'Nothing. And Downley hasn't used his credit card recently.'

She turned away in frustration. They'd moved as quickly as they could, but Kenny had always had the advantage.

'We've been trawling through the PNC,' he said. 'There's no Jonathan Moudry with any priors. We tried all spelling variations of the name.'

She rubbed her eyes. 'Public records, then?'

'There's only one Jonathan Moudry. He was born in Newcastle in 1965.'

'The age is right,' she said thoughtfully. 'Do we know where he is now?'

'Vanished, ma'am. We've checked missing persons but he hasn't turned up there, either.'

'His parents still living in Newcastle?'

He consulted his notes. 'Split up. Father left to work abroad. Mother, Janet Moudry, moved to London five years ago. We tracked her through her national insurance number, she's been drawing her pension.' He looked up. 'We've got the address.'

'Good work. We could visit Mrs Moudry now but let's call it a day. You look as bushed as I feel.'

'Just heard from the techs, boss,' said Steve, coming in. He looked intently at Larry's computer, even though it was showing the screensaver. 'Everything'll be ready by midday tomorrow. All we need now is for Hensbury to get in touch.'

And he will. She picked up her coat. *He will.*

The instant Von turned the key in the lock, she knew something was wrong.

She lowered her bag silently to the floor, and looked round the hall, trying to remember how she'd left it. The long drawer in the table was partly open, but it was always like that, the wood was warped. The coats on the pegs were in the same order. Nothing had been disturbed. Yet she knew someone had been in her flat. And perhaps still was.

Her heart hammered in her chest. Was it her imagination, or could she hear the gentle rise and fall of someone's breathing?

She slid off her shoes and padded softly into the living room. It was empty. She glanced through the adjoining door into the kitchen, ready to make a run for it. It, too, was deserted. Back in the hall, she pushed open the door to the spare room. It was as she'd left it weeks ago. Her crime novels were stacked on the futon bed and in tottering piles on the floor. The French language books were on the table. She and Kenny had talked about buying a property in Brittany and spending weekends there. She'd persuaded him to join her in language classes. He'd dropped out, but she'd persevered, and even done the assignments.

She went slowly back into the hall. Her mobile rang, making her jump.

She pulled it from her bag. 'Von Valenti.'

'Simon here,' came the smooth voice. 'I got your message.' A pause. 'I'd love to meet up, Von. Are you free now, by any chance?'

She glanced at her watch. The techs were still wiring the room. 'I'm afraid not, sir. I'm about to visit someone.'

'Ah, I'm flying to Spain tomorrow night.' A longer pause. 'You couldn't rearrange?'

'Let me call you back in five minutes.'

'Of course.'

She stood with the phone in her hand. Then she sank to the floor and put her head on her knees.

Five minutes later, she called him. 'I was unable to rearrange, sir, but I've taken the liberty of reserving a room for tomorrow afternoon. I thought, perhaps, we could have a late lunch, talk over the case, that sort of thing...' She let her voice tail off.

A gentle laugh. 'Same hotel?'

'Same hotel.'

'Perfect. My flight isn't till eight. That gives us plenty of time, don't you think?'

'Plenty of time.'

'I'll be there at two.'

'The room's in my name, sir.'

A soft chuckle. 'You know, you really will have to start calling me Simon.'

'Yes, sir.' She replaced the phone in her bag.

She was putting her shoes back on when she heard the sound. It came from the bedroom. Only then did she notice that the door was closed. She felt a tingling in her blood. That door was never closed, one of the hinges was working loose. Had Kenny returned? But why? Why had he gone into her bedroom and closed the door? What didn't he want her to see?

Her stomach cramped with fear. The sound again,

distinguishable now as a low moan. In silent terror she gripped the handle. Putting her weight against the door, she forced it open. 'Kenny,' she shouted, her voice breaking on the word.

The room was empty. And exactly as she'd left it, the bed unmade, her nightclothes scattered over the floor, the laddered tights crumpled into a ball.

Yet not exactly as she'd left it. The window was open. The sound had been the bamboo chimes, swaying in the breeze. But she'd shut the window before she left. Always did. It meant that he'd been here. He must have let himself in, heard her arrive, and slipped into the bedroom.

And listened to her conversation with Simon Hensbury.

He would know now that she intended to sleep with him. And had slept with him before.

With every sense numbed, she fell onto the bed and buried her face in the pillow. 'Oh Kenny,' she sobbed, 'I'm sorry. I'm so, so sorry.'

Too late – always too late – she recognised the depth of her feelings for him.

The technicians were giving the bugs a final check.

Von studied the layout of the room. Was it the one they'd used last week? All the rooms looked the same. All hotel rooms everywhere looked the same. She was conscious she was visibly nervous, and that it was affecting the others. She hadn't smoked for years but, God, she wished she had a cigarette.

'Let me go through it again,' she said. 'Under the food trolley, inside the phone in case he uses it, and under the lamps.'

'And behind the headboard,' said Steve. He was deliberately looking at Larry.

'It won't get that far.' She ran her hands down the sides of her jeans. 'What time is it?'

'One forty. We'd better make ourselves scarce.' He jerked his head in the direction of the bed. 'Remember, we're behind that wall.'

She tried not to look at him. When it was clear he wasn't leaving, she lifted her eyes to his. 'Steve—'

'If it looks as though you're getting nowhere, Von, don't take any risks. Pull him in. We can continue questioning him at the nick.' With a final glance around, he left, shutting the door quietly behind him.

She stood at the bathroom mirror, smoothing down her hair. She ran her hands lightly over her skin. Although she'd applied concealer, the bruise was still visible, and there were dark circles under her eyes. He might comment, she thought cynically, but once his face was buried in her breasts he'd soon forget what she looked like.

There was a firm knock at the door. *This is it. Time to rock and roll.* Blood pounded in her ears and, for a second, she felt faint.

'Simon,' she said, as he entered the room. 'Excellent timing. Lunch has just arrived.'

He smiled, his eyes moving over her face. 'Business first, is that it?'

'I thought it might be wiser.' She turned away.

'Not so quickly, Von.' He caught her by the arm. 'We've plenty of time. Let me look at you.'

The expression in his eyes softened, and she felt the familiar rush of warmth between her legs. But this was the man who'd killed Tubby. She had to keep that in mind at all times.

'Shall we eat, sir?' she said lightly.

A look of bafflement crossed his face. Careful. She'd need to be on her guard, or he'd become suspicious.

She slid her arms round his waist and kissed his neck. Praying the bugs wouldn't pick it up, she whispered into his ear, 'I'm really no good on an empty stomach.'

He extricated himself, laughing, and threw his coat over a chair. 'And we don't want that, now, do we?' He opened the bottle of champagne. 'So how is the investigation going? Have you got a prime suspect?'

'We did, but he was murdered.'

'And who was he?' he said, in a bored voice.

'Michael Gillanders. One of the cast at the Garrimont.' She piled chicken salad onto a plate. 'He stood to gain on Max Quincey's death.'

'Max had money? You do surprise me.'

'The Quincey Players is worth a small fortune.' She paused. 'But I've discounted Gillanders. I don't think Max was murdered for money. The investigation's stalled, which is why I wanted this chat.'

He forked smoked trout into his mouth. 'Fire away.'

'I've been back to the Duke.'

'And what did you uncover?'

'A hornets' nest,' she said softly.

His head jerked up.

'The more I delved into the goings-on at the Duke,' she said, 'the more suspicious I became. I discovered that DCI Harrower didn't ignore the drug-related evidence because he'd followed a false trail before. He was warned off. His daughter was threatened. She was expecting a baby.' She sipped at her champagne. 'I thought you should know, sir, as his governor.'

His face betrayed no emotion. 'Tom told me nothing of this.' He set down his plate and walked to the window. 'So how long has this been going on?' He glanced briefly at her. 'The drugs at the Duke.'

'At least twenty years.'

He returned to top up their glasses.

She watched him pour. *God, he's good. His hand isn't even shaking.*

'You're sure of your intelligence?' he said.

'It came from my snout.' She was watching him closely. 'He's never wrong.'

'Did Tubby say how he came by this information?'

She hesitated. If this was a question Simon had asked Tubby while beating his brains out, then he'd know that Tubby had told her. It would be fatal to lie.

'He got it from someone at the Duke. A man called Malkie. And there's another regular whose name we don't know.'

'Have you pulled them in?' he said warily.

'We've been unable to find them. I've come to a stop, sir. A full stop.'

'And how can I help?' he said, smiling suddenly.

'I wondered if you could tell me what you discussed with DCI Harrower.'

'It's all in the case file, Von. You know that.'

'Come on, sir, we both know that detectives discuss things that don't go into the file.' She tried to control her nervousness. 'Did DCI Harrower tell you he'd been warned off, for example?'

'If he had, then I would have taken the threat seriously and torn the place apart. That's a strange question, especially as I told you before that Tom said nothing to me about drug dealing.'

His memory's better than mine. I'll have to tread more carefully. 'I'd forgotten, sir,' she said, trying to look foolish.

'It's of no consequence. Tom and I discussed nothing that didn't go into the file, he really was a by-the-book man.' He turned the glass in his hand. 'How extensive is the drug dealing? I take it these boys who were murdered were in on it?'

'Not just the boys.'

'Who else?' he said, not looking at her.

This was the point of no return. She didn't hesitate. 'Max Quincey.'

His head shot up. 'Max?'

She was having difficulty holding his piercing gaze. 'He packaged the stuff and gave it to the boys to sell to their clients.'

'You have evidence for this statement?' he said coldly.

'We found packets of heroin in the base of his doll.'

For the first time, she saw his resolve waver. It was no more than a shadow across his eyes, but it gave her the confidence to proceed. 'Why do you find it so hard to believe, sir?'

'I've known Max for many years, and he's simply not capable of it.'

'How many years have you known him?'

He didn't reply, using the time to bring the mask back down. She could almost hear his thought processes. He'd know she had no tangible evidence to link him to Max. He'd tell her their friendship was the innocent consequence of his friendship with the Chief Super. She was never going to break him here, she might as well pull him in. But something made her go on.

'You knew Max well, didn't you, Simon?'

He raised an eyebrow. 'Are you interrogating me, Chief Inspector?'

'It's a simple question. Would you mind answering it?'

His eyes held hers. 'Richard introduced us years ago. I can't remember when exactly.'

'Fifteen years ago? Twenty?'

'I said I can't remember exactly.' He fumbled in his pocket. 'Do you mind if I smoke?'

'Not at all. Hoyo de Monterrey, is it?'

He stiffened, his hand still in his jacket.

'The same brand that Max smoked,' she said quietly.

He relaxed visibly and pulled out the pack. 'What of it? We all smoke Hoyo, even his brother.'

She saw it then, as he lifted the cigarillo to his lips. She couldn't tear her eyes from it, the evidence that, in another age, would have hanged him.

'You've gone pale, Von.' His voice was steady. 'Are you unwell?'

She dragged her gaze back to his. 'Simon Hensbury, I am arresting you for—'

He leapt to his feet, pushing the food trolley aside with such force that it toppled over. For an instant she thought he was going to hit her. She made to step back but he gripped her by the neck and pulled down the zip of her shirt. 'Are you wearing a wire?' he hissed, tearing the shirt open.

Both hands were on her throat now. She clawed frantically, but his fingers were like iron.

Lights were popping in her head when she heard the door burst open, followed by the drumming of running feet.

Steve and Larry seized Hensbury and began to prise his hands away. He released his hold on her neck, and rammed his elbow into Steve's throat. Turning quickly, he lashed out at Larry. But he'd made an error of judgement. Larry, young and agile, ducked smartly, simultaneously landing Hensbury a blow in the solar plexus that made his legs buckle.

'I wouldn't try that again, sir,' Larry said. He forced Hensbury's hands behind his back. 'It could seriously damage your health.'

Steve helped her to her feet. Her throat was on fire and she was having difficulty standing. Larry held Hensbury's arms as Steve snapped on the handcuffs.

Hensbury stared at her, his mouth working. 'You're finished, Von.'

'You first, sir,' she croaked.

Larry began to lead him away.

'Wait.' She motioned to her bag.

Steve brought it over. Seeing how unsteady she was, he opened it and held it out. She rummaged inside and brought out latex gloves and a plastic bag. With shaking hands, she pulled on the gloves. 'Turn him round,' she said hoarsely.

Steve and Larry exchanged glances. Larry pushed Hensbury so he was facing the door.

She knelt and eased the signet ring from his left hand, then dropped it into the bag and sealed it. 'Get this to Sir Bernard,' she said, thrusting it at Larry. 'I don't care how you do it, but have him start on it immediately.'

'What should he be looking for, ma'am?'

'He needs to cross-match with Tubby's DNA. That ring will contain traces of his blood and tissue.'

She motioned to him to turn Hensbury back round. 'And that will be enough to bring you down, you bastard.' She steadied herself and delivered a vicious kick to his groin. He dropped to the floor, and lay writhing and moaning softly.

'Get him out of my sight,' she spat.

Larry hauled Hensbury to his feet and dragged him from the room.

Steve took her arm. 'You need to get to a hospital and have yourself checked out.' He indicated her throat. 'You can hardly talk.'

'No time. Who knows how quickly we'll get the forensics back?' She massaged her neck. 'We may get Simon for Tubby's murder, but he'll deny killing Max or running the drugs ring. We need to break him, and we need to do it within the next twenty-four hours. Or let him go.' Steve seemed to be having difficulty keeping his eyes on her face. 'What's the matter?' she said. 'Do I look frightful?'

'Not at all, boss,' he said quietly. He lifted his gaze to hers.

Then she had it. With as much dignity as she could muster, she wrapped her shirt over her breasts and pulled the zip up over her plum-coloured satin-lace bra.

Chapter 32

Simon Hensbury threw his head back and blew smoke up to the ceiling. 'And that's the best you've got?'

They were in the main interview room. Von and Steve were sitting facing Hensbury. His solicitor, a rangy man who was balding prematurely, was sprawled in the chair next to him, a bored expression on his face.

Von had finished outlining the case against Hensbury. She'd put every fact before him save one: sleeving her aces was something she'd learnt, not from her old governor, but from her brothers. 'You're absolutely sure you never visited Max Quincey at Mrs Deacon's?' she said.

Hensbury looked as though he'd been waiting for the question. He lifted the cigarillo to his lips. 'I'd never even heard of the place, Chief Inspector, until Max Quincey's death was reported in the papers.'

She pushed the plastic bag towards him. 'Recognise this?' she said softly.

He glanced at it, and his expression changed.

'You left a perfect set of prints on the taps in Max Quincey's bathroom, Simon. They place you in his room on the day he died.'

He stared at the toothbrush. 'Impossible.'

'The jury won't think so.' She crossed her arms. 'Why did you kill Max? Did he get greedy? Did he threaten to expose you?'

He puffed at the cigarillo. 'Circumstantial evidence. You know it, and I know it. Even if I admit I visited him there, those prints could have been deposited at any time.'

'Max's room was cleaned the morning of the day he died. The landlady will testify to polishing the taps.' She brought her face close to his. 'You went to see him, Simon, and you wore a wig because you didn't want to be identified.'

'A *wig*?'

She waited till he'd stopped laughing. 'You left hairs from that wig in Max's room. We're going to find it, and when we do, you'll be up for double murder. You'll be in prison for a long, long time.'

He glared at her, hatred in his eyes.

'How many distributors were there, Simon? Max was one, but there were others.'

He drew on the cigarillo, his eyes half closed.

'Kenny Downley was another.' She paused just long enough to get his interest. 'And then there's Jonathan Moudry.'

For an instant, he froze. The mask came down quickly, but not before she'd seen the alarm in his eyes. It told her what she wanted to know, that Jonathan Moudry could identify him.

He stubbed out the cigarillo, smiling faintly. 'I've never heard of him.'

'Tell us how it works, Simon. Start at the beginning. Where do you source the heroin?'

'This is preposterous,' snapped the solicitor. 'My client has dealt with your questions. I see no point in your asking them again.' He picked up his briefcase. 'Either charge my client, Chief Inspector, or release him.'

'I have till tomorrow afternoon before I need to make that decision.'

'Very well. We'll meet then. This interview is over.' He got to his feet. 'Good afternoon.' With a nod at Hensbury, he left the room.

'Where did you get the heroin, Simon?' she said, her eyes on his.

'You can switch that machine off, Von. I'm saying nothing without my solicitor present.' He looked at her breasts. 'So are you going to accompany me to my cell and tuck me in?'

Von watched Simon leave with the constable.

'Doesn't look as though we're going to break him, Steve. Without the forensics, we'll be playing "Simon Says" all evening. Let's pray we get an answer from Sir Bernard before tomorrow afternoon.'

Steve scratched the back of his neck. 'There's an outside chance he's innocent of Max's murder. He was pally with both him and the Chief Super. He might have visited Max purely socially.'

'Not Simon. He'd have met him in a wine bar, or a hotel.' She frowned. 'But did you see his reaction when I mentioned Jonathan Moudry?'

'Aye, that got a rise. The only thing that did, in fact. I'm betting Jonathan saw him in daylight.'

'In daylight, and undisguised. Maybe Moudry walked in on them. Simon would have removed the wig in Max's room. If Moudry can identify him as the Cutter, we've got him.'

'Time's not on our side.'

She leant against the wall and closed her eyes. 'We've *got* to find him. We're so close, Steve. Can't you feel it?'

He was looking at her steadily. 'Aye, boss.'

'Come on,' she said wearily. 'Time to visit Jonathan's mother.'

They were leaving the police station when Larry caught them up.

'Something's arrived from Sir Bernard, ma'am,' he said, out of breath.

'The analysis on Simon's ring?'

'A package, the contents of Max Quincey's doll. You need to sign off on it before it's sent to the storeroom.'

'Leave it on my desk,' she said, disappointed.

An hour later, they were outside Janet Moudry's house.

'You ever been in this part of London, boss?'

'Sedate upper-class Hampstead?' Von said scornfully. 'Sorry, I don't rub shoulders with millionaires.'

'I think this area is more middle-class.' He indicated the front door, painted in royal-blue gloss, its burnished brass knocker in the shape of a bowl of flowers. 'The millionaires must live elsewhere.' He rang the bell.

A minute later, the door was opened by a stick-thin woman in a flowery skirt and hand-knitted jumper. She smiled nervously as she looked from Von to Steve.

'Mrs Moudry?' Von said brightly. 'Mrs Janet Moudry?'

'That's right, I'm Janet Moudry,' came the polite reply. She spoke in a north-east accent, her voice low. Her eyes rested on the bruises on Von's neck.

'We're police officers.' Von held out her warrant card. 'May we come in?'

Most people were anxious when police called, but what Von saw in Janet Moudry's eyes was an expression bordering on pure panic. *She's got something to hide.*

'Very well,' Janet Moudry said in a resigned tone. She stepped back, almost wincing as they brushed past. 'The lounge is to your right.'

The large low-ceilinged room was over-furnished with heavy mahogany pieces, its surfaces polished to a high shine. A lacquered grandfather clock ticked loudly, the sound mingling with the song of blackbirds drifting in through the open windows. Traces of pot pourri lingered in the air. On the floor was a bundle of Fair Isle knitting. The all-pervading atmosphere was that of sadness for something long gone, and it washed over Von like a wave.

The woman motioned to the armchairs. 'Some tea?' she said faintly.

'No, thank you,' said Von.

She smiled then. It was a smile which transformed her face. There was a softness in the wide hazel-coloured eyes which suggested that, in her youth, Janet Moudry had been a great beauty. Von had seen that smile before. She couldn't yet say where.

'Mrs Moudry, we're trying to track down the whereabouts of your son.'

The smile faded. 'I have no son.'

'Are you saying Jonathan's no longer alive?'

'I'm saying I never had a son.'

'This is an address in the Jesmond area of Newcastle.' Von held out the copy of Jonathan Moudry's birth certificate. 'Someone called Janet Moudry, with the same national insurance number as yours, lived at that address and gave birth to a son, Jonathan, on July 3rd 1965.' She paused. 'Are you denying that was you?'

The woman's face crumpled and she slumped back in the chair. 'Yes, that was me.'

'It's vital we find him, Mrs Moudry. Do you know where he is?'

She shook her head.

Von struggled to keep the irritation from her voice. 'When did you last see him?'

'I can't remember, Miss Valenti. That's the truth.'

'A year ago? Ten years ago?'

'Longer than that.'

'And where did you see him?'

'He visited me here.' She closed her eyes. 'He said he was

going away for a long time and wouldn't be in touch regularly, and that I wasn't to worry about him.'

'He can't have visited you here,' Von said annoyed by such an obvious lie. 'You've only lived here five years.'

The woman's eyes flew open. She seemed frozen with terror.

'Yes, Mrs Moudry, we know more about you than you think. Now, I suggest you stop lying to us.'

'I don't know where' – she faltered – 'Jonathan is now.'

It was time to get heavy. Von glanced at Steve.

'Mrs Moudry,' he said softly, 'are you aware that we can arrest you for obstruction?'

The woman bent over her hands, interleaving the fingers, saying nothing. Her hair was pulled back so tightly that its beige-whiteness blended with the colour of her face, making it impossible to tell where hair ended and skin began.

Von studied the bowed head. The threat of being arrested didn't seem to bother Janet Moudry. Whatever secret she was hiding, she was prepared to guard fiercely. If they wanted to get at the truth, they'd have to try a different approach.

'Do you have a recent photo of Jonathan?' she said encouragingly.

The woman seemed to perk up. 'I have ones of him as a child.'

'Could I have a look at them?'

She slid a large box out from beneath the dresser. Kneeling on the floor, she removed the lid. Inside were a jumble of items: photographs, birthday cards, children's books. She pulled out a bundle of photos and searched through them. 'This is Jo when he was twelve,' she said, pride in her voice.

The photo, taken in close-up, was of a slim-framed boy with brown hair and a shy smile. The eyes were like his mother's.

'What a lovely boy,' Von said, smiling. 'Do you have any of him older?'

She delved around in the box, removing most of the items before finding what she was looking for. 'This is him taken on the last day of school. He was sixteen.'

It was the same boy, but the face was thinner, the hair cropped close to the head. Something stirred deep in Von's memory, but refused to surface. 'What was he like?' she said. 'What did he want to be when he grew up?'

'He had his heart set on being an actor, ever since he was small. Always clowning around, putting on funny voices. Had me and his dad in stitches.' Her face became animated. 'When he was older, he took part in school plays, drama was his favourite subject. His dad wanted him to be something big in the city, but that wasn't for Jo.'

'And when he left school?'

'He went to a college in Newcastle and did drama.'

Her eyes didn't leave Janet Moudry's face. 'Did he act when he came to London?'

'He managed to get a few small roles.' She was sorting through the photographs.

'Did you ever see him perform?'

She shook her head, her attention still on her sorting.

'Which shows was he in?' said Steve suddenly. 'Did he send you their reviews?'

She lifted her eyes to his. 'No.'

'Didn't you think that strange?' he said.

'We'd lost touch by then,' she said cagily. She placed the photos in the box and gathered up the other objects.

Von glanced at Steve. He, too, was unable to comprehend the sudden change. It was as though a switch had been thrown: as soon as London was mentioned, Janet Moudry stopped wanting to talk about her son's acting.

Von picked up a children's book. The title took up most of the cover: The Giant Who Sailed to the Moon. 'Was this Jo's?'

she said.

Janet Moudry's eyes widened as she saw the book. She made as if to snatch it from Von but thought better of it. She sat back on her heels.

There's something here she doesn't want me to see. Von glanced at the inscription: To Jo, Happy Birthday from your Aunt Stella. She flicked through the pages, looking for a clue as to what had unsettled Janet Moudry. Then she saw the author's name – Stella Horowitz.

Stella Horowitz. Aunt Stella.

'What is your maiden name, Mrs Moudry?'

When the reply came, it was almost a whisper. 'Horowitz.'

'So Stella Horowitz is your sister?'

She nodded. 'She's a writer of children's books.'

Von's heart was thumping painfully. She skipped to the inside back cover. There was a photo of the author, a pretty woman in her mid-twenties. In other circumstances, she might have missed the resemblance but, now she knew the family connection, it was obvious. Particularly the eyes.

'Do you know a Chrissie Horowitz, Mrs Moudry?'

The voice was choked with fear. 'I've never heard of her.'

'I think you have. She's the manager at the Garrimont theatre.'

'I don't know her,' the woman blurted. She was trembling so violently that she nearly fell forward.

Steve put an arm round her shoulders and helped her into the armchair.

'Who is she?' Von said. 'Who is Chrissie?' She hesitated. 'Jo's sister?'

'I had only one child.'

She glanced at the publication date, then again at the photograph of Stella Horowitz. Stella would be in her late fifties by now. If Jo didn't have a sister, there could be only one explanation: Chrissie must be Stella Horowitz's daughter.

And, therefore, Jonathan Moudry's cousin.

Jonathan and Chrissie. Cousins. The last thing she'd have expected. Her mind was in turmoil. Jonathan was a distributor, so had Chrissie been involved in the drug ring with him? And after he left London, she stayed in the ring, carrying on the business with Max. It would explain the phone calls.

Steve was a step ahead. 'If Chrissie was in on the scam, boss, she'd probably be able to identify Hensbury.'

'And might also know where Jonathan is. Two positive IDs are better than one.'

He was on his feet. 'If we get a move on, we can pick her up at the Garrimont.'

They hadn't noticed that Janet Moudry was talking.

'I always knew things were different with Jo. It was the dressing-up, you see. And the roles he liked to play.' She was staring into space, seemingly oblivious to their presence. 'He didn't mix with the other children at school. I thought it was on account of the acting, his classmates were into football and stuff like that.' She picked up the knitting and began to wind the wool round a finger. 'I caught him one day. He'd been in my bedroom, trying on my clothes.' She stopped suddenly and stared at Von in bewilderment, as though seeking an explanation.

'How old was he then, Mrs Moudry?' Von said softly.

'Eleven.'

'And he was wearing your dress?'

'Not just the dress. He had on stockings and shoes. And he was putting on my lipstick. I asked him if he was taking part in a play. He just laughed and said, yes Ma, I'm in the Christmas panto, playing the part of a woman.'

She kept her eyes on Janet Moudry's. 'Did you see him in the panto?'

'He was Widow Twanky.' She smiled. 'He was good, too. When he did "There's a Hole in my Bucket", he brought the house down.' Her smile died. 'But the clothes he wore as Widow Twanky weren't like my clothes. I had nice clothes then, elegant clothes.'

'And did you see him in your clothes again?'

'He was sixteen. It was his last term at school. I thought he was out of the house – it was a Saturday – so I went into his bedroom to check whether he had anything needing washed. He wasn't good about bringing his stuff down.' She was unravelling the knitting now. 'But he hadn't gone out. He was lying on the bed, wearing my underwear.' She flushed, pressing the points of the needles into her fingers. 'He was wearing my bra and pants. He had his hand inside.'

'Did he realise you were there?' Von said, taking the needles from her gently.

'His eyes were closed. He hadn't heard me come in. I tiptoed out.'

'Did you talk to him about it?'

'Never.' She stared at Von, her eyes burning. 'And I never told his father. He wouldn't have understood. Men don't, do they?'

'What happened after Jo left home?'

'He went to college. He came back for Christmas and his birthday. And for my birthday.' She smiled proudly. 'He always came home for that. But then he moved to London and I hardly saw him.' She gazed wistfully at Von. 'I can tell you have children, Miss Valenti, so you'll know what it's like when they leave home and discover life. You have to let them go. You have to let them find their own path.'

'And what path did Jo find?' Von said, her heart aching for the woman.

'I saw him less and less. He changed, withdrew into himself.

But he must have been doing well at the acting because he was making good money. Used to send some home, to help me out. Walter had left me by then, you see.' Her lips trembled. 'Then, one day, he up and told me he was going to South America. To have it done.' She clawed at her skirt. 'The operation.'

'And have you seen him since he returned?'

'A few times.' She lifted her gaze to Von's. 'You know where he is now, don't you, Miss Valenti?'

'I think I do.' She got to her feet. 'Thank you, Mrs Moudry.'

She paused at the door. 'What colour hair did Jo have? I mean, as a teenager. The early photos show him with brown hair.'

'It was the same shade as his Aunt Stella's, but a bit darker.'

'And after the operation?'

'He went blonde. Told me he goes to the top hairdresser in London now.'

'And has his hair dyed?'

'Not just dyed. He has extensions put in.' Janet Moudry continued to scratch at her skirt. 'I looked glamorous once, with all that big hair.' She raised her eyes defiantly. 'I looked like that once.'

Von and Steve were in the Toyota, heading east. The Saturday traffic was clogging the roads, and they were moving at little more than a crawl. The early evening sun was setting behind the buildings.

'Okay, boss, all I got from that is that Chrissie Horowitz is Jonathan Moudry's cousin. And he's changed his appearance.'

'It's not that Chrissie Horowitz is *related* to Jonathan Moudry. Chrissie Horowitz *is* Jonathan Moudry.'

He turned to stare at her.

'He began as a transvestite,' she said, 'but the operation his mother was referring to was a sex change. He became a woman, and took his mother's maiden name, Horowitz.'

'You're saying that Chrissie Horowitz was once a man?' he breathed.

'It's what her mother's saying.'

'I don't believe it,' he said faintly.

'Why? Because she's so sexy? Think about it, Steve. That husky voice is unusual in a woman. Her sex-change operation was post-puberty, remember. And those slim hips.' She smiled. 'Whatever she paid the surgeons, she got her money's worth.'

'And to think I found her attractive.'

'Well, why not? You're not the first man to fancy a transsexual.'

He seemed anxious to move off the topic. 'Janet Moudry told us Jonathan was making good money, enough to send home.'

'Won't have been from bit-part acting, that's for sure. But we've been wrong about one thing, Steve.'

'Oh? Only one?'

'It might not have been Hensbury who deposited that blond hair in Max's room.'

'How do you make that out? We took a sample of Chrissie's, and Forensics confirmed the hairs weren't hers.'

'But Chrissie wore hair extensions. They can fall out or be pulled out.' She gave her head a small shake. 'We've been so hung up on wigs and toupees, we've lost sight of the fact that good quality hair extensions can also be made from Asian hair. Chrissie is now back in the frame for having visited Max in his room on the day he died.'

'I still don't get it,' he said in exasperation. 'The sample she gave us didn't match what was in the room.'

'That's because she didn't give us a sample from the hair extensions. The hair she gave us was her own. She plucked it from her fringe.'

Chapter 33

The theatre was crowded.

Steve pushed through the foyer. 'Standing room only, boss. We've come at a bad time, the play's about to start.'

Dexter was selling dolls at the table. Von tried to catch his eye but he was preoccupied with the credit-card machine, his head bent in concentration.

'There's the bell,' she said. 'It's only five minutes to curtain up.'

There was a sudden flurry of people buying dolls, then the foyer was empty. Dexter flopped into a chair, and rotated his shoulders.

'Hello, Dexter,' she said.

He sprang to his feet. 'Chief Inspector.' He stared at her bruises. 'Good grief, what happened to your neck?'

'You should see the other guy. Look, Dexter, can you do something for me? We need to find Chrissie.'

'She'll be in the wings. But the play's starting.' He smiled disarmingly. 'If it's something that can wait till the interval, I'd be delighted to offer you a glass of champagne.'

'Tempting, but can you take us to her, please? Now?'

He hesitated for only a second. 'Follow me.'

He led them through the archway and down the stairs. They heard the opening bars of 'Sex Bomb'. As they passed the dressing rooms, Tom Jones grew louder.

Chrissie, in a kingfisher-blue suit, was standing at the side of the stage, her back to them. Jools fidgeted beside her in her pink dressing gown. In the wings opposite, the actress playing the postwoman waited for her entrance.

'Shall I stay, Chief Inspector?' said Dexter.

'We'll need you to show us the way back.'

Jools whispered something to Chrissie, then slipped onto the stage, pink chiffon streaming behind her.

Von stepped forward. 'Hello, Chrissie,' she said, keeping her voice low.

Chrissie jumped, and put her hand over her chest in an exaggerated manner. 'I'm afraid my nerves are bad these days.' She simpered at Steve, her expression turning to one of confusion as he looked away.

'You need to come with us to the station,' said Von.

'That's out of the question. I can't possibly leave, the play's begun.'

'I'll have to insist, Chrissie.' She took a step closer. 'Or should I say, Jonathan.'

The colour drained from Chrissie's face and, for a second, Von thought she might collapse. She nodded to Steve, who gripped her by the arm and led her into the corridor. Dexter was watching the scene, his mouth slack.

'Can you take us back, Dexter?' Von said.

He seemed to remember himself. 'It's this way,' he said, his eyes on Chrissie.

At the front door, they watched Steve bundle Chrissie into the Toyota.

'What has she done, Chief Inspector?'

'I can't answer that.'

He ran his tongue over his lips. 'Who's going to stand in for her? What about the prompting?'

'Sorry to land you with a problem, but I'm sure the cast know the play back to front.' She squeezed his arm. 'This is your big moment, Dexter. Think of the show, and step up to the mark.' She smiled. 'You're having greatness thrust upon you.'

Chrissie was sitting in the interview room, glaring at Von and Steve.

'I don't know what this is about, but you'd better have a good reason for dragging me away in the middle of a show.' She tossed her hair back. 'So you found out I was once Jonathan Moudry. What of it? Changing sex isn't a crime.'

'Drug dealing is, though. As is wasting police time.' Von's voice hardened. 'When Inspector English interviewed you earlier this month, you presented him with nothing but lies.'

'Such as?' Chrissie said defiantly.

'You said you'd known Max Quincey for less than three weeks, you never visited him in his digs, you weren't in London in 1985.' She paused. 'Shall I go on?'

Chrissie played with her nails, not looking up.

'We have a witness who knew you when you were Jonathan Moudry. He's told us you were working with him and Max Quincey in a drug ring operating out of the Iron Duke.'

Her head shot up. 'A witness?' Her voice faltered. 'Who?'

'Kenny Downley. He's made a full confession, naming you as accomplice. And he'll testify to that in a court of law.' *Provided we can find him.*

Chrissie looked away, her shoulders sagging.

'We're going to charge you with drug trafficking. You're doing yourself no favours by not co-operating.' After a pause, she added, 'Do you want to call your solicitor?'

'What for?' Chrissie said harshly. 'A solicitor isn't going to help me, is he?'

'Do you want to tell us about it?'

'You seem to know everything already.'

'We'll talk in a bit about 1985, Miss Horowitz. I want to

know first what happened on September 12th, the day Max Quincey died.'

'There's nothing I can tell you.'

'Why did you visit Max?'

'I didn't.'

'Don't waste my time. The sample we've just taken from your hair extensions places you there.'

Chrissie drew herself up. 'I give you my word that I'm no longer dealing. I swear I've not been back to the Duke.'

'You expect me to believe that?' She motioned to Chrissie's suit. 'There's no way you can buy clothes like that on a theatre manager's salary.' When there was no reply, she added, 'The jury will be shown the phone records. You were in constant communication with Max since the day he arrived. For God's sake, you phoned him a couple of hours before he was killed.' She was struggling to keep the lid on her anger. 'So what happened on the twelfth?'

'Were you and Max meeting someone in his room?' Steve said suddenly.

A sly expression appeared on Chrissie's face. 'You haven't got him, have you?' she murmured. 'The main man.'

'You know who he is?' Von said, trying to keep the excitement from her voice.

She nodded, smiling.

'Could you identify him?'

'What's in it for me?'

'A more lenient sentence, possibly. The court will be made aware of your desire to co-operate.' She watched the play of emotions on Chrissie's face: fear, calculation, cunning. It was self-interest that won the day.

Chrissie ran her hands over her skirt. 'He was known as the Cutter. He brought us the stuff, ready mixed.'

Von tried not to look at Steve. 'You and Max?' she said.

'And Kenny.'

'What was your role? Did you help repackage the stuff into smaller amounts?'

'Only Max and Kenny did that.'

'Where?'

'They never told me.'

Jesus, just her luck. If they didn't find the rented office, the stash would stay there till the lease ran out. It might be months, even years. With no material evidence against Hensbury, they'd have to pray Chrissie could identify him.

'Tell me about the Cutter,' Von said. 'When did you first see him?'

'In Max's room. When the play was running, when I was Jonathan Moudry.'

'You got a good look at him?' she said, feeling the blood pound in her ears.

'He walked in while Max and I were in bed. Seems Max had forgotten the Cutter was arriving that afternoon.'

'Describe his appearance.'

'Tall, dark hair, blue eyes. And very sexy. I was attracted to him. I thought that, as he knew Max, he was gay himself, so I tried it on.' She paused. 'That was a mistake.'

'Was he violent?'

'He told me what he'd do to me if I ever pulled a stunt like that again.' She shuddered. 'It was the look in his eyes. I was careful not to get on his wrong side after that.' She hesitated. 'So, do you want me to work with an artist, or something?'

'Better than that,' Von said softly. 'We want you to pick him out of an identity parade.'

'All you need to do is put a hand on his shoulder,' Von was saying. 'Take your time. If you want to hear anyone's voice, then ask him to speak.'

Chrissie seemed nervous. 'He won't try anything, will he?'

'The sergeant will be with you,' she said, jerking her head at Larry.

Chrissie stared at his ponytail, seemingly unconvinced. After a quick look through the observation window, she pulled herself up and stepped into the room.

They'd managed to muster eight men who had the same height, build, and hair colour as Hensbury. Chrissie walked slowly down the line, scrutinising their faces.

Steve was leaning against the wall, his hands in his trouser pockets. 'You thinking she and Max met Hensbury together on the twelfth, boss? And Hensbury waited for her to leave before killing Max?'

'Or they left together and he returned later. We need her to tie that down.'

'She seems determined to deny she's involved in drugs now.'

'And you know why that is,' she said, her eyes on Chrissie. 'Drug running all those years ago is one thing, but admitting to still being involved puts her back as a suspect in Max's murder.'

Chrissie had stopped in front of Hensbury. They couldn't see her expression because she had her back to them, but they could see his. His look of puzzlement changed to one of interest. His eyes slid down her body.

'He hasn't the foggiest who she is,' said Steve.

'Then he's seen her only as Jonathan.'

Hensbury was speaking to Chrissie. She leant forward, apparently listening. Suddenly, she stepped back and placed a hand on his shoulder.

'Yes!' said Von, punching the air. 'Got you, you fucker.'

Hensbury stared at Chrissie with a look of stupefaction. Larry took her arm, and they returned to the corridor.

'He hasn't changed,' Chrissie said, 'apart from the grey in his hair. His voice is the same.' She peered through the window. 'So who is he?'

'A policeman. One who's well connected.'

Her eyes flew to Von's. 'Will I be safe?'

'We'll put you in the cell furthest from him.'

'There's something else.' She was watching the men leaving through a side door. 'He used to wear a ring. On his pinkie.'

'Can you remember which hand?'

'I'm afraid not. But it was unusual, gold, with a raised motif. A pair of compasses and something else. And a letter G in the centre.'

'He's a Freemason.'

'But even without the ring, it's definitely him.'

'You'll testify to that in court?' Von said, holding her breath.

'Yes. There's no question about it – he's the Cutter.'

'Thank you, Miss Horowitz.' She nodded to the duty policeman, who led her away.

'We've got him, Steve,' she said, elated. 'We'll have his solicitor in first thing tomorrow and charge him.'

'What did Hensbury say to Chrissie?' Steve said, turning to Larry. 'Did you hear?'

Larry grinned. 'You won't believe this, sir, but he told her he'd like to take her to dinner when he gets out tomorrow.'

The following morning, they were back in the interview room with Hensbury and his solicitor. Von was finishing her account of Jonathan Moudry's transformation into Chrissie Horowitz.

'And she'll testify that you provided the distributors with cut heroin, for repackaging and passing on to their sellers. I am charging you with drug trafficking, as well as the murders of Max Quincey and Tubby Wainwright.' Her voice was calm. 'Have you anything to say regarding these charges?'

After a long silence, Hensbury lifted his head. 'I'd like some time alone with my solicitor.'

She spoke into the machine. 'Interview suspended at 9.25am.' She got to her feet. 'You have fifteen minutes.'

She and Steve left the room.

'Let's get a coffee, boss.'

'I need to call The Vulture. If we can get the evidence that Tubby's DNA is on Simon's ring, he may crack.'

'I think he'll crack anyway. You saw his face.'

'He'll admit to drug-running – he knows a positive ID from Chrissie is evidence we can present in court – but he'll deny murder, because the evidence is circumstantial. I want to hit him hard.'

He raised an eyebrow. 'Again?'

'Oh, get thee behind me. I'd give my right arm to slug him.' She pulled out her mobile.

Sir Bernard answered after only two rings. 'Truscott-Hervey,' came the clipped tones.

'It's DCI Valenti,' she said, in surprise. 'I had expected Miranda.'

'I can't ask her to work at the weekend, Chief Inspector, so I've had the phone put through to the lab.'

'We have the owner of the ring here in custody, Sir Bernard.' She steeled herself for bad news. 'Are the results through yet?'

'Preliminary tests are good. The bottom line is that it's highly likely that Tubby Wainwright's blood and tissue are on that ring.'

She closed her eyes. 'How highly likely?'

'The results are entirely consistent with his profile. Enough to persuade a jury.' After a silence he said, 'Chief Inspector? Are you there?'

'Yes,' she breathed.

'We also found traces of heroin on Tubby's coat. It was contaminated with quinine, mixed in the exact proportions we found in the samples taken from Max Quincey's doll.'

'That's less significant. I sent him to the Iron Duke which is where the stuff was traded. He may have picked up traces there.'

'That's true. Well, good luck, Chief Inspector.'

'Thank you, Sir Bernard.'

Steve looked at her enquiringly. 'I take it we've got him?'

'We've got him.' She leant back, resting her head against the wall. 'The stumbling block is still Max. Simon can't deny killing Tubby, but he'll deny killing Max.'

'Then we need to speak to Chrissie again.'

'After I've dealt with Simon. And, when we do see Chrissie, I'd like Danni here.'

He rubbed the back of his neck. 'She's at the family home, shooting grouse, or something bigger.'

'Ring the Hall and see if she's prepared to come down.' She glanced at her watch. 'I'm going back, Simon's time's up.'

Larry caught her as she passed through the incident room. 'Zoë phoned, ma'am. She's left people everywhere, but there's still no sighting of Downley.'

'Get her back, then. She may as well be here for the kill.'

The detectives leapt to their feet. 'May we watch, ma'am?' one of them said eagerly.

'Provided you bring the ice-cream.'

Chapter 34

Hensbury was deep in conversation with his solicitor as Von entered.

'Do you need more time?' she said.

'I don't think so,' the solicitor said quietly.

She switched on the machine. 'Interview resuming at 9.45am on Sunday, 1st October, 2000.'

Hensbury was a changed man. His self-confidence had evaporated. He was sitting upright, but the expression in his eyes gave him away. 'Ask your questions, Von.'

There was no longer any hurry. And she'd need to choose her words carefully if she wanted him to confess to killing Max. 'Tell me about the drug ring at the Iron Duke,' she said. 'Not the outline, I want details. How long has it been running?'

'Nearly thirty years.'

Jesus. Thirty years? And no-one in the drugs squad picked this up? 'Where does the stuff come from?'

'It's sourced from Pakistan, and comes in via Spain. I can give you dates and times.'

'You kept records that long?' she said in amazement.

'Of course not.' He sounded tired. 'I meant I can tell you when and where the next shipments are due, so you can make the appropriate arrests.'

The door opened.

'DI English entering the room at 9.48am,' she said.

Steve took the seat opposite the solicitor.

'So what happens when the heroin comes into Spain, Simon?' she said.

'I mix it with quinine, in my villa. When the stuff's ready, I come into England by boat.'

'How do you get past Customs?'

A look of amusement crossed his face. 'Let's just say I'm well known there.'

'Brown envelopes change hands?'

'As I said, I'll give you all the names.'

'My client is keen to co-operate, Chief Inspector,' the solicitor said.

'And once you're in London, Simon, then what?'

'I contact my distributors. The faces change but, at any one time, there are about twenty. I bring over several kilos a throw,' he said coolly. 'I set up a time to meet, usually at night.'

'So who are these distributors?'

'Many are people I've known in the drugs squad.' A vacant expression came into his eyes. 'I wasn't the only copper for sale.'

The drugs squad. Where Simon had worked for years. She'd done the right thing in keeping them out of the investigation. It struck her that, had she contacted them, she may have lost more than just the case. The thought made her blood run cold.

'The Iron Duke was the main, but not the sole, outlet,' Hensbury was saying. 'There are two other places in Soho.'

'I notice there's no CCTV near the Duke, and hasn't been for years.'

'Nor outside the other two pubs.'

'Your doing?' She took a guess. 'You had them vandalised and made sure they stayed that way?'

The corners of his lips lifted. 'A few more brown envelopes.'

'Where do you hide your money, Simon?'

'In an offshore account in the Seychelles. I set up the operation very carefully. Everything went smoothly for years until those boys were killed.' His expression darkened. 'Tom Harrower began asking questions. It wasn't the first time the Duke had come under suspicion, but I'd always been able to pass it on to one of my, shall we say, more trusted officers who made sure any evidence was well and truly buried.'

'Then why did you allocate the Jack in the Box case to DCI Harrower? You were his boss.'

'Tom went over my head and complained he was being marginalised. I was instructed by my superior to give him the murders. But I kept a careful watch on what he was doing. I have a direct line to each of the pubs, in case things go pear-shaped. Malkie, my informant at the Duke, rang me telling me Tom was asking pertinent questions. I called him there and then and warned him off.'

'By threatening to harm his pregnant daughter.'

A new respect came into his eyes. 'I was impressed you discovered that little detail. Who told you?'

'And did DCI Harrower ever challenge you about your threat?' she said, folding her arms.

'Family is what matters to Tom. Or rather, *was* what mattered.' He looked at a point beyond her shoulder. 'He was a good officer who didn't deserve his reputation as a woodentop. And very popular with the men. He'd just won the inter-departmental swimming competition when he got the case.'

'And yet he drowned in a fishing accident.' When he didn't reply, she added, 'Was it an accident?'

'One of the drugs squad wanted to make sure of him. He even made it look as though Tom's legs had become entangled in weeds.'

'On your orders.' She made it sound like a statement.

'I know you won't believe me, but I never gave that order. Some idiot lost his nerve and took matters into his own hands. Tom's blood is on those hands, not mine.'

'And the Irish boys? Did you have them killed too? Did you ensure it was made to look like the work of a psychopath?'

He stared at her. 'To this day, those murders remain a mystery to me, Von. I have no idea why the boys were killed.'

She looked deep into his eyes, unable to determine whether he was lying.

'I swear to you,' he said, 'I'm innocent of those murders. Why would I have those lads killed? They were my outlet, after all. It makes no sense.'

'Let's park that one for the moment. How did Max Quincey become involved?'

'He was at the Duke picking up a boy, and the boy offered him heroin. Max had the good sense not to use, but he asked him where he got it. He expressed an interest in coming in. There happened to be a vacancy – one of my distributors had just retired – and the boy passed the information along to Malkie. Malkie passed it on to me.' He laughed softly. 'When I discovered it was Max, I was disinclined to take it further, partly because he was Richard's brother – Richard had introduced us some years before – and partly because I wasn't sure how Max would fare. In the end I concluded that, as he went to the Duke for boys, it would be an ideal cover.' He smiled. 'I needn't have worried. He was good. The year the play was running, I could hardly keep up with demand. It was an innovative idea using those dolls.'

'But he became careless.'

'First he let that journalist in on it.' His lips curled. 'And then there was Jonathan Moudry. Downley turned out to be useful over the years, specially when Max was away from London, but I was never sure of Moudry. For one thing, he'd seen me in the flesh. Although he didn't know my name, he could identify me.'

'Why didn't you just have him killed?' said Steve.

'I considered the idea, but when I discovered he'd been

sleeping with Max, I decided against it. I had no idea how Max would respond. Anyway, Moudry was leaving when the play finished.'

'Was Max intending to take Moudry with him?' said Von.

'He had some small bit part in Jack in the Box. He left London and disappeared. I was relieved, I thought I'd seen the last of him.'

'Till today,' she said, smiling. 'So when the play returned last month, where did you meet Max?'

'Where I always met him. In his lodgings.'

'Tell me what happened on September 12th.'

He sighed heavily. 'I don't deny I visited him. It was in the afternoon. Three o'clock.'

'How did you make the appointment? We found nothing in his phone records that linked him to you.'

'You never knew Max. He had a taste for melodrama. With all my other distributors, I'd just ring them.' He shook his head in mock disbelief. 'But Max insisted I contact him by putting an advert in The Guardian. He even devised the codes we used in the small ads section.'

'What was the purpose of the visit?'

'To drop off the next consignment and pick up the cash. I stayed an hour, maybe an hour and a half.'

'To drop off a consignment?' said Steve, surprise in his voice.

'Max and I weren't just business partners, Inspector. We were friends.'

'Did you have sex with him?'

He laughed. 'Oh, I'm heterosexual, Inspector.' His eyes wandered over Von's body. 'Your DCI can testify to that.'

'Was anyone else there?' she said, not responding to the jibe.

'No-one was there when I arrived. And no-one came while I was with Max. And, before you ask, he was very much alive when I left him.'

If he was telling the truth, then Chrissie must have met Max in his room later. But what had she been doing there? Picking up her share of the smack, probably, despite her protestations she was no longer trafficking.

'So where were you for the rest of the day, Simon?'

'I can't remember.'

'At your club? At a show?' she said impatiently. 'Come on.'

'I can't remember.'

'Did you visit your other distributors?'

'I was planning to see them through the week.'

Simon was no fool. If he'd killed Max, he'd have made sure to arrange a robust alibi for himself, perhaps involving some of his lackeys in the drugs squad. Yet he was freely admitting to not having an alibi for the time Max was killed. Either he was telling the truth, or he was playing a game of double-bluff. She decided to humour him.

'When did you learn that Max had been killed?' she said.

'When Richard rang me the following day.'

'What was your reaction?'

'I was sorry Max was dead.'

'Were you?'

A look of disgust crossed his face. 'What kind of a question is that?'

'Let me clarify, then,' she said with exaggerated patience. 'Were you sorry because he was a distributor, and his death left a hole in your business?'

He looked at her with deep dislike. 'I was sorry because he was a friend.'

'Who did you think killed him?'

'I had no idea.' He paused. 'And I still don't.'

'Come on, you're a copper. You must have a theory.'

'Fair point. Very well, I wondered if it was a rival operative, wanting to move in and take over my patch. Eat my porridge, is the appropriate term. Killing Max might have been a signal, a shot across the bows. But when I read the details of the murder, I discounted that theory.' His lips crimped with distaste. 'That thing with the eyes, and the doll. Only a total sicko would do that. And, whatever you might think about them, drug traffickers tend not to fall into that category.'

'They're businessmen, is that it?' she said, with irony.

'When I ran into you in the restaurant, and you told me you'd sent your snout to the Duke, I realised you might succeed where Tom had failed. I considered using the tactics that had worked with him.' He looked at her with interest. 'What would you have done, Von, if I'd threatened *your* pregnant daughter?'

She caught her breath. For an instant the room tilted around her. She balled her hand into a fist, but Steve caught her wrist and pulled her back. Hensbury hadn't moved.

The solicitor threw his client a look of warning. 'Maybe now is a good time for a break,' he said.

She got herself under control. 'We'll continue.' Hensbury was watching her, his eyes steady.

'Was it you who got in touch with the drugs squad, and told them about my investigation?' she said, running a hand through her hair.

'I'd hoped they'd take over, but your sergeant sent them packing. You've trained your bloodhounds well, Von.' He inclined his head. 'But then, you did have a good teacher.'

'Tell me about Tubby.'

'What do you want to know?' he said lazily.

'Why did you have him killed?'

'I didn't.'

'That's right, you didn't. You killed him yourself. We have the proof.'

The interest was back in his voice. 'Proof?'

'His DNA was found on your ring. You've been a good boy

so far, so don't spoil it by lying to us now.'

'I didn't kill him,' he said, after a silence. He conferred in low tones with his solicitor. 'This is what happened,' he said, turning back to her. 'One of my men at the Duke had informed me that Tubby was asking dangerous questions. We needed to know what he'd told you, so I had him picked up.'

'Where did you take him?'

'A lock-up garage.'

Steve pushed a pad toward him. 'The address,' he said.

Hensbury glanced at the solicitor, who nodded silently.

She watched him write, recognising his angular handwriting and remembering how, as a left-hander, he curled his fingers when he used a fountain pen, so as not to smudge the words. 'What did you do in the garage, Simon?' she said softly.

'We interrogated him.'

'For several hours?'

'We had to be sure. Once he began talking, he couldn't stop.' He sneered. 'He caved in like a cheap suit.'

'But you carried on beating him.'

'One of my distributors used to be a boxer,' he said, with seeming indifference. 'His problem is that he doesn't always know when to stop.'

She ran a hand over her eyes. 'What did Tubby tell you?'

'That you knew the details of how the ring operated, but you didn't have the names.'

'You killed him for that?' she said in disgust.

'We got little that was useful out of Tubby, so I decided to make my own investigations. I remembered your habit of taking paperwork home, so I took a look round your flat.' He smiled ambiguously. 'You really should fit bolts on your windows, Von.'

So it hadn't been Kenny. She'd had a lucky escape. What would Simon have done if she'd arrived to find him searching the place? She stared into his eyes. 'You're going down for

Tubby's murder, Simon.'

'I wasn't the one who strangled him.' His tone was indifferent. 'You won't find my prints, or any prints, on the wire.'

'The coroner's report will show that Tubby died from a blow to the head. With his DNA on your ring, and no evidence that anyone else was involved, what conclusion do you think the jury will come to?' She spoke softly. 'Don't think you'll be hightailing it off to Torremolinos. When we meet with the magistrate, I'll be requesting bail denied.'

For the barest instant, a look of fear clouded his eyes. So that was it: he'd intended to jump bail. It didn't surprise her. He knew what happened to coppers in prison.

'And Max?' she said. 'Now that you've got Tubby's death off your chest, don't you want to tell us why you killed Max?'

'Not guilty,' he said emphatically. 'You've no material evidence. And you also know, deep down, that I didn't kill him. Where's the motive? Have you forgotten everything you learnt from me, Von? Find the motive, and you find the murderer.'

Doubt crept into her gut. There was sense in what he said. But she dismissed her suspicions: Hensbury was a proven killer. She could think of any number of reasons for him to murder Max. He could have arrived in time to see Max's rent boy leave the house, then stolen upstairs and—

'There's nothing more I can give you, Von. Just the names.' He picked up the pen. 'You'll be wanting the identity of the main man.'

Her head shot up. 'Mr Big?'

'He's the one who brings the stuff in from Pakistan. I thought I made that clear.' His eyes moved over her face. 'Ah, you thought I ran the whole operation. I'm flattered, but there's someone above me. I'm loath to give him up, but my willingness to co-operate will help my case when it comes to trial.'

She held her breath, reading upside down as he wrote the

name.

'Surprised?'

'Where is he now?' she said, unable to tear her eyes from the page.

'Holed up in my villa. When I told him how close you were, he took off.'

'When did you see him last?'

'Early on Wednesday.'

The day she'd gone to the storeroom to look through Max Quincey's effects.

'I saw you take the stairs to the basement, so I followed you.' He shrugged. 'Idle curiosity. I wanted to see what you were up to.'

The man in the pinstripe. 'And was your curiosity satisfied?' she said.

'I slipped past Terry, but I couldn't find you. I left by the back door. I still have my keys.'

'I didn't see your name in the register.'

'I don't sign the visitors' book. I used to run Clerkenwell.'

After a pause, she said, 'Where's your villa, Simon?'

'I'll give you the address, along with everything else.' He continued to write, filling page after page. Finally, he put down the pen. 'I may have missed the odd name, but you'll find them all in my mobile.'

She spoke into the machine. 'Interview terminated at 11.22am.' She gazed at Simon. 'And to think I once looked up to you.' She pushed her chair back.

His words stopped her at the door. 'You'll never get beyond DCI, Von. The Met won't forgive you for this.'

His expression was hard to read, but she recognised hatred intermingled, possibly, with pity. He smiled, then, a smile that didn't reach his eyes.

'With the greatest respect, sir,' she said, 'no, actually, without

372

any respect at all, I really don't give a fuck.'

Chapter 35

The detectives pressed around her. 'Who is it, ma'am?' said Larry breathlessly. 'Who's Mr Big?'

Before Von could speak, the door to the interview room opened, and the constable appeared with Hensbury and his solicitor.

Hensbury paused. 'The one thing I didn't tell you, Von, is that neither Richard nor Max knew of each other's involvement in the drug ring.'

'I simply can't believe that.'

'Do you really think Richard would have assigned his best detective to his brother's murder case, if he'd known Max was embroiled in the very drugs ring he set up himself?' He shook his head. 'No, Richard controlled the import from Pakistan and nothing else. I was the one who liaised with the distributors. I never told Richard who they were.'

'For security?'

'Partly. But there was another reason. You may find this difficult to believe, but each of them admired the other. Max was always talking respectfully of Richard's career in the Met. And Richard was proud that his brother ran a successful touring company. He helped him set up the Players and kept an eye on it to ensure it was doing well. It was to be Max's pension.'

She thought back to the conversations she'd had about Max with the Chief Super. *In an odd way, I was proud of him. He was, after all, leading exactly the sort of life he'd always wanted, doing what he loved.*

Hensbury's mouth twisted into a faint smile. 'I'd hoped their mutual respect might continue. Unfortunately, Richard's bubble is about to burst.'

And in more ways than one. She nodded to the constable, who led Hensbury away. The solicitor inclined his head respectfully and left.

'The Chief Super?' said Larry, shock on his face. 'Mr Big?'

'Not only that,' she said gravely, 'but half the drugs squad are implicated.' She raised her voice. 'We need to move quickly, everyone. Get the arrest warrants prepared, then find the magistrate. Someone send Forensics over to Hensbury's lock-up garage. And alert the authorities in Spain.'

Zoë looked up as they hurried into the incident room. 'Ma'am, Dr Mittelberg rang to say she'll be here by noon, traffic allowing.'

Larry grinned. 'You've missed the show, Zo.'

'I take it we've made our collar, then?' she said eagerly.

'We've made our collar,' said Von. 'The others'll bring you up to speed. But first, you all need to get typing.' She caught Zoë's eye.

'Nothing, ma'am. If he's sighted, I'll be the first to know.'

She knew they were too late. Kenny had done a bunk. She'd have to alert Interpol. He'd be travelling under an alias, with Georgie. Mr and Mrs. From her office she called his mobile one last time, but was put through to voicemail. She tried her landline, in case he was lying low at her flat, but the number rang out and her answer machine clicked in. She'd have to leave it for now. There were more pressing things that required her attention.

She sat in her office, head in her hands, thinking not of what she'd just done, broken a thirty-year-old drugs ring involving senior officers of the Met, but of Max Quincey. She'd told

Simon she'd be charging him with Max's murder. His words gnawed at her. *You also know, deep down, that I didn't kill him.* Yet, Simon was the only piece left on the board.

Danni would be here soon. She'd take her to lunch, and then they'd interview Chrissie again, they still needed her to confirm she'd been in Max's room. Von rotated her shoulders, feeling the stiffness in her neck. Jesus, but she was tired. Although she'd got Max's killer, she'd failed to find the killer of the rent boys. She'd promised Manny she'd bring his attacker to justice, and she'd failed. She knew the case would continue to eat away at her. And worse was still to come. She'd have to face the press, the Chief Super's superior officer, and God knows who else. *The Met won't forgive you for this.* She'd acted with bravado in front of Simon, as though having right on her side was enough. But that wasn't true. In the space of a few days, her life had turned upside down. She'd lost Kenny and, most likely, would soon lose her job. The simple fact of her having produced the greatest triumph of her career had still to sink in.

The brown package was lying on the desk. She peeled away the tape. It was Max Quincey's doll, sent back by Sir Bernard. It would have to be deposited in stores until Simon's trial. Protocol required a second officer to check it.

In the incident room, she found Zoë staring over Larry's shoulder at the computer. 'Officers from the Met, ma'am,' the girl said, wide-eyed. 'Many of them retired.'

'Pity they weren't brought to justice before they drew their pensions.' She handed her the package. 'Can you double-check everything's here before I sign off?'

Zoë slipped on her gloves. As she placed the Jack in the Box on the desk, it fell over and the doll sprang out with its cry of: 'Jack-jack! Jack-jack!'

Von flinched. 'If I never hear that sound again, it'll be too soon.'

'Twenty packets,' Zoë said, removing the sachets of heroin from the yellow wrapping. 'All present and correct.' She handed Von the sheet to sign. She spread the yellow paper out on the desk. 'This is one of the Garrimont's programmes.'

Von glanced up from writing. 'Jack in the Box?'

'It's the programme from 1985.'

'We were looking for that at one time,' Steve said, tapping at the keyboard. 'Can't remember why, I've reused that area of memory.'

'It was to do with the timings.' Von studied the incident wall. The times of the play's exits and entrances were still there, interleaved with those of the boys' attacks. 'We made the assumption that in 1985 the start and end times were the same as now.'

Zoë laid the old programme and a copy of the current programme side by side. 'The times are identical. An 8.00pm start, one interval between 9.00pm and 9.20pm, and the play finished at 11.00pm.'

Von peered over her shoulder. 'So what did Michael Gillanders look like fifteen years ago?'

'Alas, no photographs, ma'am.' She looked from one programme to the other. 'That's odd. The 1985 programme has a man delivering the doll to the wife. He's down as a postman. But the current play lists a postwoman.' She was frowning. 'Must be a misprint, because it was a girl in 1985, too. Probably Joanne or Joanna.'

'What do you mean, probably?' Von said slowly.

'She's down as Jo. Maybe short for Josephine?' She looked up. 'Okay, why are you all staring at me like that?'

'Jo can also be a boy's name, short for Jon, or Jonathan,' Von said. 'It's both a boy's name and a girl's. Like Jools.' Her heart was beating wildly. 'What's the surname?'

'Moudry. Jo Moudry.'

He had some small bit part in Jack in the Box. Simon's words.

Her mind was reeling. Jesus, what a fool she was. She'd been too busy wringing a confession from him to appreciate the implication of his statement. She spun round and scrutinised the cast's timings, including those for the postwoman. But in 1985, the postwoman had been a postman.

'What does it mean, ma'am?'

'It means that, in 1985, there was another male character who had the opportunity to kill the rent boys. We concluded it could only have been the detective's assistant, because of the timings.' She pushed her hands through her hair. 'Jo Moudry was on at 8.01pm and off at 8.07pm. The next time he was on stage was for curtain call.'

'But, ma'am, how can you be sure this Jo Moudry is a man? Surely it's a misprint that the billing is for a postman.'

'A lot's been happening while you've been away, Zoë. The boys will take great delight in bringing you up to speed.'

She sank into the nearest chair and pressed her hands into her eyes. Jo Moudry had been having sex with Max Quincey in 1985. As a woman in a man's body, he'd wanted sex with a man. He knew Max's boys, passed heroin to them. Had he also had sex with them? And with Manny Newman? Could he have killed Gilly, Charlo, and Liam?

The door opened and Danni swept in. She was dressed in butter-soft leather boots and a tweed suit which would have cost Von three months' salary.

'You look terrible, Chief Inspector,' she said, staring at Von. 'And what the hell happened to your neck?'

'Let's skip the pleasantries, Danni. I'm about to interview Chrissie Horowitz.'

'Again?' She sighed in mock irritation. 'Is this why you dragged me down here?'

'Come on, you know you prefer being amongst the low-lifes

than at your dad's place with those nobs.'

'Point taken. So, what's been happening?'

'Are you ready for this?'

Danni said nothing as Von gave her an abridged version of the events of the last few days.

'So, you see,' Von said, 'we've come full circle. We're back with Chrissie Horowitz.'

Danni was silent for a while. 'Can I sit in this time?'

Chapter 36

Chrissie Horowitz was sitting in the interview room with her brief. She seemed distracted by Danni's presence, fidgeting and throwing her murderous glances. Finally, she turned her body so she didn't have to look at her.

Von switched on the recording machine. 'Interview commencing at 12.36pm on Sunday, 1st October, 2000. Present are Detective Chief Inspector Yvonne Valenti, and Dr Danielle Mittelberg.'

Chrissie sat tight-lipped, playing with her nails.

'I'd like you to clarify some things for us, Miss Horowitz,' Von said. 'When in 1985 did you meet Max Quincey?'

'I can't remember.'

'Okay, let's try walking through a different door.' She slid a copy of the 1985 programme across the table. 'Did you know Max before you acted in Jack in the Box?'

Chrissie glanced at the programme, and her expression changed. 'You finally found it.'

'You'd have saved us a lot of time if you'd come clean.'

She glanced at her brief, a serious woman in her late thirties. The woman nodded. 'I auditioned for the part of the postman,' Chrissie said, 'and it was Maxie who interviewed me. That was the first time I met him.'

'Date?'

'Earlier that year, 1985. That's all I can remember.'

'Did you become good friends?'

'I became involved in the drug ring, working out of the Iron Duke. It was through Maxie that I found out about it. You already know this. So, yes, we became good friends.'

'How did you get involved in the drug ring?'

She ran a hand over her brow. 'I told Maxie I was short of money, and asked him for an advance on my salary. He was sympathetic. When I did the same again a month later, he suggested I might want to join him in a venture.'

'Is that what he called it?' Von said, mockingly.

Her eyes sparkled. 'You didn't know Maxie. He never called a spade a spade if he could avoid it. Anyway, he told me the money would be good, and it would be regular, and I said yes.'

'So when did you meet Gilly McIlvanny?'

'Gilly McIlvanny?' She lifted her chin confidently. 'I've never heard of him.'

'He was one of Max's boys, sometimes known as Gilly McIlly. You passed drugs to him to sell to his clients.' She studied the woman's face. 'But perhaps you knew him under another name.' She opened a folder. 'The suspect is being shown a photograph. I admit it's not a good likeness of Gilly. It was taken after he'd been blinded. And he was strangled. That's string round his neck.'

Chrissie was devouring the photo with her eyes. 'I've never seen—'

'Never seen what? A boy who's been blinded?' She pushed the other photographs across. 'Then take a look at Charlo Heggarty and Liam Mahoney.'

A sob burst from Chrissie's throat. She drew the photos towards her and traced a finger across Liam's face, tears shimmering in her eyes.

'Did you know the boys well?' Von said, after a pause.

'Yes,' she whispered.

'There's also Manny Newman.' Von passed his photo over.

'But he survived. Did you know that?'

Chrissie lifted her head slowly and looked at Von. 'Yes, I knew.'

'He was the lucky one. Lucky to be alive, that is, although some people might not think so. He lives alone, with help from social services, in a not very nice part of London. He's changed his name because he's terrified that whoever attacked him might come back to finish the job.' She brought her face close to Chrissie's. 'His attack was so brutal that his eyes had to be removed. I don't think you'd recognise him now.'

Chrissie's breathing grew more laboured until it was the only sound in the room. 'It wasn't me,' she said, her voice so choked that Von almost misheard her. 'It was Jonathan Moudry.'

'Jonathan Moudry killed those boys?' Von said sharply.

She nodded, remorse in her eyes. 'It wasn't me.'

'Tell me how it happened.'

When Chrissie eventually spoke, it was as though a stranger had entered the room. The voice was a man's, the accent northern. She leant forward, her head lowered like a bull's, and planted her elbows on the table.

'The Duke was the best place for picking up boys,' she said, in her deep man's voice. 'At least, the type of boys I needed.'

The solicitor stared at her client with a look of horror. Von, startled, glanced at Danni, but Danni's steady eyes were on Chrissie.

'What type of boy did you need?' Danni said, breaking the stunned silence.

Chrissie motioned to the photos. 'Ones like Gilly.' She smiled. 'Gilly was very popular with everyone at the Duke. Always singing his Irish songs. When they had karaoke night, you couldn't move for people, you had to get all your drinks in at once as you'd never make it back to the bar. He had more clients than any of the other boys, he was so popular.'

'How did you come to have sex with him, Jonathan?' said Danni.

'He could sense what I was. He gave me the come-on, he could tell I was gagging for it. I tried hard not to give in but it became too much. So I made a date with him.'

'And what happened then, Jonathan?' Von said, taking her cue from Danni.

'I left the theatre as soon as my part was finished, and took the tube to Tottenham Court Road. I met him at the Duke and we went to the place he took his clients. We had to be careful, there was broken glass everywhere.' Her breathing became shallow. 'At first, I didn't want to do it. I was uncomfortable. But he was so sweet.'

'Why was there a mirror?' Danni said suddenly.

'I had to watch. I couldn't come otherwise.'

'Did you watch yourself? Or did you look at Gilly?'

'I looked at Gilly. And he looked at me.'

Von glanced at Danni, wondering where this line of questioning was going.

'He'd seen me,' Chrissie whispered. 'He'd seen me shame myself. I was disgusted by what we'd done.'

'And because he'd seen you, you had to blind him,' Danni said quietly.

She was weeping openly now. She nodded slowly, her hand over her mouth.

'For the tape, the suspect nodded. Why did you strangle him first?' said Von.

'I couldn't bear the thought of blinding him while he was still alive,' she said in a choked voice.

'Yet you knew you'd be strangling him even before you met him at the Duke. That's why you brought the string.'

'Yes, I wore gloves, and used a condom. I'd even shaved myself so as not to leave any hair behind.'

'Why did you bring the doll?' Danni said.

'I didn't. It was Gilly who had the doll.'

Of course. It would contain either smack or notes, so Gilly would want to keep it with him.

'He knocked it over by accident,' Chrissie said, sniffing. 'While we were doing it.'

'And it watched you, too,' said Danni.

The voice became more of a growl. 'I couldn't stand that grinning face, and those eyes, knowing they'd seen everything. So I scratched them out.'

Danni sat back, a look of satisfaction on her face.

'And then you went back to the theatre, and took a bow along with the other actors,' said Von.

Chrissie gazed at her, saying nothing.

'And Charlo, a few days later?'

'It was much the same. I left the Garrimont as soon as I was off the stage, and went to the place by the river, under the old Hungerford footbridge. Charlo had agreed to meet me there, it wasn't far from his flat. I pulled his belt out as he slid his pants down. I strangled him with it afterwards. Then I took a knife from the kitchen and blinded him.'

'Did you bring a doll?' said Danni softly.

'There was one there. Charlo was one of Max's boys.'

'And did the doll watch?' said Von.

'Even inside the box, it would have been watching,' Chrissie said viciously. 'I popped it and scratched its eyes.'

'And Liam?' Von said, after a pause.

'I waited till the play had ended. I met Liam outside Tottenham Court Road tube. He knew of these gents nearby that were quiet in the early hours.' She dropped her voice to a whisper. 'I left the door open so I could see myself in the mirror. I strangled him and used his penknife to blind him. Then I scratched his doll.'

Von stared in stupefaction. Nothing in her twenty years at the Met had prepared her for this.

Chrissie picked at the edge of the folder. 'After Liam, I began sleeping with Max.'

'Why Max?' said Danni. 'He was much older than the boys.'

'I thought that, if I could have a proper relationship with a man, I could stop the killing. I tried it the other way round, roles reversed, the way a woman would. But I didn't like it, I didn't like being penetrated. So I ended it with Max.'

'And went back to finding boys.'

She looked up slowly. 'Just one.'

'Manny wasn't a dealer,' said Von, 'so why was there a doll at his place?'

'The doll was mine. I'd just swapped it.'

'And Manny was the last?'

'The play ended and I left London. But, yes, he was the last.'

'Weren't you afraid Manny would identify you? You must have read he was still alive.'

'He didn't know my name. And he'd never be able to pick me out of a line-up, not blind.' A vacant look came into her eyes. 'I did think of going after him and finishing the job, but the hospital was too well guarded.'

'So where did you go when you left London?'

'Straight to Rio, to have my sex-change operation. Several operations, actually. Paid for by the money I'd made with the drugs.'

'And you stopped killing boys,' Danni said, 'because you no longer needed them.' It was a statement.

She nodded. 'I came back to England, attended a theatre management course, and became manager of the Garrimont.'

The voice changed suddenly back to a woman's. The accent was gone, the register higher and lighter. She leant back, smoothing the corners of her lips. 'I'd always loved the

Garrimont. When a job came up, I jumped at the chance.'

'And did you see Max Quincey again?' Danni said, seemingly unfazed by the reverse transformation.

'Not till a month ago. I had a call from him, asking if he could bring the play back to the theatre.'

'He didn't know who you were?' said Von.

She inclined her head, smiling prettily. 'It's taken you, a trained detective, this long to discover that I was once Jo Moudry. Do you really think Maxie guessed?' She crossed her legs. 'The play had made the theatre so much money fifteen years ago, that I thought we could repeat the success. God knows the Garrimont needed a boost. Anyway, the day he arrived he rang again and suggested we go for a drink and run through the timetable.' She smiled dreamily. 'We hit it off from the word go. He was fun personified. I've never met anyone, before or since, with such a deliciously crude sense of humour.'

'Where did you meet?' said Danni.

'He took me to a really posh restaurant.'

'And afterwards?'

'We went back to my place.'

'Was he the perfect gentleman?'

'He was. But I wasn't the perfect lady.' She fiddled with the buttons of her jacket. 'It wasn't difficult to seduce him.'

Seduce him? Where the hell had this come from? 'But Max was gay,' said Von.

'He wasn't gay. He was bisexual.' She spluttered with laughter, as though she couldn't keep the joke to herself. 'If you could only see your faces. Surely you must have guessed. He was married at one time.' She dabbed at her eyes with a handkerchief, grimacing as she saw the mascara.

I'm not convinced of my brother's homosexuality, Yvonne. He liked women. The Chief Super's words. He might have been in denial about Max and the rent boys but, on the subject of Max and women, he was spot on.

'So did you spend the night together?' Danni was saying.

'Absolutely not. It's one of my rules.' She smiled thinly. 'There's nothing worse than the cold light of day after a night of sex. You see all your partner's imperfections.'

'And he sees yours,' Danni said, her voice level.

'Did you meet regularly after that?' said Von.

'As often as we could. That's what all the phone calls were about.'

Von let out a long breath. The pieces were falling into place. 'Where did you meet?'

'Always at mine. We never used hotels.'

'Why not at Max's?'

'Have you seen the black hole he lived in?' She turned her head away, as though trying to escape an unpleasant smell. 'I remembered it from before.'

She's lying. They did meet there. And more than once. 'And that guff about the ledger entries?' she said.

'Maxie really was hopeless with figures. I did help him with the Quincey Players' books. That part was true.'

Von rubbed her cheeks hard. 'You said Jo Moudry paid for his operation using the proceeds from drug peddling. Was it all spent?'

'There was quite a bit left. I put the drug money through my mother's account.'

'And she didn't know?'

'She never uses her account. Gets her pension in cash, and probably stuffs what she doesn't spend into her mattress. I've been using her account for years, and forging her signature on cheques.' She seemed to think about what she'd just said. 'Not something I'm proud of, but there you are.'

Von felt like laughing. All those hours spent scrutinising Chrissie's financial affairs, and yet the solution was so simple.

'Let's talk now about Tuesday, September 12th, Miss Horowitz. You called Max from your office, just after six in the evening. You told me it was because you'd found another discrepancy in the figures. But that's a load of old fanny, isn't it? You were ringing him to set up another date.'

'You can't blame me for lying. I mean, you had me in your cross-hairs.' She regarded Von from under her lashes. 'No, you're right. Maxie didn't come to my office.'

'Where did you meet? It wasn't your place this time, was it?'

She stared at her hands.

'Did you go to Max's room at Mrs Deacon's? I'd advise you to think carefully before you deny it. We have the forensic evidence now.'

'We went to Maxie's digs,' she said, not looking up.

'At what time?'

'Must have been about seven.'

'When did you leave?'

'About eight. Maybe later.'

'You're sure?'

'I didn't check my watch, if that's what you're asking,' she said acidly.

'Did you have sex?'

'No, genius, I read his electricity meter. Of course we had sex. Do you want me to describe it?'

'Yes.'

She rolled her eyes. 'We took our clothes off and got under the sheets. But you want to know whether after a sex change you can still have an orgasm, don't you? Well you can, and I did. More than one. I insist on it.' She leant back, and parted her legs, stretching them under the table. 'I didn't have to teach Maxie anything. He had a gigantic sexual appetite. And the things he did. Jo Moudry never had a climax with him, but when I had sex as a woman with a vagina, wow, with Maxie it was explosive. The best of it was that he knew how to take his time.' She looked straight at the young constable behind Von. 'The advantages of sex with an older man. Michael Gillanders and I did it a couple of times in my office, but I ended it pretty quickly. He had certain – how shall I put it – shortcomings.'

So Chrissie had had sex with Max on the day he died. Forensics had concluded that the foreign DNA found in his sweat had been deposited by a man. But a gender reassignment operation, whatever it did to a person's appearance, couldn't alter the composition of DNA. There was just one more piece of the puzzle left.

'Let's get back to Max,' said Von. 'This went on for an hour?'

'We usually did it three times, front, back and sideways. We began with vanilla sex, woman underneath, man on top. Maxie liked to take control. But we soon moved on.' She ran the tip of her tongue across her lips. 'Maxie had imagination.'

'Did he get dressed afterwards?' Danni said quickly.

'He lay on the bed while I put my clothes on,' she said, her eyes lazy. 'He liked to watch, and I always did it slowly. Even though he was totally spent, he sat up while I dressed.'

Von hesitated. She was so close. She decided on a gamble. 'Why did you kill him, Chrissie?'

'It was the most unfortunate thing. He saw my birthmark.' She pulled her skirt up and peeled back the top of her stocking. Von felt a movement behind her as the constable leant forward.

Halfway up Chrissie's thigh was a butterfly-shaped birthmark, the birthmark Von remembered glimpsing that first day in her office.

'Maxie liked me to keep my stockings on in bed, so it was always hidden, but this time for some reason we took everything off. He saw it when I was dressing and commented on the shape. He didn't immediately twig that he'd last seen it on Jo Moudry's thigh, but I knew he'd remember eventually. I panicked. I thought he'd shop me to the police, and I'd be back in the frame for the boys' murders.' She stared at the table. 'I don't need to tell you the rest.'

'You do,' Von said quietly. 'We need your testimony.'

She looked at Von, an appeal in her eyes. 'He was lying on the bed, staring at the birthmark. I couldn't think. I snatched up the lamp and hit him. He fell back, moaning. I was going to hit him again when I saw the doll.' Her voice became a wail. 'My mind was still on those boys and I remembered the police had been looking for a man. I thought that, if I made it look like the Jack in the Box murders, they'd suspect a man had killed Maxie, possibly even the same man who'd killed the boys. Everyone knew that case had gone quiet.'

Von stared at the ceiling, seeing the scene unfold.

'I tied him to the bedframe. He was strong, you see. I couldn't take the risk he'd regain consciousness so I used the knot Zack had shown us, the type that can't be shaken loose. I wrapped his tie round his neck and twisted it.' The colour left her face. 'He came round while I was doing it. I could tell from the expression in his eyes he had no idea why it was happening. I couldn't look at him. He struggled and after a while he went limp. I held the tie while I counted to one hundred. Then I took my nail scissors and jabbed them into his eyes. That was the worst part, I had to make myself do it. I popped the doll and scratched its eyes too, to make it look like the old killings.' She slumped onto the table and covered her face with her hands.

'What did you do with the scissors, Chrissie?' Von said.

'They're still in my tote bag. When I got home, I threw the bag into the back of the wardrobe and forgot about it.'

'Why didn't you ditch them? They link you to the murder.'

She looked up slowly. 'I never thought I'd get caught.'

Von said nothing, waiting for her to finish.

'I wiped everything I'd touched. Then I picked up the used

condoms and shoved them into my bag. The last thing I did was to close the curtains.'

'Why?'

'I really don't know. It seemed the right thing to do. After that, I crept out. The place was deserted.' Her eyes were empty of expression. 'Not a living soul saw me.'

The silence in the room was absolute.

Von leant over the machine. 'Interview terminated at 1.58pm.'

Chapter 37

Von could tell from their faces that they'd heard everything.

Steve was staring open-mouthed. 'Who'd have thought it? Our Jack turned out to be a Jill.'

'A fascinating case,' said Danni. 'That physical transformation when Chrissie started speaking as Jonathan. I've seen only one other example.'

'But how was it possible? Didn't the operation change his voice?'

'Jonathan had his gender reassignment op while still in his twenties, after the voice had broken. Although it's possible to have the vocal cords tightened, he opted for vocal training to feminise the voice. Did you notice how Jonathan spoke in more of a monotone than Chrissie? One of the things you learn in voice therapy is to vary your pitch when you're speaking as a woman.'

'We interviewed Chrissie yesterday and confronted her about Jonathan,' said Von. 'Yet she spoke and behaved as she's always done.'

'Ah, but what did you talk about?' Danni said, growing excited. 'I'm betting it was nothing to do with the boys' killings. It's *that* that Chrissie Horowitz can't face up to. It's a type of denial. She can talk happily about Jonathan's drug dealing, but not about his being a murderer.'

Steve ruffled his hair. 'Do you think the jury will be swayed by any of this split personality identity disorder crap?'

'Gender dysphoria, you mean,' Danni said, eyeing him coldly. 'It may seem like crap to you, but it would have felt very real to Jonathan. He would have been torn between his need to blind and his desire not to hurt.' She turned to Von. 'You once asked me what the killer's state of mind was, and I said self-loathing. Once Jonathan had made up his mind to have sex with those boys, he would have been in a dark place, knowing what the outcome would be.'

'I doubt a jury will have much sympathy,' said Von. 'The boys' murders were pre-meditated. Chrissie admitted as much.'

'There's one thing I don't get,' said Steve. 'Jonathan was a woman in a man's body, right? So, why did he penetrate the boys?'

Danni didn't answer immediately. 'There was a conflict between his man's body and the need to penetrate, and his woman's psyche and the need to be penetrated. The needs of his man's body won out. But penetration disgusted him, specially as he had to watch himself. It was his gender reassignment operation that reversed that.' She hesitated. 'The mirror is what threw me. I thought he used it to watch himself killing. In the end it was to watch himself having sex. It was unfortunate for Gilly and the others that they watched him too. I don't know why I didn't come to this conclusion earlier.'

'If we're making confessions, I was wrong as well,' said Von. 'I assumed he'd brought the dolls with him.'

'An easy mistake to make. But I was right about one thing,' Danni added gleefully.

'Pray tell.'

'Mr X and Mr Y. You were convinced that the same person killed Max Quincey and the rent boys. I was right. It *was* two different people.'

She nodded sourly. *And she'll dine out on this for months.*

'Well, I'd better get back to the Hall. There's a riding gala on. I take it you'll let me have access to Chrissie Horowitz for further interviews?'

Fodder for your next book, I'll bet. 'I expect so.'

'Well, cheerie-bye, then.' She blew the room a kiss, and left in a flurry of tweed and leather.

Larry watched her go, a wistful expression on his face. 'What now, ma'am? Shall we break out the champagne?' he added more cheerfully.

'There's a large number of arrests to be made,' Von said, cuffing him playfully. 'Once you've finished typing the warrants, you can go home. We'll celebrate next week, that's a promise.'

Steve was jiggling coins in his pocket. 'We got the call a short time ago, boss. The Chief Super's been detained. There's some paperwork before we can have him extradited.'

'If he's under arrest, there's no immediate rush.' She lowered her voice so the others wouldn't hear. 'I thought you and I might celebrate at the Drunken Duck.'

He stiffened. 'Best not. We need to get on with the warrants.'

She watched him join the others at the computers, conscious that what was broken between them couldn't now be mended. She packed up the laptop wearily. Her report could be written at home.

She heard it as soon as she let herself into the flat: the steady beep of the answer machine. It could wait. She was loaded with bags. And she needed a drink. She kicked the door shut and let everything fall to the floor, swearing softly as she heard the thud of the laptop.

In the kitchen, she squatted beside the wine rack and pulled out the oldest bottle she had, a Reserve Shiraz, vintage 1992. She pulled the cork and left the bottle on the table to breathe. She ticked off mentally what still needed to be done. Any arrests that weren't made today would be made tomorrow. She'd pulled half the Met off London's golf courses to help with them. That wasn't going to make her popular, but it hardly mattered now. Tomorrow, she'd make an appointment with the Deputy Assistant Commissioner, unless he made an appointment with her first. He'd have heard everything by now, the entire force was buzzing with it. *You'll never get beyond DCI, Von. The Met won't forgive you for this.* But that was no longer important. She'd made her collar. She'd finally found the murderer of Max Quincey.

She poured a large glass, savouring the rhythmic gurgle as the wine flowed from the bottle. That damned beep again. Better answer it, she wouldn't enjoy the wine otherwise. She set down the glass and went into the living room.

If she hadn't been looking in the direction of the phone, she wouldn't have seen him. Kenny Downley was sitting in the high wing-backed chair, an expression of mild surprise on his face. His head was tilted away because the top of the chair had disappeared, along with the back of his head. Behind him, bits of upholstery, mingled with blood and shards of bone, were spattered across the sixties-style wallpaper.

On the floor between his feet was a handgun, which she only later recognised as his old army pistol.

Her legs buckled, and she sank to the floor. Unable to rise, she crawled to the companion chair and pulled herself onto it. She leant back, staring at him, her mind emptied of thought. When her senses returned, she was surprised at what came into her head first, that when you shoot yourself in the mouth with the gun pointed upwards, the top and back of your head disappear. If he'd kept it straight, the bullet would have gone through the brain stem, leaving the head intact. As an army man, he should have known that.

She became increasingly aware of the beep. He'd moved the phone to the little table between the chairs, and its light was flashing insistently.

With a trembling hand, she pressed Play.

His voice filled the room, sounding strange, distant.

'Von. It's me. I'm in your living room, calling from my mobile. I thought you might have been home today.' A pause. 'Maybe it's just as well, although I wish I could have heard your voice one last time. I think we've said everything that needs to be said, though, haven't we? But you need to understand one thing. Why I'm doing it. It's for Georgie. You see, you said you were going to put her on the stand, make her testify. It would have destroyed her. She's not strong, like you. And there's the baby to think of.' The voice became hoarse, urgent. 'But you can't make her testify if I'm not here, can you, love? You can't bring a case against me now. Not if I'm dead. Oh, Von.' A sob. 'I want you to know that, whatever you think about me and Georgie, I've never stopped loving you.'

There was a click, and a soft female voice, 'End of message.'

She sat motionless, his words carving her heart into tiny pieces. She reached across and pressed Delete, sending the message after him into oblivion. The Jack in the Box was sitting beside the phone. She'd never be certain why he'd brought it. Maybe he'd been on his way to make a delivery, or perhaps he'd wanted to present her with firm evidence so she wouldn't involve Georgie. She unscrewed the base and the little packets spilt out onto the carpet. She reassembled the doll, her movements unhurried, and stood it beside the phone, pressing the box as she withdrew her hand. The doll's head popped out, grinning, screaming 'Jack-jack! Jack-jack!'

She gripped the arms of the chair and rocked gently, watching the doll's head bob around on its spring.

Chapter 38

Deputy Assistant Commissioner Julian Somerville looked up as Von entered. Although this wasn't her first time at New Scotland Yard, she felt apprehensive, especially in the presence of a man who'd become a legend in his lifetime for the unflinching suppression of corruption in the force.

Julian Somerville pushed the newspaper away, and looked her up and down slowly. 'So you're DCI Valenti.'

She stared into the hooded eyes. 'You asked to see me, sir.'

'You've ruffled a few feathers, Valenti.' His tone was friendly. 'But you were doing your job.'

'Yes, sir.'

'Is that, yes sir I've ruffled a few feathers, or, yes sir I was doing my job.'

'Both, sir.'

'So how did it feel?' The corners of his lips twitched. 'Bringing down the whole house of cards.'

She dredged up a smile. 'Once it sank in, it was exhilarating.'

'The question is, where do we go from here?'

'How do you mean?'

'By the end of the week, half the force will be behind bars.'

'That's not my department, sir,' she said quietly.

He drew his brows together. 'Perhaps I should ask, where do *you* go from here, Valenti.'

'About that, sir, I've been giving it some thought.' She stopped, not sure how to continue.

'Come out with it. I'm a man given to plain speaking.'

'I wish to tender my resignation.'

His expression didn't change. 'Has someone suggested you resign?' he said in a soft voice. 'If so, I'd like to know who.'

'No-one, sir.' She looked at the wall. 'It's just that, in my investigation, I didn't always follow protocol, and mistakes were made. I didn't call the drugs squad in, and I didn't keep my superior officer informed. There was one time when I didn't bring evidence to the immediate attention of my staff, because—'

He raised a hand. 'I don't want the details, Valenti,' he said tiredly. He gazed at her without blinking. 'So what's the real reason you want to leave?'

She didn't hesitate. 'I'm sick to the back teeth of all of you. And of this job.'

'Now, that's more like it,' he said, nodding appreciatively.

He walked her to the door. 'I understand you've suffered a bereavement, so I don't expect an immediate answer. In fact, I don't want you to say anything, I want you to listen.' He paused just long enough for her to turn and look at him. 'Take some time off, a fortnight, a month, whatever you think you may need. Recharge your batteries and then, and only then, think about it.'

'Think about what, sir?'

'I'm putting you up for Superintendent. You'll be in charge at Clerkenwell. As it happens, there's a vacancy.' An amused look came into his eyes. 'The present incumbent will soon be spending time at Her Majesty's pleasure.'

'I don't need to take time off,' she said firmly. 'My answer will be the same.'

His eyes were steady. 'Please just think about it.'

After a brief silence, she said, 'Yes, sir.'

A large number of Kenny's colleagues were gathered around the cleft in the ground which would be his final resting place. They stood silently under the white-blue sky, their heads bowed. The minister had left, and the gravediggers were standing watching a short way away. Somewhere, a groundsman was burning leaves, the crackling sound reaching them from the distance, and the air was sharp with the smell of smoke.

From the corner of her eye, Von saw Arabella Carrington amongst the mourners. As always, Arabella was dressed as though for a wedding. She glanced at Von, then nodded, smiling, one professional acknowledging another. Von nodded back, trying to reciprocate the smile, but Arabella had already turned away.

Steve was the only member of the force attending. He stood slightly back and to the side, as though he didn't belong, his black coat taking the colour from his face. Von had exchanged only a few words with him since the inquest, but she was glad of his presence.

The voice came from her left. 'Chief Inspector?'

Zack Lazarus was smiling hesitantly. He was in a brown jacket that was threatening to burst open.

'Are you here for the funeral?' she said in surprise.

He gestured to the middle distance. 'Max Quincey's.'

A group of people was standing listening to a man in a cassock. Von recognised Jools, and the other actors from the Garrimont. And the frail-looking woman. She was without the support of the Chief Super this time, but she stood straight, her head held high, finally able to bury her son.

'I saw your car,' said Zack, nodding at the police vehicle parked on the path. 'Thought I'd come over. I heard something about—' He looked at the coffin. 'Your guy, wasn't he? I'm dreadfully sorry.'

After the silence had gone on too long, Von said, 'How

are things going with the show? The cast and crew seem to be disappearing fast.'

He smiled wanly. 'We're surviving. Our cleaner, Mrs Marks, has taken on Rose Manning's job. Not bad with clothes. Come into her element, you could say.'

'What will happen to the Garrimont, now that Chrissie's no longer running it?'

'Dexter's doing a fair job for now. Made a few changes, and for the better. He's pretty clued up, I have to admit.'

'Tell him to apply for the manager's post when it comes up. He'll be great.' She paused. 'I haven't spoken out of turn, have I? Were you thinking of applying?'

'Me? Lord no. Got other things to occupy me.' He smiled. 'Started an Open University course. I've a power of studying to do.'

She hesitated, then opened her bag and fished out a piece of paper. She scribbled on it and handed it to him. 'Here, take this.'

'An address?' He looked up, puzzled.

'The person living there needs you. And I think you need him. He goes by the name of Frankie Lowry, now.'

The expression on his face changed, and his eyes filmed over. He nodded, unable to speak.

'Good luck with your course, Zack,' she said warmly.

He nodded again, then walked slowly away, staring at the paper in his hand.

Steve had been watching. He stepped forward. 'Talking of goodbyes, boss, I'll say mine now. By the way, I hear you're up for Superintendent.'

'I'm not taking it. I'm done with policing.'

'You're not serious, surely.'

She looked into his eyes, only then appreciating what he'd said. 'What's this about goodbyes?'

'I've applied for a transfer back.'

'To Glasgow?' she said faintly.

'I think it's best.' He looked around the cemetery. 'I've never really been at home in London.'

'Are you taking your barmaid with you?' she said, trying to inject a note of cheer into her voice. 'It's Annie, isn't it?'

He looked at his feet. 'It was never Annie.'

'Steve—'

'I've been meaning to give you this.' He fumbled in his pocket. 'We've just got it back from Forensics.'

She took the plastic bag. 'It's Tubby's,' she said, the word catching in her throat.

There was little left of the spectacles, only a small glass shard stuck to the frame.

'It'll need to be produced at Hensbury's trial,' Steve said. 'It's evidence that Tubby was in his lock-up. I thought you'd like to see it.'

She nodded, unable to find the words.

'Did you hear we finally picked up Malkie and his pal? We have them all now.' He was staring into the distance. 'Anyway, good luck with whatever you decide to do, Von,' he mumbled.

Before she could reply, he turned and walked briskly away. She watched him go, realising with deep regret that a chapter of her life had closed.

There was a touch at her arm. 'Chief Inspector, we're off to the pub for a few drinks. For Kenny. Will you join us?'

'Thanks, Miss Carrington, but I need to get on. Have a glass for me, won't you?'

Arabella nodded, clearly pleased she'd been let off the hook.

The crowd of journalists dispersed and drifted away. One of the group remained behind. A woman in a severe black suit and low-brimmed hat was watching her. From the swell of the jacket, she looked about four months pregnant. Something in the way she held her head made Von's heart miss a beat.

The woman moved towards her, slowly at first, then more quickly, till she was almost running. She threw her arms round her and buried her face in her neck.

'Hello, Georgie,' said Von.

The woman released her and stepped back. She removed the hat.

'Hello, Mum,' she said finally.